INVISIBLE HERO

A NOVEL BY PETER HESS

INVISIBLE HERO by Peter Hess
Published by Creation House
A Strang Company
600 Rinehart Road
Lake Mary, Florida 32746
www.creationhouse.com

Cover design by Terry Clifton

Library of Congress Control Number: 2004112414
International Standard Book Number: 1-59185-663-9

05 06 07 08 09 — 987654321
Printed in the United States of America

Contents

Chapter 1
A Deranged Enemy

THE SHRILL, WHINING SCREAM OF THE BOMBS DROWNED OUT the loud, hysterical cries that exploded from deep inside her.

"Not again. Please, not again," she pleaded, as she pulled her knees up close to her, huddling her body as tightly together as she could, as if that would help.

She threw her hands over her ears, as she had done so many times before. It didn't matter. The noise was deafening. She stopped breathing. They were coming for her.

"Oh, no! Please! No!"

Suppose this one hit them? Suppose it killed her father?

"Please, Papa-san. Don't die yet!"

How much longer would it go on? How much more could she take? It seemed to have been going on for an eternity.

"No!" she screamed in her little girl voice.

She heard the footsteps. They were coming for her. The bombs kept falling, the guns kept shooting, the footsteps kept coming.

"No-ooooh!"

Suddenly awakening, Keiko Kobashigawa sat straight up on the mat and looked around. The room was dark. It was also quiet. There were no soldiers. There were no guns. There were no bombs. The war was over. She was eighteen, not four years old. It was 1959, not 1945. She sighed deeply. She had been having the nightmare again.

Still shaking, Keiko slipped off the mat and crawled, on her hands and knees, the few feet to where she placed the damp cloth each night before retiring, knowing she might need it. She wiped the beads of perspiration from her forehead and her face, threw the rag back to its place of safe keeping, and crawled back onto her sleeping mat.

Closing her eyes and feeling a tear slip down her cheek and onto her neck, she hoped she could get a little rest before morning dawned.

Though the war between the Japanese and the Americans had been over for years, and though the government seemed to be finally solidified under the guidance of the U.S., there was still political unrest on the island of Okinawa. Of the three major political parties—the Democratic Party, the Social Mass Party, and the Okinawan People's Party—the OPP had strong Marxist leanings and the desire to reunite Okinawa with Japan. Not many years earlier, the OPP had controlled the island's political leadership, but their government was overthrown and their leaders arrested. A great deal of animosity remained among the leaders of the OPP, and they were rumored to have joined with the Yakuza, an infamous Japanese criminal group.

Because of the Yakuza's ruthlessness, their strong-arm tactics, and their desire to dress and act like American criminals, they were often referred to as the Japanese Mafia. On Okinawa, the Yakuza had expanded their criminal activities into the black market and, in recent years, had gained control over a large portion of the island's lucrative prostitution business.

The OPP still held some mayoral positions on Okinawa but had poor relations with the U.S. high commissioner, the advisor to the civilian Okinawan government. Also, much to the OPP's dismay, they didn't have strong Communist support from the Soviet Union. The party hadn't totally sold out to Communism, and, with the US controlling the island, the Soviets weren't about to make strong moves in that direction.

The lack of Soviet backing, however, didn't deter Shinichi Murakami, an obstinate OPP leader who had been an important player in the party's political leadership after World War II, when the OPP controlled the island's administration. Though the party was still strong and fought valiantly to regain power, only Murakami was considered a true revolutionary. He was prepared to commit mass murder, if necessary, to bring the OPP back into power. He'd been to Moscow, as a guest of the Soviet government, to study Communism and to learn revolutionary tactics. While there, he met the Vietnamese revolutionary hero, Ho Chi Minh. Murakami returned to Okinawa determined to bring change to the island and be hailed as a Communist hero.

Despite the rumors regarding the Yakuza, the OPP party didn't have a relationship with the criminals, but Murakami did. He and the Japanese Mafia had met several times in recent months. The OPP madman and his bodyguard and revolutionary commander, Gunjin (the Japanese word for soldier) were the only OPP representatives who met with the Yakuza—without the knowledge of the party's other political leaders.

Gunjin, Murakami's right-hand man, was a cruel, heartless, OPP underground guerilla and a hardened criminal and murderer, without a conscience. The two men met to go over the details of their master plan.

"Gunjin, do you have the pawns in place? The Yakuza? Are you prepared for this important mission?" Murakami asked. "Are you ready to give your all for our cause?"

"I'm prepared to die, if necessary, Murakami-san. But if we are smart," he said, laughing, "we won't have to die. The Yakuza will die for us."

Murakami laughed, too. The Yakuza were pawns, ready to carry out their orders in exchange for money. Some of them would do anything for the right price. Murakami wasn't interested in money. Ideology was more important. The success of the mission depended on precise implementation of his plan. It required someone of Gunjin's ability—a criminal—who didn't care about the lives of his enemies or co-workers. Murakami had stooges in the Yakuza, and in Gunjin, he had a military commander. He would supply the brains.

The OPP leader was in his mid-forties, having lived his entire life on the small Ryukyuan island. His family had been brutally murdered during the Japanese-American invasions of World War II. Blaming the Americans, he sought revenge.

He found it in the Okinawan People's Party and worked his way into a strong leadership position. Though the bulk of the party's leaders had retreated after being ousted from the government, Murakami became even more determined to continue his quest, even if he had to do it alone.

He didn't want to wage war against the U.S., especially with all the military bases on the island. That would be suicide. His main objective would be to create upheaval in the current government of chief executive Konishi Kobashigawa. If he could create an opening in the government, he could regain a foothold. Once the OPP reacquired power, the Soviets would come to his aid, and he could use Communism to bring his party and himself back into control of the government. Then, with the help of the Japanese government, he could oust the Americans.

He would have to overthrow some of the current OPP leadership, but that wasn't an obstacle. Once the revolution was underway, Murakami would be thrust into the top spot, anyway. Who else could lead the revolution?

His plan was to launch small, quick guerilla attacks at various levels of government. That would throw the government into disarray and create unrest among the citizens. The task had to be performed in complete secrecy, which explained his alignment with the Yakuza. They would protect the OPP from suspicion and, if captured, wouldn't talk.

Murakami decided that the first of the attacks would be the largest and most devastating. If that didn't break the government, it would damage it enough so that the later, smaller attacks would complete the job. The first attack would be aimed at the chief executive, Konishi Kobashigawa. They would strike at the festival celebrating the kake damashi victory by the respected Naha shi-han Katsuo Matsumura.

Each year, top judo competitors vied in challenge matches, called *kake damashi*. In 1959, the competition was held on Okinawa at Matsumura's dojo in Naha, the island's capital city. The great Okinawan judo master, who nearly scored a sweep in the competition, was being honored in a special ceremony held at the chief executive's estate.

Murakami and Gunjin finished off their cups of warm sake, and Gunjin refilled them.

"You'll be going against Kobashigawa's guards," Murakami said. "You know their reputation. They are many and well trained. Does that concern you? Are you satisfied the Yakuza can do the job?"

"I'm surprised at your question, Murakami-san. I'm a warrior. It's in my blood. My grandfathers many times past fought against the kings of the islands to bring revolution and power to those to whom the gods granted it. If I'm not at war, I'm not at peace.

"The guards don't concern me. Death is death, and killing is killing. The Yakuza are animals and will do what I tell them. They're being paid to kill, not to think. Thinking is what you do." He laughed. "They kill, you think."

"You may have to kill some Americans," Murakami cautioned. "I'd prefer if you did. My information is that an American is being honored at this festival, too. It might be that many Americans will be there. As the Americans say, the more, the better. It might be difficult to choose your targets, but, if possible, we want to kill the government leaders and the Americans. Do you know why?"

"Killing is killing, Murakami-san. My bullets don't have names written on them. Killing an American means nothing to me, not after all our people that were killed by them, but no, I don't know why. Why do we kill the Americans and the political leaders? Are we trying to start a war with the Americans?"

"No, no." Murakami laughed. "We're revolutionaries, Gunjin, but we aren't crazy. Our purpose is to overthrow Kobashigawa's government. If Americans and important officials in his government die, then the U.S. and the citizens of Okinawa won't look kindly on Kobashigawa. They will rise up to question his leadership.

"Then we will have accomplished our goal. Don't kill Kobashigawa. Let him live, so he may suffer. He must not die. He must be hated by the people, and they won't hate him if he's dead.

"Tell no one of this mission. None of our OPP comrades are aware of it. If they were, they wouldn't side with us in our efforts. We're alone in this, you and I. The Yakuza are pawns we can use to carry out our plan, but only you and I know the full consequences.

"No matter how successful this mission, we can't brag about it or tell anyone. We can't revel in our victory or celebrate. Life is strange and sometimes difficult, my malevolent friend. It's hard to do something so wonderful and then store it away without any accolades."

Gunjin shrugged. Accolades didn't matter to him. He could see that keeping the secret would be more difficult for his boss than it would for himself.

The two OPP revolutionaries met with the Yakuza leader, a huge Japanese man with a large face and flat, ample nose, to finalize the plan. Gunjin's private name for the man was *Buta*, the Japanese word for pig. They would meet at a predetermined place off the roadway to Nago, at the northern end of the island, on the day of the festival, and the mission would unfold from there.

Everything was in place. Murakami was excited. It was a good plan that would create serious upheaval in the chief executive's government. If all went as expected, many would die, and there would be absolutely no tie-in to the OPP. His OPP compatriots would be excited by the prospects the situation afforded, and Murakami would be poised to take over the leadership of the party.

How could they refuse him? It was a masterful plan, and he felt drunk with excitement.

It was time for the much-awaited, much-heralded party at Chief Executive Kobashigawa's estate. USAF Airman First Class David "Gohan" Rice was amazed. The island had little luxury, but the estate proved the exception. Sitting on a large hill near the town of Nago on the island's northern end, it was reached by a long, winding road cut through thick forest. A pair of fancy, iron gates between concrete pillars opened the estate to the rest of the island, while a shorter concrete wall ran around the front of the grounds.

The large house was built of hand-sawn wood with beautifully painted overlays in classic Okinawan architecture. He felt as if he were walking into a two-hundred-year-old Japanese drama house. The red-tiled roof stretched out over the front of the house, creating shade for a long, brick walkway that wove around the house in the shape of an L. A perfectly manicured lawn reached to the edge of the forest, then the forest dropped dramatically down a steep cliff back to the main road.

Exquisitely crafted ceramic statues, most of which were made by local artisans, and many of which were old and treasured, were set at various places throughout the large lawn. Among them was a huge, white birdbath shaped like a giant crane. To Gohan's delight, it was being attended by two large and very real cranes as the car drove to the house.

The lawn also included large, thick, attractive, white-blossomed bushes and short, squat trees with low branches filled with beautiful maroon leaves. The trees and bushes were perfectly placed to create an attractive setting. Airman Rice was impressed. Back home were thousands of homes like that, many of which were far more luxurious, but, after he saw nothing but cold, ugly, military barracks and grass, mud, and poorly constructed wood huts for the last year, the estate was beautiful to behold.

Inside, it was equally elegant. A wood stairway wound its way to a second floor that was open most of the way around. Gohan assumed there were bedrooms on that floor or, at least, private rooms, because no one went up there. Each downstairs room was large and open. The rooms were adorned with ceramics and gold and silver items, many of which were gifts from leaders and dignitaries from around the world. Some of the gifts had been brought to the island centuries earlier, the remaining few that had survived the devastation of war.

The house was impressive. All the rooms had rich, thick carpets. One had a pure white carpet, while another had bright gold, and another brilliant green. The men's sitting room was decorated in what Gohan thought of as comfortable cream. Of course, everyone removed their shoes before entering the house.

Gohan and Matsumura were the center of attention. Gohan was the rare American that had emerged a winner in the kake damashi.

Airman David Rice first came to the island in April 1958, and he learned that the word *Okinawa* meant a rope in the sea. When he first saw the island, he thought it indeed looked like a skinny bit of rope in the middle of nowhere.

It was the largest of the Ryukyu Islands, approximately 140 small pieces of land situated in the North Pacific 800 miles south of Japan. Okinawa was south of Korea, west of China, northwest of Taiwan and Hong Kong, and north of the Philippines. The island averaged seven miles in width and was seventy miles long.

Heck, he thought, *I've seen farms in Ohio bigger than this.*

It was new, different, stiflingly humid, and, as far as he was concerned, unattractive. Initially, he hated it, but, over time, he grew to love the island and its people.

He'd been briefed regarding all that happened in the Second World War and how Okinawa was the site of one of its fiercest battles, beginning on Easter Sunday, 1945, and lasting almost three months. Many of the islanders hid in caves to survive, and some caves still held their bones. The military briefing given by a wimpy lieutenant with a high voice included warnings, dangers, and expectations.

"The Okinawan people are small, gentle, courteous, and, generally speaking, nice," the lieutenant said. "We don't have any serious problems with them. Some, however, are filled with hatred and revenge because of the war. Many Okinawans lost their lives during the war. Nevertheless, we must warn you to be courteous to them and keep your distance. You don't know who might be an enemy plant. We are not at war, but we are in the middle of a cold war, and there are things happening of which you are unaware. We must be cautious."

He cleared his throat and blushed before the next bit of advice. "It'll be difficult for many of you, but stay away from the women. Don't get involved with any of them, especially the prostitutes— of which there are many—or you could end up with a venereal disease."

How would he know? Rice wondered.

The briefing included warnings about the heat, rains, and typhoons. Rice quickly learned that the humidity, not the heat, was the problem and it was far worse than he'd been told. Rains came hard, heavy, and often during May and June, and he endured several frightening typhoons during the three and a half years he spent there.

Once he was over the shock of being on foreign soil, Rice made the best of his thirteen-month sentence. He would eventually add five six-month extensions to his original tour.

During the earliest months of his sojourn, Rice, like many of his compatriots, familiarized himself with the Okinawan bars. The longer he was there, however, the more he wished to learn the island's history. He traveled throughout the island, enjoying the unusual and attractive sights. He studied *Uchina-guchi*, the Okinawan language, and he soon became fluent.

The Okinawans liked him. He was able to converse with them, and his likable personality won him many friends. His prowess and reputation in martial arts impressed them, too. The old Okinawan proverb was true regarding his relationship with the locals. Once we meet and talk, we are brothers and sisters.

Soon, Rice reversed his initial distasteful impression of the island. With its soft, white, sandy beaches, beautiful coral reefs, and magnificently colored fish in the shallows, it was a very attractive place.

Deciding to see it all, he visited Buddhist temples, Shinto shrines, the famous Teahouse of the August Moon (made famous by an American movie), and the remains of the thirteen-hundred-year-old Shuri castle that had been perched on a massive ridge that ran across the southern width of the island. In the early days, prior to his becoming a Christian, he made friends with several priests and studied the history of the Okinawan religions.

Though he'd never shown an interest in cultural or historical things in the past, Rice became engrossed with the cultural treasures of his newfound home. It amazed him to find that the island had been inhabited for centuries, and most of that time, it was ruled by kings. Coming from America, he thought of a king as someone from medieval times—or a card in a playing deck. He was enamored with Okinawan music, art, opera, and the *nufa bushi no-odori*, the famous female love dances. He often dressed in Okinawan garb and attended the plays, thoroughly enjoying the singing and dancing and the unusual but easy-to-listen-to music.

Rice made friends with the old fishermen at Yomitan, a quiet, peaceful fishing village on the island's western side on the East China Sea. He often went out with them into the dangerous waters in their thin, rickety boats to whale watch, and he loved every minute of it. Sitting for hours, he watched the older women practice their centuries-old weaving techniques. They enjoyed his company as much as he enjoyed watching them. He went with the priests to the *utaki*, the sacred grounds in the forest groves, and he joined in the performance of their religious rituals.

He learned that the original Okinawans came from many places—Indonesia, New Guinea, Malaysia, Taiwan, the Philippines, Mongolia, and even Siberia—hundreds of years earlier. The current Okinawans were a pleasant mixture of those cultures. They were *gu choku*, a simple, pure people. Rice came to love the island and its short, sturdy, peaceful inhabitants.

Every military barracks had a man who took it upon himself to give the others their nicknames. Onna Point, where Rice was stationed, was no different. Airman First Class "Names" Hilliard collared every man in the barracks and, like it or not, saddled him with a nickname.

There was Heinie, the guy with a German last name; Drawers, the guy who lost so much weight his pants kept falling down; Arms, the guy who became drunk at a Trick Party and jumped out a second-story window in the bar they rented and broke both his arms in a cement alley; and Derriere, a guy with a big butt.

The moment David Rice was introduced to his barrack mates in April 1958, he was christened *Gohan*, which was Okinawan for rice.

Gohan started practicing martial arts the moment he arrived. He took karate-do classes at a *dojo*, or training hall, in Okinawa City, the island's second-largest city, right outside Gate Two at Kadena Air Force Base. He studied *seidokan*, an old Okinawan art that included the kicking, punching, and blocking of karate with the throwing and other techniques of aiki-jujutsu.

He progressed through the color belts quickly, eventually attaining a high level of expertise and becoming a *yudansha*, or black belt. He and his best friend, Seth Edwards, also enrolled in judo classes, starting with a small, local dojo outside Nakadomari, a small village between Onna Point, where he was stationed, and Okinawa City.

When they both reached the level of brown belt, they asked to join a major dojo at Naha, Okinawa's capital, operated by Katsuo Matsumura, a *shihan*, or master teacher, who was considered one of the top judo masters in the Far East. He had already heard of the two Americans' exploits, and, with a recommendation from their previous instructor, he accepted them at his dojo. Matsumura made an immediate positive impact on young Gohan, and he quickly became a mentor to the troubled American.

It couldn't have come at a better time. Gohan, still only nineteen years old, drank too much and was dangerous because of his marital arts abilities. He didn't pick fights when he drank, but he refused to back down. He fought anyone from any branch of the service and often took on more than one at a time.

When he came under Matsumura's influence, his fighting subsided. An Okinawan proverb said, "Your mind doesn't become disturbed by being beaten up but by beating up others," and he learned it was true.

He never fought the Okinawans, however, and went out of his way to avoid conflict with them. That seemed odd, but he respected the locals, mostly because of Matsumura, whom he greatly admired. As a result, the Okinawans took a liking to him, and his reputation spread.

The time came for the kake damashi. Every important Okinawan official and noble attended the grand event. The large, always-smiling Matsumura was extremely popular on the island and was held in high esteem by everyone. He was friendly with the chief executive, who attended the event and brought his family.

Matsumura had spoken to Gohan about the chief executive's attractive daughter, named Keiko. She was eighteen, one year younger than Gohan, and, according to Matsumura, she was attractive and had expressed interest in Gohan. During an invitation to the chief executive's house, Matsumura had been cornered after dinner by Keiko and subjected to endless questions about the young American black belt.

Matsumura laughed as he shared the story with Gohan. He knew Gohan had no chance for a romantic relationship with Kobashigawa's daughter, and Gohan wasn't concerned, either, because he didn't know the girl. Besides, he was a fierce, intense competitor who allowed nothing to interfere with his ability to perform, although the idea of meeting Keiko certainly intrigued him.

Gohan, Seth, and the other participants, who were all Okinawans, were garbed in their unattractive white dogis and sat quietly in a group to one side when the entourage of Okinawan officials and nobles entered the dojo. Chief Executive Kobashigawa led the group, and, although small in stature, he created a strong presence. Keiko was with a group of younger Okinawan women who followed her father, and Gohan saw that Matsumura was right—she was attractive.

Keiko was tall for an Okinawan girl. She stood at five-feet-six-inches, slender without being skinny, and had a touch of brown in her otherwise coal-black hair. Her facial features were extremely attractive. She looked like she had been sculpted from a classic Asian mold.

In American terms, she was a knockout. Dressed formally in a colorful floor-length kimono, she was even more attractive.

Keiko had been schooled in the arts and could act, sing, and dance, and she walked like a model. She understood politics as it pertained to Okinawa and the surrounding countries and islands. Although sophisticated, she wasn't overly so. Her father was a modest man despite his high position, and Keiko inherited that trait.

She spoke a little Spanish, fluent Chinese, and decent English. She had traveled to Japan, China, Russia, and France and taught early grades at a school in Naha. Gohan wondered why Matsumura had told him all those things, since he had no chance of becoming romantically involved with her. He did, however, notice how she, occasionally, glanced over at him while the early matches were occurring. When his time came, he didn't disappoint her, as his performance was exceptional.

Standing off in one corner, unnoticed by anyone, were two very plain, normal-looking Okinawan men, presumably waiting to enjoy the kake damashi—Shinichi Murakami and his henchman, Gunjin.

Gohan walked to an area in front of the audience, stopped in front of the mayor of Naha, and bowed, then he moved a few steps to where Chief Executive Kobashigawa and his entourage sat, stopped before him, and made a deeper, more respectful bow. He knew he was scoring big-time points with the crowd and the officials.

He looked at the rest of the audience, locked gazes with Keiko for a moment, smiled, and then bowed to the audience.

Then he went out and devastated his opponent, much to the

delight of the partisan crowd. He was careful, though, with his occasional glances at Keiko. The chief executive's guards, who all resembled Mafia hit men, spent the day staring at Gohan. He remembered Matsumura's advice and made a concerted effort not to stare at her.

The crowning moment of the event came when Gohan was invited, with Matsumura, to the chief executive's estate for a dinner and celebration. He couldn't wait for the chance to meet Keiko. As promised, she was exceptionally attractive.

Gohan, who possessed great powers of persuasion, was extremely popular among the native Okinawans. Because of the kake damashi, he was now popular even among the political leaders. If he could make a good impression during the festival, his popularity would grow. He enjoyed the attention.

It was unusual and a little shocking that he was being honored, along with Matsumura, at a major feast at the chief executive's estate. Far from being worried, though, he looked forward to it.

Katsuo Matsumura was an extremely modest man. During the opening festivities, he was quick to give credit to Gohan for reaching such a high position among his peers in the world of judo. It was rare for an American to win the kake damashi. Matsumura, who wasn't interested in accolades, anyway, was glad to pass the honors on to Gohan, who loved it.

Gohan wasn't egotistic, but he enjoyed being in the limelight, and there was plenty of that at the festivities. He was like a trained actor who said the right things, downplaying his role in the judo matches he won, giving credit back to Matsumura and even saying how humbling it was for an outsider like himself to play an important role in such an historical event.

He didn't mean any of it. He was having a blast, and he loved the attention.

There was only one thing wrong—what Matsumura said about Keiko was right. The chief executive wouldn't let Gohan near her under any conditions. Every time Gohan looked at her, she smiled. Every time he looked away, he found Kobashigawa staring at him. His look was intimidating.

Gohan decided to enjoy the day's festivities and not worry about his relationship with Keiko, which would likely never become a reality, anyway. The sight of those large executive guards convinced him that was the right idea. There were at least twenty-five of them in the house.

As a rule, Okinawans were small people, but none of the executive guards came from that school. They looked like hit men who were sumo wrestlers on the side. Gohan knew his abilities, especially in combat, but he decided early that day that he didn't want to mess with any of those guards.

Chapter 2
Sneak Attack

THE LARGE TRUCK LEFT THE MAIN ROAD AND ENTERED THICK forest with three other trucks behind it. When they were out of view of the road, the trucks stopped in a small clearing. Thirty Japanese men climbed out and began unloading rifles and ammunition. Once the trucks were emptied, the drivers turned around, drove back onto the road, and headed toward the south end of the island.

The three leaders of the group, OPP leader Shinichi Murakami, his swarthy, crusty guerrilla Gunjin, and the Japanese Yakuza Buta, gathered their men around them and went over last-minute instructions. Murakami was sharp and pointed in his mannerisms, occasionally shouting to make a point. The Yakuza men, who recognized his leadership but didn't like him, sat quietly and listened. Each was armed with a military knife, a pistol, and a rifle with ample ammunition. Some of the rifles were American M-1s stolen from bases on the island. All the men carried black hooded masks to wear once they reached their destination.

They began their trek up the thickly forested mountain, which was dotted with large, jagged rocks. It wasn't an easy climb, but

Gunjin had calculated every detail. It was the best route to reach their destination unseen. The men he led were hardened criminals who had clear instructions to kill as many people as they could other than Chief Executive Kobashigawa. No one else, including the Americans, was to be spared. They were to do their work quickly and get out.

When it was over, investigators would assume the attack had been carried out by a military group. There would be no tie to the OPP, even if someone were captured.

The idea was to create as much havoc as possible, which was much more important than protecting the men. Ideology was at stake. Gunjin, as a criminal, didn't understand the ideological aspect of the attack, but, if it was important to his boss, then it was important to him. He knew the plan was more important than the men he hired. They were expendable, but the plan wasn't. Murakami had made that very clear.

When the massacre ended and their mission was accomplished, there would be men, women, and children in place to transport the Yakuzas—with changes of clothing—to predetermined places on the island. They would travel by bicycle, motorcycle, and car.

The plan was flawless, and Gunjin was satisfied. Murakami had seen to every detail. He accompanied them for a while, then turned the operation over to Gunjin and Buta. After waving the men off with a word of encouragement, he returned to the clearing, where a young Okinawan woman waited with a motorcycle. They embraced, then she lit cigarettes for both of them before they rode off, leaving the rebellion to Gunjin, Buta, and their men.

Buta, feeling they were behind schedule, wasn't happy.

"Gunjin, you've given us a nearly impossible task," he complained. "Murakami's information was wrong. They'll meet for the festivities in less than an hour, and we'll barely get there in time."

"Murakami is never wrong, Masaru-san."

Buta's given name was Masaru. Gunjin never used the man's nickname to his face. Buta was much larger than he, and, though Gunjin feared no one, he didn't want to create unnecessary problems.

"Murakami has this mission planned to the smallest detail," he continued. "We'll arrive exactly at the time we should begin the massacre."

"No," Buta answered. "This isn't good. You can't drive men up a difficult mountain, tire them, then expect them to be expert sharpshooters without rest. You and Murakami haven't planned this to the smallest detail. We'll have to move at a faster pace so we can arrive early and rest before our mission."

Gunjin, who decided not to argue, didn't know if they were behind schedule, and it didn't matter how tired the men were when they reached the house. Gunjin could kill under any conditions.

Buta gave the order to move more quickly. The men would be tired when they arrived, but there was little choice. He glanced, menacingly, at the Okinawan. He wanted to beat Gunjin's face. Maybe, when the mission was over, Gunjin could meet with an accident. That was worth thinking about.

He hoped to bring his men to their destination quickly enough to rest a little before starting the war. Otherwise, executing the mission properly would be difficult. Although a criminal, Buta was still a professional. He exhorted his men to move quickly.

Gohan sat in Indian fashion on the floor at the dinner table, pleased to find Keiko almost directly across from him. Every time he looked up, she was looking at him. When she caught his eye, she smiled.

Seeing her so close, he saw that she was even more beautiful than he thought. Her complexion was perfect. He had never heard of an eighteen-year-old with such flawless skin.

He was so excited he could barely finish his meal. The chief executive was busy talking with the other officials, giving Gohan a little more freedom to flirt with Keiko. To his delight, there were no guards in the room.

It was a delicious dinner of pork, chicken, seafood, sweet

potatoes, cold matted rice, various vegetables, and a wonderful dessert that had pineapples, bananas, and other things Gohan wisely didn't ask about.

After they left the dinner table, the men moved to the sitting room with the comfortable cream carpet, where they rested and toasted the occasion with small cups of heated sake, the bitter Okinawan rice wine. Gohan was careful not to drink too much, especially since he had nearly stopped drinking due to Matsumura's encouragement. He wanted to impress Keiko, not ruin his chances.

Eventually, the entire group went outside onto the lawn. There, after various speeches that Gohan didn't completely understand, the award ceremony began. He noticed Keiko had moved to the side of the lawn with some of the other young women, but he was careful not to stare at her. He hadn't completely digested his dinner yet, and the executive guards were close by.

The ambush team was in position, twenty to fifty feet from the far edge of Kobashigawa's lawn. Because of the sharp drop-off at the edge of the lawn, Gunjin, Buta, and their men were well hidden. The Yakuza leader turned and, with a nod of his head, signaled Gunjin that they were ready. Gunjin took two steps up the hill, leveled his rifle, and slowly squeezed the trigger.

As Matsumura accepted a golden plaque from one of the Okinawan officials, a sharp crack was heard that stunned the group. Blood oozed from one of the officials standing next to the popular shihan, and the man fell limply to the ground.

O God! Gohan thought. *He's been shot! What's going on here?*

Kobashigawa's guards reacted quickly. Two grabbed the chief executive and dragged him into the house. Guests scattered in all directions, creating chaos on the grounds. Others among the chief executive's guards grabbed metal shields and moved toward the edge of the forest, from where the gunfire had come.

Shots came in rapid succession. Gohan saw Keiko standing alone, screaming, as the other women had left her, running toward the house. With the heavy gunfire splattering the lawn, he wondered if the house was too far away for her to reach.

He sprinted across the lawn, knocking over one of the guests attempting to reach the safety of a small building next to the house. As he did, he saw that the closest protection was a large bush situated at the edge of the lawn. He grabbed Keiko around the waist and ran toward the bush, keeping as low as he could. He dived behind the bush holding Keiko above him so that she wouldn't be injured. He gently placed her on the ground behind the bush. They were safe for the moment.

Though the bush was near the woods, it was a fair distance from the enemy, but it was also far from the house and the protection of the guards.

He squeezed Keiko in close to the bush and looked around to get his bearings. The guards, who had taken sheltered positions throughout the estate, returned fire rapidly. Although the bush was large enough for two to hide behind, he realized they were safe only as long as no one realized they were there. It wouldn't offer much protection against bullets.

He forced his way in until he could see through the thicket, quickly realizing how close he was to his unknown enemies.

Who were these people? he wondered.

From that side of the lawn, the forest dropped off sharply and was full of jagged rock and thick trees down to the road. The gunmen had good cover there. He surveyed the area and began to pick out enemy locations. One man was hidden behind some rocks, and another was firing away from behind a tree. He saw two or three more moving up the hill, shooting at Kobashigawa's guards. He realized that if they reached the lawn, many would die. What could he do? He didn't even have a gun.

He crawled back out to the lawn and looked down at Keiko. She lay on the ground, huddling near the bush, clearly terrified. He knew she spoke some English, but it wasn't as good as his

Okinawan. He smiled weakly, touched her hand, and spoke in her native language.

"It'll be all right, Keiko. I'll protect you. I won't let anything happen to you. I promise."

She threw her arms around him, looked longingly into his eyes, and nodded. That was all he needed to take on the world.

He climbed back into the bush for another look. The attackers he saw wore black hooded masks. There were still some political difficulties on the island, but Gohan didn't think they'd go far enough to provoke an armed attack.

Don't they realize they'll end up fighting the United States of America? he wondered.

He didn't have time to worry about that. He had to stop them. But how? They were making steady headway toward the edge of the lawn. Once they reached it, the guards and he and Keiko would be vulnerable.

Out of the corner of his eye, he saw one of the hooded men moving cautiously toward his bush from the far side of the hill. He quickly pulled Keiko into the bush with him to get her out of the man's sight. There were sharp thorns that had already stabbed him repeatedly in his arms, but he had to protect her. She wisely threw her hand over her mouth so that she wouldn't yell. When she saw the hooded man slowly approaching, she froze, her eyes wide with fear. Gohan put his finger to his lips, not wanting her to scream and give away their position. She nodded.

They watched as the man slowly reached the top of the hill, closing the gap between them. Gohan made his decision. He glanced at Keiko, who covered her ears. The sound of gunfire was terrible, and she had never heard anything like it before.

He was too involved with the action around him to let the noise affect him. The hooded man was only thirty feet away, still on the forest side of the lawn and out of sight of most of the guards. He looked ready to make a dash for Gohan's bush, then use it for cover to ambush the guards.

His heart beat fast. In a few moments, his and Keiko's lives would be in his hands. He knew what to do, and he had the ability to pull it off, but that didn't make it any easier. He was ready and had no fear, confident in his abilities. He glanced at Keiko and smiled.

Don't worry, Keiko, he thought. *I won't let anything happen to you.*

He motioned her to be quiet, then watched as the hooded man reached the edge of the lawn. He'd make his run toward the bush at any second. Gohan tensed.

"Keiko," he said softly, "watch that man and tell me the moment he starts running toward us."

He moved outside the bush, to the side closest to the house. His only weapons were his hands, but that would be enough.

"Gohan, Gohan," she whispered, waving at him.

Here he comes, Davey boy. Get ready.

He crouched behind the bush, poised to strike. He felt the ground pounding and knew the man was near. Suddenly, he leaped, and the hooded man, surprised, froze for a second. That was all it took. Gohan sent a powerful right fist into the man's throat, smashing his Adam's apple. He tried to scream but couldn't.

Gohan had him down in another couple of seconds and crashed repeated karate chops into his neck. The man went limp. Gohan didn't have time to think about what he'd just done. He retrieved the rifle and ammunition, then rolled the man onto his stomach so Keiko wouldn't see the gruesome sight.

Now he was ready to go to work. *You guys were going to use this bush to thin out the guards. Now I'll do the same thing to you.*

He suddenly realized he was holding an American M-1. *How the heck did they get these?* he wondered.

He crawled back inside the bush with Keiko. Seeing blood on his hand, she moaned with fear, but he smiled, comforting her.

"I'm fine, Keiko," he said in English.

He poked the M-1 through the bush and said softly, "OK, boys. The party's over."

He checked the clip, flipped off the safety, and positioned himself. He was comfortable with the light, 30-caliber carbine, and he knew he'd do some damage. He eyed a hooded man thirty yards away who was moving toward him, got him square in his sights, took a deep breath, and slowly pulled the trigger.

The Yakuza jerked and fell, rolling down the steep hill and out of sight.

You just killed two men in less than two minutes, Davey boy. How does it feel?

He didn't have time to think about it. He saw another hooded man working toward him. He was about forty yards away. He breathed deeply to calm himself, then squeezed the trigger smoothly.

He too went down, falling onto a large, jagged rock that appeared to rip off his head. Gohan didn't waste time watching. More of the enemy was moving into view. As the reality of the situation set in, Gohan began to tremble.

Get a grip, man! he told himself. *This isn't target practice. This is war!*

He saw another hooded man moving from tree to tree, gaining ground on a couple of Kobashigawa's guards, who were protected only by the metal shields they held in front of them.

The guards were spread out throughout the lawn. They all carried the metal shields. The guard closest to him, about twenty-five feet away, stopped and slipped his shield, which had sharp iron posts protruding from the bottom of it, into the ground. Using it as cover, he lifted his rifle and fired at a Yakuza who was stationed behind a small tree. The shot him hit right in the head.

Good shot, man! Gohan said to himself, congratulating the guard.

His eyes went back to the edge of the lawn. The man he had been watching was over fifty yards away, but he centered his sights on the middle of his face and pulled the trigger.

The man continued moving.

Gohan slapped his forehead. He was a good shot and knew he shouldn't have missed the hooded man. He took a deep breath and calmed himself. *Take your time, Davey, and do it right.*

He reset his sights. His last shot was high. He made the adjustment, relaxed his body and arms, and fired. The man jerked forward, turning toward Gohan as if to ask, "Where'd that come from?" before falling backward down the hill.

Gohan pulled back and looked at Keiko, who still had her hands over her ears. He forced a smile, and so did she. After loading another clip, Gohan turned back to the fray.

Whew! OK, Davey, get your bearings. Who's next?

As the guards moved much closer to the edge of the lawn, the enemy started backing down the hill. The firepower coming from the guards was enormous.

He concentrated on some movement that caught his eye. Four or five of the attackers were moving away from the top of the hill, toward him. He chose the closest one, hoping to pick him off without the others realizing where the shot came from. The man was down the hill, standing in front of a large rock, making him an easy target.

He aimed and fired, then heard the bullet ricochet off the rock. The Yakuza jumped away from the rock, started to run, then froze. He turned toward Gohan and grabbed his side and fell over. The other men with him ran further down the hill and slipped in behind the large rock.

He pulled back and glanced at Keiko again. Despite her fear, she was being a real trooper. Her expression showed him that she trusted him with her life.

He took another deep breath. The guards had reached the edge of the lawn. He saw another hooded man who'd reached the same rock where the other Yakuza were hiding.

He shot the man through the neck.

He saw another man roll down the hill and knew one of the guards must have shot him. They were retreating more rapidly. He quickly chose another target as a man came straight across the hill below the lawn's edge, directly in front of him. He aimed and fired, but the bullet missed.

The hooded man whirled toward Gohan and fired wildly, bullets whizzing through the bush. He fired back quickly, drilling the Yakuza with successive shots, felling him. He dropped his weapon and turned, reaching toward Keiko. He saw quickly that she was

OK. For that split second, he realized that any of those stray bullets could have hit her. A tear slipped out of his eye. She reached over and touched his arm, letting him know she was OK.

"Oh, Jesus!" he said to no one in particular. He had been raised a Catholic, and though he wasn't a practicing Catholic at the time, he did believe in God. It struck him that for the first time since the attack had begun, he was calling on God for help.

What took you so long, idiot? he chided himself.

He put his mind back to the task. He eyed a hooded man moving down the hill. He was injured and was moving slowly. Many of the attackers had begun to retreat. He had a clear shot at the man and slowly pulled the trigger. The man fell and bounced into a tree stump.

Suddenly, chaos erupted. The rest of the hooded men charged from behind rocks and trees, firing wildly, shouting and running down the hill. There weren't many left, and Gohan knew the attack had been broken. He fired a few more times but missed. Kobashigawa's guards, in better position, had better success.

As quickly as it had begun, the skirmish was over.

Gohan and Keiko crawled out from under the bush, and the guards, all at the edge of the lawn, continued firing at the fleeing men until they were out of sight. Six guards held their position while the rest pulled the dead men into a pile at the edge of the lawn.

Gohan, exhausted, sat down, looking at the cloudless afternoon sky, almost unable to comprehend what happened. His head and arms hurt. He hadn't realized how tense he'd been during the skirmish. He was cut in many places from the bush's sharp needles.

Keiko sat beside him, her arms wrapped tightly around him. She wiped blood from his arms with her kimono, then laid her head against his shoulder. She too was emotionally exhausted. The touch of her head on his broad shoulders brought Gohan back to reality. He squeezed her shoulder lightly and smiled at her.

Kinjo, one of the chief executive's guards, walked toward them. Gohan and Keiko stood and met him halfway across the lawn, where he addressed Gohan in English.

"Gohan-san, you are hero to Okinawan people and to master,

Konishi Kobashigawa. I see what you do. You save life of Kobashigawa-san's daughter, Keiko, and you make enemy run because
you excellent shooting. I tell Kobashigawa-san what you do."

Suddenly, Gohan was an even bigger hero than before, and he
had his girl, too. The chief executive couldn't refuse him now, and
Gohan knew it.

Keiko knew it, too.

Chapter 3
Unrest in Indochina

Fort George G. Meade
Baltimore, Maryland
September 1960

Senator Warfield Nye of Georgia was a special liaison from the office of the president. His presence at the meeting was largely due to the fact that the National Security Advisor was out of the country and unavailable. His assistant wasn't available, either, and someone in DC decided to send Senator Nye.

Bob Nagy, a senior official with the CIA; retired General Adam Horring from NSA, the National Security Agency; and Major General Marshal Winthrop, U.S. Air Force Far East Commander and head of SIGINT operations, rounded out the group. The atmosphere was tense. The two generals and Bob Nagy had been involved with the situation with Indochina for a while. Senator Nye, a novice, wasn't very well known or liked.

Coffee was served, though Senator Nye chose a brandy, which he found in the cabinet in the corner of the room. He hadn't bothered to ask to use it. That wasn't a good way to impress important people, none of whom knew him well. The men waited until

General Horring's secretary left the room before speaking.

"Gentlemen, let's get right to it," General Horring said. "We have information to discuss and to take back to our respective bosses, and it's not pretty. The situation in Indochina isn't good, and it may have just gotten worse.

"Let me bring you up to speed. As we all know, Ike is concerned about the spread of Communism in Vietnam. He has predicted, probably correctly, that the country will be the base from which Communism will spread throughout the entire area. The Viet Minh, under Ho Chi Minh, have taken over northern Vietnam, and we can assume that area is lost.

"Ho Chi Minh isn't a common household name yet, but it will be, thanks to the press, who are making him into a hero instead of telling the world he's a daggone Communist. Some of us believe he's the most dangerous man in Indochina.

"That's part of the problem. He's a hero to many and a savior to the Vietnamese. He got the Japs out of Vietnam—with the help of China and America, of course—and he got the French out, too, so he looks like a hero. The truth is, he's a dangerous Communist revolutionary who's a capable catalyst for the spread of Communism throughout Indochina unless we can stop him.

"I'm not convinced we've done our best job over there. The CIA program didn't work. Sorry, Bob, but you know that."

Bob Nagy shifted in his seat. He couldn't deny the CIA's inability to accomplish its goals with a propaganda program in Vietnam and attempted coups in Laos. What he didn't say in front of the group, mainly because of Senator Nye, was that they were still in Laos, still trying to help control the topsy-turvy government there.

"Part of the reason was because it was done clandestinely," Horring continued. "We don't want the world to know how deeply involved we are in Vietnam's problems. Now we send our military into the south to train Diem's troops and build up South Vietnam's armed forces. We've done the same thing in Laos. We won't hide that from the world. This isn't 1940. Anyone who's interested in these things already knows what we're doing. Where does that leave us in the eyes of the rest of the world?"

He shook his head in disgust as he spoke. It was clear he wasn't in agreement with American military policy in Indochina. He wasn't convinced that his country had handled the mess in Vietnam and Laos very well.

"Anyway, the bottom line is, we're trying to stay out of the mix—or make it look that way. In the meantime, Ho Chi Minh is preparing to take the rest of Vietnam. We expect him to infiltrate the south with a major effort soon. We just hope our people can hold him off again. This isn't an easy situation for America. As you know, we have detractors in this country who say we need to get out before it's too late.

"As is usually the case, those who yell the loudest don't know all the details. South Vietnam can be saved from Communism. We believe it, and so does our government, or else we wouldn't be there. If we want Southeast Asia to be anti-Communist, then South Vietnam must be protected. As Ike predicted, Vietnam could be the most vital position in the Far East for either Communism or democracy.

"The Viet Minh just keep on coming. We aren't doing a good job of stopping them. It would be nice to have help from somewhere else, but that won't happen, either."

"Why aren't we solicitin' help from other institutions, general?" Senator Nye asked. "What about SEATO? Can't we get help there? Pressure from peer nations would certainly have a positive effect on Vietnam. Why hasn't anyone thought of that?"

Bob Nagy, who didn't like the Georgia senator to start with, felt the man didn't belong in the room. He answered quickly. "SEATO is useless, Senator. The countries that we need to join the alliance refuse, and Laos, Cambodia, and Vietnam can't participate in the discussions. Left in that position, SEATO is weak. Adam's right. Our best hope right now is to keep southern Vietnam anti-Communist. It won't be easy, but there are ways, including new elections, military buildup, and other plans that are already in progress."

General Horring nodded, sipping his coffee, and continued. "Ho Chi Minh has won the hearts of the Vietnamese people. He single-handedly directed the long tug of war between Vietnam and France, and he gave the Vietnamese the only hope they had. He ousted France. The ol' guy's been around a long time, spreading his pro-revolutionary, pro-Communist message. That will be very hard to overcome. We have to pitch anti-Communism to people who look up to a Communist hero. How easy does that sound? Now it appears that our man in South Vietnam might not be the right person for the job after all."

"I assume you're speakin' of President Diem," Senator Nye said. "Why, he's a democratic leader. We installed him to bring about democracy. Why are you sayin' he's not the right man? Who else do we have? Isn't he doin' what we want?"

"With all due respect, Senator," General Winthrop said in his strong Texas accent, "you appear to be a little naïve in these discussions. Possibly you weren't briefed."

Like his father before him, General Marshal Alan Winthrop was a lifetime military man. He served in World War II and Korea and spent two months in a prison camp. He had two purple hearts and more other decorations on his uniform than the fat little Southern senator had pockmarks on his face. He was a little miffed that a dishonest politician who lived in the tobacco industry's pocket was invited to the meeting. The material was too sensitive.

Since that was out of his control, he continued his explanation.

"Senator, Ngo Dinh Diem was allowed to run South Vietnam because there wasn't anyone else we trusted. Yeah, that's right. He's a Catholic ruling over a country that's 95 percent Buddhist. How popular do you think he is? We know he rigged the elections and proclaimed himself president. We also know he has assassinated all those who opposed him. Now granted, he has fought Communism and done it pretty well, but Shorty's country isn't a democratic nation any more than ours isn't run by a king. You understand me, Senator?"

Nye looked surprised. "You know him well enough to call him by a nickname?"

Winthrop laughed. "You've obviously never met the man. He's

so short that when he sits on a chair, his feet don't touch the floor. That doesn't make him a bad guy, and I probably shouldn't have called him that. No disrespect intended.

"Diem's rule is more authoritarian than democratic. Democracy in South Vietnam is practiced on paper only, Senator. Diem has lost the respect of the Vietnamese in the south. He appointed members of his family to high political positions instead of appointing those who were most competent. His idea of democracy is for the state to control everything.

"That's not democracy, Senator. We want to see capitalism bring individual prosperity, but it's not happening in South Vietnam. The problem is, we learned all this too late, and not all those who need to know have found out. We're fightin' a losin' battle over there, and my guess is that General Horring has even more bad news. I have an inkling of it from my contacts in Okinawa. Right, Adam?"

Horring nodded and sighed. They didn't have all the right people at the meeting, and important items had to be discussed. Although it was still considered preliminary information, that didn't diminish its importance.

"We're missing something here, gentlemen," Nagy said. "Before we toss Diem out with the dishwater, let's remember why we kept him in power. I agree he might not be the ideal man for the job, but who would be? The fact is, he has reduced Communist pressure in South Vietnam, and he has fought Communism fervently. He made clear inroads against the Viet Minh. Most importantly, he's kept Ho Chi Minh and his guerrillas out of the country. That's why he's in control. Whether he forms a democratic government isn't essential, but keeping Communism out of South Vietnam is. His anti-Communist programs have worked, and, under his control, South Vietnam is still anti-Communist."

"Until recently, yes," Horring said. "As you know, Bob, Ho Chi Minh doesn't remain stagnant and never has. He's always got something working. If Plan A doesn't work, he moves to Plan B. He's been infiltrating South Vietnam under our noses. They're killing people like crazy, and there are lots of problems stemming from that. Diem is staggering. As Marshal said, he doesn't have the respect of his own people. If anything, Ho Chi Minh has the upper hand, and that's not good."

General Winthrop stood and began pacing. "Here's the bottom line, boys. Vietnam's a trouble area. The book's still out on Diem. He's fightin' Communism, but he's not winnin' over his own people. That creates an opening that Ho and his boys will drive through like a Mack truck through Jell-O. You can bet your rear end on that.

"We have a lot of good people over there right now tryin' to retrain Diem's troops so they can fight like guerillas, because that's what they'll have to do to keep Communism out. Those Viet Minh won't stay in North Vietnam and settle for half. No, sir. They've already proven that.

"Diem needs us now more than ever, but he's getting harder to work with. Not a very pretty picture, is it? Not only that, but our attention's bein' divided several ways, what with Russia and Cuba goin' on and this thing in Laos. It's not clear if any of that's been intentional. I wouldn't put it past Khrushchev to try to divert our attention if he's buddyin' up with Minh. Adam, it's been hot in Laos for a while now. Some of our people have felt that Laos might be more strategic than Vietnam."

"General," Senator Nye said, "if we're training President Diem's troops to fight the guerrillas, then we should be able to win. After all, America is the greatest fighting nation on earth, isn't it?"

The general was very tired of the White House idiot. Politicians like Nye kept America from moving forward. There were plenty of good politicians across the river, but Nye wasn't one of them. He wondered how they got stuck with him.

He turned toward the senator. "Honorable Senator, you've never been in the service, have you? Never mind. You don't have to answer, because I know you haven't. Senator, we can train Diem's troops better than our own, and it won't make much difference. Diem has the final say over assignments and promotions.

"He has already placed favored people in critical positions and bypassed those who were more highly trained. Why? Because loyalty is more important to him than victory, and that's because he's enamored of the presidency. All the rich folks in South Vietnam are part of his family, and they're loyal to him.

"Maybe I'm bein' a bit too hard on Diem, but darn it, his country's about to be taken over by someone who doesn't like him much, and I'm not sure he even knows. I'm tellin' you, boys, Diem will lose the people of South Vietnam the way things are goin'. We're slippin' badly over there."

"General, that's a very unfavorable position," Bob Nagy said. "Worse, it's very unpopular. The American press is making Diem out as a hero. We have a little more information than the rest of the American people, but most of them give him a favorable grade so far."

"I understand that," Winthrop answered, "but let me ask you something. If I stuck a hand grenade up your butt, and the American press told the American people you're doin' a heck of a job at the CIA, that won't make your butt feel any better when the grenade goes off, will it?"

Horring shifted in his seat. He had to take control of the meeting before it got out of hand. Bob and Marshal could disagree without rancor, but Nye kept interrupting. The situation could turn nasty.

"You're right, Bob," Horring said. "In fact, you're both right. I'm afraid it won't be any better after I tell you the latest development. We all know Ho Chi Minh has made inroads into Laos and has an alliance with the Pathet Lao insurgents. Bob can tell you that the CIA backed a couple of coups over there, but they ultimately failed. The government there is weak even with our backing.

"Ike's concerned about our prospects in Laos, and he should be. He's as much concerned with that as with South Vietnam. If Ho Chi Minh gets Laos, he also gets South Vietnam. We're beginning to get information that military support for the anti-American forces in Laos isn't just coming from North Vietnam and Ho, which we expected. It's also coming from the Soviet Union, which was not expected."

"Whoa!" Senator Nye said. "What the devil's going on here? We can't fight the whole stupid world!"

No one responded to his outburst. The situation was clearly beyond his understanding. He knew there were problems in Vietnam. Anyone who watched TV could figure that out, plus he received important information from his White House contacts. However, he'd just been told more in half an hour than he could handle. He didn't know what it meant, but it was definitely important.

"This information came from our U-2s. They fly low over Laos and pick up coded signals, signals too weak to be picked up from our normal operations. We've got enough info to concern us, but not enough to tell us what we need to know. We're still missing a lot. There's a lot of information being passed that the U-2s can't even get."

The telephone rang. General Horring answered and listened, occasionally shaking his head unhappily. General Winthrop used the respite to get up and pace throughout the room. Senator Nye poured himself another brandy.

Captain Marcel "Mercy" Brown took a swig from his canteen and leaned up against the Quonset hut. He was assigned to the Green Berets to help train the Royal Laotian Army recruits. The U.S. Navy had given the Royal Lao government a number of LCVP and LCM landing crafts to help them control the Mekong River. Mercy and his friend, Niko Rizzi, a Navy UDT specialist, had worked with the RLA and, specifically, with a group of local farmers, known as the Hmongs, training them in the use of the Navy vessels.

Rizzi had since been reassigned back to Vietnam, but Mercy remained in Laos, continuing to work with the Laotian Hmongs. He was, in military terms, "short." He had only a few weeks remaining in his military life, and he looked forward to it.

"Whatdya think, Captain?" a Green Beret sergeant asked. "These guys gonna be any good?"

"Well, I like those Hmongs," Mercy answered. "They learn quickly, and they're tough. They already know the jungle. They can survive without much training. They just have to learn how to kill. They don't think like military, but once the Commies start killin' their brothers and sisters, they'll get angry enough to do the job right."

"You hear the rumors?"

"You mean about the Lao Commies joinin' up with Ho Chi Minh?"

"Yeh."

"They've been joined at the hip for a long time, sarge. Maybe it's just becomin' official now. But, then, that's why we're trainin' these guys—so they can protect their own country. We don't really wanna get in this war."

"Yeh, but we're gonna, aren't we?"

Mercy Brown laughed. "That's why I'm getting' out, sarge. Korea was bad enough. Then this little mess we had over here the other month—that nearly got my buddy Niko killed. It's time to go with the odds."

"So this is it for you, huh, Mercy?" a Green Beret colonel asked, joining the conversation.

"Yes, sir. I thought I was gonna stay in forever, but I've had enough. Time for me to say good-bye to the army. Like sarge said, we're gonna end up in this war, Colonel. You know that, don't you?"

The army colonel sat down on a crate of ammunition. "Well, I guess the jury's still out on that, Mercy. The politicians say no, and so do our superiors. But those of us in the trenches aren't quite as optimistic. Remember, the reason we're training these locals is so we won't have to get involved."

Mercy Brown laughed. "Yeh, right. You think the Vietnam thing is gonna creep over here into Laos, too?"

"It already has, Mercy. But the hope is that we can keep Laos out of it. We'll see. So, whatdya gonna do, Mercy, when you get out?"

Mercy Brown took another swig from his canteen.

"Remember those Thais and those Chinese guys we met—the

ones that were guarding all the dope coming through Thailand and Laos?"

"Yeh, what about 'em?"

"Well, that's what I'm gonna do, Colonel. There's lots of money in drugs. As long as somebody has to make it, it might as well be me."

The Green Beret colonel laughed. "What, you're gonna sit on the border with those guys with a rifle slung over your shoulder? Doesn't sound like you, Mercy."

"No, I ain't that dumb, Colonel. I know how to fly, you know."

"Yeh, what about it?"

"I'll fly that stuff from one place to another. I just need to make the right contacts. That won't be difficult. I'll get myself a little plane, mount some guns on it for protection, and who knows? I'll probably become a millionaire."

"Your momma's not gonna be real thrilled about that, Mercy."

Mercy Brown thought for a moment before speaking. "Yeh, I could go back to Alabama and get a job in the cotton fields or somethin'. But I ain't interested in being a martyr for the cause, Colonel. There ain't nothin' back there for a black man. I'd end up in prison. You know what I do best? I'm a trained killer. That's what I do best. A black man in Alabama that's a trained killer ain't gonna last long, Colonel. No, I got aspirations above and beyond the cotton fields. Survival, Colonel—that's the magic word. And I'm good at it."

"I thought you were tight with the CIA. You tellin' me they're gonna let you do that?"

"I ain't tellin' you nuthin', Colonel." He laughed. "I'm short, real short. But don't worry 'bout me. I'll be OK."

"Yeh, well, I hope you stay alive long enough to enjoy that million dollars you're gonna make, Mercy," he answered, laughing. "In the meantime, let's see if we can teach these locals how to survive and be trained killers. That's the only way they're gonna make it, you know. The word is that the Viet Minh are gonna be coming through here. If these boys aren't ready to defend their homeland, Laos is gonna bite the dust.

"You're awful good, Mercy. Teach 'em what you can before you become a criminal, OK? Their lives might depend on it."

He slapped the 6'5" black man on his back and went on his way. Mercy Brown yawned and rubbed the back of his neck.

"Didn't get much sleep, Captain?" the sergeant asked.

"Never get enough sleep, sarge. Too much pain. All those injuries. That's why I'm getting' out. C'mon, let's go to work."

Warfield Nye was an egotistical man whose parents and grandparents were filthy rich. His good fortune had been handed to him when he was born, although he acted as if he'd earned it—or deserved it. Everything he did politically had personal gain attached. That was the only way he knew how to operate. He really believed that with his money, position, and American citizenship, none of the events in those puny little countries could possibly affect him.

He knew he had some responsibility for those things, and he showed outward concern, but he didn't really care. Unfortunately for his country, men like Nye had far-reaching responsibilities. That meant that someone, somewhere, would be adversely affected by his actions. Luckily, not all politicians in America were like Nye.

The senator wondered with whom he should share some of the new information. He had to be careful. It was likely none of the others in the room would talk, because they were military types. He didn't want to be known as the man who leaked information.

General Horring hung up the phone, and General Winthrop began speaking.

"Adam, this Laos stuff came from our boys on Okinawa, right? We have some good ones over there."

"Yes, Marshal." Horring looked at the CIA chief. "Bob, you and Senator Nye probably aren't aware of this, but we have a group of people at a number of intercept sites on Okinawa who are giving us vital information regarding events in Laos. They picked up a new Russian network that passed some astounding intelligence regarding Russian intervention in Laos. We're watching it closely. That phone call was an update, and the situation is deteriorating. The scary thing isn't that the Russians are willing to support the Viet Minh in Laos, but it looks like they're ready to send troops in, too. Our U-2s verify some of that."

"Oh, poop!" Nagy looked at General Horring. "That's the first I've heard of that. The cold war was supposed to be easy, Adam. What happened?"

"Maybe it's not cold anymore," General Horring replied.

There was stunned silence in the room as the men realized the prophetic aspect of the general's statement. General Winthrop turned to his NSA counterpart.

"Adam, this is a little scary. We all know how shaky our position is over there. If Russia gets involved at a high level, we'll be forced to make some serious decisions that won't be very popular. How about laying it out in clear, precise detail? I want the right picture in my mind before I sit down with my people and try to make recommendations."

"Sure," Horring replied. "Let me get more hot coffee." He buzzed the outer office, and a pleasant, middle-aged woman came to retrieve the nearly empty pot. The men stood and stretched, walking a bit and making small talk during the short break.

In a few minutes, the door opened, fresh coffee was served, and the secretary relocked the door on her way out.

"I've studied the goings-on in Laos for some time now," Horring said. "Laos is like the little boy who grew up on the wrong side of the tracks, with gangs and criminals all around him. His parents tried to protect him, but the gangs got him in a stranglehold. Finally, one day, they walked up to him and said, 'OK, son, you've seen all we've been doing for years. Now you either join us, or we beat your brains out.'

"That's what's happened to Laos. They were under French control, just like Vietnam. They saw how Ho Chi Minh pushed the French out, and he walked up to them and offered to do the same thing. He joined forces with the Pathet Lao to drive out the French from Laos. The U.S. saw the problem and intervened, and Laos began operating in a pro-U.S. fashion, at least to some extent. Then Ho and his gang walked up and said, 'We're back, and we're taking over. Join up, or we beat your brains out.'"

"Where did this Pathet Lao come from?" Nye asked.

"They've been around for almost thirty years. Prince Souphanouvong, a nephew of King Sisavangvong, formed it. They started off as a nationalist revolutionary group like their Vietnamese counterparts, trying to get out from under French control. They ended up as Communists. That's what makes them dangerous.

"Getting back to the present, the Laos government, led by Prince Souvanna Phouma, chose to make concessions to the Pathet Lao. We didn't like that. He formed a coalition government and included the Pathet Lao Communists. The CIA got involved and tried, and failed, to control the elections. Prince Souphanouvong, the Pathet Lao leader, took control again, so we cut all military and economic aid.

"Prince Souvanna Phouma resigned, and the coalition government fell. The new government was backed by the U.S. and was led by Prime Minister Phoui Sananikone. The Pathet Lao leaders were ousted. Prince Souphanouvong, along with some other top Pathet Lao leaders, was imprisoned.

"Then Prime Minister Sananikone resigned. The CIA backed a coup led by General Phoumi Nosavan. That government took control less than a year ago, and the new prime minister was Prince Somsanith.

"A few months ago, Souphanouvong and the other Pathet Lao leaders escaped from prison. Now there's been another attempted coup. That happened back in August when Captain Kong Le attempted a takeover. Incidentally, he was trained in America. The king got involved and assigned Souvanna Phouma as prime minister. Kong Le retreated. The king asked General Nosavan to stay on as deputy prime minister, but he refused and formed a counter coup backed by the CIA.

"Now it seems that Prince Souvanna has turned to the Soviets for help. Kong Le has since joined the Pathet Lao. Are any of you still keeping score?

"Laos is ripe for the picking. Ho Chi Minh knows it, and so does his Communist sponsor, Nikita Khrushchev. We have major decisions to make, but we need more information. Thanks to our intelligence programs, we're getting it. Every day we learn more, but time is against us."

General Winthrop stood and began pacing again. "So Laos has a pro-American government and a group of insurgents who are anti-American but not necessarily pro-Communist, though they receive support from Communists. We also have Khrushchev's boys thinkin' about comin' to their aid, but we don't know how, when, or if. That's clear as a bell, Adam."

Horring laughed. "I hope it doesn't sound that bad. Here's where we are now. It appears that the Soviets and North Vietnam are pre-paring to enter Laos to help the Laotians overthrow their govern-ment again. That doesn't make any sense, because we would have to get involved. Khrushchev isn't that stupid—I hope."

"Adam, suppose they're not goin' in there to help the Laotians overthrow the government. Suppose the Russians are goin' in there just to help Ho Chi Minh."

"That's what we think, too. Our information is very sketchy on this, which means we're guessing, but it looks like the Russians want us to think they're helping the Laos insurgents to keep us on military alert in central Laos. That forces us to put more effort into working with the RLA. If they truly intend to help Ho Chi Minh make a move on South Vietnam, they'd like us to be short-handed, and we can't afford that.

"The other concern is that if Khrushchev intends to aid North Vietnam physically, they're asking us to become physically involved. We could be talking a major war, gentlemen."

Bob Nagy fidgeted in his seat, then slammed his fist on the table. "Adam, the Russians can't be that stupid! We know every-thing they do, and they watch us just as closely. They have to understand that we'll find out what they're doing and will respond in kind."

"History tells us that the Soviet military leadership doesn't always make the wisest decisions, Bob."

Bob Nagy smiled, walked to the table with the coffeepot, and poured a cup, then he walked back to his chair and set the cup on the table next to him. "Yeah, you're right, but, right or wrong, they have to know we'll find out. They don't want to start a war with us. Doesn't that tell you something?"

"I don't know. Spell it out."

"The Russians know we're on the brink of becoming involved in the Vietnam problem. They know we're training Diem's forces. Maybe they've determined that we're already in it up to our elbows, so there's no reason for them not to be involved a bit, maybe on the perimeter. Maybe they figure there's no danger doing what we're doing.

"The problem with that is why are they being so secretive? How long has this been in the planning stages, yet we didn't find out until now? That doesn't sound right. It looks like they've been trying to keep it from us. As you say, our information is sketchy, but do they really think they can do something like this without our finding out? It appears they believe it, and we know our intelligence isn't complete. We don't know for certain that the Russians are moving into Laos, do we? This is a major undertaking, and we don't have enough intelligence. Why?"

"That's a fair question," Horring replied. "It appears that they aren't passing the information normally. They change frequencies a lot, and there are whole new nets springing up where they switch the information. By the time we find them, we don't know how much information we've lost.

"Maybe you're right, and they're trying to disguise their communications so we don't know exactly what they're doing. The bottom line is that this is more than just a threat. At this point, we're prepared to advise that the Soviets are moving into Laos and will be taking a supportive role.

"As you've indicated, we have to understand that the Russians aren't granting us information. We have to step up our attempts to get it. It's too vital to miss. We have some SIGINT sites in that region. We can put all of them on it if that's OK with you, Marshal."

"That's fine," Winthrop said. "This is too important. We'll switch over anyone we can to get what you need."

"We'll continue getting more information," Horring continued. "We'll keep everyone updated daily. Right now, it's important to get this into Ike's hands—and to your people's hands, Bob.

"We don't have to reach a decision yet. There isn't enough information for that, but the guys across the river will want to know what we've got. We need to get this into the right hands, then we need to get our people onto this and stay with it. Do you agree?"

The others nodded.

"OK. Here's where we go from here. Bob, your people need to get as much additional information as you can, especially regarding how the Soviets might make this move if that's really what they're up to. Are you all right with that?"

"Sure. Let me talk to, uh, Ken Damsteegt. One of us can get back to you tomorrow if that's OK."

"Thanks. Senator Nye, the information you've heard here must reach the president ASAP but no one else. Mr. Eisenhower can take it from there. Because this is important, I'm going to repeat myself. I know you don't usually work in these circles. That information goes only to the president. There are no exceptions. We know the National Security Advisor won't be back for almost a week, and it can't wait that long. You also can't share any of this over a phone line. Do you understand, Senator?"

"Sure, general. What do y'all think I do, sit in my office and smoke expensive cigars all day? I know what's goin' on. Don't worry. I'll take care of gettin' this info to Ike immediately."

"Marshal, if you think it's worth it, you might want to stop at Onna Point on your way home. Our friend Sergeant Rice might need a little pep talk. He's very good, and we need him more than ever. It'd be good to keep him focused.

"I can't remember your commander's name out there, but he needs to know how important this network is. Keep Rice on it twenty-four hours at a time if necessary.

"In the meantime, I'll make sure we stay on top of it here. Every word the Soviets say to each other will have an impact on our decision-making process. It's my gut feeling that we have only 50 percent of what we need. We'll know when we have the other 50 percent. Then we'll have to move fast. That's why we have to keep our friends at the top fully informed.

"Thank you for coming, gentlemen. We have work to do."

Senator Nye was insulted by General Horring's remarks. He had to think carefully before deciding what to do. The president was away and might not return for twenty-four hours. Should Nye wait, or was there someone else to see? He'd have to think about that. He didn't need a military man telling him what he could or couldn't do.

General Winthrop looked forward to his trip to Okinawa. He always enjoyed the island and its friendly people, and he was proud of the work being done at Onna Point. Lately, that had become a feather in his cap. Sergeant Rice was becoming the Willie Mays of cryptology. The man was cocky but pleasant, and Winthrop was anxious to see him again.

Bob Nagy left immediately. He wanted to find Kenneth Damsteegt and discuss the new information. He had some ideas of his own, but he wanted to formulate them better. He'd think them over during lunch.

General Horring made a mental note to speak to someone about Senator Nye. The information was too sensitive to have a self-centered politician involved. He doubted Ike knew that Nye had been sent to the meeting.

After glancing at the empty room, he buzzed his secretary. "I'm sorry, Nancy, but can you come in and clean up a little? I don't know what it is about these meetings, but no one ever cleans up his mess."

"I know what it is, sir."

"Yeah? What's that?"

"They're men, sir."

Chapter 4
Ho Chi Minh

Nguyen That Thanh was a Vietnamese and a nationalist. He was born Nguyen Sinh Cung in central Vietnam in 1890.
At the age of ten, his name was changed to Nguyen That Thanh,
which meant destined to succeed. As a young man, impressed by
the Communist revolution in Russia, he was determined to bring
change to his own land using the same means.

Early after World War I, he changed his name to Nguyen Ai
Quoc, meaning Nguyen the Patriot. After betraying a peaceful
Vietnamese activist for $10,000 Hong Kong, he stopped using
that name. Over the years, he used many aliases, but the most
important name change came in 1941. At that time, he changed
his name to Ho Chi Minh, a name taken from an old beggar he
met. It meant Ho, the Enlightened One. Ho was one of the found-
ers of the French Communist Party in 1920.

Ho Chi Minh lived and studied in Paris in his early years.
While there, he wrote a book about the French colonies and their
problems, a thinly veiled stab at the French suppression of his
Vietnam. He also published an anti-French newspaper.

Beginning in 1923, he spent considerable time in Russia,

training in Communism and learning revolutionary tactics. He studied political theory at Moscow University, then traveled in China in 1924, where he started a revolutionary group instructing the exiled Vietnamese who lived there.

After substantial training from Ho, they were sent back to Vietnam to begin what would become a long, powerful revolutionary movement in his country. As the movement grew, new leaders emerged, and they too were sent to China to train under Ho, the Enlightened One.

When the Chinese authorities under Chiang Kai-Shek forced the Communists from China in the mid-1920s, Ho returned to Russia to continue his revolutionary work. In 1928, he became the Southeast Asia representative to the Communist International Organization. In 1930, he led the Indochinese Communist Party from Hong Kong. He was arrested in Hong Kong in 1931 by the British for his role in the Vietnamese riots against the French, but, having already established a reputable name for himself, he was released after one year. While in prison, Ho contracted tuberculosis.

In the early 1940s, Ho returned to China where he once again trained revolutionaries in the hope of liberating Vietnam from the French. Though he spent many of his previous years in hiding, moving from country to country like a shadow, he openly began leading his movement.

He sent emissaries into Vietnam with a new purpose—to create unity among the Vietnamese people to draw them to himself in the process.

"Forget our dear Communism for a while," he told his followers. "Strive for unity among our people. Once we've been liberated from the outsiders and rule our own country, then we can move forward with our Communist movement."

His strategy worked. He created an organization called the League for Independence of Vietnam, shortened to Viet Minh. To no one's surprise, the Enlightened One became its leader and spokesperson. By the mid-1940s, the Communist movement was strong enough in Vietnam for Ho to leave China, where he had endured additional arrests and imprisonment. Finally, he could lead his people from his own homeland.

Once there, it was easy to convince the inhabitants of northern Vietnam to side with him and his Viet Minh. The choice was simple. The Japanese overlords, who had moved in during the Second World War, would soon be driven out, and then the people would have to choose between French or Viet Minh rule. He knew they didn't want to continue under the French.

Ho's revolution operated under the generalship of Pham Vam Dong and General Vo Nguyen Giap, who had learned guerrilla warfare while in China from Mao Tse-tung. Ho's army established its headquarters in Hanoi, and soon Emperor Bao Dai abdicated his government to Ho and the Viet Minh.

Soon thereafter, the French military took control of southern Vietnam, arresting and killing many Communists, forcing the Viet Minh underground. The remaining Communist leaders escaped to the north.

In 1946, the first major military action between the Viet Minh and the French occurred when the French attacked the city of Haiphong. Nearly 6,000 Vietnamese died as a result. From then on, the Vietnamese people rallied around Ho, who, since he appeared to give them their only chance to escape from French rule, became even more popular. Even those who disapproved of his Communist leanings felt they were better off with him than the French, whom they hated.

At the turn of the decade, in late 1949, Mao Tse-tung and his Communist movement took control of China, and the Viet Minh immediately took advantage of their strong relationship with their Communist allies. That gave them a safety net in the north where Ho's troops could rest and be resupplied. It also created a training center for the Viet Minh guerrillas, who learned from the master, Mao Tse-tung, and his commanders.

The Viet Minh and the French fought for control of Vietnam for eight years. Ho warned the French that their superior military expertise was no match for the massive number of men in his army.

"For every ten of my men you kill, even if I kill only one of yours, I'll still win," he told the French commanders.

In the early 1950s, the French created a stronghold at Dien Bien Phu to keep the Viet Minh from entering Laos, and, eventually, South Vietnam. When Ho found out, he ordered his top commander, General Giap, to attack and overtake Dien Bien Phu at any cost.

In the spring of 1954, General Giap, with tens of thousands of troops, used brilliant maneuvering strategy over many months to completely annihilate the French at Dien Bien Phu. Nearly 20,000 Frenchmen died, were wounded, or were captured in the all-out assault. Soon thereafter, the French withdrew from Vietnam. Ho Chi Minh had carried out his warning, and he and his Vietnamese Communists had finally triumphed.

In the mid-1950s, Ho and his Viet Minh invaded neighboring Laos to oust the French from that country, too. They recruited a Laotian left-wing nationalist group called the Pathet Lao, operating under the leadership of Prince Souphanouvong and Kaysone Phomvihane. The Pathet Lao joined forces with Ho Chi Minh to help them gain independence from the French. Ho's purpose, however, was to establish Communism in Laos and to use that country as a way to move his Viet Minh into South Vietnam. Though Ho and the Pathet Lao were able to oust the French from Laos, the U.S. stepped in soon thereafter, and Ho backed off.

The Americans, led by President Dwight Eisenhower, gave economic and military backing to South Vietnam and its new leader, Ngo Dinh Diem, making it difficult for Ho and his Viet Minh to infiltrate, but Ho wouldn't be denied. He fought for years against the south, and finally, in the late 1950s, he began to win. The Vietnamese people in the south rebelled against President Diem's way of running the government. He cared little for his people, and it was only a matter of time before they realized it and rebelled. He turned his back on the small villages, which, for centuries, had been the backbone of the country, and his people soon turned their backs on him.

That made it easy for Ho and his armies to win over the people, because their loyalty was already broken. By 1960, Ho had seriously infiltrated South Vietnam.

Ho was seventy years old by then, a thin, frail, emaciated man who stooped from age and infirmity. The powerful Vietnamese leader ate seldom and then only vegetables. His once-thick black head of hair, thinning and turning gray, combed to one side, accented his baldness. His mustache and goatee, part of his appearance his entire life, were also gray.

In his earlier years, he'd been known to rant and scream while he trained and taught his revolutionary followers, using them as an outlet for the frustration caused by his passion for Vietnamese independence. He grew calmer with age, but he was still ruthless and calculating. Though appearing docile to the masses, where he was commonly called "Uncle Ho," he ruled with an iron fist behind the scenes, where his followers called him "The General."

"Get up, prisoner. You not can lay on ground. Get up, or you die!"

Lieutenant Harold Baker slowly climbed to his feet and stared at the Korean soldier. He hadn't fallen because of weakness. He was strong and in excellent shape, though he, like his POW compatriots, had become weaker because of the torture and the starvation tactics of the Communists. He had simply tripped, attempting to walk through the muck and mire.

He sloshed on through the mud. The camp was only a quarter of a mile away, not that things would be any better there. But at least they rested there, sometimes. Baker, being an officer, was interrogated constantly. If that was their plan again, there'd be no rest.

He sighed. His faith in God had kept him alive thus far, and he'd continue to trust Him. Like all POWs, he constantly tried to find ways to deter the enemy and to escape from the camp, but no one had escaped this camp yet—and stayed alive. He knew his chances were slim, if there was any chance of escape at all. But he belonged to God—and if God wanted him to die there, he'd accept it. If not, somehow he'd get out.

Being forced to build the bridge that they had just finished working on was not only hard work, since none of them were allowed to eat properly, but it was also demoralizing. They were helping the enemy. He wondered how many Americans or allies would die because of what they were doing.

Of course, he and his friends made sure that the bridge wasn't built as well as it should have been. That's about the only thing they had control over—that, and their own minds. Baker was lucky. Well...fortunate. God protected him. Most of the men turned to the Lord there, but not all. Of the ones that didn't, many lost control of their minds. They didn't have that extra strength to stand against the tricks of the devil. And the Commies were definitely the devil. At least in that camp.

He noticed Sammy Carlisle, the young army corporal, fall in front of him. He moved quickly to help him. The Korean soldier wouldn't allow it.

"Let go. If he not strong to get up, he can die. Move! Move!"

Baker couldn't do it. He wasn't raised that way. He was a Negro, and Carlisle was a white man, and not a white man that had gone out of his way to make Baker comfortable. After all, Carlisle was from Mississippi. But it didn't matter. They were both American soldiers. And Corporal Carlisle needed his help.

He paid no attention to the Korean soldier but reached down and grabbed Carlisle by his arm, pulling him to his feet. Suddenly, he was pushed hard from behind and knocked face first into the smelly mud. He turned toward the Korean soldier and watched him kick Carlisle in his groin. Baker got up to his feet and pulled Carlisle up with him.

The Korean started toward the army corporal again, but Baker moved between them.

"He's OK. I'll get him back to the camp. You need him to help build the bridge. He's a good worker. I'll take care of him."

Holding the corporal around his waist, he continued on, moving fast to catch up to the rest of the POWs.

"I said leave him," the Korean shouted.

Baker turned to see the Korean level his rifle at him.

"Leave him."

Baker closed his eyes for a quick second, asking the Lord for guidance. If they killed him, he couldn't help any of the other men. But he couldn't turn away from the boy from Mississippi. He knew they'd kill him.

He turned, his arm around the corporal, and continued walking to catch up to the rest of the group.

The Korean ran up behind him and whacked him behind the knee with his rifle. Baker, again, fell into the mud, Corporal Carlisle falling next to him. The Korean soldier pushed Carlisle away from Baker and stood between them.

"Get up, Lieutenant, and go with others."

He then pushed Carlisle down into the mud, face first, and kicked him in his ribs..

"Move! Move!" he shouted to Baker.

The lieutenant, knowing he had no other choice, ran to meet the rest of the men, slipping and falling twice. When he got up the second time, he turned and stopped. He wanted to see what was happening to Carlisle.

The soldier kicked the army corporal again.

"Get up, prisoner, or you are dead man," he heard the Korean soldier shout.

Carlisle tried to get to his feet but couldn't. None of the Americans had been fed well, and Carlisle wasn't a big man. He faltered quickly. Lieutenant Baker saw the Korean raise his rifle. He knew what was coming next. He turned and ran toward the rest of the POWs, not willing to watch another of his compatriots fall at the hands of the enemy. He heard the shot and screamed, "No, God!"

Baker woke up, drenched in perspiration. He sat up and looked around, recognizing that he was not in Korea. He was on Okinawa. He shook his head, wiped the perspiration from his face, and jumped down from the upper bunk. It was semidark in the room. Everyone else was sleeping. He grabbed his wristwatch from the table next to the bunk, pulled a towel out of the top drawer, and left the room, walking to the shower area. He stripped and took a short, cold shower, then checked his watch. It was 5:00 A.M.

He walked back to the barracks room and got dressed. He'd be getting up soon, anyway. Grabbing his Bible, he walked outside, ambled over to a bench from where he could see the beach and the water, and sat down. He leaned back against the bench and sighed.

Okinawa! He didn't know much about the place except that it was a small island and that they wanted him there to prepare for another assignment. He thought about his family back in Houston. A black man married to the most beautiful white woman in Houston, Texas, and they hadn't strung him up yet. He smiled. It sure helped that most of the people he knew there were Christians. God had gotten him through Korea and had helped him survive the POW camp. And he didn't have those dreams that often anymore. Now, it looked like there might be another assignment. That was probably what prompted the dreams again. At least America wasn't at war, although, like many of his military friends, he wasn't convinced America could stay out of the Vietnam problem very long.

He opened his Bible to the Book of John and read quietly. After a few minutes, he stopped, looked out onto the green sea, and prayed. "Lord, You sent me here. Not the Navy. You. If they want me to get involved in another major assignment, I'm ready. But Lord, bring me someone. Someone that needs You. Let me be a catalyst in someone's life. Let me make a difference."

Pleased with his prayer, he sighed.

"Amen."

He reopened his Bible to John and began to read again.

Dressed in his familiar faded khaki pants and loose, rubber-tire sandals, Ho Chi Minh was joined for dinner by his trusted aide, General Vo Nguyen Giap.

"Giap, it's time to give our Vietnamese brothers in the south a different look. They need something new to keep their minds free of the sadness that pervades our land. You told me you had some ideas. What are they?"

"Our people love the revolution, but they must also believe in it," Giap answered. We can create for them a new league. We'll give them a reason to rebel, a tool to oust their American-backed president. They already have a reason to free themselves from Diem, and now we will give them the way."

"Do you have a name for this league?"

"You're so much better at that than I, my dear Ho. It will be a means for the people of South Vietnam to be liberated from the pro-American Diem."

"Then we shall call it the National Liberation Front." He glanced at his friend for approval.

"I like that very much."

"Good. Now tell me more," Ho ordered.

"We'll plant our revolutionaries in South Vietnam. Their purpose will be to gather up those who are tired of Diem, who are disillusioned by his empty promises and greedy decisions. We'll promise them independence and a change for the better, including better leaders, government, villages, schools, money, food, and control over their land and possessions.

"They will cling to our words. That's what they need and want. We will offer the proper solution at the proper time and will draw them into the new National Liberation Front. With our help, they will overthrow Diem and his puppets.

"It is highly important that we overthrow Diem without the American imperialists knowing that we're doing it. The National Liberation Front, though fueled by our revolutionaries, will be empowered by Diem's own people. It will appear to be a revolution among the South Vietnamese, and the world will say, 'Look, the South Vietnamese have finally had enough of President Diem and his American backers. They have risen up to overthrow his government. Good for them.'"

"Ingenious, my friend," Ho said happily. "You've done it again. We make an excellent team. I will formulate and create a plan for you to implement."

Giap laughed. "I like this idea very much, my friend. The revolution must go forward, and Communism must prevail. You must form an ideology for the masses so we can indoctrinate it into our own people. We must rid ourselves of the Americans so we can accomplish our goals. Shall we begin our planning?"

"There's time for that later. We must look into the length of this idea and estimate its impact."

"I can tell you its impact. We will assassinate thousands of Diem's officials, infiltrate their armies, and will devastate their controlled villages. Diem and his government will be overthrown, and the Americans will be helpless. Diem's puppet government will fall with a loud crash."

Ho Chi Minh smiled and clapped. "Bravo, Giap. Now on to more timely matters. I have conferred with my friends in the Soviet Union. They're prepared to offer support for our just cause and will create a physical presence if we deem it necessary, which we do.

"With the help of our friends, Prince Souphanouvong and Kaysone Phomvihane, we have overtaken a small village settlement in the mountains of Laos. It's far enough from other activities that the Americans will never know what we're doing. The Laos government, already in disarray, won't care. They have their hands full, and, as I will explain, they'll have them even more full soon. What you don't know is that we have created a communications and intelligence site at that location."

Giap raised his eyebrows in surprise, and Ho laughed.

"Giap, you are always a revolutionary, but even revolutionaries must change with the times. You would have us fight as your hero Napoleon did. You would choose one of his battles, mastermind it for the jungles of Vietnam, and make it work. You're a genius, but today, wars are fought differently. Success is still measured in blood, but, when the wise man watches his adversary build a bridge, he must recognize that swimming is no longer needed to cross the river. We have won many battles by sheer numbers, but now we will also use intelligence.

"A senior member of the KGB, Nikolai Ivanovich Nikolayevich, along with several Soviet military personnel, will operate that camp. We will place a small contingent of our Viet Minh there for protection, and there will be some Pathet Lao, too. We have created a small dungeon for prisoners and a small hospital."

He paused, noting the general's lack of understanding.

"I see your questioning look, general. The dungeon is primarily for the intelligentsia, as Nikolai refers to them. Those from the village who could create difficulties for us will be placed in a position where they can't. There are several officials in the village who have wisely chosen to accept the change in leadership. As a result, they can continue to manage the village under us.

"There are others, however, who have chosen to rebel. Of that group, there are a few who could create difficulties. We can't allow them continuous freedom. We promised the village leaders we won't harm those who oppose us, but we will protect our interests by separating them from the rest of the village. Isn't that a nicer way than saying they are imprisoned?"

"What of the Laos government? You say they won't care, but they are still backed by the American pigs. Will they and the Americans just sit by idly and allow us to do this?"

"Nikolai has assured me that the Americans don't know of the camp and its purpose. They have altered their communications abilities so that the Americans can't intercept their information. As far as the RLA is concerned, I assure you that our friends, the Pathet Lao, will keep the government troops so busy that they won't know there's anything going on in this remote village. We'll meet them soon to plan the diversions.

"This is only the beginning, Giap, of what we intend for our neighbors from Laos. That country is the most direct way for us to reach South Vietnam. From now on, everything we do in Laos will bring us closer to our ultimate goal."

"Aha! Didn't I say that very thing when we discussed the issue earlier, dear Ho? Laos is our means to infiltrate South Vietnam from the standpoint of an all-out war. It will be good to have a camp as a stopping-off point."

"We will visit Ban Na Lom camp soon," Ho continued. "I'd like you to meet Nikolai Nikolayevich and Major Ustinova, the top Soviet military officer. I haven't met the major yet, but I assume he must be a good soldier if he's been put in charge of the camp.

If they are willing, they can learn from you, my friend."

"May I ask what is the primary purpose of this camp? What kind of communications and intelligence will they create?"

"I'm glad to see you taking such a keen interest in the technology of future warfare. Information, my friend, is like an automobile. It moves us from one place to another more quickly than by walking and allows us to plan better. When we know exactly where the enemy is, what he is doing, and why, when, how, and with whom he does it, it becomes much easier to plan our attacks. Information is a tool forged with brains, not muscle.

"Think about it for a moment. We've always had information. The more we have, the easier it's been for us to carry out our operations flawlessly. We've used methods that require much manpower, time, and effort to gain the information we need, and now we will learn how to gather information through communications.

"Right now, we don't need to understand how it is done as long as we can use what our friends, the Soviets, provide. They've been collecting information for me for some time, part of the friendly relations we have from our mutual efforts on behalf of Communism. Now, with the efforts being made at the new camp, we'll participate more fully in the gathering of information.

"We wish to know exactly what the Americans are doing and where they intend to do it. We need to know if and when and how much they will become involved in this war, and what is happening in the southernmost portion of Laos. Then we can make our plans to move through Laos into South Vietnam. Isn't it wonderful that we can find the answers to such questions at a location that is en route to our final destination?"

He was tired, but having meetings with the general was necessary. He accomplished his goals through General Giap, a brilliant strategist in his own right, but the man was easier to control when they spoke together, making him part of the bigger picture.

"Have you had enough to eat, general?" Ho asked.

Giap knew his superior well enough to know that the meeting was over. "My dear Ho, I have had more than sufficient food.

You are very kind. If you do not mind, I would like to retire for the evening. Please inform me of tomorrow's activities at your leisure. Thank you."

Ho nodded his approval. The general, bowing to him, left the room. Ho clapped once, and a servant immediately removed the food and dishes before bringing Ho another cup of hot, sweet tea and a small cup of rice wine, setting them on the small table beside the couch where Ho liked to rest in the evening. The Communist leader walked to the couch and sat, watching steam rise from the teacup.

There was much to do. Would he see the task completed before he died? He thought back to the earliest years of his sojourn. He longed for independence for his country, and, through years of training, fighting, imprisonment, and frustration, he won that independence, but only in part. Because of the negotiations at Geneva, he was awarded only North Vietnam after he defeated the French. Now he fought to bring freedom to his entire people. With it would come Communism, because that was the vehicle through which independence would be wrought.

The Americans had made the situation difficult for him. Years earlier, they once dined across the table from each other and planned to free Vietnam from the Japanese. It was advantageous for the Americans to help Ho then, but then they turned on him, becoming his enemy. He wondered if that was how the world was supposed to operate.

He wished they'd let the Vietnamese resolve their own differences. It wasn't necessary for the Americans to become involved in Vietnam's civil war. In America's Civil War, the two sides fought, and the stronger side won. The Americans didn't want that to happen in Vietnam. He wished Eisenhower would leave them alone, but he knew it would never happen. The Americans were there to stay.

He sipped his tea and wine, then laid his head back on the comfortable couch to rest. At seventy years of age, he wasn't in very good health. He was tired, but he would see the fight through to the end.

General Giap went to his private quarters and poured a much-needed drink, then sat quietly at the window, staring at the dark night.

He wondered what was happening to their great leader. Had Ho reached the age where he was no longer capable of leading the revolution? Revolutions were always won with blood and strength. Giap could provide both. For strategy, he needed Ho's support.

His friend was slowing down in his thoughts and actions. It would take a major war to brighten both their spirits.

He poured another glass of American whiskey without recognizing the irony. He wanted companionship while he drank, but he knew that wasn't possible.

Perhaps Ho should retire. He might no longer be able to lead the Viet Minh as he once did. Perhaps he should find a young Chinese woman to care for him. She would gather vegetables for Ho every day and would pour him a small glass of rice wine at night, which Ho sipped like British tea. Giap would send daily messages to Ho, telling him how the revolution went, while the woman could bathe and massage Ho.

Giap poured another drink while smiling at his thoughts. He knew they were fantasies. Ho was still a powerful leader, as he should be. Giap's negative thoughts were fueled by the frustration he felt because the revolution wasn't going fast enough. He would do whatever Ho said, though, because it was his duty.

Giap was a history teacher who loved military history in particular. Napoleon Bonaparte was his hero. Giap had memorized all of Napoleon's battles and used some of the French general's strategies during his own military engagements. Giap had been Ho's military strategist since the early 1940s, and, though he experienced many failures, he was the brains and the brawn behind the victory at Dien Bien Phu.

Giap was more ideologically aligned behind Marx than Mao and was far more anti-American than Ho. Hardened by personal tragedy, Giap had lost all his ability to be compassionate. His men called him Nui Lau, the ice-covered volcano. He considered that a positive attribute for his position.

Why did the wretched Americans have to get involved in something that wasn't their business? Why did they care if Communism spread through that part of the world? They had enough trouble in their own country to keep the military busy. Life for Giap would have been much easier if the Americans went back to Chicago and listened to Elvis Presley.

He laughed at his thoughts. There was a good chance he'd be fighting the Americans soon. They didn't frighten him. He had already overcome overwhelming odds to defeat the French, and he could do it again. The Americans would fight a war they didn't understand. They would be unwilling participants fighting against an army that had a reason and will to win. He hoped the Americans would come, bringing their sideburns and Coca-Cola, neither of which would help them in the Vietnamese jungles.

He topped off his drink and downed it in one gulp. Ho might be weak of body, but his mind was still strong. He prayed his friend would remain strong. Together, they would win the war.

He capped the bottle and put it in the cabinet in the far corner of the room, then went to his bed, undressed, and sat on the bed thinking about Ho, the new Soviet camp in Laos, and the hated Americans.

"To the victor, go the spoils," he spat in American slang as he retired for the evening. "So, what spoils do you have for me, Ike?"

The general laughed aloud, pulled the covers up to his waist, and closed his eyes.

Chapter 5
The Admiral

Gohan had just finished the day trick, working three consecutive days from 8:00 a.m. to 4:00 p.m. at the Onna Point Compound. Now he had seventy-two hours off, then he would work the 4:00 p.m. to midnight shift. He looked forward to the extra time off as he changed into his civvies and hopped onto the bus outside Onna Point that would take him to his house a few miles south of the military compound. After he and Keiko married, Gohan rented a small hut in Nakadomari, a village just west of Ishikawa Beach.

He was hungry, so he got off at Ishikawa Beach near the U.S. Marine base. He stopped at the Little Las Vegas and took a seat at the bar. The Okinawan bartender, recognizing him, nodded hello.

He ordered a bowl of tomato soup and, though he no longer drank like he used to, a San Miguel beer. There were a dozen marines in uniform scattered throughout the small, dimly lit building. Most were alone or with a buddy, although one group of five was getting a bit rowdy. None looked older than Gohan, and he wasn't even twenty.

Across the room, sitting alone at a table, was a black man in his thirties. He wore civvies, and Gohan guessed he wasn't a marine. The rowdy group was starting to bug the man pretty hard.

I hope they aren't riding him for his color, Gohan thought. *This could get nasty.*

One of the marines was black, and that made Gohan feel a bit better. He couldn't hear everything they said, but he heard the words *mermaid* and *pee-swallower*, which made him assume the man in civvies was from the navy. Then he noticed an anchor tattoo on the man's arm.

Gohan planned to stay just long enough to eat his tomato soup and go home. It also took an edge off the day. The situation was becoming intense at the compound. He'd been on two separate Russian radio nets for the past few weeks and picked up some pretty good information that had NSA's attention. Two or three of the crypto guys hung around his workstation constantly.

He remembered when he first started working at the compound and was told that intercept work, while important, could be pretty boring. During the cold war, each side intercepted the other's messages, decoded them, saw they weren't important, and took a nap. The following day, it happened all over again. Occasionally, someone uncovered a troop movement, and that got the attention of the NSA guys, but they soon decided it was just internal war games, then everyone went back to sleep again.

But occasionally, things got hot. Recently, a U.S. reconnaissance plane was shot down over Russia, and that woke up everyone for a while. That was exciting, and Gohan was assigned to all the networks that had anything to do with the incident. Somehow it was determined that the event had been an unfortunate accident, not an international incident.

The two cold war enemies still hated each other but understood what happened and forgot about it. It never even reached the American newspapers. The official word from the military was that it had been an unfortunate accident.

Gohan didn't believe it. He felt the Russians had shot down the plane, killed the survivors, rewarded those who did it, held a celebration in their honor, gave the citizens free vodka, then acted astonished, saddened, shaken, concerned, and regretful as they met President Eisenhower's emissaries.

Sorry, Ivan, Gohan thought, *but I don't buy it.*

That wasn't the first time, either. More than once, Russia shot down an Air Force plane and never returned the survivors. There were supposedly over twenty men missing in action that way, probably in Soviet prison camps. Gohan wondered who called the conflict the cold war.

Then, just recently, a U-2 was shot down. From what Gohan understood, the pilot had parachuted out and was captured. The brass were still arguing over that one. He didn't know if it reached the newspapers back home, and he wondered how lucky the pilot would be.

Now the Russians were at it again. Gohan didn't know what was going on, but the stuff he copied was receiving a lot of attention. It had something to do with Indochina, wherever that was.

He took another sip of his San Miguel, ready to leave for home. Keiko was pregnant and due soon, and they were excited about the coming baby. She was spending the day with some of her friends and would be home around six.

He and Keiko had been married at the chief executive's house. Gohan wanted the marriage to be formal, through normal Air Force channels, but he met a major obstacle. Since Keiko was considered a foreign national, and because Gohan held a top-secret crypto security clearance, the military disallowed the marriage.

He had spoken with Major Richard Parsons, the commander of Onna Point, a man Gohan had never liked because he was too young to be a major and apparently thought he was better than everyone else. Someone said his father was a famous general, which helped him move quickly through the ranks. That made it even easier to dislike the man.

"Airman Rice, we have an unusual situation here," the major said. "You've become a very important member of a top-secret team of radio operators here at Onna Point. General Winthrop, the Far East commander, has recommended you for a special citation because of your work.

"Please understand, Rice, that as long as I'm commander of this base, no one receives any special recognition without my approval. The fact is, the only reason you haven't been busted or court-martialed is because of your high standing at the base—and with General Winthrop.

"You carry the highest security clearance in the U.S. military. Though you're completely aware of the standards, rules of conduct, and guidelines regarding foreign nationals, you completely ignore them. You cavort with Okinawans as if you were their long-lost brother. You used to be a drunk, and I don't buy it that you don't drink any more, and now you want to marry an Okinawan girl who just happens to be the daughter of the chief executive!

"I'm sure you're in love, Rice, and I'm sure she's a wonderful girl, but, from a security standpoint, she could easily be an enemy. More likely, she could be used by the enemy to pry information from you that would be detrimental to U.S. security. Do you understand me, Airman?"

Gohan enjoyed tormenting his superiors. He still had a rebellious streak that hadn't yet been put under control. "You mean I can do it, sir? Oh, thank you!"

"Sit down, Airman! You know what I'm saying. No, you can't marry a foreign national while you carry that top-secret crypto clearance. The answer to the next question is also no. You're too important to our work. You aren't allowed to drop your clearance just to marry this girl.

"You might become a hero someday, Rice, but you'll be a single one."

That didn't stop Gohan. He simply bypassed the military, went to his prospective father-in-law, and arranged to be married in an Okinawan ceremony. That was more to his liking, anyway.

Of course, he didn't go directly to his father-in-law. He went to his friend and shihan, Katsuo Matsumura. Matsumura, as Gohan's friend, went to Konishi Kobashigawa with a gift of food and sake. They discussed the arrangements, and a suitable day of good omen was chosen. The ceremony would take place only when the tides were right.

The fact that the U.S. government didn't recognize the marriage didn't bother Gohan. In Okinawa, he was a husband. In the Air Force, he was single.

Keiko had been gorgeous in her kimono and *takashimada*, her wedding headdress. She entered the house during the rising tide according to custom, and, as the ceremony progressed, two young girls poured sake for the couple. Each took three sips, signifying the number nine, which meant they would be together forever.

Then everyone became drunk, but that was OK, because that, too, was the custom. Gohan, true to his new nature, drank a little sake, but stayed sober.

Moscow, Russia

"General Samsonov, the orders I'm about to give you are confidential at the highest level. Recently, you were told to have a military commander ready to move at a moment's notice. And I believe you were given the details of the assignment. Is that correct?"

The general nodded. "*Dah.*"

"So, are you ready?"

"Yes, sir. I'm ready."

"Good. This should not be a difficult assignment. Our purpose is to give aid to our ally Ho Chi Minh. He has determined to take over South Vietnam by entering it through Laos. We have found the ideal location to create an intermediate depot, which will double as a communications depot. We will need to build a compound there. And we will supply a small medical team. Other than that, our presence is to create numbers. We will be working, in a joint effort, with troops from General Giap and also a contingent of Laotian Communists."

"What is the purpose, sir? Rest and relaxation for General Giap's troops?"

"Partly. We intend to build a compound in northern Laos that will act as a rest center, with a small hospital, for troops coming and going, primarily for those returning. But the communications is as important, if not more so. From that location, we can move information quite secretly.

"The compound will be manned jointly by Viet Minh, Pathet Lao, and our own troops, under the control of whomever you place in charge. Have you decided?"

"*Dah.* Major Ustinova."

"Hmm. Ustinova. That will certainly assuage his father. He's been pestering us about the major's minor role in things. Ustinova's not an imbecile, is he? I've heard the stories."

General Samsonov laughed. "No, sir. He's actually a learned military man. He just doesn't have experience. He's been primarily a desk man. I think this is a perfect assignment for him. I agree with you; it will get his father off our back."

Major Aleksandr Ustinova was a life-long military man, like his father before him, though he hadn't had the same success as his father. In recent years, the desk work to which he'd been relegated dismayed his father. The elderly Ustinova attempted to use his position to put pressure on the military generals to get his son a prime assignment. But none had been forthcoming.

His immediate superior, General Alyosha Gregoriev Samsonov, saw the upcoming situation in Laos as a way to satisfy the elder former General Ustinova without compromising the mission. He saw Major Ustinova as an incompetent, but the Laotian mission required bodies, not skill. Besides, a KGB officer was to be assigned to the compound. He would, ultimately, be in charge.

Major Ustinova was ushered in to General Samsonov's office and offered a small glass of vodka.

"Major, sit down. I have something to discuss with you."

Ustinova had always considered himself an able soldier. But he had never been given an opportunity to prove himself. Though he hoped, again, this was such an opportunity, he had been disappointed many times before. He sat quietly and accepted the general's glass of vodka.

"Major, what I'm about to share with you is of the utmost secrecy. You cannot share this information with anyone, not even your father."

Ustinova smiled. Whatever it was, he assumed his father already knew about it.

"We, the Soviet Union, have a strong interest in the things that are happening in Vietnam. As you likely know, we have a good relationship with Ho Chi Minh, and we are in constant communication with him. He is ready to embark on a mission that could turn the tides of the civil war there.

"I am sending a contingent of soldiers into Laos to aid Ho Chi Minh in this regard. I would like you to take command of the military group. We will be moving shortly. Please take care of whatever personal matters that need your attention, and report to me early Wednesday morning. You will be leaving soon thereafter."

"May I ask what the assignment entails, general?"

"We'll go over that Wednesday morning. Suffice it to say that it shouldn't be a difficult task. I don't have all the details yet myself. However, I'd take a chessboard if I were you. There may be lots of idle time."

Ustinova didn't play chess. He would prefer an assignment right in the thick of action. He wanted an opportunity to prove himself as an able commander. He'd studied all of the great Russian military commanders, and he was confident in his ability. He wondered if they were, once again, passing off a minor assignment to him to get him out of their way.

He thanked General Samsonov as he stood, finished the glass of vodka, turned, and left the general's office.

The group of rowdy marines were hassling the navy man pretty hard. Considering the situation, the sailor was very calm.

Across the room, two other marines sat and drank quietly.

"You know who that guy at the bar is, Marty? That's the Air Force guy they call Gohan."

"I've heard of him. What's he doin' at a marine bar?"

"Well," the tall marine said with a laugh, "first, he ain't afraid of no marines. Besides, we get along good with him. He comes in sometimes, and we sit, drink, and shoot the bull. Haven't seen him for a while though. He's pretty neat, and he never picks fights. He just won't back down from one."

"You think we should warn those guys?" Marty asked.

"No. They ain't giving Gohan any grief. Just because they're marines don't mean they aren't idiots. Real marines don't act like that. They'll butcher that poor navy guy, and all he did was come in to have a drink. It might do those guys good to tangle with Gohan. It would teach 'em a lesson they'd never forget."

The situation soon got out of hand. The tallest marine, who'd been doing most of the harassment, tossed bottle caps at the sailor and made disparaging remarks about the man's family. The sailor stood, turned his back on his tormentors, and walked out.

Good for you, Gohan thought. *Those guys are too dumb to notice, admiral, but you have a lot of guts and a lot of class.*

"Hey, look! The wimpy mermaid's runnin' away. Let's go see where he's goin', guys. Maybe he'll take us home to meet his wife."

As the marines followed the sailor out, Gohan decided it was time to leave. Once outside, he wasn't surprised to see the five marines in a semicircle taunting the sailor from a distance of twenty feet. Gohan walked up to the sailor and stood beside him with a smile.

"Well, admiral," Gohan said quietly, "looks like you could use a little help. How many of those jerks can you handle?"

"Two, maybe more."

"Two's enough." Gohan looked at the marines. "Boys, you're obviously lookin' for a fight. It's a little unfair when the odds are stacked like this. What do you think?"

The tall marine and his buddies walked forward slowly. "What is it, mouthy? You don't like five against two? What do you want, a couple of us to sit and watch so it's two against two?"

"Oh, my goodness, no," Gohan said. "You got me all wrong. I was thinking the odds are stacked in our favor. Five of you twerps will be like a midnight snack for the admiral and me. Now, I'd prefer that you just go away, and my friend and I will do the same. But if you're insistent on getting your brains knocked out, then let's get on with it."

The smart-mouthed marine jumped at Gohan and took a wild swing. Gohan sidestepped, grabbing the man's arm behind the elbow and yanked him forward. He snapped the arm at the elbow, then, in the same motion, karate-chopped with his free hand in the back of his ribs. He kicked the man's feet out from under him and threw a hard right into his chest, toppling the marine onto his back.

Screaming from the broken elbow and ribs, he quickly rolled away. The entire exchange took only a few seconds.

A second marine jumped Gohan's back and beat his fists into his head, and a third man came up to Gohan in front, intending to attack him while he was held from behind.

Gohan kicked him in the groin, sending him sprawling as he clutched himself, moaning in pain. The follow-through from the kick sent Gohan flying backward, as intended, where he landed on his back on top of the marine who still clung to him.

He jumped up and saw the marine gasping for air, so Gohan grabbed his shoulders and pulled him to his feet. A quick look over the marine's shoulder told him the sailor might be in trouble—he had one man hanging on to his legs and another throwing punches at his head.

Gohan threw a hard right uppercut to the marine's jaw and walked off as the man dropped limply to the ground. By that time, the second marine managed to get to his feet. Gohan ducked his lame punch, kicked the man's legs out from under him sideways, and flipped him through the air to land hard on his back.

Gohan pointed at him. "If you try to get up again, I'll hurt you. Stay there. You'll be fine in the morning."

Meanwhile, the navy man was doing all right. He had a good cut on his face, but the marines looked a lot worse. The one hanging on to the sailor's legs had been beat up pretty good. The navy man had popped him in the stomach three or four times, then turned and drop-kicked him in the gut, finishing him off.

The second marine was losing his boxing match with the sailor, but the navy man had been handicapped by the man holding his legs.

Gohan walked over and pulled the guy off the sailor's legs. When he saw the man's condition; however, he just tossed him to where his three buddies lay in a pile, nursing their wounds. A few seconds later, the sailor finished off the last marine.

It wasn't pretty. The marines would wonder what happened to them. Later, they would find out with whom they tangled.

"Well, friend," the navy man said, shaking Gohan's hand, "I need to thank you. I'm Harold Baker. Your help was greatly appreciated. Can I ask your name?"

"Most everybody calls me Gohan, admiral."

"Ha! I've heard about you. You've got quite a reputation. I guess those guys didn't know who you were, or they would have had second thoughts. By the way, I'm a captain, not an admiral."

"I guessed you were in the navy."

"Yeah. Navy UDT. I could use another drink. Where you off to?"

"I live in Nakadomari. That's near here, on the east China Sea side of the island. There'll be another bus coming along soon."

"No buses for us, man. I have a bike. Why don't I give you a ride? Is there some place we can get a drink?"

"Yeah, but just one. I have a pregnant wife at home, and I don't want to be late."

"That's good stuff, brother. A man who takes care of his family is number one in my book. Besides, if you'll notice, I was drinking a coke, not hard stuff. Follow me."

Captain Baker and Gohan walked around the bar and saw a beautiful blue and yellow English BSA motorcycle parked there.

"Wow!" Gohan said. "Where'd you get this baby?"

"Just bought it. Had it sent over from England. Nice, eh?"

"Boy, I'll say."

The captain started the bike and motioned Gohan to sit behind him. They left for Nakadomari, shouting conversation as they went.

"You got a family, admiral?" Gohan asked.

"Yep, a wife and two boys. They're six and three. They're back home in Houston, Texas."

"You don't have a Texas accent."

The captain laughed. "It's not against the law to move from one state to another. I didn't say I was born in Texas."

They finished the rest of the ride quietly and arrived at the American Beauty bar, a small wooden hut in Nakadomari near the trail that led back to Gohan's house. The two men ordered Coca Colas and sat at one of the four small tables.

"I'm originally from Costa Mesa, California," Captain Baker said. "I met my wife while traveling in the navy. She's the most beautiful girl in the world, Gohan. I'm the luckiest man alive." He took a picture from his wallet and showed it to Gohan. "You can see Vanessa's a white woman. I hope that doesn't upset you."

"Admiral, if you were really concerned about that, you would have asked me before you married her. Now I have a question for you. Does it upset you that my wife is an Okinawan?"

Baker laughed. "I get the point, Gohan. Thanks. Vanessa's from Houston. After we married, we decided to raise our family there. Her dad's a pastor in the Full Gospel Church of Houston. It's a great little community, very comfortable. We like it."

"What's full gospel? I never heard of that. I was raised Catholic."

"Do you go to the Catholic chapel on the base?"

"No. That stuff doesn't do much for me, admiral. I guess I'm not that religious. You know, when we were growin' up, we had to go to church. There wasn't any choice, because we'd get a weepin' willow switch wrapped around our legs if we didn't go. I never got much out of church, though. It was hard for me to believe it. First it was a sin to eat meat on Friday, so we ate fish. Then it was OK to eat meat on Friday, and it wasn't a sin anymore. What happened to all the Catholics who ate meat before the rules got changed? Are they burning in hell?"

Gohan paused to see if Baker had an answer, but the captain didn't speak.

"They did the same thing with Communion," Gohan continued.

"First you couldn't eat anything for several hours before Communion, because that was a mortal sin. Then you could, and it wasn't a sin anymore. Come on. How are we supposed to know what's right or wrong?

"There are too many rules for me. Once I was old enough to get away from the church, it was history for me. All I remember from those years is that Saul became Paul and was from Gaul."

Captain Baker laughed.

"Anyway, I'm not that interested in chapel. I've been to the Shinto shrines on the island and met a few Buddhist monks. I'll tell you, admiral, their stuff is more interesting than anything I learned in Cincinnati. I hope that doesn't bother you."

"Not at all, Gohan. Real Christianity is a relationship with Jesus Christ. It doesn't have anything to do with rules. Those are man-made, not from God. A lot of folk leave churches for the same reason, and I don't blame 'em. I'd like you to remember that a church is a building, and religion is a noun. Christianity, though, is a relationship—you and God, or me and God. I'd like to talk to you about that some time."

Gohan thought about the little war at his father-in-law's house. He had called out to God then because he was afraid he and Keiko were going to die. He told the captain about it.

"Do you realize what that means, Gohan?"

"I don't know. What are you getting at?"

"You can't call out to God unless you realize He exists. Some of what you learned as a youngster took hold. And by the appearance of things, it looks like He heard you. You got out OK, and now you're married to the young girl you saved."

Gohan was thoughtful before he responded. "Yeah, I guess you're right. I never thought much about it. I guess the one thing I did was realize that I needed to clean up my life some. I think I've done that. Now, of course, I'm gonna be a father. I really want to do things right."

"Will you raise your child in the church?"

"Hadn't thought much about it, admiral. Keiko's a Buddhist, but she'll do whatever I say. At least, I think so."

"Think about it, Gohan. It's a monumental decision that will have a major impact on your child's life."

Gohan wanted to change the subject. "Are you stationed there at Ishikawa?"

Captain Baker smiled. It was clear Gohan didn't want to hear any more about Christianity. "Temporarily. I'm in a holding pattern. There's the possibility of a special mission, and this is a central place for me to wait until then."

"Special mission? What are you, a one-man wrecking crew? What's this UBJ stuff?"

"UDT. That stands for Underwater Demolition Team. We're specialists. Mostly underwater stuff… Blowin' things up… We did some work in Korea."

"What will you do, blow up Okinawa? Man, if you need water to work in, we've got enough to keep you busy for a while."

Baker laughed. "No, I'm not doing anything here. They just want me here, because it's a good drop-off point. We can reach a lot of places from Okinawa pretty fast. Sometimes, we prepare for a mission that never happens. We get to continue our training that way. I'm doin' some preparations now. It's good to be ready if you need it, you know?"

"So what happens if you're trying to blow up something underwater, and war breaks out above? You know how to fight, so do you fight underwater?"

Captain Baker sipped his Coke. "Yeah, I've had to fight underwater before. Mainly, we're the guys for difficult or special missions that others aren't trained for. UDTs are highly trained, kind of like you. We made a pretty good team back there. Maybe we should get you transferred. They could call us Salt and Pepper."

Gohan laughed. "No chance, admiral. They've got me locked up at Onna Point. We're involved in special assignments there, too."

Finishing their soft drinks, they went outside. Gohan shook Captain Baker's hand. "I hope our paths cross again, admiral. I wish you the best with your special-duty stuff."

"Thanks for bailin' me out back there. When will you and your wife have the baby?"

"In about a week. Man, I can't wait, and neither can Keiko. We're excited."

"What do you want, a boy or girl?"

"Keiko wants a girl, but I don't care. I just want it to happen."

"I've been there, brother. I'll pray for you, your wife, and your baby. I hope we meet again soon. Take care."

He jumped on his bike and drove back to Ishikawa Beach to write a long letter to his family. Gohan walked through the woods to his house, where Keiko was waiting anxiously.

Chapter 6
Bear in the Jungle

Laos
October 1960

"Nikolai Ivanovich Nikolayevich, I brought us some good Russian soup loaded with potatoes. Look at this thick, black bread! The new cook is just what we needed. We may stave off starvation yet."

"You're a good man, Pavel," Nikolai replied. "Did we get the good vodka I requested?"

"Oh, yes," the young Soviet KGB clerk said shyly. "I was able to bribe a female supply clerk who I...knew...before. You know, we dated. I promised her that when I return, I'll bring some souvenirs and will keep her company." He smiled, thinking of that reunion. "She put two cases in with the potatoes."

"Comrade Zortov, if we were in Moscow, I would now be talking to Dr. Mokheyevich, the KGB psychiatrist, about your propensity to coerce lower-ranked females to do your bidding in exchange for money or favors. We would be very concerned that a KGB employee at any level would fatten his wallet at the service's expense."

73

Pavel Zortov froze. "But Nikolai, you asked me to get the vodka. I was following your orders."

Nikolai laughed. "Of course, Pavel. You needn't be so concerned. Your secret's safe with me. When we return, maybe I should meet this female clerk. If we don't frighten her, she might think she can do this again, and that wouldn't be good. Do you agree?"

"Oh, yes, Nikolai Nikolayevich! When we return, and you're ready, please let me know. I'll arrange everything."

"You're promising your lady friend souvenirs, Pavel? Just what did you plan to take her, a bowl of rice, an asp, or an opium leaf? There's nothing here, comrade. We'll be happy to take ourselves back, nothing else. Let's enjoy this good potato soup and have the vodka later."

Pavel was concerned. He'd worked with the KGB long enough to know that any agent could turn on another at any time. Nikolai, his superior, had a terrible reputation. He was one of those who, in the middle of the night, went to citizens' homes, yanked men or women out of their sleep in front of their families, and sent them off to prison, sometimes to never return. He wasn't someone any man willingly crossed.

Though Pavel's work was administrative rather than operative, he was still KGB, which meant someone watched everything he did all the time. It never occurred to him when he asked Irena to steal the vodka for them that someone else might find out. He'd been stupid. Now he had to strengthen his relationship with Nikolai and hope the man wouldn't turn him in during a fit of anger. He had to be very careful what he said to his superior.

The two men were among the Soviets who'd been sent to the makeshift camp in the jungle near a mountaintop in Laos. As difficult as life had been in Moscow, with its economic woes and food shortages, it was like heaven compared to Laos. Pavel spoke only Russian, so the only people he could speak with were the other Russians. It was beneath him to spend too much time with the lower-ranked soldiers. He could have become friendly with the Russian radio operators, but they were in their own world, and Pavel hadn't learned how to break through that barrier.

He spent a lot of time alone, and he visited his superior officer, Nikolai, as often as possible.

The Pathet Lao soldiers were a strange breed. Though they were allies, Pavel didn't like them. They were guerillas, scruffy and unclean, who constantly drank and smoked. Many chewed opium leaves or stems, and sometimes smoked them. When they did, they looked deranged.

They were very rough on the Laotian prisoners who were being held in the makeshift dungeon. Those were mostly members of the Laotian intelligentsia who weren't pro-Communist. That made it necessary to imprison them, though they were probably harmless. Most were too old to fight physically and, as long as they were imprisoned, couldn't fight psychologically or intellectually, either.

The Pathet Lao guerrillas, however, beat and starved their own countrymen. That part of the revolution was something Pavel didn't understand. But, as a member of the KGB, he accepted it.

Nikolai, however, liked the way the Laotians operated. It sent a strong message to the rest of the village and would eliminate further rebellion. The one thing the KGB man didn't want was interference from anyone.

The camp had two purposes. It was a home base for an elaborate communications network that had other stations in, among other places, inland China and on a merchant ship on the South China Sea. They obtained information regarding troop movements in South Vietnam and about President Diem and his top officials. They also watched for sea movement on the Gulf of Tonkin to the Gulf of Siam and kept a close eye on the Americans. Gathering information from Mao Tse-tung and the Pathet Lao leaders, Prince Souphanouvong and Kaysone Phomvihane, as well as from their own beloved KGB, they centralized and coordinated the ideas of Ho Chi Minh.

The camp was built within the village of Ban Na Lom, and the inhabitants either became part of the program or were tossed into a cold, damp, underground dungeon built to house those that rebelled. The dungeon had smooth, even walls and would have been difficult to climb out of even if it were open at the top. With the thick, bamboo-laced door that covered it, escape was impossible.

The Communists also built a small hospital staffed by one Russian doctor, one Laotian doctor, who had since been put into the dungeon, and some Laotian nurses.

The camp was guarded night and day by combined Soviet, Pathet Lao, and Viet Minh troops. All inhabitants were kept under close observation.

The camp, situated near a proposed route the Viet Minh would soon use, would become a meeting place for the leaders of the various Communist revolutionary groups and a quiet place of solitude where ideas could be discussed and strategies determined. It was a significant post, a vital cog in the move to promote Communism worldwide, something that Comrade Pavel Zortov was proud to be a part of.

His superior, Nikolai Nikolayevich, was a lifetime KGB man. An avid Communist, he landed a position with the Committee for State Security or the KGB after finishing his schooling at the university and been recommended by a professor who was friends with a KGB officer. Nikolai learned later that the same professor had turned in several students for their anti-Communist leanings, which meant the professor was in favor with the KGB.

Nikolai never understood why anyone would rebel against the Communist state. Many had been brainwashed by American propaganda, but not him. He was proud of being a staunch Communist.

He was assigned to the 5th Chief Directorate in the Ideological Section of the Committee for State Security. During the time when many citizens were imprisoned for little or no reason, Nikolai built an unenviable reputation as a mean-spirited policeman. He was transferred to the 1st Chief Directorate of Foreign Intelligence and recently moved to Department Six, which covered Laos and Vietnam.

Nikolai was forty-five years old and had never married. He was a big man—six feet tall and weighing over 250 pounds. Though he was balding, he still sported a heavy, brown, unkempt mustache that curled thickly over his lip and became an advertisement for whatever he ate or drank. Slob was an accurate word for him. During his years of service in the KGB, he learned how to operate in KGB circles to his best advantage. Among peers and those of higher rank, he was quiet, circumspect, attentive, and respectful. Among those of lesser rank or not within that circle, he was rude, overbearing, and a KGB bully.

He took his assignment seriously. While he was the superior KGB officer at the camp, nothing would be done that would violate the KGB code or interfere with the primary goal of the Communist party. He didn't care much for the military personnel, even though he recognized their importance.

The commandant, Major Aleksandr Ustinova, was a blithering idiot, but Nikolai had to put up with him and control him. It was Ustinova's responsibility to mold the three small armies—Soviet, Pathet Lao, and Viet Minh—into a solid military unit. Knowing that Ustinova faced a difficult task, Nikolai was interested in seeing how good an officer Ustinova really was.

Nikolai was satisfied, however, with the Russian doctor who was in charge of the hospital. He was a good man who came highly recommended for the position. A loner, he was perfect for the assignment. He would do a commendable job operating the small hospital. In his spare time, he was writing a book, so the assignment seemed to fit him perfectly.

Nikolai had to find something to keep himself busy. They were in the middle of the jungle with nowhere to go after work. He had plenty of vodka and knew where to get more, but there wasn't much else to do so far from any sizable city. From the reports he'd been given, Laos didn't have cities anyway, at least none that could compare with Moscow or Leningrad. That didn't matter. He was a loner. Even in Moscow, he spent most of his idle time in his apartment, though he sometimes strolled through a park or bought bread at a nearby store. If he wanted, he could always find a nice bar in which to drink away the hours.

He did that far too often, and it became a serious problem. He was cited more than once for drunkenness, lewd behavior, and even attempted rape. He wasn't an attractive man, and, when he drank, he did things he never would have attempted were he sober.

He was called in and disciplined by his superior officer, then was sent to a KGB psychiatrist. He assured the doctor he'd been framed as part of a conspiracy against him due to his KGB status. He lived in an area that was well known for its criminal activities.

The charges were dropped, and Nikolai controlled his drinking. He hoped that being sent to a jungle outpost wouldn't make him revert to his bad habits. It would be nice, after a difficult day in that godforsaken camp, to walk to a bar and order a sausage and small bottle of vodka as he listened to loud music waft through the smoky room.

That wouldn't happen at Ban Na Lom. There would be too much leisure time, and he had to fill it somehow.

He found his answer when he walked through the village. There were many young Laotian Hmong girls, and he had control over them. Suddenly, he had something with which to fill his idle time.

Chapter 7
Onna Point

October 1960

Sergeant David "Gohan" Rice's best friend, Seth Edwards, was his roommate. Seth was a short, powerfully built farm boy from Missouri. There was no reason for the two men to become friends, but they did. Although they were totally different, they became inseparable.

Seth was a classic Missourian. Everything he did was done slowly—work, walking, and talking. His slow speech accentuated his Missouri drawl. As good as Gohan was at the top-secret compound, Seth was just as bad. He couldn't get the hang of the dots and dashes, especially when someone was sending at one hundred words per minute. Gohan bailed him out countless times, and Seth's reputation remained intact. He, like Gohan, extended his tour and stayed on the island almost as long as Gohan.

Seth and Gohan were like Mutt and Jeff. Seth was five-feet-six-inches tall and didn't look as strong as he was. Gohan was six-feet-one-inch tall, thin, and muscular. Seth had average looks, but Gohan was good looking and knew it. He didn't have a girlfriend back in the States, because he'd been too busy playing baseball to worry about girls. Seth had a girlfriend, but he soon received a Dear John letter from her that linked him with servicemen throughout the centuries.

Though both young men were raised in strong religious households, they took different paths once they left home. Seth was still a strong Christian who attended chapel each week, read the Bible, and prayed daily. Gohan became involved with the Okinawan religions, but only because he was interested in the island, not religion itself. Seth was amazed at his friend's knowledge of local religious history.

They stood on a hill at Bise, the westernmost point on the island, looking into the East China Sea. There was a small island in the distance, another of the Ryukyus, called Ie Shima, or Ie Island. It was nearly four miles away but on a clear day, it could be seen with binoculars. Gohan had visited it with some of his Okinawan friends.

"See that island?" he asked Seth. "That's Ie Shima. It was once a famous Ryukyu island. There was a *tenteishi*, a heavenly granchild that emerged from the first generation deities. He had three sons and two daughters. The eldest son founded the Tenson dynasty, which was the first of the Ryukyuan kings. The second son was *anji*, the first lord, and the third son was the first farmer. The first daughter was *kikeo-ogimi*, the first high priestess, and the younger daughter was *noro*, the first community priestess.

"There was a Japanese sun goddess named Amaterasu who lived in a cave there. Back more than one thousand years ago, the islands had kings, not governors and their staff like they have now. All the Ryukyus were ruled by kings.

"In those days, gods and goddesses were everywhere. They lived on the islands with the people, and Amaterasu, the sun goddess, taught them how to worship. The big gods, the head gods in heaven, sent smaller gods down here. They had a bunch of little kid gods, or whatever they were. Those were the ones I just told you about. The noro is the same noro that helps run the religious ceremonies today. I've been there. I know."

Seth smiled. He occasionally spoke to Gohan about Jesus but

knew his friend didn't want to hear about it. Most of the time, he kept his Christianity to himself. At times like that one, when Gohan went on about the gods, he was trying to get Seth's goat. Seth prayed harder and longer for his friend.

They went drinking together often in the early days, but Seth never had more than two beers, and he never touched sake, the local drink of choice. Gohan had stopped drinking, however, much to Seth's delight.

As different as the two men were, they shared a love for the martial arts and both became proficient.

Onna Point was the site of a top-secret Air Force installation, an extension of Kadena Air Base, the main Air Force base on the island. The facility at Onna Point was in the middle of the island on the East China Sea, its primary purpose to intercept cold war military transmissions to keep the cold war cold.

The base, surrounded by a high, steel, electric fence, was protected every hundred yards by cannons and military guards. The entrance gate was heavily guarded, as was the compound where the top-secret work was conducted. Except for the administrative and support personnel, the airmen assigned to Onna Point worked at the compound. Gohan, like many of his contemporaries, was a Morse code intercept radio operator.

Because of the many months he spent on the island, Gohan became the most-experienced and most proficient operator. There were times when the transmissions came in so fast, often at a hundred words a minute or more, that most of the operators could not keep up. Gohan could.

Some of the enemy Morse code operators had what he called clump fingers. Their transmissions were garbled and difficult to copy. When one of those came in, Gohan was called in to help.

When new cold war enemy networks were discovered, it was important to locate the outstations, places where the base sent information. Sometimes, it took days or weeks to track the complete circuit. If it was an important new net, Gohan was brought in to locate the outstations quickly and complete the network so it could be copied. Then someone higher up could determine how significant the information was.

Gohan and other top copiers had what some called sweet fingers. They could roll their receiver tuners through many frequencies, listening to transmissions that sounded like they were on top of each other and still find the outstations that were communicating with the base they were copying.

When it was known in advance that impact transmissions were coming, Gohan was one of a handful of operators who was called in to guarantee correct copy. The cryptology experts at the NSA, which worked with SIGINT, were aware of Rice's abilities. His skills as an intercept operator were well documented. Major Parsons, the camp commander at Onna Point, appreciated the man's talents although he disliked his strong rebellious reputation. Sergeant Rice didn't exactly follow the rules.

His many early drunken escapades were noted in his record. Were it not for his unparalleled skills, Rice would have already been court-martialed and dismissed from the Air Force. In reality, he was the best they had, and he didn't appear to be a security risk—so far. By the time his personal record of atrocities reached serious disciplinary levels, his exemplary work had reached vital U.S. interest levels, too. As a result, he spent much of his early military life barely hanging onto his job. The Air Force had him right where they wanted him, and he knew it.

"Where's Major Parsons?" one of the intercept operators, nicknamed Spike, asked. "We got some serious stuff goin' on here. Has anyone sent for him?"

Lieutenant Thiebold answered. "He's off the base, Spike. I've sent for Captain Foust. He'll be here soon. I also sent for the NSA guy who's been hanging around. I'm sure he'll want to be here, too."

"Lieutenant Thiebold?" Sergeant John Mancini called out.

"Yes, sergeant? What is it?"

"We can't stay on top of this, sir. They must be sending 150 words a minute, and they're all talkin' simultaneously. They must have two people at each station, one to send, the other to receive. It's difficult, sir. Our guys are having trouble getting this done. I'm sorry, sir."

"OK, sergeant. No apology necessary. Getting the job done is what's necessary. Your people can only do what they can. Tell 'em to keep on it and get what they can. This is more important than anything else we're doing right now. Our cryptos and NSA people are good enough to figure this out. You just get the copy." He slapped the sergeant's shoulder in encouragement.

Another airman stepped into the room and got the Lieutenant's attention. "Lieutenant? I've got Mr. Sinclair from NSA on the horn. He asked for that guy Milton, then Major Parsons, and then Captain Foust. I told him the captain was on his way. He wants to know who's in charge, and I guess that's you, sir."

Lieutenant Dan Thiebold went into his office to take the call. As he did, Captain Peter Foust, still fighting sleep, walked into the compound center.

"Hi, sergeant," Captain Foust said. "What's goin' on? I understand you sent for Steve Milton, too?"

"Yes, sir, Captain. Sorry they had to wake you, sir. The lieutenant's on the phone with Mr. Sinclair from NSA. I don't know what that's about. The net we've been tracking, the one they've been so hot about, just exploded half an hour ago. Our guys copied it OK for a while, then whoever those Commies are, they just went crazy, sending number messages faster than we could copy 'em. Then, everybody on the net started up—all four outstations— and it got even worse. We couldn't figure out who was doin' what. We've got more guys on it now, but you know we hate to do that, Captain. It won't copy as well."

"Has anyone thought about calling in Sergeant Rice? If this stuff is that important, I'm sure Steve Milton will say we need our top people on it."

"I know, sir. The first thing Lieutenant Thiebold did was send two guys and a Jeep to Nakadomari. Gohan should be here soon."

"What about Major Parsons?"

"He's off base, sir. The lieutenant figured it would be better to have you here."

"The way Major Parsons and Gohan get along, Dan's probably

right. We don't need a fight between those two right now. OK, sarge. Keep your guys on this and do your best. That'll be good enough. As soon as Gohan arrives, get him on it, too. Someone make sure you've got a hot cup of coffee for him and some food. Whatever he wants, he can have. Where's Dan? In his office?"

"Yes, sir. Like I said, he's talking to some guy named Mr. Sinclair from NSA."

"OK. Keep up the good work, sarge. You're doin' fine."

Weeks earlier, the Onna Point operators picked up copy that got NSA's attention. It was information regarding Russian military troop movements into Laos. The information was sketchy, but it suggested there was a small contingent of Soviet troops ready to move into a remote village in that country. U.S. intelligence tracked down the approximate location but didn't have much more.

Captain Foust put Gohan on the net, and, within a few days, he located four outstations that were in communication with the base station. The net produced good, solid information for a while, allowing intelligence to get an idea what the Soviets were doing. Then, just as quickly as it began, the information flow stopped.

The network was still alive, but it wasn't producing any significant data. NSA felt there was another live network operating somewhere, passing along information that military intelligence wanted and needed. Gohan searched the net constantly but couldn't find it.

Then, almost instantaneously, the five-station net shut down.

Around that time Steve Milton, a senior NSA official, arrived at Onna Point. He spent most of his time with the officers and crypto boys. They all believed that more vital information would come soon. The Soviets had to communicate, but the question was how. If they used Morse code, Onna would locate it, and NSA had its top people poised to break down the information.

Then, after weeks of silence, the entire net came alive again, with all five stations talking simultaneously. The copy was pulled and worked on. NSA was apprised of every message that was sent. Along with NSA, the news was sent to top officials in the CIA, the U.S. National Security Advisor, and SIGINT command.

Gohan checked in with the duty guard, who hid his comic book when he saw someone approaching.

"Hey, Sergeant Rice, you too, eh? What's goin' on in there, man. It's like Grand Central Station here, and this is the middle of the night. You're not homesick for this place, are you?"

Gohan smiled at the airman and walked into the compound, where he found Sergeant John Mancini pacing and waiting for him.

"Gohan! Man, are we glad to see you! You thought you had seventy-two hours off? Sorry, but think of all the overtime you'll get for this."

"Yeah, right, sarge." Gohan laughed. "Two times zero is still zero, isn't it?"

Sergeant Mancini laughed with him. "Come on in, man. They need you in there. Why don't you get settled, and I'll rustle up some breakfast for you. What would you like?"

"Black coffee, please, and lots of it. How about some SOS with that, too, as long as that big cook who sweats in it isn't working tonight? I'm not that hungry."

"Gohan, you're the big hero here. That's why you're workin' a double shift for free. We'll keep you happy, Mister. Don't worry. If I have to, I'll cook the stuff myself."

Gohan did a double-take. "Did you say what I thought you said? Maybe I ought to stick with just coffee."

"Go get 'em, Gohan. I'll be back with a gourmet breakfast in a flash."

Gohan walked to his workstation. It had five separate receivers so he could copy the five net stations. As he walked in, he greeted the men gathered around the three operators.

"Hey, Captain, what's going on? Is Ivan the Terrible invading DC?"

"You got that half-right, Gohan," Captain Foust replied. "Thanks for comin' in. It's the same net you found for us a few weeks back. It's gotten hot again just when we thought it was dead. Looks like pretty serious stuff. They're masking it and making it darn hard to copy."

"You'll have a ball with these guys, Gohan," Zak, another operator, said. "Man, they're sending a hundred-plus words a minute number messages, and the stupid outstations are all doing the same. They've been going like gangbusters. I don't know how much we already missed. Right now, they seem to be taking a break."

"Crypto doesn't think they're finished, though," Captain Foust said. "From what we've gotten so far, they think they might be moving their network to another location, so this might be the last time we hear from them for a while. We'll have to see."

"If you ask me," Zak said, "they're probably tryin' to cook down that stupid ditto machine. It must be burnin' up at that speed."

"Were you doing most of the copying?" Gohan asked Zak.

"If you want to call it that," the young airman replied. "I was tryin', man, but it was a nightmare. I got some stuff. I hope I didn't screw it up too badly."

"You did fine, Zak," Captain Foust said. "Don't get down on yourself. Gohan, these guys can fill you in better than I can. They've been here working with this for the last hour or more. When I came in, it was going hot and heavy. They were really cooking."

"Speaking of cooking," Gohan said, "where's sarge with my breakfast? Man, I'm starving."

"It looks like this stuff is what we've been waiting for, Gohan," Captain Foust said. "Let us know if you need anything. We want you to be happy."

"Is that right? Captain, if you wanted me to be happy, you wouldn't have come and got me."

Foust smiled.

"Who knows, Captain?" Gohan asked. "Maybe this is the start of World War III. Will I get a special medal for predicting that?"

"Sure. I'll put it in for you. While I'm at it, I'll put in for a medal for Sergeant Mancini, too, for goin' for your breakfast. He's a heck of a guy. You know that, don't you?"

"You're right, Captain. Johnnie told me that if there weren't anyone in the kitchen, he'd cook that SOS himself. If he gets a medal for that, so should I, because I have to eat it.

"Reds, yank that thing off your head and let me in. If I gotta be here, I might as well do something."

The young redheaded intercept operator removed his headset, sighed, and wiped perspiration from his forehead. "Wow, Gohan. You should've been here. All five of those Commie perverts were goin' at the same time. It was nasty. We couldn't keep up. Hondo and Zak did the most. I feel like I just played a football game. I guess the boys in the back will let you know if we did any good. It sure was tough. We might've wrecked it."

"No sweat, Reds," Gohan said. "I'm sure you guys did all right. Now let me on this thing. How about rehookin' the receivers and give me all five? I want to know if anybody's talkin' to anybody else. Then you can take a break. When you're done, come back in case we start smokin' again."

Gohan saw Lieutenant Thiebold enter the operations center. "Hey, Captain Foust, these guys did a heck of a job," Gohan said loudly. "Maybe you should promote all of them to lieutenant. We need a few more of those around here."

"I heard that, Gohan!" Lieutenant Thiebold said.

"Hi, Lieutenant. You and Captain Foust runnin' this show tonight?"

"It looks that way. Milton from NSA just arrived. Please cooperate with him, Gohan. This could be really important stuff."

"You disappoint me, Lieutenant. As long as my favorite major isn't here, I'll get along fine with everybody. Uh-oh. Here comes Ivan the Terrible."

Gohan began copying while some of the men watched. Captain Foust put an arm around Stan Petrzak's shoulders. "Tell sarge when he gets back to take over here. Lieutenant Thiebold and I will be with Mr. Milton in the office if you need us."

Sergeant Mancini brought Gohan's coffee and hot plate of creamed chipped beef on toast. He also brought coffee and doughnuts into Major Parson's office, where Lieutenant Thiebold, Captain Foust, and Steve Milton were huddled. Soon, General Winthrop, the U.S. Air Force Far East commander, joined them.

"Boys, I hear we've got somethin' cookin' tonight," the general said. "Is that right?"

"Yes, sir," Captain Foust said. "How are you, sir? We're sorry we had to wake you, but we knew you'd want to be here."

"You're darn right I do. Thanks. Milton, how are you?"

"I'm fine, general. Still trying to wake up, though, like the others."

"OK, men. As you know, not everyone needs to be here. Captain, are you in charge?"

"For now, sir. Major Parsons is off base, and we didn't call him."

"My information is that he doesn't get along that well with your ace. Why don't you stay on, Captain. Lieutenant, I'm sure you understand, don't you?"

"Yes, sir. No problem, sir." Thiebold left the room and rejoined the men in the operations center.

"Captain," General Winthrop continued, "I'm going to clear you for this, because you need to know what your boys will be looking for. Things are getting tight, and time becomes more important every day. OK, Milton, where are we?"

"Kenneth Sinclair is one of the senior supervisors in our branch at NSA, general," Milton began.

"Yes, I've met him. Go on."

"He's been on this project since these guys located the net a few weeks ago. Actually, he's been heading it up for over two months. Back when we started getting info about the Viets and the Russkies joining forces, he started watching it.

"What we know right now is that the Soviets have sent a small military group into Laos. We're still trying to pinpoint their location, but we know it's in a small village somewhere in the middle of the jungle. Isn't that great? Does anyone know how big that daggone jungle is over there? Given enough time, we'll pin it down. The CIA's working on that. We know a senior KGB officer is in on it, and that means Krushchev's pushing it."

"As opposed to whom?" Captain Foust asked.

"The Soviets operate differently than we do, Captain. If this were strictly a military operation, there wouldn't necessarily be a KGB presence. If the purpose is to spread Communism, the KGB is always out front, and they usually control the operation. That sometimes creates problems. The Russian military doesn't get along that well with those guys."

"So, you're saying, general, that this may not be a military operation?"

"No, I was just hopin'. Truth is, Captain, that's probably exactly what it is. We don't like it when Russia sends troops anywhere. If this isn't a military operation, why are they sending troops into Laos? It could be just moral support, but if not, this is a scary situation. We could be goin' to war with our old friends, the Russkies. What else have we got?"

"We don't have a bottom line yet, because there are too many holes in our intercept information," Milton answered. "We can tie this move in to Ho Chi Minh and his Viet Minh guerrillas. If the Soviets are going into Laos, it's because Ho wants to use Laos to get to South Vietnam and attack Diem. Laos gives Ho a back door.

"The question then becomes why are the Soviets there? Are they offering support in the way of arms? We don't think they're there to train the Viets. Those guys know more about guerrilla war than the Russkies will ever know."

"Don't the Soviets know we're backing South Vietnam?" the captain asked. "Do they really want to mess with us?"

General Winthrop laughed. "Captain, there's not much we do they don't know, and vice versa. No, they don't want to mess with us. They're smart enough to know that if we back South Vietnam without actually fighting there, they can do the same thing in the north."

"That's right," Milton said. "They know Diem's our man. They also know we support the government in Laos. It's obvious they don't want us to know what they're doing, or they wouldn't go to so much trouble to disguise it."

"That's where we come in, Captain," General Winthrop said. "It's clear we're not getting all the information we need. Those people are passing information we don't see. I'll hand the rest of this off to you, Captain. Your boys need to find out what's goin' on over there. If this stuff is so important they keep changing frequencies and network bases, then it's important to us, too.

A knock came at the door.

"Yeh," bellowed the general.

A short, middle-aged man, not in uniform, opened the door and handed the general a piece of paper, then shut the door and left.

"Is he out of uniform?" the general asked.

"Yes, sir, he is," Captain Foust answered.

"OK, just wanted to know," the general replied, laughing.

"Civilian," the captain added.

General Winthrop quietly read the report.

"Well, crypto just got us some more information. It looks like they're definitely sending in troops—thirty men, doctors, communications people, and the KGB. They're already on their way. In fact, they're probably already there.

"I know you've got good men in there, Captain. They need to keep playin' around with this until they find out where that information is coming from. We have to know, Captain."

"It's also complex, general," Captain Foust replied. "Obviously, it's not easy, or we wouldn't be having this conversation. I'll make sure Gohan and Zak understand. They're the best men we've got." He turned toward Milton. "Steve, what about the communications people the general just spoke about. Why would they be going with these troops?"

"What do you mean?" Milton replied.

"Your people are saying that the Soviets probably have an alternate communications network, but we haven't been able to find it. It's probably a small base with a weak signal, right?"

"Yeah. What are you getting at?" Milton asked, but he already knew what the Captain was saying.

"Suppose the alternate communication site is in that camp in Laos? If it's small, we probably wouldn't be able to pick it up from here."

"Uh, without compromising anything, we can pick up anything

on the ground from our spy planes, Captain," Milton answered.

"Well, without sounding like a smart-butt, sir, have you?"

General Winthrop smiled. "Captain, that might be the answer we've been looking for. Right, Milton?"

"Yeah, it's possible. We discussed that idea earlier, but it wasn't considered very likely. We've gotten a lot more information since. No doubt MI is on top of this, so I don't think it'll come as a surprise. Maybe I should contact Sinclair to make sure.

"With the Soviets' intelligence capabilities, they could give Ho a big boost just by providing a better communications system. Those guys might be guerillas, but they're as sophisticated as the Soviets. They aren't backward. If they knew what everyone else was doing, they'd have a tremendous advantage.

"Let me take a break and call Sinclair. I'd like to discuss this with him. Do you mind, general?"

"No. Go right ahead. We'll go visit Gohan. How about it, Captain?"

They found Gohan leaning back in his chair, balancing precariously on two legs with his feet on the work desk, busy chatting with two of the night-shift operators.

When he saw the two officers walk in, Gohan immediately dropped his chair to the floor, smiled, and saluted.

"Not necessary, Gohan," General Winthrop said. "That's for other people to see. We're working tonight. At ease."

Gohan propped his chair up again.

"Everything quiet now?" Captain Foust asked.

"Yeah. It was crazy for a while, but not as bad as these guys had it earlier. I guess Ivan the Terrible took a nap. That's life, Captain."

"Gohan, General Winthrop has suggested," Captain Foust said, "and I agree, that you and Zak must be on the receivers all the time, looking for an alternate network. It'll probably be a very weak signal, and it might be outside our area. It's very important to find it. I'm guessing it'll be the same five guys on different frequencies and equipment. Think you can find 'em for us?"

"Like an anteater in a termite hill, Captain."

"What did you get earlier?" the general asked.

"Not much, sir. Just hello, how are you, how's the wife and baby? No messages."

General Winthrop nodded.

"Speaking of which, how's that new baby?" Captain Foust asked.

"Absolutely beautiful, Captain. I always thought all babies looked alike, but it's a lot different when it's your own. She's wonderful. I can't wait until she walks and talks."

"Just remember, son," the general said, "daughters aren't like sons. Once they begin talking, they never shut up."

Gohan laughed. "I've got a ways to go before that, general. All I know is, it's really neat to go home from work and have a wife and daughter waiting for me. I like it so much, I might get married again and have another baby next week. Sumi's pretty sick right now, so once we get this thing squared away, I want to get home, if possible."

"We can work that out," Lieutenant Thiebold said, walking into the operations center. "How old is she?"

"Just over two months. You have a little girl, too, right?"

"Yeah. April was eight months old last week. Prettiest little girl you ever saw. What's your daughter's name?"

"Sumiko Leah."

"Really?" the captain asked. "What does it mean?"

Gohan's face took on a sly look. "It means three cabbages and a baseball glove careening over a waterfall."

"What?"

"Come on, Captain." Gohan laughed. "How the heck would I know what it means? It's a name. We just like the sound of it."

General Winthrop laughed as hard as everyone else. Suddenly, the net became active again.

"Later, guys," Gohan said. "Here we go."

His chair dropped to the floor in front of his electric typewriter, and he tuned the main receiver before typing very, very fast. The message lasted more than twenty minutes, and all five stations were involved. There were several fast number messages, but Gohan managed to get all of them.

The crypto guys arrived, leaning over Gohan's shoulder as he typed. They tore off the copy one sheet at a time as Gohan punched it out, then they sat at the large, flat table in the corner and began working on it. To the naked eye, it looked like someone typed with his fingers on the wrong row of keys.

Gohan was amazing. No matter how fast the information came, he typed it in the correct format and set the messages off-center so they'd be easier to read. He pecked away as the base station and all four outstations conversed for over an hour. Many messages were sent, keeping the crypto men busy almost all night.

Steve Milton divided his time between the telephone, the crypto department, and meeting with General Winthrop and Captain Foust.

Major Parsons eventually arrived, pulling into Onna Point at 4:30 that morning. Parking his Jeep, he walked into the compound, then ordered a fresh pot of hot, black coffee and breakfast. He joined Captain Foust and Steve Milton, who were talking in the major's office, and was quickly brought up to date. General Winthrop had gone back to his quarters at Kadena.

"More and more," Milton said, "it looks like they've installed a communications site in the jungle in Laos. Peter was right about that. We know the Russkies and North Vietnamese are in cahoots, and we can assume the Pathet Lao are involved, too. Whatever they're doing, they began passing information this evening. It stopped a couple of hours ago.

"We can tell by the responses from the outstations that there's more info being passed, but we can't find it. We think they're sending locally, using signals that are too weak for us to pick up. That's bad news, major. That information could drastically change the makeup of Indochina and might mean a major war.

"We'd like you to give this top priority. The big shots will tell us what the next moves should be in a day or two. There are plenty of possibilities, but frankly, once I started asking questions, the situation became hush-hush. That probably means they know what they want to do, but they aren't ready to tell us.

"Your instructions are to stay on the net. We'll keep your

golden boy, Gohan, on the job as much as possible. Let him roam to see if he can locate the other net, but don't kill him with work. We have to give him some time off. He's got family."

"Bull crap," Parsons snapped. "The guy's an enlisted man in the U.S. Air Force, and we own him. He does what we say. I don't care about his family. He's not legally married. I warned him about getting entangled with foreign nationals. If we need him here, we'll just keep him. If he weren't married, we wouldn't be so lenient."

"You're right, major," Captain Foust said. "We can do that, but remember, we need him. He's vital to this operation, even if that puts him in the driver's seat. This is more important than protocol. If Rice cops an attitude and refuses to work, what will you do? Force him? Please remember, he's a solid, hard-working sergeant, not a troublemaker. If we keep him happy, he'll bend over backwards to get this done for us.

"He has a wife and two-month-old little girl, major, and the girl's pretty sick right now. He needs his personal life. If we treat him right, he'll do a better job for us."

"Yeah, maybe, but I don't like the guy," Parsons admitted. "He's got those black belts and speaks the local lingo. If he likes it that much over here, he should slant his eyes and buy a coolie hat so he can work in a rice paddy. The U.S. won't miss him. I sure won't."

"Major," Milton said, "I'm not a military man, and I don't want to interfere in military matters, but Captain Foust is right. We need Gohan. No one else can copy this stuff like he can. The big boys are making some major decisions that could be earth shattering, and it's coming from the stuff Gohan's getting for us. We need that boy happy, warm, fed, loved, and ready to produce. Like it or not, he's the best, and we need him."

Major Parsons frowned in displeasure, but he was a good commander and nodded. Then he stood and walked to the door, opening it before whistling. "Send the lieutenant in!"

Lieutenant Thiebold quickly joined the group.

"Lieutenant, we were just discussing our friend, Rice," Major Parsons said. "The men seem to think we need to let him go home to his family. What's going on out there right now? Do we need him?"

"Things are pretty slow right now, sir. Why don't we let him go home? We can put him on special assignment so he doesn't have to come in unless we call him. We can even have someone run him home or loan him a Jeep. That'll keep him happy."

"No Jeep, Lieutenant. All I need is that jerk getting plastered and wrecking an army Jeep under my command. The guys who supply that stuff have no idea what's going on in Indochina and probably don't care. Captain Foust?"

"I like Dan's idea, and I agree with you on the Jeep. We don't need to give him a Jeep. I'll give him a ride home. I'm too awake to sleep right now, anyway."

"OK, go ahead. I'm here now, so I might as well finish out the night. Why don't you guys get some rest? If something pops, I'll send for you. You, too, Dan," Major Parsons told the Lieutenant. "Get some sleep. We'll be on weird schedules for a while. Let's take advantage of it."

As the men left, Major Parsons wondered why they liked Rice so much. Sure, he was a whiz with the radio equipment, but he wasn't God. He was just an E-4, and he was belligerent, mouthy, and rebellious. Parsons had been against Rice's recent promotion to sergeant, but he was outvoted and eventually had to approve the application.

He'd be glad when Rice's tour of duty was up, and he finally left Okinawa. Parsons walked to the door and called, "Who's running the coffeepot tonight? I can't run this shift without that black goo. Someone please get on it."

He didn't see the three airmen who were on break shrug and flip a coin to see who'd be the major's flunky for the rest of the night.

Chapter 8
Ban Na Lom Camp

October 1960

THE BUILDING AT BAN NA LOM CAMP WAS FINALLY COMPLETED. The layout wasn't exactly what Nikolai preferred, but it would work. The main compound included his office, a twelve-by-sixteen room with a desk, six chairs, a couch, two mosquito-netted windows, and two metal cabinets, one of which held an ample supply of Russian vodka. The office was large enough for him to sleep in it if he wished. It wasn't Moscow, but he was stuck in the Laotian jungle. All he could do was hope it wouldn't be a long assignment. If things went well, he would send reports to Moscow detailing his accomplishments. If necessary, he could feign illness and be sent back home.

Next to Nikolai's office was a smaller room where Comrade Pavel Zortov handled the administration and supply details. It, too, was an unassuming room, but he had a desk, typewriter, file cabinet, and, thankfully, a window. He shared his office with the communications experts, usually a Russian soldier named Gerkov. He was the top communications man assigned to the camp and received transmissions over one receiver, copied them by hand, then turned his back on Zortov so the other man couldn't watch while he sent messages out using his hand-held Morse code transmitter.

He also communicated with the other stations using a second receiver. He constantly changed frequencies, depending on whom he was sending messages. The situation was very confusing and disconcerting to Zortov. He didn't care for Gerkov and occasionally watched him work, which upset the soldier, who had instructions to be as secretive as possible. Zortov made sure Gerkov knew he was a member of the KGB and had ties to Nikolai and other men of even higher rank. Nikolai, as the KGB chief, knew about the secret messages but didn't bother telling Comrade Zortov anything.

When Gerkov wasn't working, Shikin, the other Russian soldier, was. Without meaning to, Zortov intimidated Shikin, and he enjoyed it when Shikin handled the communications chores. Unfortunately, that didn't happen very often.

Zortov spent many evenings alone in the office. After the communications men left at the end of the day, Zortov could relax. He despised his assigned living quarters, where he was forced to live and sleep with military men, around whom he felt very uncomfortable. Most nights, he stayed in his office as long as he could, sitting and daydreaming. When he was ready for bed, he returned to the barracks, although there were many nights when he slept on two chairs in his office.

Next to Zortov's office was a larger room that was cold and damp, with a small table, two chairs, and no windows. It could have been used for storage or converted to additional sleeping quarters, but it remained empty for the moment.

Along the back of the building were two long rooms that were barracks for the soldiers. The inside room housed the Soviets, including Major Aleksandr Ustinova, who roomed with his men by choice. Much to Zortov's dismay, that included him, too. The outside room was used by the Pathet Lao and Viet Minh guerrillas. Nikolai had a private bedroom at the far end of the building.

A twenty-foot tower stood at the upper end of the compound,

housing two guards who watched the village and camp. They kept a large, battery-powered spotlight in the tower, and, at night, they swept the area with the light to make sure no one sneaked up on the camp. During the day, the guards took eight-hour shifts in the tower, while at night, they worked only four hours at a time.

On the other side of the compound, closer to the village, was a large dugout dungeon twenty feet square and twelve feet deep. The smooth sides were impossible to scale, and the thick bamboo door on the top was tied into four posts hammered into the ground. The inhabitants of the dungeon were pro-American Lao Hmong dissidents and villagers who had strong affiliations with the American-backed Lao government. Others were labeled enemies because they stood up to the Communists when they invaded their homes. The Pathet Lao, along with Nikolai, became the judge and jury for all dissidents. If Nikolai labeled them enemies of the state, which he did in every case, they were sent to the dungeon.

There were currently eleven men in the underground jail, including the village headman, the local doctor who'd been building the hospital when the village was taken over, three village elders, and a visiting Buddhist monk.

The dungeon had no waste facilities or drainage, so it stank. Dysentery was rampant. When it rained, the prisoners huddled against the walls but couldn't stay dry. They were fed once a day, although the food was poor. Though most had been in the prison for only a few weeks, all had lost weight and were becoming sicker and weaker by the day. They knew that without outside intervention, they would die within a month. That created a strong bond between them, but none had any hope of rescue. Their American allies probably didn't even know about the situation.

One hundred feet from the dungeon was a small, poorly equipped hospital that was responsible for aiding the Viet Minh guerrillas who would travel the nearby Laotian route to South Vietnam. The hospital was already in use, because some of the villagers had become ill or injured and were being treated there. A competent Soviet doctor was in charge, a compassionate, understanding man who seemed truly interested in tending the sick.

Below the hospital, near the village settlement, was a storage area that contained large wooden bins filled with boxes of ammunition. The bins were locked and secured, and the area was patrolled by two soldiers.

There was a large clearing, approximately eighty yards wide, between the compound and the jungle that ran the length of the compound. A tall, barbed-wire fence surrounded the camp, separating it from the rest of the village. One small area near the village wasn't fenced, partly because three large trees grew together there, and it wasn't possible to erect a fence around them. The site was far enough from the compound that no one was concerned. Besides, since guards patrolled there during the day, it was deemed safe.

The camp had twelve guards on duty at all times—two in the tower, two near the dungeon, two near the ammunition stores, and six men who patrolled the village in three pairs.

Ban Na Lom was a large settlement near the Annamite Mountains in the area where Laos and Vietnam met. The village had several hundred inhabitants—large for a Hmong settlement. The villagers, all Hmong, were part of the Lao Sung, meaning Lao up high. Their rice, corn, and opium fields stretched for miles. They also grazed cattle and buffalo, and almost all families raised pigs, which were used more for sacrifice than for food. They had vegetable gardens, from which they harvested most of their food, which also included rice, chicken, and fish. Because it was such a large village, there were many houses, most built from wooden planks with bamboo or thatched roofs. Each house had an altar on the wall for ancestral spirit worship.

The Hmong were a polite, shy people, content to live by themselves in their mountain villages. They grew rice to eat, corn to feed their livestock, and opium for pain relief or to exchange for money or necessities. They didn't need much, and they didn't ask for much. They had no calendar or clocks, and most didn't even know when they were born.

In their belief system, evil spirits caused illness, and there were shamans in each village to pray over and tend the sick, casting out evil spirits. Opium was used to relieve pain and comfort the dying. Major illnesses were almost always fatal.

Ban Na Lom, however, was fortunate to have a medicine man, Dr. Boua Thao, who studied in the U.S. and was in the process of building a medical clinic for his people. Though his methods were unusual to the Hmong, his success rate was astounding. All the villagers looked forward to the completion of the clinic.

Life was simple for most Hmong in Ban Na Lom. It would never improve much, but it also didn't get worse. Then came the Soviets, the Pathet Lao, and the Viet Minh.

One of the nurses at the hospital was seventeen-year-old Ka Moua, the daughter of the headman, who'd been arrested and imprisoned by the Soviets. Because he had multiple wives and an extended family, his family shared three houses. As a result, the Soviets and the Pathet Lao didn't know that Ka Moua was his daughter. She was a secret member of a grass-roots, under-ground, anti-Communist guerilla movement led by her brother, Cheu Moua, who had been trained by the American Green Berets and UDTs.

When the Pathet Lao, aided by Viet Minh guerrillas, captured their village, Cheu Moua and a few others escaped. He formed a small army of twelve guerillas, some of whom also had previous military experience, but the rest were rice and opium farmers.

In 1959, the U.S. smuggled Green Berets into Laos to train the RLA, the Royal Lao Army. Several Hmong joined the RLA and became its best soldiers. Cheu and his second in command, Vu Xiong, were among that group.

He and Vu took their small band deep into the mountains to train them. Cheu was determined to take back his village and release his friends who were being held captive by the Pathet Lao and the other foreigners.

Starting with only a few rifles and very little ammunition, they procured additional weapons from other villagers who were will-ing to aid their cause. They also stole weapons and ammunition from the Americans and the local police, amassing a small arsenal of American M-1s, Browning automatics, .45-caliber pistols, and Russian SKS-45s and AK-47s. Cheu intensified his efforts to build up his small army.

Ka Moua worked during the day at the small village hospital, assisting the Russian doctor. She tried to learn what she could about events happening within the compound—when new groups came, who left and why, and anything else she could overhear. At night, she sneaked out of the camp, climbed through the three trees at the edge of the village, and ran the four miles to her brother's camp in the mountains.

She shared whatever information she gleaned, spent the night at the camp, then ran back down the mountain to take her place at the hospital. She wanted to give her brother better information, but she wouldn't prostitute herself, and Cheu didn't want her to, either. She disliked the Soviets, but she loathed the Pathet Lao. Still a virgin when many other Hmong girls her age were married and raising families, she devoted her life to medicine and would wait 'til later for marriage. Without compromising her virginity, she gained what information she could and was satisfied with that.

Ka was born in the settlement, though it had moved a few times during her lifetime. When she was thirteen, while most of her friends prepared for marriage, she moved in with relatives in a village outside the city of Vientiane, known as the City of a Thousand Temples. It was a long trip, but Ka, after speaking with Dr. Thao, had decided to become a nurse. Her only desire was to move back to her beloved Ban Na Lom and help the doctor care for her people.

For the next few years, she split her time between her city residence, the home of distant relatives of one of her stepmothers, and her beloved village, and loved it. She had the best of both worlds. She liked the hustle and bustle of the city, particularly because she knew it was only temporary. She liked visiting markets and stores even when she couldn't buy anything.

Mostly, she liked the city, because it gave her the chance to learn and train, but she loved her village and its people even more. She wanted desperately to return and make a difference. She could have studied English instead of nursing, but she wasn't planning to visit America and saw no need to learn the language. She did, however, study Russian, because she intended, eventually, to go to Leningrad to become a doctor.

It never occurred to her that she might need money for that. She was content, at the time, to return to her village and help nurse the sick. Nursing was an unusual occupation for a girl, and that broke with her Hmong traditions. Accepting the encouragement of her friend, Dr. Thao, she was determined to follow through with her dream.

Though her country was torn by civil strife, and there was terrible fighting around it, that didn't affect Ka. Her world centered on her village, and no matter how close the political upheaval and war might be, to her, it seemed as if it was over 1,000 miles away.

Unfortunately, her comfortable world, like that of her relatives and neighbors, was soon uprooted.

When the Pathet Lao and Viet Minh took over the village, Ka escaped with Cheu. They talked for a long time about what Ka should do. When she decided to join his underground, she knew the decision might lead to her own death. If her secret were discovered, the Communists would have no mercy on her. She would be murdered, but, like her brother, she embraced the danger.

The plan was for her to sneak back into camp and volunteer to work in the hospital. Construction of the small clinic had been started by Dr. Thao and the villagers, but progress was slow, and it was never finished. When the Viet Minh and Pathet Lao took over, they, under Soviet tutelage, finished the hospital, then claimed it for themselves. Ka was allowed to work there, and the plan she and her brother created worked well at first.

Nikolai Nikolayevich, the large, unsightly KGB officer who ran the camp, took a liking to the young Hmong girls in the village. One by one, he coerced them into his quarters and took them by force. Later, he frightened them by promising to kill them and their families if they refused him or told anyone what happened. He didn't ask their age and didn't care. He took turns with several girls whenever he was in the mood, which, fortunately, wasn't that often. One girl was only ten years old.

Nikolai liked Ka a lot. She became apprehensive when the KGB officer summoned her to his office one evening. She was just preparing to leave for her brother's camp when the word came. Ka knew that denying the man's request would be a serious offense. She didn't know why he wanted to see her. Perhaps he needed an interpreter for the Hmong. But then she realized he wouldn't know she spoke Russian.

Apprehensive, she made the short walk from the hospital to the KGB man's office, hoping to learn valuable information for her brother.

Within minutes of her arrival, she knew why she'd been summoned. Terrified, she tried to fight him off, but to no avail. When he finished with her, she left his office, stumbled through the camp and into the jungle, then ran to her brother as hard as she could. Fifteen minutes later, with tears streaming down her cheeks, she sat on a fallen tree and vomited.

She stopped by a small stream, and, undeterred by the dangers in the water, she bathed. That helped. She was very late reaching her brother's camp, and Cheu was concerned.

Ka told him she had a fever, had no information to report, and wanted to sleep. She never admitted what happened, but she didn't have to. He knew. He hated his enemy already, but that hatred grew. What happened to Ka only strengthened his love for her and his resolve to drive the perverted Communist leeches from his village.

As time passed, Ka gained an immense amount of information from Nikolai, although she hated every second with him. He never discovered that she understood Russian, so he spoke in her presence often, assuming she couldn't understand a word. And since he spoke no Tibeto-Burmese, the Hmong language, he never tried to converse with her.

Cheu, though he gained valuable information from Ka, was greatly outmanned by the invaders and knew there was little he could do to fight back. He and his men continued training, believing the right time would eventually come to drive the Communists from the village and keep them from any neighboring villages. So far, there had been no attempts to take over any other settlements.

Cheu and his valiant team added to their numbers and trained hard. Perhaps someday the compound would be undermanned, making the odds more favorable for an attack. Then he could liberate his village. For the time being, though, he practiced patience.

Captain Harold Baker was handed a large envelope and told to study it. He retreated to the private quarters that had been arranged for him. He made a pot of coffee, laid a pack of peanut butter crackers out on the kitchen table and began pouring over the material.

"Ban Na Lom?" he repeated, thinking aloud.

He laid the series of maps out on the table and pinpointed the location of the Communist compound. He then read the report slowly.

The information was sketchy. He guessed the U.S. was having difficulty getting good intelligence on the Communist operation. He knew enough to be concerned. North Vietnamese troops, Pathet Lao troops, and Soviet troops manned the outpost. It appeared to be under Soviet control. That wasn't good.

Their purpose was to get close enough to intercept communications. He would have a five-man team, three Marines for cover, and...

"Well, I'll be darned," he said aloud.

Gohan was the communications expert. David Gohan Rice. It had to be the same guy. He read on. It indicated he was a capable warrior stationed at Onna Point. Yep, he was going to team up with his fighting buddy, Gohan. He nodded his approval and continued reading the report.

They would parachute in under the cover of darkness, land a mile or so away from their point of contact, then hike to that point. They'd build two temporary housing units high in the trees, set up their equipment, then let Gohan go to work.

Five days maximum would be spent in Ban Na Lom, depending on what information they got, then they would return to Okinawa. According to his schedule, that should be his last assignment. He was due to go home for an extended leave, then he would have to make a decision as to what his future would be.

He had strongly considered getting out of the navy and working with his father-in-law at the church. It would be different, but he wanted to be with his family. He had spent far too much time away from them. There was still time to enjoy the boys, play baseball with them, and be an influence on their teen years. He looked forward to it.

So, how dangerous was the mission? According to the report, they expected no difficulty at all. But, he was too experienced to take that as meaning a routine assignment. No mission was routine when you were in the same vicinity as your enemy.

He looked over the rest of the information they had provided him—a forty page report on the late history of Laos, a report on guerilla warfare in Laos, and a story about life in Laos' jungle.

He poured himself a cup of coffee, slipped a cracker into his mouth and started with the history of Laos.

Chapter 9
Secret Mission

October 1960

GOHAN WAS WORKING AT ONNA POINT WHEN WORD CAME there was a Jeep waiting to take him to Kadena Air Base.

"I don't know what it's about, Rice," Major Parsons said. "I got a call from Kadena. General Winthrop wants you at a high-level meeting down there, but that's all he said. He told me he'd give me the details later."

The driver didn't know anything, either.

"Hey, buddy," he said, when Gohan asked, "I'm not the information director. I'm Colonel Hoke's driver. When the colonel introduces me to a three star, and the big guy tells me to come up here to get you, that's what I do. That's why they like me. I follow orders, and I don't ask questions. That's what you should do. As far as you're concerned, I don't answer questions, either."

Great, Gohan thought. I'm going to meet the top brass, but I don't know why, and I get the Air Force's number-one jerk driver as an escort.

The driver pulled into Kadena Air Base and drove through every alley and side street it had until they finally arrived at a small, nondescript block building. Two MPs met Gohan at the curb and escorted him in. A pretty WAF lieutenant looked up from her desk and smiled warmly.

"Sergeant Rice?"

"Yes, sir. I mean, ma'am. Sorry. We don't have women officers at Onna Point. I'm not used to addressing…."

"That's OK, sergeant." She grinned. "Please have a seat. I'll see if the gentlemen are ready to see you."

Gentlemen? he wondered to himself. *What's going on?*

In a few minutes, she returned and motioned him to follow her. "This way, sergeant. We're just going down the hall."

At the end of the hall was a closed wooden door with a sign on it that read Private. Like all the other doors in the building, it had no glass panels. The lieutenant stopped at the door and knocked.

"Yes?" a voice boomed.

"Sergeant Rice is here, sir."

Gohan heard the door being unlocked from the inside. The door swung open, and a loud voice echoed into the hall. "Come in, sergeant. We've been waitin' for you."

Gohan walked in and recognized Major General Winthrop. He knew and liked the general, but didn't know the other men. The second man was introduced as a top official of the CIA, though Gohan didn't catch his name. There was also a major general from the marines, General Emilio Mancini. Gohan walked forward and shook the men's hands, then sat down wondering if the general was related to John Mancini at Onna Point.

The CIA man looked like he hated the world. He didn't smile, and, when Gohan shook his hand, he merely nodded without speaking.

Is he mute? Gohan thought. *Naw! I couldn't be that lucky.*

"Gohan," General Winthrop said, "we're waiting for one more person to join us. I believe you know him. It's Captain Harold Baker of the Navy UDTs."

Gohan's eyebrows shot up. *Wow! The admiral will be in on this, too, whatever it is.*

After the encounter with the marines at Ishikawa Beach,

Gohan met the admiral one other time, and they spent some time together. Gohan liked him a lot and remembered him saying something about being sent there for a special mission. Perhaps it was coming up. *Whatever it is,* he thought, *I'm glad the admiral's in on it.* He nodded to the general. "Yes, sir. I know Captain Baker."

"Gohan, both Major General Mancini and Captain Baker have been briefed regarding your work at Onna Point. Mr. Damsteegt and I are already aware of it. Due to the nature of this meeting, there won't be any secrets among us. These men know what you're doing, including the recent information regarding the Soviet move into Laos.

"I know you men aren't often informed about what it is you intercept, but this time, you have a need to know. You and your friends at Onna Point are responsible for getting us critical information about Russian troop movements into Laos. That's what we're here to discuss."

There was another knock at the door.

"Yes?"

"Captain Baker's here, sir."

General Winthrop unlocked the door again. Captain Baker walked in and saluted.

"Captain Baker, you know everyone here," General Winthrop said. "Please take a seat."

The admiral shook Gohan's hand firmly. "Good to see you again, Gohan."

"Likewise, admiral."

"Let's cut to the chase, men," General Winthrop said. "From this moment on, everything that's said in this room is the highest, top-secret priority. Gohan, your company commander knows nothing about this, and you can't tell him under any circumstances. You can't even tell your best friend or your wife, nor can you mention it to your judo buddy, Matsumura. When we say top secret, we mean it. You've just moved into a special echelon in the intelligence world. Tens of thousands of lives could hang in the balance. Do I make myself clear?"

Gohan gulped. He hadn't anticipated such a thing, but he didn't shy away from it, either. "Yes, sir."

"Captain Baker is more familiar with the rules of this kind of game. He's been in it before. From the time you leave this building until you leave on your mission, you aren't to set foot in any bar anywhere. Is that clear?"

Gohan nodded, wondering what the word *mission* meant.

"I'm going to repeat that, Gohan. This is a very important assignment, and I know this is your first involvement with this kind of thing. You flat out can't talk about it once you leave this room. That's why I said no bars or drinking allowed. Got it?"

He wanted to tell the general that he'd already stopped drinking, but he didn't.

"Yes, sir, general. I get the picture."

"Good. Now I have to bring you two up to snuff on what's happened so far. I want you to know the background of this situation. Captain Baker, from what I understand, is doing some research on Laos and its history to get an even clearer picture.

"I want you two to understand why we're in this predicament and how we plan to get out of it. This information isn't available to anyone else. I can't say that often enough, and you'll hear me say it again. Whatever we say in this room stays here."

The general shifted positions in his chair, then he stood and began speaking as he paced, occasionally turning toward the men to drive home an important point.

"Vietnam's a major trouble area for the U.S. and has been for a long time. The Communists have been tryin' to get into South Vietnam for over forty years. You've probably heard of Ho Chi Minh. If not, you'll be hearing a lot about him from now on. He's a Vietnamese Communist revolutionary who studied Communism in the Soviet Union and in China. His friends are everyone we aren't friends with.

"He started out just wantin' to get his country out from under the French. But he became so involved in the revolution, he couldn't stop even when the French were gone. He's a professional guerilla who isn't happy unless he's fighting.

"We've got our boy, President Diem, in South Vietnam to keep Communism out. Ho and his troops, which he calls the Viet Minh, are camped in North Vietnam. That's fine if it stays that way, but Ho isn't satisfied with just the north. He's startin' to get into Diem's territory, too.

"Diem has held him off pretty good so far, but Ho's gotten a foothold. You see, boys, President Diem is a Vietnamese, not an American, and we have only limited control over him. Things aren't going along over there the way we'd like. Don't get me wrong. Diem has done a good job 'til now, and he's kept the Communists out, but an all-out attack by Ho Chi Minh could be devastating. Diem might not hold up under that much pressure.

"That puts us right smack in the middle of the war we're tryin' to stay the heck out of. If that happens, we have big problems, but that's not our concern. We have people prepared to handle the consequences if we go to war.

"Our concern is peripheral to the current Vietnam situation, but it's essential to the overall problem. We have the chance to play a big role in the outcome of this conflict, which depends on what exactly is goin' on over there. That's what we have to find out.

"The best route for Ho to get his Viet Minh guerrillas into South Vietnam is through Laos. The Lao government is backed by America, and Ho isn't stupid. He's got friends in there, too. There's a group of Communists called the Pathet Lao—same folks, same ideology, same methods, but a different name. If you took the Pathet Lao and the Viet Minh and put 'em into a bag and shook it, when you poured 'em out, you wouldn't know which was which. Get my drift?'

Gohan and Captain Baker smiled and nodded.

"Unfortunately, it gets worse. We've found out that the Soviets are getting involved. At first, they just sent supplies to the Lao insurgents. Other than arms and supplies, they've pretty much stayed out of things until now, so we looked the other way and pretended we didn't notice. Not anymore.

"Somebody—the Soviets, Ho Chi Minh, or the Pathet Lao—took over a small village in the mountain jungle of Laos. That's part of the stuff you were getting us at Onna Point, Gohan. We've just recently learned where the village is. It's call Ban Na Lom, close to the Vietnam border, and the Communists have built a compound there.

"It's manned by about fifty troops, including Vietnamese, Pathet Lao, and Soviets. It's also a small communications site, but I'll talk about that in a few minutes. There's a small hospital, and they even have their own KGB man. It's a perfect drop-off point for troops entering and leaving South Vietnam.

"The villagers are Hmong. I see you noddin', Baker. You been readin' about them?"

"Yes, sir. It appears the Hmong are pro-American, at least most of 'em."

"That's right. The Hmong are mountainous Lao people who live in similar settlements throughout the country. They're good people. Most are pro-American, and some fought for us in the RLA, the Royal Lao Army. Word was, they were the best troops in the whole dang army.

"We don't know what the Communists did with the villagers. Our intelligence is limited, because we can't get that close. It's a pretty big village, though, with a couple hundred people, so we doubt they killed 'em all. That would be crazy."

He paused, then glanced at Ken Damsteegt, the CIA man, and nodded. "Ken, you want to add anything to this?"

"Just so you guys don't think you're in there alone," Ken said, "there's a lot of top-secret stuff goin' on that's affecting this operation. For example, years ago Chiang Kai Shek sent a large army into southern China to protect it for the nationalists. Unfortunately, the Communists beat 'em to it.

"The KMT army slipped into Burma and hid out for years. The Burmese eventually found 'em and contacted Peking, and about six thousand of the KMT forces were sent back to China. The rest, about the same amount, moved into northern Thailand and are still there. They operate an important intelligence network for us.

"They teamed up with some bandits in Burma, because they had no choice but to stay clandestine. And the bandits, who are opium smugglers, are the key players in the intelligence network. They tell us what we need to know, and we let them get away with their smuggling. It's not pretty, but it works.

"Anyway, they told us about the Chinese Communist movement in Laos and what the Pathet Lao are doing. Recently, they confirmed the Russian movement into the mountains and the taking over of the settlement.

"That's important, because you guys need to know that our information is accurate and verified. Other than that, forget you just heard it."

General Winthrop took over the meeting again. "Thanks, Ken. Boys, we're hesitant to send American troops to Ban Na Lom, because we might start somethin' that'll come back to haunt us. From a military standpoint, we're actin' like we don't know what's going on. From an intelligence standpoint, it's a different story. We not only know they're there, we need to do something about it.

"This communications site is the one we've been looking for. Gohan, you and your boys at Onna got us some stuff recently that helped us figure out what they're doin'. As Ken said, it was verified through other intelligence networks. They've got a small base station in that village. It has a weak signal, which is why you boys can't hear it. However, they can communicate with their own little group, which probably covers a couple hundred miles, but no one can intercept what they're sayin'.

"Here's the problem. If Ho Chi Minh takes thirty, fifty, or a hundred thousand of his guerrillas into South Vietnam through Laos, we'll have a major war on our hands. The good ol' U.S. of A. will be right smack in the middle of it. That's not our problem. Other people will make those decisions, but they can't unless we get 'em the right information. Right now, it looks like the information is comin' from that camp. Gohan, we want you to go in there and get it for us."

The room became silent as the two generals waited for Gohan to reply. The CIA man remained unmoving in his chair. He hadn't even crossed his legs or cleared his throat.

Captain Baker knew his own role from when he met with the men the previous evening. He was glad that Gohan was part of the team. He felt that Gohan was the best choice for the mission, not just because of his intercept abilities, but because he knew how to fight—calm and deadly.

Gohan, however, was stunned. As he listened to the general's story, he assumed he'd become more involved, but at Onna Point. He hadn't anticipated going into enemy territory.

OK, Davey Boy, what are you gonna do? he asked himself. *They're waiting for you. You ready for a war? Ready to visit Laos?*

Gohan didn't even know where Laos was. He wasn't any braver than anyone else, but he didn't run from danger, either. When he signed up, he'd known a war might be coming. That was part of the risk.

Now it looked like they wanted him to go into a jungle in enemy territory and copy code. He didn't have all the issues clear in his mind yet, but he knew the answer.

"First, where's Laos?" he asked. "Second, what do I do when I get there? Third, when do we leave?"

The two generals relaxed. The CIA man didn't move. General Winthrop nodded approvingly.

"Good, Gohan. Major General Mancini will walk you through the mission. Emilio?"

The mustachioed marine general had a high-pitched voice that took Gohan a few moments to become accustomed to, but the situation was too serious to dwell on anything but his words.

"Captain Baker is in charge of the mission. You'll have a five-man team, with three handpicked marines to accompany you. One of those men, Sergeant Oscar Gomez, is responsible for getting your information back to us. You, Gohan, are responsible for getting the information to Sergeant Gomez.

"We chose a site a few miles from Ban Na Lom, far enough away from everything so that you can get in unseen. The jump will be at night, and you'll use black parachutes. Once you've disposed of your paraphernalia, you'll hike to an area about a mile from the enemy camp and set up your copy sight.

"This is mountainous jungle, loaded with poisonous snakes, tigers, elephants, panthers, leopards, and lots of friendly animals, too, that might eat flesh. There's jungle, mountain, and rain forest. The area we want you in is thick with trees, some strong enough to support two or three men. You'll build temporary housing in the trees, and you two will live together. The marines will do the same in another tree. That area's thick with monkeys, so you'll have plenty of company. You never know, sergeant. One might even be related to you."

"Well, I'll be a monkey's uncle," Gohan said.

The men laughed, then General Mancini continued.

"Your first priority, Sergeant Rice, is to build a suitable platform for your radio equipment. You'll need to keep it dry. The treetops are thick enough to protect you from aerial surveillance.

"Once you're situated, your objective is to get the Ivans on your equipment and copy everything they send back and forth. That's all we need from you. Sergeant Gomez will transmit the information back to us. We don't have the luxury of sending a typewriter along, so you'll have to do this by hand. We've been assured you can handle that."

"I'll go one step further," General Winthrop said. "Not only can Gohan do this, he's probably the best man in the U.S. military for the job."

General Mancini nodded. "Sergeant Gomez is the radio operator. He has his own instructions. When he asks for what you've received, you give it to him. The three marines will travel back toward your original landing site and transmit from there. Then they'll return to join you.

"This is a five-day mission. We believe we can learn everything we need in that time. If that changes, you'll be notified. The onus is on you, Sergeant Rice. We need you to locate that net immediately after you arrive. Send us everything they say. We want to know when they blow their noses and when they pass gas. If you do this right, five days will be enough. Then we'll bring you out.

"You must understand that this is an extremely dangerous

mission. You have quite a reputation, sergeant. Captain Baker told us about your little escapade together, and we're aware of your heroics at executive Kobashigawa's house. Now you'll be in the mix again. You have to look at this as war.

"Captain Baker has the experience to command this mission, and he has the final word. He's run similar operations in Korea, and he's very capable. In you two men, we believe we have the best the U.S. military offers. Every man on this mission was our first choice. That's how important this is.

"We'll meet again tomorrow afternoon at two o'clock right here to go over the details. Make sure you're rested and alert. You'll eat dinner, have a short nap, and fly out tomorrow night. Marshal?"

"Thanks, Emilio. Boys, I know this is short notice, but it can't wait. We need to get over there as quickly as possible. Gohan, since you have family here, we'll let you get out in a few minutes. You know the rules, but I'm going over them one more time.

"You can't tell your wife where you're going or why. If necessary, you can say you're being sent on a mission to another country for a little while. If she insists on knowing where, say Germany. You can say you hope to finish your work quickly and should be back in a few weeks. If she asks about danger, shrug it off and tell her it's the same thing you're doin' here, just in another location.

"Your friend, Seth Edwards, could be a problem. Don't talk to him at all. Once you're gone, he'll ask questions at Onna Point, but your commander knows what to tell him. It'll coincide with the story you give your wife. If she goes to Seth with questions, he could make this sticky for us, because we don't know how he'll react to the information he gets from your major.

"I suggest you cover it with your wife. Tell her this came up quickly, and you won't even have time to talk to Edwards, so he won't know what's goin' on, either. If he comes by to ask her, tell her to tell him what you said. Got that?"

Gohan nodded. "Look, general, I need a moment to think. This is a lot to throw at me in a hurry. You're telling me to walk out on my family without any notice. I have a sick baby at home. I need to digest this."

General Mancini looked at General Winthrop. Gohan noticed the look they exchanged.

"General, I didn't refuse to go," Gohan said. "You can wipe off that concerned look. All I said was I needed to digest this. I walked in thinking you'd give me a piece of candy, and instead, I was handed a poisoned apple. That's all."

"OK, sergeant," General Mancini said. "You have the right to take a moment to think about what's been said. How about if I order coffee?"

"Thanks, sir. I could use a cup of coffee." Gohan took a deep breath as the admiral patted his shoulder. The other four men left the room. Gohan was glad to see that the CIA man was still alive.

Once the door shut, the room became very quiet. Gohan wasn't sure he wanted to be alone, but he needed to think, although he didn't know why. He knew how important the mission was, and he knew he'd go through with it, but he didn't know how to break the news to Keiko. He didn't want to leave her and Sumi. The whole thing would have been easier if they'd given him two weeks' notice.

Part of him itched to accept the assignment. He felt good about having the admiral along, partly because he liked the man, and partly because he was an old hand at undercover operations. He also like the fact that the admiral was such a religious man. The generals seemed to have all the details worked out, and it wasn't likely that the team would be very close to the camp or the Russian soldiers.

They'd go in for a week or so, get the information, and get out. He could handle that. He wondered why it was so much easier to accept a dangerous assignment that carried the possibility of death than to break the news to Keiko. He knew the answer to that but didn't want to admit it. If she were an American, he could make her understand. But she wasn't, and there was the chance she wouldn't understand at all. He didn't know how to handle that.

I'll just have to follow the general's orders and tell her I'm goin' to Germany and will be back in a couple of weeks, Gohan thought. What difference does it make if she doesn't handle it? I still have to go.

He considered that. *Man, that ain't good enough, and you know it, Davey Boy.*

He needed Keiko to understand. The last thing he wanted was to leave on the mission with her doubting him. He shook his head, upset at his inability to resolve the dilemma.

Gohan had plenty of confidence, feeling he could do anything he set his mind to. The more he thought over the situation, the more he realized he'd handle it somehow. All he needed was time to think—the one thing the generals weren't giving him.

Maybe I should walk back to Nakadomari, he thought. *That would give me time to figure this all out. The general indicated they'd let me go home from here. I can get some fresh air and think.*

He felt better. When someone knocked on the door, he opened it and nodded to the men. The admiral held two cups of hot, black coffee and handed one to Gohan.

"Thanks." Gohan waited for the others to seat themselves. "The only question I have, general, is should I bring anything special with me tomorrow or just show up?"

General Mancini sighed, and Winthrop laughed. He knew Gohan pretty well and would have been surprised if he balked at the assignment. The CIA man resumed his unmoving position.

"Boys," Winthrop said, "it's a go. The name of the operation is Operation Gohan, but no one knows that except us. There are a few others you haven't met who will have some of this information, but there are less than twenty in the world who know about this mission. We need to keep it that way.

"Because of the support people we'll be using, some people will know certain parts of this but not the whole deal. Be careful. The only ones you can safely discuss this with are each other, General Mancini, and me. Nothing is to be said while you're on the plane. The Marines accompanying you know of the danger and understand their individual responsibilities, but they don't know everything. Do you understand?"

Gohan and Captain Baker nodded.

"OK, captain, you've heard this before, but Gohan, you haven't, so listen carefully. If you're killed, no one will admit to sending you out there. We don't have any idea how you got into Laos or why you went. There will be no record of this mission. Understood?"

Captain Baker nodded. Gohan noticed he didn't seem too concerned, so he nodded, too.

"If you're captured, it's the same deal. We won't know how you got there or why you went. We won't have any record of a mission of that kind in that part of the world. One of the reasons the marines know less than you do is because, though the danger of capture is slight, they'd be more likely to be caught than you two. If so, they don't know enough to hurt us.

"If either of you are captured, you need to beef up your courage. Captain Baker spent time in a Korean prison camp, and he can tell you about that, Gohan. You'll have time to discuss it. There won't be much to do up in those trees unless you can speak monkey.

"You both understand, right? This is the part I don't like thinkin' about, but, because of the possibility, no matter how remote, we must address it. Are we together on this?"

Gohan and Captain Baker said, "Yes, sir."

"OK. Finally, assuming everything goes as planned, you both come back in one piece and face a major debriefing. You'll be almost stripped of your ability to remember any of this." He looked at the two men and felt satisfied they could do the job. "Very well. The rest of the day is yours. Gohan, don't return to Onna Point. Go home and spend the evening with your family. It'll be your last chance for a while. We'll see you tomorrow."

Captain Baker and Gohan stood, shook hands all around, and walked out after saying good-bye. They walked past the pretty lieutenant's desk. They left the building and walked down the sidewalk toward the admiral's BSA motorcycle.

"Want a ride?" Captain Baker asked.

"No, thanks, admiral. I'll walk. I need time to think things out. I have to tell my wife, and she doesn't speak perfect English."

"You'll handle it. Just take your time. You were given a lot this afternoon, and you'll be thinking about it all night. That's normal, but don't waste time trying to figure out why. Instead, spend your time preparing to handle all that might happen. Think about livin' in a tree for five days.

"Once you know in your mind that you can do it, carrying it out is a lot easier. We'll have plenty of time to talk once the mission starts. Right now, give some time to your family. Enjoy 'em. It'll be a while before you see 'em again. I'll be praying for your little girl, Sumiko."

He shook Gohan's hand and patted his shoulder. "See you tomorrow at two. So long, brother."

Captain Harold Baker felt good about having Gohan along on the mission. He was young, but Baker learned years earlier that experience came quickly in war. Gohan respected Baker and would listen to him, which would help. In a worst-case scenario, Gohan wouldn't give up or run. He was a warrior, just like Baker.

Baker got on his bike and decided to return to barracks to finish studying up on Laos. He wanted to know as much as possible about the area.

Gohan began the long walk from Kadena toward his house at Nakadomari. He should have plenty of time to sort out his feelings and figure how to break the news to his wife. It was hot out, so he removed his shirt and slung it over his shoulder, waving to the admiral as he zoomed past on his bike. Gohan wasn't looking forward to the next hour.

Chapter 10
Difficult Communication

October 1960

GOHAN HAD A LOT TO THINK ABOUT, BUT HE KNEW HE WAS going to Laos. There was no turning back. He'd had a lot of information stuffed into his head in a short time, though, and he still didn't have it sorted out. He wanted to think about the mission, its dangers, and the possibilities of capture or death. One of the ways he always prepared for danger was to consider the possibilities and prepare for them in advance. The problem was, he didn't know anything about Laos and had only minimal information about the true dangers he would face.

The most pressing need, however, was how to tell Keiko and make her understand without giving her any top-secret information. He stepped off the curb to cross the street and waited for a passing Jeep, which screeched to a halt beside him.

"Soldier, you're out of uniform," the young lieutenant admonished. "I'd like your name and rank and an explanation."

"Yes, sir." Gohan saluted. "My name is Sergeant David Rice, sir, from Onna Point. I just met with Major General Winthrop, the SIGINT commander, and Marine Major General Mancini. They told me to take off my shirt and walk back to camp while I thought over some things we discussed. We're meeting again tomorrow. You can verify that if you wish, sir. We met in Building 203, back down the street and to the right."

"Suppose you tell me exactly what you discussed, sergeant."

"Sorry, sir. Top secret. I'm under specific orders from the SIGINT commander. As a matter of fact, sir, I shouldn't even be talking to you. You'd better check with the general, sir. I need to keep moving. I have my orders. Sorry, sir."

Gohan walked in front of the Jeep, crossed the street, and walked toward the north gate. The lieutenant sat in his Jeep, watching him go and wondering what to do. A moment later, Gohan heard the Jeep drive off. He smiled.

Man, if he goes to the general, I'll be in deep manure, he thought. *Oh, well. It's an important mission. Maybe the general will cover for me.*

He laughed, and his thoughts returned to the mission. He wanted to see Katsuo Matsumura, his friend and mentor and the wisest man Gohan knew. He'd helped Gohan straighten out his thinking more than once. Unfortunately, that was out of the question. Gohan had to work this one out alone. He wanted a beer.

He wondered where that thought came from. He didn't drink much anymore at all. And he knew what the general had just said about drinking. But, he was thirsty. He'd stop and get a Coke to drink on the way home.

Besides, he wasn't going to tell anyone about the mission. He'd been in top-secret crypto for three years and hadn't leaked anything yet.

I might be young, but I'm responsible, his thoughts continued. *If I weren't, I wouldn't be on this mission. I'll get a Coke, but I won't stay in the bar to drink it.*

He decided to stop at the Sunset Strip—a little, green, cinder-block bar outside the north gate—and pick up a bottle of Coke.

Wow, he thought, *a top-secret mission in the jungles of Laos. I might end up a hero or something.*

He thought about that for a moment.

No, Davey Boy. Heroes jump on hand grenades. They don't copy code. Besides, you were a hero at your father-in-law's house, remember? That was it for you. One per customer per lifetime.

As he walked, he thought about Keiko.

How do I tell someone I love that I'm goin' off somewhere for a couple weeks, but I can't say where, why, or how long? How do I tell her that I know our baby's sick, but this is more important? Suppose she won't accept it? No, that's crazy. I can't think about it that way. Keiko will be OK. I have to stop makin' this worse than it is.

He would tell her what General Winthrop suggested, that he was being sent on a special mission that would last about two weeks, then he'd be back.

She can handle that. She won't like it, but she'll be OK.

He imagined their conversation.

"Where you go, Gohan-san? You go far from Okinawa?"

"Well, honey, I'm going to Europe, to Germany. We'll fly there, so it won't take long to get there, and I'll be back soon."

"But why you go? Can send someone else?"

"No, honey. I'm very good at my job. That's why they want me."

"You tell about sick Sumiko? Maybe go later, not now?"

"I tried that, honey. They need it done right now. It can't wait. I'll bring the doctor tomorrow. Sumiko will be OK."

"Not understand, Gohan-san, but OK."

That should work, but he knew it wouldn't be easy. Why was he so good at things that others cringed at, yet things like the present situation were so difficult for him? He wished he could sit down and talk with his parents. Not only would they understand, they'd help. Dad would understand the military aspect and would be proud of his son. He'd encourage him and tell him not to worry. Mom would pinpoint exactly the right words, inflection, and time of day to talk to Keiko.

Well, Mom and Dad, you're there, and I'm here. I guess I'll have to work this out by myself.

It dawned on him that he was twenty years old and he suddenly had a lot of responsibility. He walked through the gate, waved to the guard, and walked to the Sunset Strip bar. After returning the greeting from the Okinawan bartender, Gohan ordered a Coke and began the long walk north to his home, wondering what the general told Major Parsons. It did Gohan's heart good to know the major wasn't a part of the mission. The man was a jerk.

Maybe when Gohan returned, he could rub the situation in the major's face. He sighed. He knew he'd never be able to talk about it, but that was easy for him.

A bus roared past, and someone shouted his name. Gohan stopped as the bus halted farther down the road, then someone got off and ran toward him. He saw it was Seth, who was panting hard when he finally reached Gohan.

"What are you doin', man?" Seth asked. "Why are you walkin' down the road like this?"

"I had a meeting in Kadena, and I decided to walk back. I needed to think about some things, that's all."

"A meeting? About what?"

"Can't say, man. You know how it is."

"Oh, that stuff you're doin' at the compound?"

"Yeah."

"You goin' home?"

"Yeah, I'm goin' home. Sumi's sick, and I want to spend some time with my family."

"Gonna stop along the way?"

"No. I picked up this Coke when I left the base. Here. Have some."

"No, thanks. I don't need anythin'. You seem a little weird. You OK?"

"Yeah, just tired. They've had me in there all hours of the night lately. I'm a little bummed about Sumi not doin' so good."

"She ain't gettin' any better?"

"I think so, but I don't understand it. I remember watchin' my younger brothers get sick, sometimes for days, but they always got better. That's what happens with kids. It's harder when it's your own kid, I guess."

"She'll be fine. We just need to pray her through it. I'll keep prayin' for her. Somebody said the stuff you guys are copying is pretty nasty, maybe could lead to a war. Is that right?"

Gohan looked at his friend. Not only did he have to lie to his wife, he had to lie to his best friend. "I wouldn't pay much attention to such talk, Seth. You know as well as I do that the cryptos won't tell us anything important. That's probably a rumor someone started. Who knows?"

"You haven't been to the dojo much lately. Matsumura was askin' about you. He wanted to know if everything was OK. I told him you had a lot of work at weird hours, and that Sumi was sick. He understood and told me to say hi."

Gohan smiled, glad to have such friends. "Tell him it doesn't look like it'll get better anytime soon. I don't know when I'll be back, but I will. I enjoy it too much to stay away long.

"Seth, I need to do some thinking. When I get home, I need to be alone with Kay and Sumi. I hope you don't mind, but it's important."

"What kind of friend would I be if I didn't understand?" They slapped each other's shoulders and parted company. Seth took the road to Yomitan, where he could catch another bus.

Gohan reviewed the upcoming conversation with Keiko in his mind. He knew it wouldn't be easy, but it would be OK. She always understood. It wasn't easy for her, and he didn't like it when she struggled against their cultural or language barriers.

He arrived at Nakadomari and walked down the path through the woods to his house.

Halfway there, he saw something rustle in the leaves to his left and immediately froze before turning toward it slowly. Fifteen feet away was a six-foot habu, the poisonous snake indigenous to the island. Once he'd seen Matsumura walk up close to a habu, stand perfectly still, then, moving faster than Gohan had ever seen, grab it behind the neck and toss it away like a worm. Gohan had often wondered if he could do that.

It wasn't the time to find out, especially with his mind being so distracted. He watched the snake for a few minutes, then moved away slowly toward his house, remembering the general's warning about danger in Laos from snakes and animals.

Gohan and Keiko lived in a small, wooden house in the village of Nakadomari, a small wooded area north of Yomitan and Kadena but south of Onna Point. Their part of the village, on the edge of the island, facing the East China Sea, consisted of only fifteen houses.

Though Nakadomari was a larger village, it was broken up into many small groups. Their settlement didn't have a name, so everyone called it Nakadomari. Gohan was the only American who lived there.

The house had three rooms, a bedroom, living room, and kitchen. It was surrounded by many fukygi trees, which offered protection from typhoons and created an enjoyable place to sit outside to eat or rest. Gohan and Keiko did that often. He paid ten dollars a month in American money to one of the local bar owners to rent the house.

The house gave him the chance to raise his family in privacy. Keiko's father had offered them the chance to live with him, but Gohan and Keiko wanted their own home. They were happy, especially after Sumiko was born.

Sumiko Leah Rice was a doll. She had a hint of Okinawan in her round face, but she had her father's blue eyes and light-brown hair with tints of red. He wondered if she'd be as beautiful as her mother when she grew up. Of course she would. Sumi smiled and laughed a lot and became the joy of their lives.

Gohan was a happy man who loved roaming the island, learning about local culture, exploring caves, scuba diving off the cliffs, and visiting and talking with the locals. With Keiko, they did a lot of that together and thoroughly enjoyed traveling across the island. She took him to places he hadn't known existed, and he learned about the war from a different perspective as she shared stories her father told her.

The locals called the war *tetsu no bofu*, "the typhoon of steel." One out of every three Okinawans died in the war, more than 60,000 total, of which more than 45,000 were civilians. After hearing Keiko's stories, Gohan understood why so many island-ers disliked or hated Americans. He was amazed that so many were pleasant and respectful to him. Maybe that was because of Keiko. He believed it was a combination of the islanders' gentle natures, the fact that Gohan married the chief executive's daugh-ter, and his own love for the land and its people.

He and Keiko attended plays and dances. They watched the Okinawan bullfights, which were very different from Mexican ones. On Okinawa, two bulls fought, not a bull against a person.

Gohan and Keiko walked hand in hand through many sugar cane fields, enjoying the sweet scent. They visited shrines, and he participated, with her, in the Shinto rites and festivities. They loved the old village festivals, traditional tug-o-wars, and habu-mongoose fights. Gohan was amazed at how the little rat always won. Festivals were presided over by the village noro, or priestess, and they always ended with prayers for good fortune and abun-dant harvests. There was a lot of superstition on the island, and Gohan enjoyed learning about that, too.

He and Keiko took boats to many of the nearest islands, most of which were uninhabited. They spent their days exploring, sit-ting on beaches, eating picnic lunches, and enjoying the par-rots, monkeys, and magnificent birds. They accompanied locals in dugout canoes to where they watched whales playing in the ocean. He didn't think he could enjoy life more.

Before he reached the house, he heard Sumi wailing. He knocked, like a guest or salesman would, and Keiko opened the door to find him waiting.

"*Konnichi wa. Chaabira sai?* Good afternoon. Pardon me, may I come in?" he asked.

"*Mensore. Dozo ohairi kudasai.* Welcome. Please come in," she replied, smiling.

They laughed. Gohan walked in, gave Keiko a big hug and kiss, and picked Sumi up off the bed to hold against his shoulder. She immediately quieted down.

"How's she doin', Kay?" he asked.

Concern showed on Keiko's beautiful face. "Oh, Gohan-san,

what we do? Sumiko sick. You feel."

He kissed her forehead. "Yeah, she feels sick. She's really warm. OK. I'll get the doctor early tomorrow and bring him here. He'll take care of her, OK?"

"Yes. *Arigato. Oishasan* take care of Sumiko, Gohan-san." Keiko smiled.

Gohan was glad. He knew the sickness had taken its toll on her, too. As young as he was, Keiko was even younger, and Sumi was their child. Keiko couldn't bear to see her baby suffer. Having the doctor visit would help.

"Come on. Let's go to Shizuko's and have dinner."

"Sumiko *byoki*... sick. She maybe cry. You sure?"

"Yeah, don't worry about her. They love her at the restaurant. I'll hold her and keep her quiet. She likes me, remember? I'm her dad."

Keiko smiled. "Yes, you dad. Can wait? I change clothes."

"Sure. Take your time."

Gohan sat in the small rocking chair he bought when Keiko was pregnant and put Sumi on his lap so she could look up at him as he gently rocked her. Her little face was flushed with fever, and she seemed hot. Gohan didn't understand it. He was raised with four brothers and sisters, all but one younger than himself, and childhood illnesses always passed. He hoped this one would, too.

He sang to Sumi, making her smile, but it was clear she was tired. He laid her against his shoulder again and continued rocking, softly patting her back. She always responded to him. He lifted her head and kissed her cheek, then allowed her to nestle against his shoulder as he sang Keiko's favorite Okinawan lullaby.

> *The evening shadows slowly fall, and pale the sky.*
> *Now from the mountain temple, sounds the bell on high.*
> *Clasping each other, hand in hand, on this path below,*
> *Together with the flying crows, homeward let us go.*

Sumi slept throughout the dinner, and Keiko enjoyed the respite. Everyone at the restaurant loved the child. She was more popular than Shizuko's famous lemon fish soup.

They finished their meal and walked slowly back to their house, where Gohan gently placed Sumi in bed, thankful she didn't awaken. He went into the next room, sat beside Keiko, kissed her cheek softly, and sighed.

"Keiko, honey, I got word today I'm being sent on a special assignment."

"What mean, special assignment?"

"You know my work at Onna Point?"

"Yes. You do Air Force work."

"Yes. Well, they need me to do this work in another country."

"What? You go far away?" Her face showed lack of understanding.

"Yes. I have to go to a foreign country. It will be for a short time, just two weeks."

Keiko sighed, and Gohan saw relief return to her face. She took his hand and held it tightly. "Gohan-san, I not understand. You go away two weeks. Where you go?"

"Germany."

"Germany? In Europe?"

"Yes, but for only two weeks. Then I'll be back."

When she showed concern again, he knew he wasn't explaining himself very clearly. He had to be patient and calm, giving her time to understand. The worst was yet to come.

"Gohan-san, Germany far away. Not close like Japan."

He smiled and softly kissed her lips. "Honey, remember this is 1960. We have airplanes. We can go to Germany in less than one day."

She smiled and understood. "Yes. Sorry. I forget. Why you go? Can send someone, not you?"

"No, Kay." He paused to think of the right words. "My work at Onna Point, I am *ichiban*, number one. They're sending me, because I'm ichiban. Understand?"

"Yes. You ichiban." She kissed his lips hard, then smiled. "You ichiban with Keiko, too," she said, trying to smile. "I understand but don't like."

He laughed. She was precious. He pulled her closer and held her. "You know what, honey?"

"What?"

"I really love you. You're the cat's meow."

"I what?"

They laughed, momentarily breaking the tension. It was a welcome respite, but Gohan knew there was more to discuss, and he wanted to finish before Sumi awoke.

"I need to be sure you understand, honey," he said. "I'll be leaving for Germany and will stay there two weeks. Do you understand that?"

"Yes, think so. You go to Germany, come home two weeks. Gohan-san, how you say... *abunai*?"

"Dangerous? No, honey. It's the same work I do here at Onna Point. I'll be OK. There's one more thing."

Keiko saw the concern on his face and knew he was about to tell her bad news. Knowing it was important to understand him, she concentrated, but she was frightened, too. She nodded before laying her head against his chest.

"Kay, I leave tomorrow."

Keiko jumped back and stared at him. "No. Gohan-san, you have sick *akanbo*, sick Sumiko. No go Germany now. Later, yes."

She spoke emphatically as if determination alone would make a difference. She didn't understand the control the military had over her husband's life and that he had no choice in such matters.

She looked at him, wanting desperately for her concern to make a difference.

"Kay, I can't say no. I must go to Germany tomorrow."

Keiko began to cry. Before they married, Gohan explained to her and her father that the U.S. government wouldn't accept their marriage as legal. As a result, the U.S. records would list Gohan as single. Though their Okinawan ceremony was a perfectly legal one in Okinawa, Keiko knew that Gohan could leave her at any time if he wished. Over time, her fears subsided, primarily because of their love for each other. They loved being together and doing things. Hearing his unexpected news brought her old fears back to the surface.

She didn't understand why he couldn't refuse, especially with a sick child. She knew his work was secret, and he couldn't tell her about it, and she had learned to trust him when there were things she wanted to know, but he couldn't tell her.

Matsumura was a great help and a good friend of the family. He knew Gohan better than any other Okinawan. He explained to Keiko how Gohan's work was secret, and, if he ever spoke about it to anyone, he would be put in prison. Keiko felt better when she learned that Gohan couldn't have told an American wife what he did, either.

She learned to trust him and realized she had to do that again. Wiping tears from her face, she put on a brave expression and looked at her husband, then started crying again.

"Gohan-san, hold please?"

He held her closely without speaking. They sat quietly, enjoying each other's company. Keiko allowed Gohan's physical and emotional strength to carry her through this tough time, just as she had done in the past. It was a great comfort to her.

Finally, she pulled away and sighed, the issue over. "OK, Gohan-san. Please tell what to do."

Sumi cried in the next room. Gohan took Keiko's hands in his and kissed them. "Tomorrow morning, I'll bring oishasan, Dr. Kentsu, to look at Sumi. You do whatever he says. If she needs medicine, he'll get it. Sumi will be fine. I leave tomorrow afternoon and will be back in two weeks."

He got up from the sofa, turned toward the bedroom, then looked back at Keiko. "Honey, would you rather stay here while I'm away, or go to your father's house?"

"I speak to father tomorrow. Is OK I go to Nago?"

"Of course. If you're more comfortable there, that's a good idea. Two weeks won't be long."

"OK, Gohan-san. *Watashi-wa anata-o aishimasu.*"

"I know. I love you, too, honey. Look, it's late. I want to rock Sumi in the rocking chair. Why don't you get some sleep?"

"No. I rock Sumiko. I wife. You husband. I stay Okinawa. You go Germany. I rock. You sleep."

She stood and kissed his forehead with a smile. Gohan shook his head in admiration. "I have a lot to think about, honey. I won't sleep, anyway. I want to do this for Sumi, OK?"

Keiko nodded, and they undressed, then Keiko climbed into bed, and Gohan pulled the rocking chair into the next room. He sat with his little girl in his lap, rocking gently. She was so pretty. It was sad she didn't feel well. He was glad he agreed to bring the doctor to the house. That would make Keiko feel better, too.

Sumiko smiled at her father as he gently rocked her on his knees. She was tiny and beautiful, just like her mother. He tried to envision what she'd be like in a few years, starting school, but he just couldn't imagine her a little older.

"Well, Sumi, honey, I'll just have to wait. Tell you what, though. You'll be a looker, just like your mother."

For the rest of the night, Gohan sat in the small rocker, entertaining his daughter. Occasionally, she cried because of pain. Then he laid her against his shoulder, rocked the chair, and sang quietly.

When she slept for short periods, he held her in that position, enjoying her scent and the feel of her against his chest and shoulder. When she was better, he put her on his knees where she could look up at him. Then he rocked, talking quietly to her, enjoying her beautiful smile.

He couldn't imagine there being a more beautiful baby anywhere in the world. As the night wore on, he realized how short and precious those few hours were. As important as his mission was, he didn't want the night to end. He was enjoying Sumi more than ever, and he knew he was a lucky man. The world was filled with unhappy, crazy, or angry people, and he had met many of them. But at that moment, he was as happy as a man could be. He had a lot to return to and felt able to handle his new assignment.

Then he considered the possibility of capture or death and realized, if it happened, that was the last time he'd see his daughter.

He sighed, unwilling to consider that possibility. But it existed, and he had to consider it.

Can you understand any of this, honey? he wondered. *How old do you have to be before you can understand what's going on in your old man's head?*

Sumi lay on his legs, looking up at him, and she smiled. It wasn't as pretty as her smiles without the fever, but it was still beautiful. Gohan smiled back, remembering the Okinawan poem Keiko taught him.

He kissed Sumi and quietly sang it to her.

> *Wakaritin tageni*
> *Guyin atikari ya*
> *Ituni nuku hana nu*
> *Tsiriti nuchumi*
> *Even after we part,*
> *Shall fate have it so,*
> *We will be like flowers*
> *Linked together, never to be torn apart.*

Don't you worry, Sumi, he thought. *Your daddy will be back. I promise.*

Sumi smiled again. He didn't know if she was old enough to know if she loved him or not, but he thought so.

Looking at his watch, he knew he and the admiral would soon be on their way to Laos. As he thought about that, he laughed to himself. He still didn't know where Laos was.

Chapter 11
Operation Gohan

October 1960

AS THE FIVE HIGHLY TRAINED SOLDIERS REACHED THE END of their descent toward the lush, green jungles of Laos, Captain Baker saw something was amiss—he noticed a small village near their landing point. He hit the ground hard, rolled to a stop, quickly gathered his chute, tied it into a neat bundle, and hid it in the bushes.

He sat on a tree stump, waiting for the rest of his team. Within fifteen minutes, they all arrived. No one was injured, and their equipment was fine. There was no movement in the surrounding jungle, so Baker chose a spot where the bushes were thick and buried the chutes there.

The three marines patrolled the area, then returned to help. Digging in the soft, wet ground was easy and quick. Captain Baker looked around, trying to get his bearings. They were supposed to be miles from the enemy camp, but he wasn't so sure. The village he'd seen from the air had no fences around it, so that meant he wasn't too close to their target, but there weren't supposed to be any villages at all. That meant he wasn't sure where they landed.

Since their mission didn't require them to investigate the enemy camp or even come closer than necessary, he decided to go with the original plan a little sooner than intended. That would bring them close enough for Gohan to work. If Gohan still couldn't pick up his target, Captain Baker would think of something else.

He just hoped he was right.

After the men finished burying the chutes, they packed the ground down evenly, checked their equipment, and were ready to move out.

"OK, men, listen up," Baker said. "We're goin' north but only about two miles, not the original three. We landed a little off course. Keller, you take point, then Gomez, Gohan, me, and Bowie. No idle conversation. This isn't our backyard. We don't know who lives here, so let's not wake anybody if we don't have to. Like Roosevelt said, we'll walk softly and carry a big rifle." He smiled. "Let's go."

Their information proved correct. The area was full of mountains and Baker guessed they were on one of them. The jungle was thick with bushes and trees, and there was a lot of noise from birds and monkeys. As they neared the target area, much of the thick brush disappeared, and high trees blocked the sun almost completely.

It took almost an hour to walk the two miles. They were careful, quiet, and alert. Finally, Baker halted his men to rest for a few minutes, then the three marines went ahead to scout the area.

"All clear, captain," Sergeant Bowie said a moment later. "Nothing but jungle."

"That's good. How far did you guys go?"

"About a quarter mile, captain."

While they were away, Gohan set up his dual mini receivers and tried to listen to the Soviet network. After fifteen minutes, he heard a familiar "fist"—the same sender he copied back at Onna Point. He nodded to the admiral, then shut down his system.

"OK, then. We're set," Baker said. "Gohan's got his boy. Let's build a couple houses and a radio platform. Three of us will work, while

Bowie and Keller each take a point. We'll trade off in an hour."

For the next few hours, working in the dark, the men cut down trees and built camouflaged platforms high in the trees, as quietly as they could, that would serve as their home for the next few days. They worked quickly and without speaking. At one point, Sergeant Gomez questioned their location. He'd heard their original orders and wasn't sure they were in the right place.

"I know it's your call, sir, but are you comfortable with this location?" Bowie asked. "I didn't remember it this way from our instructions."

"You're right, Oscar. Did you see that little village half a mile east of our landing spot? It was clearly visible."

"No, sir. I came down on the other side."

"We were supposed to land in the middle of the jungle without any villages nearby. The closest ones should have been to the south. If there's suddenly a small village to our east, that means we drifted southwest, or we're completely out of the area, beside a village we didn't know existed."

"Yeah, or there's a village out here nobody knew about. You ever think of that, Captain?"

"Hmmm. Yeah, that's possible, too. Still, we ought to be safe. If that's the case, and we landed in the right place after all, we still came in the right direction. We just stopped a little short. As long as Gohan gets the info we need, that's fine. If, as I think, we landed out of our area, we were too far west. That means we'd still have to march in this direction. Then the enemy camp would be to our east, not our west. That make sense?"

"Yes, sir. We're OK as far as this location goes. Do we start right away?"

"As soon as these houses are finished."

As dawn slowly brought life to the jungle, the team finished building their treehouses. They climbed into their nests, and Operation Gohan began. The three marines kept guard two at a time while the third man slept. Baker was Gohan's assistant when the net was busy. When it wasn't, he rested or stood guard. Their camouflage served its purpose, keeping the treehouses from being noticed by casual observation. If someone were looking into the trees, however, specifically to see if anyone were there, they'd have a fight on their hands.

The first day went well. Gohan got the radio system up quickly, though several hours passed before he heard any transmissions. Then copy came in by the bucketful. By two o'clock that afternoon, he had eleven handwritten pages filled.

Sergeant Gomez signaled from the neighboring tree that it was time to transmit to base. Captain Baker acknowledged, and the marines met Gohan and the captain at the base of the trees.

"What's it look like, Gohan?" Sergeant Oscar Gomez asked.

"We got lots of stuff, Oscar. I've got writer's cramp."

"Anything good?"

"Man, we should've brought along one of those NSA guys. He could tell us if we're doin' a good job. I don't know. I can't interpret this stuff. There was a feeling of urgency in the transmission, and that's not common. From the give and take between the outstations, I'd say it sounds important. For all I know, the guy had to pee, and he hurried to finish sending."

"Not that I have to know, but what do you do with this stuff once you send it off?" Gohan asked.

"If everything goes right, we burn it and bury the ashes. If it don't go right, we add some salt and pepper."

Gohan laughed. "Right. Gotcha, sarge."

"OK, men," Captain Baker said. "Get back to that rendezvous point and do your thing. We'll hold down things here."

The three marine sergeants left to fulfill their part of the mission. After stretching their legs, Gohan and Baker climbed back into the treehouse, and the captain took over guard duty. The radio was quiet for several hours, letting the two men talk.

"What do you know about this place, admiral?" Gohan asked. "I mean, about the whole thing over here?"

"I'm a history buff, Gohan. When I learned that I might be comin' over here, I started readin' about Laos and its history, especially the recent part. I told General Mancini I wanted to spend as much time as possible learning about our involvement. He gave me his OK, so I spent my last night readin' some of the secret stuff.

"As far as Vietnam goes, it all started years ago. By the way, we're only a couple miles from the Vietnam border. Comforting, isn't it? Ho Chi Minh, the guy General Winthrop talked about, was like the rest of the Vietnamese. He wanted out from under French rule and to gain independence for his country. Back then, this was called French Indochina. Anyway, Ho became a Communist and fought for Vietnam's independence under the Communist flag. That's why the U.S. is worried.

"Some of this might be top secret, but back when Vietnam was overrun with Japs, right after World War II, we came in quietly and helped Ho get the Japanese out. Then, when he tried to oust the French, we supported the French. I had a buddy who flew for a supply outfit back then. They were dropping supplies to the French at Dienbienphu while General Giap, Ho Chi Minh's top man, was routing them. That was the battle that did the French in.

"Back about twenty-five years ago, here in Laos, one of the local princes with a name I can't pronounce—something like Soup Du Jour—formed the Pathet Lao, an insurgent group with the purpose of helpin' Laos gain its independence. Ol' Ho came runnin' to the rescue to help them out. The Hmong, like the folks in the Ban Na Lom village, were split over the idea of the Pathet Lao. One group of Hmong, led by a guy named Faydang Something-or-Other, joined the Pathet Lao. Another group led by Touby Lyfong joined the French. It wasn't because they didn't want independence. They just didn't want Communism.

"So this war over here's been goin' on a long time. For the last few years, it's become really confusing. The American OSS (Office of Strategic Services) got involved, although now it's called the CIA. There have been a couple of coup attempts, some backed by us, others by the Communists. The government Laotian has bounced back and forth between Communist leadership and U.S. so often in the last few years, you'd need a scorecard to keep up. Right now, the government's backed by the U.S. That's why we were brought in secretly. We don't want to mess up whatever our government's doin' with theirs."

"What are they doing?"

Baker looked at him for a long time, then shook his head. "Gohan, I can't answer that. It's clear we want to keep Communism out of Vietnam and Laos. These are strategic places in this part of the world. I think mostly what we're doin' is trying to protect these countries from Communism, but it isn't goin' our way."

Gohan thought that over. "Let me see if I have this right. We're puttin' our lives at risk for a bunch of people who are half-Communist and half-unable to protect themselves without us. That doesn't say much for 'em, does it?"

"That's one way to look at it."

"Although maybe these Hmong are OK. At least, from what you said, they sound like good folks. Now the Commies came in and took over their village, and who knows what else they did. If we don't help 'em, maybe no one will. I feel a little better about that now. Tell me about Korea. I might as well be prepared in case the worst happens."

Captain Baker was an extremely humble man, one of those men everyone wanted as a friend, because he cared about people. The thirty-three-year-old Navy UDT had a wealth of experience and was very tough, but only those who knew him knew it.

Baker married the prettiest woman he ever met, and they had two sons. His family was in Houston to be near her parents, where he'd join them as soon as the mission ended. He had a strong reputation as a leader who wouldn't crack under pressure—quiet, religious, smart, and very tough.

While serving in Korea, Baker was captured and spent three months in a Korean POW camp. He didn't like to remember those days, but it was important for Gohan to know something about it, because there was always the chance Gohan might be captured, too.

"First, Gohan, this is a pretty safe mission. We don't want to dwell on negative things, like being captured. But it's important to be prepared if something happens. It's like being a baseball player. You said you were pretty good at baseball, right?"

"Yeah, I guess."

"A good defensive player prepares himself to be ready for anything. He looks at who's on base and decides what to do if the ball comes to him. He also thinks about the ball going over his head and what to do if he catches it. He tries to be totally prepared for anything, right?"

"You must've been pretty good with a glove, admiral."

"I played, but then, most everybody does. That's what kids do. Anyway, we have to do what the outfielder does—be prepared for anything the enemy comes up with. If he does it, we can handle it. That's why I'm willing to discuss being captured and put in a prison camp. OK?"

"OK. Let's have it."

"First, don't try to convince yourself that you're invincible. No one is. You're pretty tough, brother, but you're human. You have to remember that. The strongest in body aren't the ones who survive. It's the strongest in mind that survive.

"If you're captured, you'll be tortured. That's how barbarians act. Learn to embrace the pain. Pain sends a strong message, and that is that you're still alive.

"You'll probably be kept isolated. They don't like prisoners getting together unless there are too many to handle. If we're captured, there probably won't be any other Americans, so the first thing they'll do is separate us. They don't want us talking and making plans for the interrogation sessions.

"If you're alone, you have to learn to live with it. That's not that easy. Learn how to care for yourself. Don't let a bad wound fester and cause infection. Clean it as best you can. Spit works wonders. Cover it with whatever you've got. Check it and clean it every day.

"Keep your mind sharp. Sometimes, you have to play games to keep your mind active. Every day, think about what time it is and how many days you've been there. Create your own calendar and stay with it. Measure off your cell or room. You might be kept underground. Learn every square inch of it. That could be important someday. Mainly, keep your mind alert. The more on top of things you are, the less chance you have of breaking down.

"When you're in the enemy's camp, he wants to make it negative for you. He wants to break you and will use every physical and psychological ploy he can. Nothing's out of bounds. You can forget the Geneva Convention. It doesn't exist in war.

"Everything you do that's positive is a plus. This is like a game. There are lots of negatives, so you have to create positives. It doesn't matter how little they are. They're very important. Enjoy any positive reinforcement you can find. Something as little as a tiny crack in the wall that lets in daylight is enough. Record those events in your mind and remember them every day. Think them over a lot. Keep looking for positives and continue to create them. That kind of stuff is what will get you through.

"Your mind is your best weapon. They'll try to destroy it, but it's yours. They can't do anything to it that you don't want 'em to. They'll have control of your body, but that's temporary. When your life is over, Gohan, someday maybe sixty years from now, your body will die, but not your mind. That might be hard to understand, but it's true. Your soul, spirit, and mind live on, maybe in a different body or maybe none at all. God knows, but we don't have to.

"So if the Commies try to destroy your body, what have they really done? In the overall scheme of things, not much. The only way they can really destroy you is to destroy your mind. They can't do that unless you let 'em. Do you understand?"

"I think so. What about interrogation and torture?"

"You can count on it. They'll automatically think you're America's number-one spy who has military information they want. They'll try to get it out of you. If possible, ignore what they ask. Everything they try will be to break you down. They know you're strong and that whatever you tell them early on is probably a lie. That's part of the game.

"They'll use your own lies to break you down. Everything they and you do will be used against you. Once they've broken you, they'll consider believing you.

"So what can you do? Give them as little as possible to use against you. No matter what they ask, all you say is your name,

140

rank, and serial number. That's it. No matter what! That's not easy, but prison camps aren't for wimps. They're for heroes. Every prisoner in a camp is a hero, even the ones who break."

Gohan had never considered that before. He'd seen movies, but real life wasn't like that. Every prisoner in a prison camp is a hero, even the ones who break, he repeated in his mind. "How do you handle the pain?"

Captain Baker smiled slightly, remembering his own ordeal. He remembered the torture and the pain, but he didn't want to go into it. He shifted position on the treehouse floor.

"You have a strong mind, Gohan. That's what you need to survive torture. Pain is relational. If you stick a knife in your finger, you'll scream, because it's painful. If someone's pounding your head with a hammer, and brains splatter all over your face, then he sticks a knife in your finger, you won't scream, because it won't seem as painful."

"Thanks. That's real comforting. I'm sure I can handle anything now."

Baker laughed. "The point is, Gohan, you have to look at pain with that understanding. There's a scripture from the Bible that says God won't let you go through anything that's more than you can handle. If you ask Him, He'll give you the strength you need to handle it all—pain, torture, loneliness, anything."

"What happens if you're not religious? Does God just watch you suffer?"

"Not at all, Gohan. One of the beautiful attributes of God is that His love is unconditional. It isn't based on any requirement you have to meet. Christianity isn't a set of rules. It's God choosing to love us, no holds barred, no requirements, brownie points, black or white, smart or dumb, strong or weak, whether we deserve it or not. When we reach heaven, if we find out God's white, we'll also find out He didn't love you more than me because you're white. When I call you brother, it's not a figure of speech. I mean it."

"And if He's black?"

"Then we'll have a good old-fashioned Harlem prayer meeting, Gohan."

The two men laughed.

"Maybe you'd better teach me some of your hymns, admiral," Gohan said. "I don't want to end up there without knowing the songs."

"We can do that, too."

As they laughed again, Baker grabbed two K-ration cans and tossed one to Gohan. "Dig in. This is a business dinner. We can write it off on our taxes."

"Do I have to leave a tip?"

"Only if it's the best meal you ever ate. Let's get back to our talk. The way we respond to God's love is what determines the kind of life we live. A lot of men don't believe in God and don't pray, but none of them are in prison camps."

"Did you pray a lot when you were in prison camp in Korea?"

"Oh, yeah. I was raised in the church, Gohan. We were Pentecostals. Man, we sang, danced, pranced, and shouted. We even jumped over pews. I couldn't wait until I was old enough to get out of there."

Gohan laughed. He knew exactly what the admiral meant. To a much lesser degree, he had the same experience.

"I'll tell you somethin' funny, though," Baker continued. "When you find yourself in a prison camp, you're awfully glad for that upbringing, 'cause it comes back to you. You know why? 'Cause God's faithful even when we aren't. I prayed a lot, Gohan, and God answered my prayers with faith. The longer I was in there and the more they starved, interrogated, and beat me, the more I knew I was in God's hands and that He loved me more than they hated me.

"I didn't know we'd be rescued. I often thought I'd die there. Don't get me wrong. I had hope. We're taught that when we're in prison camp, all our thoughts should be directed toward getting out. We did that, but there wasn't any way out. If my American buddies didn't come to get me, I wasn't getting out. But they did. In reality, I expected to die there.

"In the meantime, I prayed for my family, friends, old girlfriends, the guys I used to play ball with, the other prisoners, and their families. One thing you've got in there is time. You can pray for a lot of people if you want. The Bible says to pray for your enemies." His voice caught, and he paused to regain his control. "I couldn't do that, Gohan. I hated 'em. I don't hate 'em now, but I did then. I prayed, and somehow, God saw me through. I wouldn't have made it without Him.

"Don't let your pride keep you from speakin' to the Lord. All that stuff we were taught as kids about God is true. He really is everywhere all the time. He knows everything about you, what you do, think, like, and hate. You can't hide anything from Him. If you're scared, He knows. If you're puttin' on a front, it's a waste of time, 'cause He knows what's in your heart.

"I don't think that will happen here, Gohan. This is a pretty safe mission, but if something goes haywire, and you're captured, you'll need to use your mind to protect you from fear and pain. Play games in your mind to keep yourself sharp. Don't give the enemy any quarter, and remember to pray."

"It sounds a lot easier than it is, right?"

"Yeah. The truth is, it's hard even to talk about it, but that's easier than havin' to live through it. The other side of the coin is that if you somehow blow it, forget it and start over. They'll use that against you, too. There's no shame if you cave in under the pressure. As corny as it sounds, at bottom, we're American soldiers. We have information they'd love to know, but we can't give it to 'em under any circumstances. That's heroism."

The network became busy, so Gohan started copying furiously. Captain Baker, glad to stop talking, concentrated on guard duties and tried to keep his buddy dry as rain began to fall.

Chapter 12
Death in Laos

THOUGH EVERYTHING SEEMED ON SCHEDULE, NIKOLAI NIKO-layevich was uneasy. The communications network worked beautifully, for which he took full credit. They were sending vital information to General Giap. Kaysone Phomvihane, the Pathet Lao leader, visited Ban Na Lom camp and gave his approval—as if Nikolai needed the approval of a Lao general.

Within a few months, Minh's army would strangle the American-backed government in South Vietnam, and Communism would prevail. Still, the KGB man didn't feel fulfilled.

Because of the nature of guerilla warfare, it was difficult for Nikolai to perform at his best. His strong suit was bullying subordinates using party rules and regulations. His current assignment, however, was different. He had to deal with unsophisticated, uneducated backwoodsmen and rice farmers. He didn't like his assignment or the people he met.

Major Aleksandr Ustinova was a Soviet military man to the core. He loved being a soldier and would have served in that capacity for free if asked. He worked with his men every day, a poorly trained group of Soviet soldiers who'd been handed to him by General Alyosha Gregoriev Samsonov, a total idiot. To add insult to injury, they added angry Vietnamese soldiers, Viet Minh, and untrained Pathet Lao from Laos. The major had only a short time to transform that unlikely menagerie into a capable war machine.

As he thought about how far he'd brought his band of ragamuffins, he felt satisfied with their progress. They weren't fully trained, and they would never have satisfied General Samsonov, but then, nothing ever did. Besides, he wasn't there. He was relaxing somewhere in a steam bath in Moscow.

Aleksandr was a strategist. He studied Russian military history fervently and believed there were few in the Russian high command who had more ability when it came to the proper utilization of troops. He had several strategies worked out to keep his troops at a high level of intensity and readiness. Skirmishes had been reported throughout Laos. Though none were close to his camp, he wanted to be prepared for anything.

He didn't take his assignment lightly. He did a masterful job of preparing the unsophisticated guerillas. When he finished with them, they would rival the best Russian troops in the motherland. As commander, he would have a high grade, too.

What Major Aleksandr Ustinova didn't know was that General Samsonov had handpicked him for the assignment but not for his abilities. It was because he was considered inept. Ustinova was a lifetime soldier as was his father before him. However, his father had been a great soldier. For some time, General Samsonov sought an assignment for Ustinova that would satisfy his superiors, who were under pressure from Ustinova's father, an old, retired general. The communications site in Laos was perfect.

It was important enough to assuage the old man and easy enough that Ustinova couldn't fail. Better yet, he couldn't destroy anything. The assigned troops weren't likely to see any action. Guarding a communications site and hospital in one's own backyard wasn't very dangerous. Best of all General Samsonov was happy to be rid of Ustinova.

Major Ustinova didn't like Nikolai, his KGB superior. Nikolai displayed a condescending attitude toward all Soviet soldiers, including Ustinova, though he clearly had no military background and didn't understand military matters at all. Ustinova wondered what the bully wanted as he knocked on the man's office door and waited.

"Yes? What is it?" Nikolai called.

"Major Ustinova."

"Come in, major."

Major Ustinova walked in and asked, "Nikolai Ivanovich Nikolayevich, how can I be of service to you today?"

The KGB man didn't even turn to face the major. He finished writing at his desk before standing, turning, and looking down at Ustinova. "Major, it has come to my attention that you're planning a military exercise. Has it not occurred to you that I must approve every military activity of any kind? Do you think I'm here because I like rice?"

Major Ustinova didn't answer. He knew why the KGB officer was there, and he knew what he did in his spare time. Ustinova hated him for it. Some of the girls Nikolai amused himself with were children. It made Ustinova sick.

"I apologize if I should have brought this to your attention," Ustinova replied. "You see, it isn't really a military exercise. It seems wise to have a small contingent of men comb the area outside the compound each day. It will be good for them. It's hard to keep men sharp when there's nothing to do. Secondly, it affords better security."

"Hmmm." Nikolai liked the idea. He doubted anything would happen in such a remote outpost, but it was good to keep the men alert. Maybe he should give the major more credit. He might not be as incompetent as Nikolai thought. "I agree, major. Proceed as you intended, but I want clear, detailed reports each day. Bring them to Zortov next door. He'll bring it to my attention if necessary."

With a brush of his hand, he waved the major good day.

Major Ustinova sent for Sergeant Dmitry Cherkov, a lad from

Novgorod. He was young, energetic, and the best soldier he had. The two men met in the clearing outside the main compound and sat on one of the crude, wooden benches.

"Sergeant Cherkov... may I call you Dmitry?"

The tall, powerfully built sergeant nodded.

"Dmitry, I'm sending you out on a small mission. I want you to form a scouting party of six men, including yourself. Be sure to include some locals and Vietnamese. I want you to cover the area around the camp for about a mile each way. Be alert. You aren't looking for anything in particular, just to make sure the camp is safe and well protected.

"Your purpose is to make certain there is no activity in the area that shouldn't be there. Beware of animals and snakes. Have a Laotian lead you, because they know the area. Explain to the men this will be a daily exercise. We want the men alert without becoming trigger-happy. There could be villagers out there. We must remember that this isn't our war. We must show restraint, and, if necessary, we must also restrain the Lao and Viet soldiers, who are accustomed to killing.

"I want you to understand that the main purpose of these exercises is to keep the men sharp. They'll rot away inside this compound if we don't find action for them. I don't fear outside interference, but don't tell that to the men. This is good exercise for them. It's not dangerous duty, but it's important to assure our commander and troops that the compound is safe. Alternate the time of day and begin the first one today. Any questions?"

"No, comrade major. I can start immediately after the noon meal if you wish."

"That would be fine. We won't be upset if you bring back a nice deer for the cook, too. It would be nice to vary our menu. The Laotians know where to find them."

"Yes, sir. I understand the deer are very large here. They have a name for them that I can't recall right now. What if we meet enemy soldiers? There are Americans in Laos, and the Royal Lao Army has soldiers throughout the land."

Major Ustinova realized how young Sergeant Cherkov was. "It

would be very unusual to encounter soldiers here. We're in the mountain jungles of Laos. The fighting is all in the provinces. For the moment, though, let's assume you meet enemy soldiers.

"You must act like a soldier. Your first responsibility is to protect yourself and your men. You must also remember, as I said before, that this isn't our war. You will, therefore, try to capture the enemy and bring them back. There's the possibility you might meet villagers from other tribes who mean you no harm. If so, we want no gunfire. If something unusual happens, and someone is killed, destroy the evidence. We don't want other tribes coming after us. Ask the Pathet Lao for advice in that case. They'll know the best way to get rid of a body in these mountains."

"As you wish, comrade major. May I suggest, sir, that I use different men each day? That way, all will be able to participate. I agree it'll be good for them to have some meaningful activity."

"An excellent suggestion, Dmitry. Be off, then."

For three days, the American soldiers lived quietly in the trees. They weren't happy or rested, and all wanted to return to Okinawa. Other than Gohan's work, it was very boring.

Then, at midmorning, they heard sporadic gunfire in the distance that lasted for fifteen minutes. They assumed it was target practice at the enemy camp. That meant the camp was much closer than they first thought.

Later in the day, they heard gunfire again. The five Americans discussed the situation but decided not to change their plans. Their mission was more than half-completed, and so far, it had gone smoothly.

"Gohan!" Captain Baker shook his partner, who was napping during a lull in transmissions. "Oscar's signaling. It's time to send what you have. Let's take a break and stretch our legs, brother."

The two men climbed down and met the three marines.

"Captain, this might not be dangerous duty, but I'm tellin' you, a couple more days in that tree, and they'll have to cut off my legs for lack of circulation," marine Bob Keller said.

148

"I know, Bob," the captain replied. "This isn't as exciting as we first thought. But don't forget we have enemies out there, and they're a short distance from here. The minute we forget that, we'll lose our edge."

"You know, I've been thinkin', captain," Sergeant Bowie said, "if you were really concerned about havin' enemies in your territory, you don't signal 'em by havin' loud target practice twice a day."

"That's right, Willie. If anything, that shows they think they're safe. That's another reason we should do our jobs quietly and get the heck out of here."

"You got anything for us, Gohan?" Sergeant Gomez asked.

"Yeah. Transmission's pretty constant now. It's not like the first day, but all five stations are talking regularly. It looks like they're passing information along. It must be important, but I can't tell what it is from what they're doing. There were two long number messages in this batch. Maybe headquarters can make something of it."

"Two more days, right?" Gomez asked.

"That's the plan, amigo," Captain Baker said.

"You won't run out of paper, will you?" Gomez asked Gohan.

"Not hardly, man. They sent enough paper for five months."

"You don't think...?" Gomez asked.

"No. They wouldn't do that to us, would they, captain?" Willie Bowie asked.

"No, Willie. If they said they were comin' for us in five days, then they're comin'. Unless we tell 'em differently, that's the plan. OK, guys, do your thing. We'll be right here."

"Yeah," Gohan said. "Don't get trampled by any elephants. We'll be waiting at home sweet home."

"You mean tree sweet tree, don't you?" Gomez laughed. "Let's go, men. We have to say hi to Mom and Dad."

The marines left. Gohan and Captain Baker remained on the ground for a few minutes to enjoy their break.

"How about a little hike, admiral?" Gohan suggested. "I could use some leg exercise."

"Me, too. Remember, my main job's to protect you. We go

together. Let's walk a few minutes this way, then circle back toward where the men went. That's probably safe enough. Like you said, we don't want to be trampled by elephants."

The two specialists enjoyed the respite. They recognized the importance of their mission, and they did it well. But considering the difficult circumstances, it was very tedious.

"Are we allowed to eat anything from these trees?" Gohan asked.

"Absolutely not. You know the rules. Don't play games with me. We have good, home-cooked K-rations waiting in the kitchen. What else could you want?"

"I don't know. Maybe a little filet mignon and a baked potato, and some lemon meringue pie for dessert. That's all."

"Well, why didn't you say so? I believe there's some filet mignon K-rations upstairs with grits and collard greens. I'll rustle up some later."

"Really? How come I didn't see those? They aren't hiding in the can labeled Spam, are they?"

Captain Baker laughed. Joking was good for both of them. After a ten-minute hike, their legs loosened up, and they walked back toward the treehouse.

"Enough exploration for today, Gohan. Let's go back upstairs and get to work. We have only two days left. Let's get all the information we can."

"OK, boss. I'm ready."

Climbing back into their treehouse, they resumed their positions, trying to become as comfortable as they could. Gohan put on his headset and listened for activity on the net. Captain Baker, rifle in place, swept the area with his eyes, making sure they remained hidden.

Within minutes, the stations began transmitting, and Gohan was busy again. He copied for about twenty minutes before the receivers were quiet.

Sergeant Oscar Gomez finished transmitting the coded information Gohan prepared and was glad their assignment was almost over. He had only two months left in the marines, but, because of the current mission, he'd be discharged as soon as he returned to Okinawa. Then he'd fly to San Diego to meet his fiancée so they could be married. He could hardly wait.

Sergeant Willie Bowie was a lifer. He liked the marines, and they liked him. He saw no reason to return to Alabama and put up with the same stuff his dad and all the other black men put up with for years. Everyone told him to move north, but it wasn't his nature to run from a problem. He could remain a marine for up to thirty years, then move back to Alabama. With luck, he could make a difference then. He liked the assignment in Laos. That was what being a marine was about.

Bob Keller didn't know what he wanted. He leaned toward staying in the marines. He married while he was stationed in Hawaii and brought his wife and son to Okinawa. But he and his wife weren't getting along, so she and the baby went to live with her family in Hawaii.

He'd have to face that problem soon and try to fix it. But the truth was, he'd been running from it for months and jumped at the chance for a special assignment. He needed something to get his mind off his problems.

The last few days, he had plenty of time to think. He'd be back in Okinawa in a few days. He wanted to call Mandy and try to patch things up with her.

Sergeant Keller turned to say something to Gomez when someone shouted, "Halt!"

Keller raised his rifle as he turned. Fifty yards away, in a cluster of trees, were soldiers. He quickly determined they weren't American and began firing. He saw one, then another of the enemy fall from his outburst, but the Communists returned fire, riddling Bob Keller with bullets. He went down immediately.

Bowie knew Keller shouldn't have fired, but it was too late. He went to his knees, making himself as small a target as he could and fired into the enemy group. He, too, hit one of the enemy and watched them go down. The marines were at a terrible disadvantage, in the open without any cover.

Gomez, who was the most exposed, jumped up and ran a few feet to hide behind a large fallen tree. As he began running, he saw Keller lying in a pool of blood. He dove to the ground and reached for his weapon, which lay a few feet away. He turned and began firing, realizing he was still exposed. He couldn't see Bowie and didn't know if he was alive or dead. The enemy soldiers were moving toward him. He lay prone on the ground, aimed and fired, felling one of them. He then felt the searing hot pain as bullets drove into his leg, then into his shoulder. He tried to roll away, but bullets kept tearing into him. Mercifully, he died quickly.

Sergeant Bowie saw that he was the only one left, but there were only two of the enemy soldiers remaining, too. He got up from his crouched position and ran toward a group of trees twenty yards away, hoping to find better cover.

"Ahhh!" A bullet slammed into his left leg, and he screamed, dropping his rifle as he fell. He cursed, realizing he'd lost his weapon. It was behind him. The bush was in front of him. He had a pistol in his side holster, so he crawled toward the safety of the bush.

As he dragged himself along, screaming encouragement to himself, he suddenly saw a pair of boots. They were quickly joined by a second pair. He looked up into the face of a white man and guessed he was Russian.

The other guy was considerably smaller, probably a Vietnamese or one of the Pathet Lao.

"You American?" the Russian asked. "Negro American?"

Willie thought of a lot of nasty replies but didn't say anything. Instead, he reached down to tear off a piece of his pant leg to tie around his wounded leg. The Viet Minh soldier kicked Willie's hands away.

"What you plan to do, let me bleed to death?" Willie shouted.

"We take you to camp," the Russian shouted, pointing at the smaller soldier, then motioning Sergeant Bowie to come with them.

"Viet Minh speak no English," the Russian said.

That meant Willie was captured by a Russian sergeant and Vietnamese grunt. They weren't dumb enough to carry him, because that was too dangerous, and he couldn't walk with his wounded leg. He would drag behind, slowing them down, but that wouldn't last. Once they figured that out, they'd shoot him, anyway. He might as well die fighting.

"Get up, Negro!"

As he tried to stand, he yanked his knife from his belt and lunged at the enemy soldiers. The Russian shouted and jumped back as Willie's knife cut into his hand. As Willie turned toward the Vietnamese, the man's gun barrel came up and pointed at him. As it fired, Willie looked at the soldier's face. The last thing he saw was the Vietnamese laughing at him.

"Wow. I thought those guys would never shut up," Gohan said. "Man, I got a toilet full of stuff here. Hey! What's that?"

They listened for a moment.

"Sounds like our friends are having target practice again," Baker said. "Wait. Where'd that sound come from?"

"Back where Gomez and the other guys went. Admiral, that wasn't target practice. That was a couple quick flurries, then it quit. Daggonit!"

"OK. Hold on, brother. Let's not get ahead of ourselves. We don't know what it was. Even if it involved our guys, we don't know who shot whom. Besides, there's nothing we can do about it. If we go lookin' for 'em, we're openin' ourselves up to whatever's out there.

"Give me a few minutes to think, Gohan. Keep a lookout, especially in that direction."

They heard one more shot from the same direction. Gohan looked at the admiral, who sadly lowered his head.

"Let's not speculate," Captain Baker said. "They could have been shootin' a tiger or something."

They knew that wasn't the case. Gohan gave Captain Baker the time he needed to think while he steadied his rifle against a tree limb and scanned the area behind them, ready for anything.

"The bottom line is, we have to wait," Baker said finally. "Our first responsibility is to keep you alive. The second is to get this information back to headquarters. Then, we can take care of each other.

"We'll stay here and keep a sharp lookout, giving the men a little more time to return. If they don't, we'll make some decisions."

"Whatever you say, admiral, but I don't like this."

"Me either, brother."

They sat quietly for an hour, but there was no more gunfire. Fortunately, the net was quiet, too. Normal jungle sounds returned, but not the three marines. Captain Baker and Gohan became increasingly concerned.

"Gohan, stay on the receivers, but keep your weapon ready," Baker said. "Don't make any quick or loud moves. I'll keep my eyes on the area where the men went. You watch this side where I used to be. If the net comes on again, nudge me, and I'll watch both sides."

For an hour, they scoured the area around them, but there was no activity. The jungle was far too quiet, and they feared the worst.

"What'll we do, admiral?" Gohan asked. "We can't leave them out there. They might be injured or holed up, waiting for help."

"You're right, but we can't walk into an ambush, either. If the men are hurt, then whoever's responsible won't assume they're alone. We have to wait a little longer. Assuming there's an enemy out there, he can hunker down and wait as long as he likes. It won't help our men if we walk into a trap.

"We might have to wait all night. We'll take turns on guard so each of us gets some sleep. Early in the morning, before dawn, we'll try to find our men."

Gohan sat quietly, trying to settle his mind, but it raced out of control. He wanted the net to stay quiet so he could help his friend. The last thing he wanted at the moment was to copy code. It was time to be a soldier, so he wanted to concentrate on that.

"OK, admiral. What should I do if shooting starts?"

"Do exactly what you did at the chief executive's house that time. Think things out when you can, react when you must, and make every shot count."

"Is it wise to stay up here? If we're seen, we're dead. You know that, right?" Gohan asserted.

"Yeah, but we don't know where they are or how many. Right now, we're safe, 'cause they don't know where we are, either, or if we even exist. We probably have a better chance of not being found here than on the ground."

"OK. That's why you're a captain and I'm a sergeant. I'm ready. As far as I'm concerned, we can ditch these receivers anytime. I'm ready to become a marine."

At 10:30 that evening, Ka Moua left Nikolai's bedroom. As was her custom, she sneaked through the camp until she found the area right behind the hospital where she could run into the jungle without being seen. Then, as she did every other time she left the brute's room, she ran as hard as she could to the little stream on the way to her brother's camp.

When she saw the big shale rock, she slowed to a walk. Breathing heavily, she walked past it, sat on a fallen log, leaned over, and vomited until she felt she'd rid herself of the filth and taste of the horrible man. She stripped and stepped into the cold water, completely unconcerned about poisonous snakes and large cats in the jungle. She washed until she felt clean. Then she dried herself with the large rag she left hidden there before dressing and running the rest of the way to the camp.

Cheu was concerned for his sister. He knew what was happening at the camp, especially because of the nature of the information Ka brought. He would love to blow off the heads of every soldier in the camp. His group of Hmong guerrillas had grown to twenty. He felt they were strong enough to invade Ban Na Lom

155

and overthrow the Communists, but he didn't know what that would gain him.

He assumed he would die in the attack. He couldn't raise enough men to completely overtake the Pathet Lao, especially when they were reinforced by Russians. If they ever caught Cheu, he'd be tortured and killed. But he wanted revenge before he died.

Ka finally arrived after midnight. One look at her and Cheu knew what happened, but he swallowed his anger so she didn't see it. To protect her pride, she kept her secret. Cheu didn't want to destroy that.

He brought her into his tent and prepared hot soup and vegetables for her. "Are you all right?" he asked. "They're working you too hard at the hospital."

She smiled. She loved her brother and was proud of what he wanted to accomplish. "I can put up with the work if it helps bring information to our cause. I have very important information tonight. There are American marines somewhere in the mountains."

"What? Are you sure? Who told you? How do you know?"

"No one. It's secret information. Remember, they don't know I understand Russian, so they talk openly around me."

"What happened? Tell me about the Americans."

"Major Ustinova, the commanding army officer, sent out a patrol made up of Soviet, Viet Minh, and Pathet Lao soldiers. I'm not sure why they were patrolling the jungle, but they met three American marines about a mile from the village."

"Did they capture them?" Cheu asked in excitement.

"No, they killed them. They met suddenly. The marines opened fire, but there were too many soldiers from the camp. Four of them died. The other two, Sergeant Cherkov, the man in charge of the patrol, and a Viet Minh soldier, stayed out to look for more Americans, but they found none.

"Sergeant Cherkov was injured slightly, and I tended him in the hospital. That's where I learned most of this. They said the

Americans had communications equipment and were sending messages somewhere, but they didn't know what the messages were or where they went. They don't know if Sergeant Cherkov and his men met them before they could send their messages, but they didn't think so. They found ashes on the ground nearby and assumed the Americans burned the messages.

"They said they'd spend all day tomorrow searching the mountains for more Americans, but they don't think there are any more. The KGB man said the Americans always use groups of three for spying. He seems to understand how the Americans work, but I think he just likes to hear himself talk."

Cheu, seeing the look of contempt in his sister's eyes, wondered if that was the man who was destroying her or if there were others. He wanted to kill them so badly. As he looked at her face, compassion filled his heart. He wondered why she gave so much for their almost-hopeless cause, but then, so did he. He was proud of her.

"Well, dear brother, what does this mean?" Ka asked.

"I don't know. It's exciting to know the Americans are here, wanting to help. But if they're dead, how do we let the other Americans know? Where are the others, or were all of them killed? I'd like to talk to my friends in the RLA. They might know more. They'd certainly like to know about the killings, but they're too far away to reach. There isn't enough time. We're making our plans to attack the camp, but we might have to wait to find out about these Americans. There's a lot to think about. I'll decide by tomorrow morning.

"I'm sure you'll learn more tomorrow. I'd like to know where those Americans came from. Sending messages doesn't make any sense." He smiled at Ka. "I'll think better after some sleep. You must finish eating and sleep, too. You're doing too much for our cause."

Chapter 13
Captured

GOHAN AND CAPTAIN BAKER CLIMBED DOWN FROM THEIR treehouse at 4:30 the following morning. The marines still hadn't returned, and they knew there was serious trouble, but they didn't know exactly what it was. Captain Baker decided to shut down the mission and search for their friends. Gohan had an extra transmitter. From his position in the treehouse, he sent copies of everything he received during the past twelve hours, but he didn't know if it reached its destination. He added a special code to notify their superiors about the missing marines.

They took a roundabout route to the rendezvous point in case the enemy was still waiting. From there, they would search a mile in each direction until they found the missing men. That was their top priority. Hopefully, the material they'd sent to the base had been enough. Their obligation now lay with their missing friends.

Arriving at the rendezvous point, they hid in thick bush. All was quiet, and nothing moved. After fifteen minutes, they were satisfied it was safe and walked into the small clearing.

"Admiral! Come quick!"

Captain Baker ran over and looked where Gohan knelt. "That's blood, all right."

"Look, admiral. There's blood everywhere. Daggonit!"

Captain Baker jumped to his feet, his weapon ready.

"What's the matter?" Gohan immediately raised his gun.

"Sorry. I'm a little jumpy. We need to be careful, Gohan. We're kneeling, looking at this mess, and that makes us easy targets. This is war now. We need to remember that."

Gohan was right, though. They found traces of blood all over. Captain Baker began thinking out loud.

"This isn't good, man. What happened here? Darn it, those were good men."

"Look," Gohan called. "There's blood here, too."

Captain Baker nodded. "There was a fight here. This is where those shots came from that we heard. With all this blood, they must've taken some of the enemy with them, but where are the bodies? Maybe the men are still alive. We have to learn more.

"Let's get out of here, Gohan. I don't feel comfortable. Let's pull back half a mile and think."

Sergeant Cherkov, his injured hand bandaged, led the next patrol of four Soviet soldiers, four Viet Minh, and four Pathet Lao down the same route they'd taken the previous day. Their assignment was simple. If they found more Americans in the jungle, they had to bring them back alive.

Major Ustinova and Comrade Nikolayevich were upset with the result of the encounter with the Americans. Once they heard the full story, they knew that Sergeant Cherkov and his men had little choice but to return fire.

Cherkov's report was straightforward. When they confronted the marines, before anyone could speak, the Americans fired on them, killing the two Pathet Lao soldiers in front. The patrol fought back in self-defense, killing all three marines. Two more members of the patrol died, including Sergeant Cherkov's Soviet friend, Pyotr Kholakova. Dmitry was fond of Pyotr's younger sister, Natalya. Now he had to return and tell her that her brother had died protecting the motherland.

Major Ustinova and Nikolai were stunned by the report. Even with a badly bloodied hand, Sergeant Cherkov and the one remaining Viet Minh soldier managed to drag the seven bodies to the river's edge and left them half-in, half-out of the water. Between the flesh-eating animals that came to the river to drink and the dragons, the bodies wouldn't last.

Sergeant Cherkov didn't know what the dragons were, but the major and KGB man didn't press him. Nikolai made a mental note not to stray too far from the compound. Until the Viet Minh began troop movement toward South Vietnam, he didn't want any signs of trouble in his area. There were plenty of American soldiers in the more populated areas of Laos. If word got out that Americans had been killed, the situation would become very difficult. No one wanted any American bodies cropping up. Though neither commander would have thought of such an ungodly manner to dispose of the bodies, both realized it was probably for the best.

That was the first person Dmitry ever killed. He didn't know how he felt about it. They weren't supposed to kill Americans, especially when they weren't supposed to be involved in the civil war. If he went home to brag about it, spies might hear him, and then what?

He had enough worries at the moment. Comrade Nikolayevich made it clear that unless there was absolutely no alternative, they weren't to kill any more Americans. If there were more in the area, which the KGB man doubted, he wanted them alive.

That troubled Dmitry. He knew he could kill if necessary, but he wasn't sure how to capture someone, especially if the man was trying to kill him.

He and his twelve men walked to the place of the massacre and spent time looking for clues to see if there were any more Americans in the vicinity. They found tracks, but there had been so many soldiers there already, it wasn't clear if the tracks were fresh. No one had any knowledge of the local area, and they found nothing important.

"Let's rest a few minutes," Sergeant Cherkov said. "Spread out in groups of three and rest in those bushes. Then we'll move toward camp."

"Sergeant!" a Soviet soldier called. "Look here!" He pointed at two cigarette butts ground into the soft earth. "Were any of the marines smoking yesterday? If not, this might mean there are more Americans nearby."

Sergeant Cherkov stooped to examine the cigarette butts. "Comrade, look. Americans don't roll their own cigarettes. These belong to someone else, either one of our own men, who roll their own, or one of the villagers who might have passed this way."

Nikolai was sure there were no more Americans nearby. His KGB experience gave him a feel for such things, and he told Cherkov to patrol the area but not to waste a lot of time.

Major Ustinova, however, was adamant that the three marines weren't alone. The Americans wouldn't send out a group of three and have them standing around, waiting to be captured. His instructions were to scout the area in detail.

Cherkov knew he could appease both by being detailed and quick. He motioned his men to break up into groups. After a short respite, they walked back toward camp.

Gohan and Captain Baker retreated farther into the jungle than intended, then sat behind a cluster of tall trees, large bushes, and thick vines that kept them well hidden.

"Gohan, we have to know where our men are," Captain Baker said. "Then we have to decide what to do about it."

"I guess the bodies were dragged back to the camp, right?"

"That's a natural assumption, but did you see any drag marks? I didn't. Then again, we're dealing with people who are accustomed to this land. They could have covered their tracks, but why?"

"If our guys are still alive, maybe the Communists don't want us to know. Besides, didn't you say they'd take our guys back to camp for questioning?"

Baker nodded, deep in thought.

"So we can assume they're alive, right?"

He looked at Gohan in concern. Gohan realized he was interrupting the man's thoughts. "Sorry, admiral. Look, these guys might have given their lives for this assignment. If need be, I'm ready to give mine, too. I'm sorry if I'm talkin' too much, but I'm still young. Maybe I'm a little scared. I have a wife and baby at home waiting for me. I'd like to see them again."

"I know, Gohan. So did Bob Keller. He had a one-year-old son. Oscar Gomez was engaged to be married in two months. He planned to return to San Diego to marry his high-school sweetheart. Life's unpleasant sometimes."

Gohan swallowed hard. He was working with a pro, but he wasn't handling the pressure very well. "I hear you loud and clear, admiral. I'll do what I have to do. Right now, that means I'll shut up so you can figure out what's next."

Baker allowed himself a half-smile, then patted Gohan's knee. "Keep a lookout, brother. I want to shut my eyes and ask the Lord for directions."

Gohan raised his rifle and looked around. He didn't understand all the stuff about God that Baker talked about. It would be easy to think about God if he were captured, but he didn't think it was right to ask Him what to do in the jungles of Laos when three of their buddies had been blown away.

Come on, admiral, he thought. *Think back to the stuff you learned in Korea and officer's school. You'll figure out something.*

Fifteen minutes later, Captain Baker stood, rested his weapon on his shoulder, looked at Gohan, and nodded. "Let's go, mister. We have some men to find."

"Great. What's the plan, admiral?"

"We're going back to the treehouse to destroy our equipment. From there, we'll move toward that camp and see what's going on. This is dangerous stuff now, Gohan. Are you prepared to put your life in God's hands?"

"Sure, just not in Ivan the Terrible's hands, or those of that Ho Chi Chi guy you mentioned."

Baker smiled. "OK, brother. Let's go get 'em."

They returned to the treehouse without difficulty and quickly destroyed the receivers before hiding them under heavy bushes. The treehouses could remain where they were. If the enemy found them, he would assume that was where the three Marines lived.

"Admiral?" Gohan asked.

"Yeah?"

"I know we're prepared to die, but, if you don't mind, I'd like to be an optimist. How about I bury this transmitter without destroying it? Then, if we survive, we can at least let Mom and Dad know where we are. Maybe they can come pick us up after the movie's over."

Baker smiled. "Good idea, Gohan. Just make sure you remember where you bury it."

"Hey, man. I'm like a dog burying a bone. This is our future. I won't forget."

When they finished, the two warriors started toward Ban Na Lom camp, moving slowly and alertly, looking for anything that would give them a clue about the fate of the three marines. They stayed in the thickest part of the jungle and didn't encounter anyone.

Baker wondered if the enemy had decided to remain home. If they had the marines and were interrogating them, they might not want any more confrontation. The Commies wouldn't know how many Americans were in the jungle. He just hoped Oscar, Willie, and Bob would hold up under interrogation.

They traveled half a mile when Baker raised his hand and stopped. He looked around, then motioned Gohan closer.

Gohan, his weapon ready, looked around and whispered, "What's up, admiral? Hear anything?"

Captain Baker grinned. "No. I just wanted to make sure there were no models prancin' around out there in bikinis. I have to go to the bathroom real bad."

Gohan laughed. "What are you trying to do, give me a heart attack?"

"Listen. I won't be long. Stay alert. I'll go a few steps away to protect your nose." He walked back toward the treehouses. Gohan leaned against a tree to stand watch. Like the admiral, he felt the enemy was probably back at camp, interrogating the marines.

The Pathet Lao guerrilla tapped Sergeant Cherkov's shoulder, and Cherkov turned. The guerrilla pointed into the jungle to where an American stood against a tree, his rifle ready.

Cherkov motioned his men to get down and stay there. He quietly reminded them not to kill the American if possible, then he sent three men to the American's right so they could get within fifty feet. Three others were sent left. Then three men crawled on the ground straight ahead. Another three were twenty feet away, hoping to close in and capture the American. The thick brush kept the Communists well hidden.

Gohan wondered how far they were from the enemy camp. They had to be close and they'd have to be careful. It wouldn't help their friends if he and the admiral were captured.

He also wondered if the admiral brought along any toilet paper.

I sure hope he doesn't grab some poison ivy or somethin' like that to wipe with, he thought. *He'll be itchin' and complainin' for weeks.*

He thought about walking toward Baker and joking with him about it. *No. I'd better stay here. Like the admiral said, this is war.*

Then he heard movement ahead and aimed his rifle at it, but he didn't see anything.

"American! Many soldiers around you! Put down gun. We not kill you. Do now!"

Gohan stood his ground, aiming toward the voice. He'd take as many of them with him as he could. His heart was beating so fast, he wondered if he'd faint. But he quickly gained control of his emotions.

When something moved in the bushes ahead, he fired. Gunfire

came at him from all sides. He dived to the ground, relieved he hadn't been hit.

There must be at least ten of 'em, he thought. *That was a lot of gunfire. Why didn't anyone hit me?*

"American, we not kill you. If we want you dead, you be dead now. Put down gun!"

Gohan realized he had only a few seconds to decide. He'd rather meet them face to face. If there were only four or five, he had a chance, but he suspected there were more. The admiral was behind him somewhere, too.

He took a deep breath. "OK! I'm puttin' down my gun!" he shouted.

Captain Baker quickly finished dressing and got as close to the action as he could without being seen. He saw how badly his friend was outnumbered. At best, Gohan could take four or five of them. But, then, they'd likely finish him off. He decided to wait and see what happened. He only hoped Gohan didn't try to be a hero. He crouched as low as he could get behind the thick brush and watched.

After laying the gun on the ground, Gohan slowly straightened up. Men stepped out from the bushes all around him. When he saw how many there were, he realized he'd made an error in judgement. If he'd known how badly he was outnumbered, he would have died fighting. With his gun on the ground, he was at their mercy. He quickly made a plan.

OK, boys, come nice and close, he thought. *I don't have a reservation at your prison camp, and I don't want to become a guest. I'd rather die right here, only I won't die alone. I'll take at least three or four of you with me.*

Sergeant Cherkov and his men surrounded the American. Gohan made a quick count and saw he faced eleven soldiers. Then he saw an Asian soldier come out of the bushes carrying another Asian.

Good, Gohan thought. *At least I got one of 'em.*

One of the Viet Minh soldiers picked up Gohan's weapon, and the others moved closer. The Russian sergeant stayed back. He was the spokesman.

"How many Americans?" Dmitry asked.

Gohan remained silent.

"How many? Answer!"

A Viet Minh soldier tapped the butt of his rifle into Gohan's chest.

"Four," Gohan said.

"Four?"

"Four. Three marines and me."

"Ah." The Russian smiled. "Four." He realized that accounted for everyone. He assumed the American didn't know about the other three men he and his soldiers had already killed. "Come. We go."

The small Viet Minh soldier smacked Gohan in his face with the rifle butt hard enough to draw blood, but Gohan stood his ground. Another kicked his leg below the kneecap, and he fell. Then another kicked his ribs and motioned with his hands, yelling in some language Gohan didn't understand. Gohan knew they wanted him to stand up. At that point, he made up his mind that he'd battle them to the death.

He slowly rose. Once he was on his feet, he threw a powerful kick into the Viet Minh's ribs, breaking several. He smashed a hard right open fist up and under the nose of one of the Pathet Lao, shoving his nose into his head.

One more down, Gohan thought. *He's definitely dead.*

He knew they'd kill him after that, but he didn't care. He'd get as many as he could before they stopped him.

His quickness and power held off the inevitable for a while. He kicked another Viet Minh in the midsection as hard as he could. As the man fell, Gohan whirled and slashed a powerful karate chop into another soldier's neck. Something struck the back of Gohan's head, and he wondered if he'd been shot, but then he didn't care.

His momentum swung him toward a Pathet Lao soldier swinging his rifle butt at Gohan's face. He ducked and came up, firing a straight knuckle jab into the man's throat. When the man gasped,

Gohan knew he'd been incapacitated. He tried another kick, but his left leg didn't respond, because someone was holding onto it.

The back of his head throbbed terribly, but he didn't have time to worry about that. He threw a wild roundhouse punch at one of the Russians and saw the man's face blossom red like he'd been cut with a knife. Blood ran down Gohan's back like water when someone struck him. He didn't know how much longer he had.

He tried to throw another chop, but his arm wouldn't work, then there was another crushing blow to the head, and he keeled over. As he fell, he tried to shout, "God bless America!" but nothing came out.

The ground seemed much closer. Part of him wondered why he wanted to say those words. It seemed to take a long time for him to reach the ground. Then, everything went black.

Chapter 14
Interrogation

Though rendered unconscious by two powerful blows to the head from rifle butts, Gohan slowly regained consciousness while being dragged back to the camp.

I guess I'm not dead, he thought.

His head throbbed with pain, and his back and arms ached from being dragged by his feet. Deciding to keep his eyes closed, he willed himself not to groan or make noise. Maybe he could learn something if they thought he was still unconscious.

Finally, after what seemed like hours, they reached the camp. He heard men moving around and a lot of talking. By the accent, some of it was Russian. He had no idea what the other languages were. They ran together and were spoken quickly.

The voices stopped while a gate was opened, then Gohan was dragged into a room and dropped onto the cold damp floor.

After a few minutes, the noises stopped. Gohan assumed they'd left him alone, but he didn't want to open his eyes to look. The only thing he knew for certain was he hurt.

He lay perfectly still for a long time, at least an hour. He wondered if they'd gotten the admiral, but he hadn't heard any more shots. He wondered if his friend was dead, alive, or captured.

I hope you got away, admiral, he thought. *You'll come get me. I know you will.*

His reverie was interrupted when he heard someone enter the room. He remained still, trying to get his mental bearings and overcome the pain.

Suddenly, his face was drenched in cold, bitter liquid. Reaction forced his eyes open, and his eyes immediately burned. A few seconds later, his face burned, too.

What the heck is that stuff? he wondered.

He fought to remain composed. When he looked up from the floor, he saw a huge man towering over him.

He must be Russian. I ain't very smart, but if the Viet Minh and Pathet Lao look like that, I'm nuts.

The Russian barked an order, and two men grabbed Gohan, lifting him and throwing him into a chair in front of a small table.

Gohan almost fell off. Two of the men grabbed him and roughly forced him into a sitting position. That created more pain. He glanced around quickly. They were in a closed room that was cold and damp, with no windows.

Several people stood around him, probably soldiers. He didn't turn his head to look. The back of his head hurt even more, and he wondered if he'd been shot. Whatever happened, it was unbelievably painful. He took a deep breath, trying to prepare himself.

The big Russian sat across the table from him. He was ugly as sin and looked like he hadn't seen a barber in months. His coal-black hair was unkempt, and a big, thick mustache hung down over his lip.

Without moving his head, Gohan glanced to the side and recognized the tall Russian from their earlier encounter. His left arm and hand were bandaged. There were an unknown number of Viet Minh and Pathet Lao soldiers in the room, too.

The big Russian leaned over Gohan and smiled, exposing brown teeth. Gohan's head was spinning. He forced himself to be calm. He had to be able to react properly.

"Water?"

Despite the friendly tone, Gohan knew the man wasn't a nice guy. He remembered his conversation with the admiral, who had advised him not to give in, agree, play games, answer questions, or accept anything from his captors. If he did, his words would come back to haunt him.

He didn't reply.

"I asked if you want water," the Russian said in good English. "I'm trying to be kind. Please answer."

Gohan didn't answer, and the Russian's demeanor changed. "OK. You think you're a hero. Therefore, that's how we'll do the questioning. Listen carefully. I won't be nice to you. I won't smile, and I won't give you food or water. What I will do is give you the chance to answer questions. If you don't, I'll beat out your brains. Do you understand?"

You won't win me over with kindness, Ivan, Gohan mused, *so you might as well stop tryin'.*

He thought he'd better give some sort of answer. The Commie might be serious.

"Sergeant David M. Rice, United States Air Force, 13631452."

Displeased, the Russian turned to a Russian soldier and shouted an order. Then he turned back to Gohan, lit a cigarette, and blew smoke into his face. Gohan assumed that was supposed to bother him and make him want a cigarette, but he didn't smoke.

Chalk one up for the good guys, he thought.

The Russian, smiling, spoke very softly. "Sergeant Rice, if that's who you are, neither you nor your marine friends had American dog tags. That means you're on a secret mission. You have me at a disadvantage, because I don't know your name. But I'll call you Sergeant Rice, since that's what you said. Would you like to know where your friends are?"

Gohan wanted to know that very much, but it was probably a ruse. He repeated the admiral's words in his mind. *Don't give in, Gohan. No matter what they say or do. Don't give in.*

"I ask you question, sergeant, but you don't answer. So I think we play little game. I will enjoy little game, but you will not."

He barked out an order. Someone brought him an ashtray. He took another deep drag on his cigarette, then placed it in the ashtray after blowing smoke in Gohan's face. "I ask questions, Sergeant Rice. If you don't answer, I burn hole in your hand."

The Russian laughed heartily as a soldier entered the room with a bottle of booze and a glass. If that was a test, they were wasting their time. Gohan didn't drink and even if he did, he wouldn't take a drink from that jerk.

The big Russian poured a drink and took a big gulp without offering any to Gohan. Another Russian lit another cigarette and placed it in the ashtray.

"Comrade Nikolayevich." He nodded to indicate the cigarette was ready.

Now I have a name, Gohan thought. *This guy's a comrade, whatever that is.* He thought he remembered reading that Communists called each other comrade, sort of like *mister* in America.

"Sergeant Rice, I ask again if you'd like to see your marine friends."

"Sergeant David M. Rice, United States Air Force, 13631452."

The Russian motioned to his men. Four held Gohan's arms and wrists and held his right hand open against the table. The interrogator took the lit cigarette and held it against Gohan's palm.

Gohan had already decided he could handle what was coming. In the past year, he had quietly and secretly studied *ninjutsu*, the ancient mystic art of the ninjas, from his sensei, Matsumura. Different from the other martial arts, ninjutsu was created for offense or war. Therefore, it was the art of killing. Defensively, it teaches balance, perception of danger, and mind control over situations. Gohan knew he would be put to the supreme test. Prepared by his training, he relaxed his body completely, and thought of Keiko, his beautiful wife, and Sumi, his precious daughter. He envisioned them sitting in his day room at home. Keiko was beside him, her arm around him. He balanced Sumi on his knees. She smiled up at him.

The pain in his right hand was excruciating, but he was able to experience it as if from a distance. It didn't make it less painful, simply easier to control. *Not easy*, he said to himself, almost smiling, *just easier*.

A part of him wanted to scream, but he overcame the thought as perspiration rolled down his face. He smelled burning flesh and called out Keiko's name in his mind repeatedly, allowing her pretty face to slide into the forefront of his thoughts. He did the same with Sumiko.

The intensity of the pain increased. He became aware of a battle in his mind—wanting to yield to God, as the admiral had told him, and wanting to allow the mystic power of ninjutsu to carry him through the ordeal. Common sense won out.

God, I don't know much about You other than what the admiral told me, but I trust him. Please help me here, God. This pain is almost too much for me. I'm not much of a Christian, but I'm scared. Please, God, please!

The smell of the burning flesh was so acute, it began to make him ill. He slowly took a deep breath and, just as slowly, exhaled, relaxing his body as much as he could. He hurt from his other injuries, too. He knew the more he concentrated on it, the more it would all hurt.

Suddenly, it stopped—not the pain, but the torture. He opened his eyes and glanced, only for a second, at his tormentor. He knew he was perspiring heavily. The back of his head throbbed. He rememberd what the admiral said about pain being relative. Were the circumstances different, he would have laughed.

Well, admiral, you're wrong. They just burned a daggone hole in my hand, and it didn't make my head stop hurting.

The big Russian smiled at him. "Sergeant, you have a hole in your hand. It's pretty, don't you think?"

Gohan's eyes locked on the KGB man's, but he refused to look at his hand. He didn't want to give the man the satisfaction. The KGB man barked an order, and two men grabbed Gohan's head and forced his head down until he had to look. The pain in his head increased until it was worse than the pain in his hand.

It wasn't pretty. There wasn't a hole all the way through it, but there was a hunk of flesh missing. It seared, continuing to burn away flesh.

He needed to gather himself together quickly. The situation would only become worse, not better. He needed enough guts and willpower to handle whatever happened. Remembering the admiral's promise that God wouldn't let more happen than someone could handle, he prayed that would be true.

The Russian screamed something, and Gohan looked up.

"Sergeant Rice! That's better. When I call your name, you look at me. That's how we play game. Understand?"

Gohan stared at him but didn't answer.

Nikolai smiled, speaking softly as if talking to a dear friend. "How many Americans with you in Laos, Sergeant Rice?"

In an equally soft voice, Gohan said, "Sergeant David M. Rice, United States Air Force, 13631452."

Nikolai slammed his fist against the table and nodded to his aides, who quickly forced Gohan's hands to the table palm up. Gohan didn't fight. He relaxed his body and mind and allowed them do what they wished. Nikolai shoved the lit end of a cigarette into the center of Gohan's other hand. He allowed his mind to slip away. The admiral came to the forefront.

He must have escaped, Gohan thought. *He'll go for help. He'll find some other Americans. They're all over Laos. He's working on it right now. Just hang on. Remember, no negative thoughts.*

Gohan didn't know if the admiral was still free. The Communists might have gotten him, too. But he knew where the transmitter was buried. He could send an updated message back to Okinawa, that is if he knew how to use it.

His mind was jerked forward. The pain was almost unbearable. Perspiration poured down his face and into his eyes, burning them. He tried to think about where the admiral might be, but he couldn't concentrate. Much to his disgust, he allowed his thoughts to be brought back to the present. The barbarian's coarse voice brought his eyes open.

"You're a strong man, Sergeant Rice," Nikolai said. "Most men scream. Since you don't, maybe we cut out your tongue.

Then you can't scream." He laughed.

Gohan took another deep breath and slowly exhaled. The KGB man might do it, and Gohan wondered how he'd handle that, having his tongue cut out. He tried to remain strong.

Did you prepare me enough for this, admiral? How about you, Matsumura? Can I really handle anything they do?

He didn't know.

My head feels like it's been cut off. The throbbing is so intense, I feel like I'll die. They just burned two holes in my hands and those ache worse than anything I've ever felt besides my head. If they cut out my tongue, can it get any worse? How much more can I take before I die?

He didn't feel he was doing very well handling the pain and the pressure. He knew God was the answer.

God, I feel like I'm gonna die. I know men have undergone worse than this. Where's all the extra strength and stuff You're supposed to give me? I'm sorry. I'm not trying to be nasty or anything, but I'm not doing real well. Please, help me!

Even as he thought his prayer, he realized he was still alive and in control of his mind. Maybe God had given him the extra strength. Many before him, including the admiral, had endured far worse and survived. The admiral told him that the human body could survive a lot more than people thought. Matsumura was even more adamant about that.

"Sergeant Rice! I'm tired of shouting at you. Have you lost your hearing?"

Again, Gohan was brought back to the present. The KGB man poured another glass of vodka and gulped it, then motioned off to Gohan's right and pointed at something.

Gohan heard the men clanging around, and he knew he had to prepare himself. Whatever it was, it was going to be worse.

OK, Gohan, he continued to himself, *it doesn't matter what they do next. You can handle it. Grit your teeth and think about those you love. There are three other guys here who probably have it a lot worse. Hang in there. The admiral's probably working out a plan to get you out of here right now.*

The Russian gulped more vodka, then he leaned over and poured some into the burns on Gohan's hands. It was all he could do to keep from screaming, but somehow, he didn't.

"Now, sergeant, I ask you question again. If you answer, you get nice food and rest. If not, tomorrow, even your mother won't recognize you." He laughed softly.

"Sergeant Rice, we have three American marine friends of yours. They tell us much about your mission. If they lie, we kill them. If they tell truth, they live, and you can visit them. If you don't answer me, then I say they lie, and they die. It will be your fault. You are responsible for their deaths. Think about their wives and children. You must explain why you kill them, because you refuse to talk. If you answer question, maybe they tell truth, then everybody happy. Maybe have drink together, good food, hospital for injury.

"Sergeant Rice, Soviet Union and United States not enemy, but you kill many soldiers. I must know why. Then maybe we can be friends. Why you and marine friends in Laos? Sending coded messages? Sending to where?"

He paused, clearly proud of his tactics. Gohan stared at him without speaking.

"Sergeant! Sergeant Rice! Answer question now!"

"Sergeant David M. Rice, United States Air Force, 13631452."

That was all Nikolai could take. He stood, slamming the chair into the wall behind him and shattering it. He poured another drink, gulped it down, and motioned to the men.

Two big Russians grabbed Gohan and threw him to the ground. He lay there, on his stomach. Remembering the admiral's advice, he considered it a positive—a respite—so that he could get his bearings and decide what he would do. He didn't think they'd leave him alone there. He could hear them working, building something. How much time did he have? It didn't matter. He had to make good use of it.

Don't tense your body. Relax. You're not in a position to thwart anything the enemy does. You have to allow your body to handle what it's dealt.

Again, he turned heavenward.

God, he prayed, *I haven't been a good Catholic or, like the admiral, a good Christian, either. There's a lot I don't understand, but if You don't help me here, I'm dead. I know that much. Please give me strength to handle whatever they're going to do. Help the admiral get me out of here. And please, God, help me handle this pain. I've never had this much pain before.*

Two of the men grabbed him and dragged him to the far wall, where there were hooks and chains. He realized they intended to chain him there but didn't know why.

Two men held him against the wall while two others pulled his right arm as high as they could. Then they clamped a hook around his right wrist. When they released it, he felt as if his arm was being pulled from its socket. They did the same thing with his left arm, then stretched his legs down until his toes touched the floor. The pain in his armpits was excruciating, but the pain in his head was worse. Still, he was determined he could handle it.

They chained his ankles with hooks, too, spreading his legs until he looked like a big X against the wall. There was more to come. He saw the soldiers talking among themselves.

Some left the room and came back with six or eight pairs of boots. Several men took off their own boots and put on new ones. Nikolai walked over to Gohan, looked at him, and laughed. He had a bottle of something that he showed to Gohan. It wasn't in English, but it looked like the label read Vinegar.

What? He wants me to drink that? Come on, Nikko-Witch, or whatever your name is. I drank worse than that in high school.

Gohan was wrong again. Nikolai didn't pour it down Gohan's throat. He poured it into the searing burns on his hands. Then he grabbed the bottle of vodka and his glass and walked out.

The latest pain was almost unbearable. There was nothing Gohan could do but close his fists. He couldn't move his body. Trying to grit his teeth, he bit his tongue. Feeling and tasting blood running down his throat almost helped.

Oh, God! Oh, God! Oh, God! he screamed silently.

Now his hands really did hurt more than his head. Perspiration rolled down his face and into his eyes. Trying to blink away the sweat, he felt totally helpless.

You're wrong, admiral. My hands are killing me, and my head doesn't hurt any less. What did they do to you in Korea, slap your wrists?

That was a terrible thought, and he knew it. The admiral probably went through much worse than Gohan's present torture. He needed to remember good thoughts about his friend. He might need them later.

Gohan watched as the eight men got into a line on his left with strange expressions. Whatever they planned, they looked like they would enjoy it. They were in no hurry, though, and that was part of the game. They kept talking together while Gohan prepared for the worst.

I won't give in no matter what they do. I've already handled more pain than I ever thought I could. Remember, Davey Boy, pain's relative. That's what the admiral said. Come on. Get ready. Create positives. Keep your mind sharp. Relax your body. Allow it to absorb whatever's coming. No tenseness.

The door opened, and the KGB man walked in with another bottle of vodka and eight plastic cups. He walked to Gohan, laughed derisively, and left the room.

So you're letting them have a drink before they do me in? Go ahead, Nikko-Witch. I'll handle everything you throw at me and more.

Gohan tried to build up his bravado, but he wondered if it was a game. How brave was he? *Come on, you bunch of drunks,* he screamed inwardly. *Let's get on with it. There's nothin' you can do that I can't handle!*

Each man poured a full cup of vodka for himself. Most downed theirs quickly. The first man, a large Russian, walked up to Gohan and stood directly in front of him. He wound up like a pitcher throwing a baseball and kicked his steel-toed boot into Gohan's midsection. It felt like being hit by a sledgehammer.

"Ohhh," he groaned.

It angered him that he'd made a sound, having already decided he wouldn't give in. He wouldn't let them know when he was hurt.

He had no idea they'd kick him, though. At least he understood why they changed boots. The new ones had steel toes.

Gohan had no more time to think. The next guy was winding up.

"Uhhh," he groaned again.

It felt like pieces of him were being torn away. He could feel his bones being crushed. At least, that's what he thought. Maybe it wasn't that bad, but it felt that bad. Almost immediately, the next man stepped forward. When the third kick landed, Gohan was able to keep quiet, but the pain drove right through him.

He had to think fast. He didn't know how long they'd keep it up, but he couldn't take much more. He was already badly beaten. He had to get a grip on things fast and hold on. Biting into his lip, he tasted more blood as it rolled down his throat.

The fourth man was an even bigger Russian. His kick felt like it went completely through Gohan's stomach.

God, there won't be anything left of me down there, he thought. *How will I have more children?*

Then, just as quickly, he realized that he probably wouldn't live long enough to father any more children, anyway.

"Ohhh," he groaned again.

It was worse than the pain in his head. Every new kick seemed to rip flesh from his body. It was the most extreme pain he ever felt, and his body felt ready to come apart. He could feel blood run down his legs. The pain was unbearable, but somehow, he had to bear it. He refused to give in.

Here's number six. They won't even let me take a breath. God, I don't know if I have what it takes to handle this.

He tried to think about his family. Since he would probably die, he wanted to die with thoughts of them on his mind. It didn't help. The soldiers kept battering him.

Oh, God, there's too much pain, God! he screamed in his mind.

He decided to play a game like the admiral told him. He would count the kicks so he'd know exactly how many times they tried to destroy him. But no matter what they did, he wouldn't give in. He'd concentrate on counting the kicks to keep his mind off the pain.

Look at 'em having such a good time.

They were laughing and enjoying themselves. He forced himself to think of Keiko. But almost immediately, the next kick tore his mind back to reality.

Ohhh, that's eight. God, it feels like all the bones in the center of my body are broken. I'll never be able to go to the bathroom again. What a stupid thought that was.

Please, God, this is too much. I'm not sure I can handle this. Please, God! I've never had pain like this before. Please!

He thought of Keiko and how he loved her.

Ohhh! Number nine.

They enjoyed life together as much as two people could. He thought of their times together and remembered how excited she was when they visited the remains of Shuri castle. She was proud of her heritage and the history of her homeland. She made it come alive so that Gohan felt as if he were part of it, too. It was hard to imagine the castle had been built more than one thousand years....

Ahhh! What is that, ten? God! How much more can I take? Please, God! he screamed.

He took a deep breath and exhaled slowly. He forced himself to relax his body again, but it was difficult. He forced himself back to his reverie. Tears from the pain rolled down his face. Thoughts were darting back and forth in his mind. He concentrated on his body, recognized that his neck muscles were taut, and relaxed them. He saw that his chest was tight, and forced it to relax.

Thoughts of Keiko came quickly and easily. He was immensely moved when Keiko talked to him about the recent war. She'd been just a baby when their island came under attack, but her father was an unwilling participant. She grew up hearing the stories of the war. There wasn't any family on the island who hadn't lost someone, yet the Okinawans were peaceful, kind people. It touched Gohan deeply and was one of the reasons why he loved that place.

Did they suffer as much as I'm suffering? he wondered. *Yes. Ohhh! That's eleven.*

Don't make more out of this than there is, Davey. The admiral probably went through worse. Willie, Oscar, and Bob might be goin' through more, too. The Okinawans went through more....

Uhhh!, That's twelve. I'm sorry, admiral, but I'm not as brave as you were. I feel like all the skin's been torn off the middle of my body, and my bones are just sitting there, waiting to be broken into tiny pieces—if there are any left that aren't broken. I'm tryin', admiral. God, I'm trying.

As the positive and negative thoughts warred in his mind, he realized that he had, in fact, been handling the torture pretty well. He had survived more pain than most people felt in a lifetime. His body jerked as another kick tore into his midsection. But, he would make it. He would make it.

Did you hear that, Nikko-Witch? I'll make it! You can get the biggest, fattest, heaviest, strongest men in Russia to play football with me, and it won't matter. I'm gonna make it.

Oooh, number fourteen. That guy must have weighed 500 pounds to have that much force. Listen to 'em. They're so drunk, they don't care if they kill me. In fact, they probably hope to.

He heard a Russian talking, but it wasn't Nikko-Witch. All the men cheered. Gohan forced his eyes open and saw a younger, smaller Russian who placed another bottle of vodka on the table. He walked over to Gohan and looked down at his midsection, fear showing on his face. Then Pavel, the KGB assistant, turned and left quickly.

The pain was destroying Gohan. Maybe with luck he'd go numb and wouldn't feel it anymore. He hadn't known that anyone could endure such pain, and he wondered why he was still alive. If he somehow survived the torture, he would be as belligerent as before. Nikko-Witch had better have something else to try, because he had just met his match.

Ohhh, fifteen. Ha! I'm still alive, aren't I? What do you think of that, you drunken slobs?

He opened his eyes again. He'd kept them closed to try to centralize the pain, but he wanted to look at the soldiers and let them know they were losing. He stared at them as they drank, and he saw some were already drunk. One of the Pathet Lao soldiers saw Gohan looking at them and pointed, shouting something.

Another little Pathet Lao man walked up to Gohan as Gohan stared at him. The little man glared, then screamed and gave Gohan a flying kick into his midsection that almost pushed him through the wall.

God, am I crazy? Help me keep my eyes closed. Please don't let me do that again. Ohhh, God, was that sixteen?

He needed good thoughts again and forced himself to remember when he and Keiko decided to marry. Hand in hand, they walked beside one of the large sugarcane fields, then stopped and sat on a rock. It wasn't working. He couldn't control his thoughts.

Relax! he screamed to himself.

Keiko again slipped into his reverie.

"Keiko, this is silly. With the way we feel about each other, why don't we marry? I know it's unusual because of your father's status, but it's not unheard of. Let's do it."

Another kick attempted to destroy him, but he wouldn't allow it.

"Gohan-san, I love you very much and know my father will agree. He loves you very much, too. I talk to, what you say, monk? Bukkyo?"

"The Buddhist monk? Yeah. That's right."

"I talk to monk and to father, get signs. Then we get married."

She looked radiantly happy. He wished he were back with her again.

Ohhh, that was seventeen. You filthy slime-balls, if I ever get out of here, I'll come back and turn your faces into scrambled eggs.

When would it end? How much more could he take? Taking a deep breath, he prepared himself for more.

"Nikolai Ivanovich Nikolayevich, may I speak to you, please?"

"Yes, Comrade Ustinova. Come in. What is it?"

"Have we gotten any valuable information from the American?"

"If I had, comrade, it wouldn't necessarily be something I would share with you, would it?"

"Nikolai, it was my plan that put us in the position to kill the three marines and capture the other one, wasn't it?"

The KGB man thought for a moment and drank some vodka. "Yes, comrade. That was a good idea. I'll be sure to mention it in my report. As for the Americans, they are highly trained specialists sent here on a secret mission. I'm certain of it. The first three are dead and can't help us. This one, I don't know. We won't get anything from him yet. He's stubborn, but I'm even more stubborn.

"He's being tortured right now. When we finish this lesson in diplomacy, he will certainly wish to talk to us. We'll see, comrade.

"Major, please fill a couple glasses of this good vodka and walk outside to enjoy the rest of the evening. I have other work to do. When you go into the courtyard, please send Comrade Zortov to me. He sits out there and reads each night."

Major Ustinova was pleased. Not only had he made a positive impression on the KGB officer, he would also be able to enjoy two glasses of good Russian vodka. That was a nice way to finish off his day.

He poured two glasses, thanked Nikolai, walked into the clearing, and found Zortov as instructed. He passed on the order and sat on one of the benches with the two glasses in front of him, feeling relaxed and satisfied with himself.

He would enjoy the evening. He'd done a masterful job, and Nikolai knew it. What would Samsonov say when he saw that report? His father would certainly hear about it and would be proud. That might even put enough pressure on the old man to get Aleksandr out of that horrible place and into a better assignment.

Good things would come. For the moment, he was content to enjoy his vodka.

Zortov rapped on the door, heard his superior's voice, and entered.

"Comrade Zortov, did you take the extra bottle of vodka to the soldiers in the interrogation room?"

"Yes, comrade. Are you aware what they're doing to the American? They might kill him. I've never seen anything so cruel."

"Zortov, you don't understand interrogation work. That's why you're a clerk. Don't worry. They know when to stop. And when they do, the American will be ready to talk to us."

"But, sir, he didn't look like he was going to survive when I was in there and that was ten minutes ago or more. Please, sir. I don't think we want to kill an American by torture. That could have far reaching ramifications."

The KGB officer flung his glass at the young clerk, splashing him with vodka, then slammed his fist against the table. "Comrade Zortov, have you forgotten who you are and who I am? You will never plead with me like that again, or I'll send a report to headquarters that will destroy your career. For the things you have done with your Irena and the items you've stolen from the supply stores, I could have you sent to a prison camp for the rest of your life. Is that what you want, comrade?"

"Of course not, comrade. I'm sorry. I wasn't thinking. Please forgive me, comrade."

Gohan couldn't believe he was still alive. He felt as if his lower body had fallen away. His vision blurred, and he blinked without being able to focus. It seemed even his tormentors had grown tired of the game. Their kicks lacked their former drive. They'd been at it a long time and were very drunk.

He hurt badly. He wanted to scream, but that would create more pain and bring satisfaction to his enemies. He accidentally bit his tongue again and tasted blood.

Why not? he wondered sarcastically. *They'll cut it off, anyway. Now I know what it tastes like.*

What would Keiko do when she learned he was dead? Would they say he'd been a hero? No. They wouldn't even admit he was in Laos. General Winthrop made that very clear.

Ohhh. Was that sixty-two? Yes. Oh, God. Oh, God. Oh, God. Please, I can't take anymore.

What would they do when they tried to kick him, and there was nothing left? He had reached the point where the pain from all his injuries ran together in his mind, and he couldn't separate them. He no longer knew what did or didn't hurt. There wasn't an inch of his body left that didn't feel great pain. He wondered why he was still alive.

God, the admiral said I should pray. Well, I'm prayin', and I'm just like him. I won't pray for my enemies, not those... I'm prayin' for Oscar, Bob, Willie, and the admiral. Then I'm prayin' for Keiko and Sumi. God, help me through this. This is terrible.

Keiko, I love you, honey, and I love you, too, Sumi. Daddy wanted to be there to see you grow up. He really did. I'm so sorry, honey.

Tears ran down his face.

Ohhh. Sixty-three.

Suddenly, everything started fading. He couldn't see the Russians, the Viet Minh, or the Pathet Lao soldiers. His eyes were open, or so he thought, but everything was black. The pain was still there, so he was still alive. Then it, too, disappeared.

The last thing he remembered was sixty-three.

Chapter 15
Tragedy Back Home

KEIKO MOVED BACK INTO THE FAMILY HOUSE IN NAGO. SHE had a separate room where she stayed with Sumi. Her father arranged for Dr. Kentsu to treat Sumiko, who was severely ill and growing worse each day. He also arranged for a private nurse to stay at the house until Sumiko regained her health.

It was very difficult for Keiko. Seth Edwards, Gohan's best friend, visited her before she left Nakadomari. She asked Seth many questions, but he had no answers. She also saw Katsuo Matsumura, but he, too, was unable to assuage her concern. He explained it was common for a country like the United States to have secret assignments for its top military people. Gohan was one of the best soldiers the U.S. had, and he couldn't be exempt from such assignments.

None of that helped Keiko. Her baby was sick, and Keiko was frightened. She wanted her husband with her and couldn't understand why he couldn't be. Though Gohan was held in high esteem on Okinawa, especially after the attack on her father's house, there were still some who didn't like Americans, including a few who worked at her father's house. They used the opportunity to fill her mind with negative thoughts about Gohan.

With all that going on, Keiko wasn't strong, and it took very little negative influence to weaken her resolve. Matsumura and her father did what they could to help Keiko remain balanced in her mind. Both men cared deeply for Gohan. They understood the situation.

She felt better after listening to them and felt she could wait, patiently and longingly, for Gohan to return. When Sumiko was at her worst, Keiko left her with her nurse and spent hours at Shinto shrines, bowing low in prayer, hoping for good health for her child and a quick return for her husband. She saw the *yuti*, an Okinawan shaman, to ask for healing for her baby.

She tried everything she knew, but nothing seemed to work. She and Gohan talked often about what they'd do when his tour of duty ended. He told her he wanted to go to America and would stop with her in Japan, then Hawaii, and, finally, San Francisco. He talked so much about his home in Cincinnati, Ohio, that she almost thought of it as a village outside Naha.

"The country's flat, honey, not like Okinawa. You can get on the highway and drive for miles. It's just straight, no hills or mountains."

Because she was educated, she already understood some of the things Gohan explained. When he told her that driving from Cincinnati to the next major city, Cleveland, was farther than from one end of Okinawa to the other, it was difficult to comprehend, even though she knew it was true. He promised she'd love his parents and his younger brother, who was only five years old. Gohan assured her many times that the others would love her, too. She wanted to believe it. Maybe, in time, it would come true.

She enjoyed hearing about the farm where they raised cattle, sheep, goats, pigs, turkeys, chickens, and geese. They also had horses and donkeys, and there were occasional attacks by mountain lions. It was fascinating, and Keiko couldn't wait to experience it for herself.

One of the things that helped her was the way Gohan accepted Okinawan culture. He immersed himself in it, enjoying it immensely. Because of that, she felt she could do that with Ohio.

Gohan told her about baseball. She knew he played baseball on Okinawa on the Kadena Base team. Seth said Gohan was very good. In America, they would attend many baseball games.

They would also see plays and dramas like they did on the island, though they would be different in America. They also had many Asian plays, many with Japanese actors. If they weren't too far away, they'd see those, too. She looked forward to it.

Keiko sighed. She thought about those things a lot and missed Gohan terribly. She wondered what would happen if she went to America and Gohan had to leave again. She wouldn't have her father to visit, and the thought frightened her. She was very insecure without Gohan at her side.

She loved him very much. If he went to America, she would accompany him—unless she could talk him into staying. After all, he loved Okinawa. When he returned from his assignment, they'd discuss living on Okinawa and maybe visiting America occasionally. She hoped he would agree. If they could stay, she would be very happy.

As she rode her bicycle up the long, winding road to her father's house after a tour of the island, she pondered those things. She'd been visiting various places, trying to build hope and find healing for the baby. She saw Matsumura, and, as always, he encouraged her. After spending more than an hour with him, she went to the shrine and told her woes to the gods, the caves, the ocean, the wind, and anyone else who cared to listen.

She rode all the way to the south end of the island to Shuri castle, which Gohan always enjoyed. They often sat there for hours, talking. After Shuri, Keiko visited the old fishing village and stood at the top of the hill to look at the island's southern end.

As she thought of Gohan, she remembered a poem she learned at school. As she sang it to herself, tears rolled down her cheeks.

Karaya tsji nubuti
Mafe nkati miriba
Shimarura du miyuru
Satu ya miran.
Climbing to the top of Karaya hill
I looked toward the south.
I could see only the shape of the village,
No shadow of my loving husband.

She visited many places she'd seen with Gohan, and the tour helped her spirits. As she finished the ride toward her father's house, she felt better and was anxious to spend time with her sweet, sick Sumiko.

As soon as she arrived, Kinjo, one of her father's guards, motioned her inside immediately. Her father met her at the door.

They hurried upstairs and into the bedroom where Sumiko lay in her crib. The doctor listened to her through a piece of apparatus, and the nurse wiped her forehead with a damp cloth. She was flushed red, but she wasn't crying.

Keiko walked to the crib and looked down, then at the nurse, who looked away. When she looked at the doctor, he smiled weakly.

"What is it, Dr. Kentsu?" she asked. "Is she worse? Can't you help her?"

"I gave her more medication, my child. That's why she isn't crying. She doesn't know she's sick. That's the best we can do now."

Keiko began crying. She had refused to recognize Sumiko's steady decline, holding tightly to every small positive sign she noticed. She wanted desperately for her child to recover.

Now she realized it had been false hope. She finally understood how serious Sumiko's condition was. For the first time, she allowed herself to see that her daughter's life was in danger. Keiko felt frightened and lost.

She looked at the doctor as tears streamed down her face. "What should I do?"

"Kiss your child, Keiko, then go downstairs with your father."

She looked at him, trying to understand what he meant. Finally, she leaned over the crib and kissed Sumiko's hot face. The child didn't respond. Keiko's tears slipped from her chin onto Sumiko's face, but she didn't react to that, either.

The young mother lifted her head, raised herself from the crib, and looked at her father. He took her arm and gently led her into the main sitting room, then ordered tea. He sat on the deep, comfortable couch with Keiko beside him. She buried her head against his chest and sobbed uncontrollably.

Konishi Kobashigawa had endured much in his lifetime. Only in his mid-forties, he was appointed as the island's chief executive by the U.S. high commissioner. There was a great deal of political turmoil, and his life was in constant danger. He'd lost his wife four years earlier to an internal disease, and two older brothers were killed in the war. His only son, Keiko's older brother, died in a boating accident at the age of fifteen. He loved Keiko dearly and knew she would soon leave for America. Now he knew that the life of his only grandchild hung by a thread.

Regardless of his personal misfortune, Konishi had to be strong for Keiko. It was an extremely difficult time for her, and Gohan was away on an important mission. Konishi assumed that Gohan didn't even know of his daughter's condition. If he were on a special assignment, the U.S. military wouldn't keep him informed of such matters. He wondered if even the military knew about Sumiko and guessed not.

Keiko lay her head against her father's chest and cried for a long time. When she had cried herself out, he raised her head, ran his fingers through her hair, and smiled lovingly at her. "Drink some tea. It will help."

She took the cup and sipped the hot, sweet liquid, then leaned against her father again. She'd grown closer to him over the past few years. They were the last members of their family.

"Do you think I'll hear anything from Gohan in Germany?" she asked.

"I know this is difficult for you, but you must understand that he's on a military assignment. I'm sure he doesn't know about Sumiko. If he could write you, he would, probably every day. That means he isn't able to. He doesn't know how difficult the situation is. As a military man, he must obey his orders, even if he doesn't agree with them.

"He said he'd be away for two weeks. I'm sure he'll be back then. You'd like him to be here now. If he knew how sick Sumiko is, he'd want to be here, but he can't."

He smiled at her, and she returned it. He was a kind, considerate father who cared deeply for his people. When Keiko needed him most, he was with her.

She heard movement on the stairs and saw the doctor and nurse coming down. Keiko and her father stood quickly and met them at the bottom of the stairway.

The chief executive knew immediately what happened, but Keiko still held onto a last flicker of hope.

"Sumiko?" she asked.

They looked at her without speaking, then the doctor looked at Konishi and shook his head. Keiko's eyes widened.

"Sumiko!" she screamed.

She ran upstairs with her father right behind her. When she threw open the bedroom door, she stopped, because the sound of her child's heavy breathing was missing. The room was totally still.

She walked slowly to the crib with her father beside her, holding her hand, and looked down. Her baby lay, eyes closed, and, for the first time in weeks, with a peaceful, painless expression. Keiko slowly touched Sumiko's face. It was no longer hot with fever, but it was lifeless.

"She suffers no longer, Keiko," her father said gently. "She's at rest. Don't try to understand right now. Come downstairs with me. I'll sit with you for as long as you wish."

She looked at him, uncertain she'd heard his words. When she leaned forward to pick up her baby, her father stopped her.

"Remember her as she was, not as she is. There's nothing you can do."

Her hand moved away from Sumiko's face, then Keiko backed away from the crib. Her father wrapped his arm around her waist, gently leading her from the room and down the stairs.

Chapter 16
Underground Warriors

CHEU MOUA TOOK SIX MEN INTO THE JUNGLE BETWEEN HIS camp and Ban Na Lom. Ka told him about the American who'd been captured and brought to the compound, but that was all she knew. Cheu decided that if there were more Americans, he had to find them. They could do far more working together than alone. Pooling information and resources would help both.

After searching until noon, they still had found nothing. Finally, they reached the Americans' original rendezvous point, and Cheu and his men noticed dried blood on the ground and other signs of a fight.

"There was shooting here," Cheu said. "There's lots of blood. Look around closely for more clues. We need information. Take your time. We aren't in a hurry."

The Hmong guerrillas searched every inch of ground.

"Cheu, look what I found!"

Two of his men found some branches tied together.

"It looks like someone made a broom to sweep the ground. Maybe they were covering up something."

"Look!" Vu Xiong, his second in command, said. "Something heavy was dragged along here. You're right, Xang. It looks like they tried to cover it up."

"It goes toward the river," Cheu said. "Maybe it means nothing." He looked around.

"Why would they cover the trail unless it was important?"

"You're right. Let's follow it and see where it leads. Maybe we can learn more. Did Ka say the marines that were killed were taken back to Ban Na Lom?"

"I don't know," Vu replied. "When you told me about it, you didn't say anything about the bodies of the dead marines."

"Then maybe we've found something. Let's go."

As they approached the river's edge, one man noticed a piece of cloth on the ground, and the others inspected it closely.

"What do you think, Vu?" Cheu asked.

"It's probably clothing, but I don't know whose. It looks as if someone was dragged to the river, and...."

"...thrown into the river?"

"Yes. Doesn't it look like that to you?"

"But why? If they wanted to destroy the bodies, they should leave them out. Dragons and tigers would eat them."

"Yes, but it looks like that's what they did."

"Think about it, Cheu," Jou Pang, another man, said. "If you wanted dragons and tigers to destroy dead bodies, what better place than the river? All animals go there to drink. I'd place the bodies half in the water, then all the animals could participate."

"You're right. We'll walk the riverbank for a while and see what we find."

The armed patrol moved along the river toward Ban Na Lom. Farther downstream, they found another piece of clothing and the grisly remains of some body parts with dark skin. Cheu nodded and continued looking.

They left the river and moved back toward Ban Na Lom, searching the area where the Americans made camp. One of Cheu's men noticed the ground cover was altered, as if someone had spent some time in the area.

"Search this area carefully," Cheu told everyone. "Something happened here."

Soon, the men saw the camouflage up in the trees. Four men aimed their rifles at the area while two more climbed up to investigate. They discovered empty K-rations, a few pencils, two large pads of paper, and wads of leaves tied together, probably for pillows. They climbed down and reported their findings.

"So this is where the Americans lived," Cheu said. "I wonder how long they were here and why." He shook his head. "How many were there, Vu?"

"Two in each tree, although there's room in one treehouse for another. Maybe four or five men all together."

"OK. The Communists killed three and captured one, according to Ka. We might be looking for one man, my brothers. Or none. We'll continue for now."

During the shooting, Captain Baker had feared the worst. He had climbed into thick brush and watched the fight. He saw Gohan on the ground, alive. Then he watched the enemy soldiers cautiously approach. He witnessed Gohan's impossible attempt to take on the entire patrol, and he saw them beat him into unconsciousness and drag him away.

He only hoped he was still alive.

Baker retreated farther into the jungle, hoping to escape danger. He tried to create a plan all morning, but nothing came to him. He had to do something, but what? He wasn't worried about his own life. He was a survivor and knew it, but what about his men? They were his responsibility. How many, if any, were still alive? What could he do to find out and offer help?

He had no answers.

Sitting quietly on a flat rock, he listened to the sounds of the Laotian jungle. It rained gently, and it was beautiful in its own way. As part of God's creation, that was only natural. Baker wanted to lie down and take a nap, but he couldn't. With a deep sigh, he looked around at the false serenity and prayed,

Lord, we've been here before, haven't we? You got me through that one and can get me through this, too. Lord, You're God. There isn't anything You don't know. You know if those men are still alive, and You know where they are and how much danger they're in. You also know how to get them out. That's what I need, Lord. I need that wisdom.

I'm not just asking for my own protection. There are four men out there somewhere. If they're alive, I want to get them out. Lord, please protect them. Give them the strength to stand up to whatever the enemy might do. Help them not to give in. Lord Jesus, please help me. I need it. I'm not John Wayne. I'm just me. You know my strengths and weaknesses, Lord, and You know my heart. I'll do whatever's necessary to save those men, but I need Your direction.

Lord, somewhere in Laos are more Americans. If I can find them, we can get this done. I can't do it alone, Lord. I'm no hero. You can put it all together, though. Please give me some direction, and I'll obey. I'm prepared to make the full sacrifice if necessary. I don't want those men left to such a fate.

Lord, I don't believe I'm asking too much. I'll move ahead now and let You guide me. Thank You, Jesus. Amen.

He knew the possible consequences of his request and thought about Vanessa and his two children, Samuel and Jordan. For a black man in a somewhat-prejudiced world, he'd done pretty well for himself. He was highly thought of in his field. What would others say about him if he didn't return? They wouldn't call him a hero. General Winthrop would make certain of that.

Baker didn't think of himself in those terms, anyway. He had a job to do and would perform at the highest level he could. He chose his profession and didn't expect special accolades when he did something right. No one applauded a factory worker when shoes were made properly. That was expected.

He realized he couldn't rescue the men alone. His smartest move would be to get help. There were Americans in Laos somewhere, but he didn't know if they were a few miles away or several hundred.

I guess there's only one way to find out, Lord. I'll start walkin'.

I'd appreciate it if You'd let me run into some Americans real soon. Amen.

He decided to leave the mountainous jungle and head for more civilized parts of the country, where he might be able to contact his people in Laos. There was danger in that idea, because the generals might have already decided the mission was over. They'd probably be willing to rescue Baker but would leave the other men behind. His only hope was to assure them that the men were alive, and it was wise to rescue them before they talked. The generals might consider that, because Gohan was the most important man in the mission.

If he met American troops in the meantime, they could devise a plan to rescue the men from Ban Na Lom. Baker would still need to contact Okinawa, but it would be easier to convince Generals Winthrop and Mancini to make the attempt if Baker had troops with him first.

He cleaned up his area and began his trek deep into the jungle mountains, where he moved southwest, the best direction toward a city. He walked quietly, quickly, and alertly, realizing he was in unknown territory, and his rifle was ready with a silencer attached.

The area was beautiful. From thick jungle bush to canopied trees to mountain clearings, he felt he was walking through three different countries.

After an hour, he came to another large clearing with a river on the far side. Beyond that he saw a thickly forested mountain. Though it presented danger, he decided to cross the clearing, rest at the river, and go up and over the mountain.

Four sets of eyes watched as Captain Baker crossed the large, grassy meadow.

When he finally reached the edge of the small river, he rested. The mountain looked bigger at close range, but it wasn't insurmountable. He decided he'd rather cross downstream. There would be more cover, too.

He walked farther until he stopped suddenly, surprised and elated to find a swinging bamboo bridge that crossed the river. It was built in an area full of trees and bushes, offering some protection, and he wondered if he was near a village.

He slowly crossed the bridge and found it a harrowing experience. *That was scary*, he thought as he finished. *I wonder if people use that thing? It wouldn't hold more than two or three.*

He stared up at the mountain without seeing a human being, rice field, village, or any other sign of life and wondered how long it would be before he met someone.

He found a trail leading through some rocks that appeared to go straight up the mountain, so he followed it. It took a while to reach the top. But now that he was far from his starting point, he relaxed a bit. The enemy forces wouldn't stray that far from camp. He didn't know who else was out there or whose side they were on. So all he could do was hope that his American fatigues wouldn't automatically make him an enemy.

Finally, he reached the top of the mountain and was surprised to find another large jungle there. He looked around and decided to go west. An eighth of a mile later, he saw what appeared to be a clearing. It was hidden by thick bush and trees.

Approaching cautiously, he saw it was a village, because he saw the tops of tents. He moved farther to his left, hoping to approach the village from behind and investigate. Thirty yards away, he hid behind thick brush and stopped.

Several men moved in the village, presumably all Laotians. If they were a mountain tribe, they would be Hmong, and that might mean they would be friendly. He watched for a while and realized there were no women or children. That was bad. He scanned the village carefully, noticing a stack of rifles lined against the back of a long wooden box. Some looked like old muskets. He wondered if that was possible.

What have I stumbled onto? he wondered.

Then he sensed movement behind him, turned fast, and froze. Three Hmong guerillas held rifles aimed at him. It looked like Captain Baker would soon find out what the village was about.

"American?" one asked.

Baker carefully placed his weapon on the ground and slowly stood, his hands atop his head. The three men motioned, and he walked through the brush with them following. A few minutes later, they were in the clearing. Another twelve men were waiting for him, all dressed the same. Since they didn't have uniforms, they had to be guerillas. Baker prayed they weren't Pathet Lao. He'd heard terrible stories about them.

"American?" the guerilla repeated.

The situation was odd. The guerillas didn't seem mean. Maybe they didn't know what Gohan and the men had been doing. The more Baker looked, the more he felt he wasn't seeing an organized guerilla army.

The self-appointed leader of the group motioned Baker to sit, and he obliged. Then to his surprise, someone brought food and drink.

Baker was amazed. *Could these be friends?* He'd been through enough in Korea not to take anything for granted, so he didn't react. They set down some fruit, nuts, and a cup of liquid beside him. Three men sat on the ground ten feet away with their rifles pointed at him. The rest went about their business.

They stayed that way for an hour. No one tried to force Baker to eat, nor did they ask questions. He assumed the real leader was on his way, and the others were waiting for him. Then he would know what he had found.

Soon enough, the group stirred, and Baker turned toward the edge of the clearing. A small group of men walked into the village. One of the guards ran to them and began talking.

Captain Baker looked at the bearded man in the middle of the group. He was medium-sized, strong, and young. He had to be the leader.

The newcomers approached. Baker saw the leader was five-feet-eight-inches tall and probably weighed 170 pounds, but it was hard to tell with the clothes he wore. He had a full beard, but he seemed around thirty, maybe younger.

He walked over to Baker, smiled, and held out his hand. Baker was stunned. Then the bearded man spoke to him in broken English.

"Mr. American Soldier, I Cheu Moua. Friend."

Baker looked at him. "Hmong?"

"Yes." He smiled, wondering how the American knew.

Baker shook Cheu's hand, and immediately reached for the food and drink. He was starving. Cheu took him to one of the larger tents, gave some orders, then sat down while three men continued to guard the American. Cheu offered Baker a drink, which he accepted gladly. But when he sipped it, he almost choked.

"Wow! That's strong! What is this?"

Cheu laughed. "Rice drink. Strong, yes?"

Baker tried to talk through the burning in his throat. "Yes. This will last the rest of my life. Thank you, but no more."

Cheu laughed again, then became serious. "Name Cheu Moua. You name?"

"I'm glad to meet you, Cheu Moua. I'm Captain Harold Baker of the United States Navy."

"Captain? Navy? Good. You know other Americans?"

"Yes. There were five of us." He held up five fingers. "Do you know anything about the others?"

"Yes. Five? Yes. Three marines killed by soldiers of Ban Na Lom camp. One American in camp."

"Three killed?"

"Yes. Dead."

"The other is alive?"

"Alive before…." Cheu shrugged, and Baker assumed he didn't know if he was still alive. "Captain, we fight Ban Na Lom camp. You fight?"

"Yes. I'll join you." He realized that was the Lord leading him. He thought of going to a city to contact his superiors in Okinawa, but God led him to a group of Hmong village guerillas who were after the same thing he wanted—to take that compound and get their people out. Maybe he wouldn't need American troops after all.

"First, I need to know about the American at the camp," Baker said.

Cheu nodded. "Cheu Moua sister work hospital. She come, tell…." He shrugged.

"That's OK. We're doin' all right. Your sister works at the hospital in Ban Na Lom?"

"Yes. Sister in hospital."

"OK. Does she come here to stay with you?"

"Yes." Cheu smiled and nodded.

"OK. Will she be able to tell us about the American?"

"Yes. Sister tell."

Captain Baker felt much better. At least Gohan was alive. As soon as Baker could speak to Cheu's sister, he would learn more. He hoped she spoke better English than her brother.

"Does your sister speak English?"

"No. Sister no English."

He sighed. He would have to communicate through Cheu. It seemed the man understood more than he spoke. The longer they conversed, the more they would understand each other. Baker decided to speak with Cheu as often as possible.

"Do you have a plan to attack Ban Na Lom camp?"

"No. Captain help?"

He sighed again, but maybe it was better that way. He had more experience than the villagers. He nodded. "Are you and your men from Ban Na Lom?"

"Yes. No. We run."

Baker assumed that meant some were, and some weren't. "You're all Hmong?"

"All, yes."

"Good. I assume you know the area well?"

"Yes. Cheu, Hmong, same."

"Cheu, are you and your men proficient?" He stopped, wondering why he had used such a big word. Was he trying to impress someone? He tried again, asking, "Do you and your men have experience in war? Do you know how to use your weapons?"

Cheu understood and looked inquisitively at the American. "Captain, know Vang Po?"

"Vang Po? Isn't he one of the leaders of the Royal Lao Army?"

"Yes. He Hmong captain." He held up two fingers side by side and pointed at them one at a time. "Vang Po. Cheu." He smiled.

"You and Vang Po were in the RLA together?"

"Yes."

"Good. Thank you."

That meant that at least two of them had military experience, he and Cheu. He had recently learned about Vang Po from the CIA reports. He was a Hmong leader who had been trained by the U.S. Green Berets. That was very good news.

Seeing the weariness on Captain Baker's face, Cheu motioned him to sleep. Baker nodded, then a man came in with food. Baker didn't know what it was, but he no longer cared.

You provided for me, Lord, he thought. *Thank You for this meal and for answering my prayer and leading me to these men. Amen.*

The food was all vegetables, but that suited Baker fine. He ate heartily, sipped the rice drink, and allowed Vu Xiong, Cheu's lieutenant, to direct him to a small tent on the far side of the camp, where he laid down and was instantly asleep.

Chapter 17
Left to Die

GOHAN AWOKE BUT REFUSED TO MOVE. HE HAD NO IDEA WHERE he was. At first, he wondered if he was dead, but the pain assured him he wasn't. He hurt everywhere, but the pain around his midsection and the tops of his legs was more than he could bear. He wanted to scream but didn't. His memory returned quickly.

He had been tied to a wall. Then they kicked his groin area until they almost killed him. He remembered counting in an effort to keep his mind sharp. After sixty-three, the kicks either stopped, or he fainted.

Where am I? he wondered. *Am I still chained up? No, I guess not.*

The tearing pain in his arms was missing. They ached, as did his head, and he wondered what happened to his head. He didn't know if he'd been shot or just beaten. He remembered blood running down his back when he was first captured.

How bad are my injuries? he wondered. *If I'm not chained to the wall, where am I?*

He stopped thinking and concentrated on the stillness to see if he could learn anything. He quickly realized he wasn't alone, but he didn't know if he sensed breathing or just knew someone was nearby.

All right, Nikko-Witch, what will you do now? You want to cut out my tongue? Why not? That's the only part left that doesn't hurt.

He wasn't sure if he could take any more torture or if he was even able to move. He hadn't tried, because he didn't want anyone to know he was conscious. That might be his only respite. How long could he remain there? When would they come and pour that cold, bitter stuff over him again?

He needed as much information as possible to survive. He wanted to know where he was, partly because it had a terrible stench. In a different setting, it would have been sickening to smell something like that. But in his condition, the odor wasn't much compared to the pain he felt.

He needed to open his eyes. He didn't know what they would do to him if he were awake, but he doubted they could hurt him much more. There wasn't that much left to hurt.

He slowly opened his eyes, hoping no one would notice. As his vision focused, he was startled to see a face only inches away from his. He jumped. It was an older man with a sad, wrinkled face. The longer Gohan studied him, the less old he seemed. It was clear the man wasn't one of the perverted soldiers.

Though Gohan couldn't move his head, he realized there were several people in the cold, damp room with him, and the smell was even worse than he first thought. He allowed his eyes to meet the older man's gaze. There was compassion in those eyes and a lot of pain.

Light came from bars high above. Gohan realized he was in a prison dungeon, probably a ditch or hole in the ground. The sunlight seemed very distant, hidden by a lid of some sort. He tried to look around, but his head hurt so badly, he couldn't move his neck without excruciating pain.

The old man gently brushed dirt from Gohan's face. Suddenly, Gohan realized how skinny the old man was. The people in the dungeon were being starved to death.

The skinny man looked at the sunlight, waited a moment, then leaned close to Gohan's ear and spoke in almost perfect English. Gohan thought the man might be a plant, but one look at his emaciated frame told him otherwise.

"I'm Dr. Boua Thao, a Hmong. I was educated at UCLA in America." He glanced upward, then spoke even more quietly. "We can speak only when guards aren't close. You've been hurt very badly."

"How badly, Doctor?"

Dr. Thao looked at him with a sad expression. "Very badly. You probably will not walk again. The upper portion of your legs and center of your body have been almost completely destroyed. I'm afraid there's very little left. Didn't you see what they did to you, or were you unconscious?"

"I was chained to a wall. I couldn't see, just feel."

The old man shook his head as tears streamed down his face. "God have mercy."

He put a finger to his lips, warning Gohan to silence. After a few seconds, Gohan saw a shadow pass overhead. Once it was gone, the doctor resumed talking.

"I won't ask your name. The less I know, the better. Your condition is grave. I'll try to help in any way I can, but I have no medications. I'm a prisoner, too. I'm not sure what I can do."

"Can't I recover with time? Won't I heal eventually?"

Gohan was pleading. And from what he had just heard from the Hmong doctor, he was frightened. Suppose this guy wasn't a doctor. But then, why would he give him no hope. He looked up as the man answered his question.

"Son," he said, placing his hand on Gohan's shoulder, "look at me. Do I look like I'll get better with time? No. I'm getting worse, and you're in the same situation. They don't feed us very well. Occasionally, the nurse will look at us, but there's little she can do. Your only hope is to be taken to the hospital."

Gohan was awake enough now to realize several things. The horrible smell was human waste. Though he didn't try to move his head, he saw there were many men in the dungeon, and all seemed to be starving.

With his senses sharpening, Gohan felt increased pain. He couldn't believe how much he hurt. It was hard to think. He wanted the doctor to keep talking, anything to keep his mind active.

"Doc, if that's my only hope, how do I do it? How do I get into the hospital?"

"Please don't misunderstand me, son. I didn't say you could get into the hospital. I said that was your only hope. I'm not sure they'll let you be hospitalized. They haven't shown any willingness to help us, and some of us are dying. It's possible, since you're an American, they're more concerned about you than about rebellious Hmong villagers."

"Right now I'm in such pain, doc, I can hardly think. If they take me back for more torture, I'm not sure how long I'll live."

The realization suddenly hit him. He had known all along, while he was being tortured, what was happening. But only now, lying next to the mild-mannered starved doctor, did he realize the extent of his own condition. He began to cry but quickly took control of himself.

"They are crazy men, my young friend, but even they must realize they can't do much more to you. If they want information from you, they must let you recover."

"That's it, doc!" Gohan said, excitedly.

The doctor turned to speak to the other men in another language, then turned back to Gohan and nodded for him to continue.

"How do we get them to understand I'll be more valuable to them alive than dead? If they put me in the hospital, maybe they can get information from me. Of course. If they put me in there, and I recover, I can escape and help the rest of you. I promise I'll do it, doc."

"My friend, have you seen what they did to you?"

"No. Should I?"

"If you're strong enough to attempt an escape, you're strong enough to see your condition. You need to know that so you can plan. If you're so weak you don't want to know your condition, you won't be able to escape anyway."

Gohan wondered if the doctor was trying to psyche him out. It didn't matter. He was right. Gohan knew he was strong enough to escape, so he had to look.

"OK, doc. How? I'm not sure I can move."

The doctor tried to help Gohan sit up, but he was weak, too. Gohan's pain was so intense that any movement was devastating. He managed to move his upper body by pushing with his hands. What he finally saw almost made him faint.

Gohan's fatigues were ripped apart. His body was bare from below his chest to his knees. The doctor had placed a piece of cloth over Gohan, but he tried to remove it when Gohan tried to sit up. The cloth stuck to Gohan's body.

His stomach and lower chest were raw. In some places, he saw ribs and bones sticking out. All his flesh was gone. He assumed his ribs were broken. But because he couldn't separate the different pains he felt, he didn't know for sure. He couldn't raise up high enough to see lower than that, but what he saw was enough to make him ill. He motioned Dr. Thao to lower him again. It took him more than a minute before he could speak.

"What's the rest look like, doc?"

"Do you want the truth?"

"Yes. I need to know."

"What you have seen, unfortunately, is the best of your condition. Everything else is far worse." He motioned Gohan quiet as the guard returned over head.

"How do I get into the hospital?" Gohan asked when it was safe to talk again, as tears streamed down his face. "Where is it?"

Dr. Thao thought for a moment, then sighed. "Because I'm a doctor, I can say you'll die unless they put you in the hospital. It's only a few feet away, but it's here at the camp, in Ban Na Lom. You can get better treatment if you wish."

Gohan was confused. "What? Why wouldn't I want better treatment?"

"These soldiers are barbarians, young man. I'm afraid your condition is such that you might never recover. I'm amazed to find you still alive. Your powers of survival are strong. If you recover, it will only be so they can torture you more to make you talk. You must decide if you want that."

Gohan thought for a moment. There were things he needed to know, and maybe Dr. Thao could help. He tried to ignore his pain and continue talking. "Look, I had three friends, marines, who may have been captured. Are they here? Do you know anything about them?"

"No. There are no other prisoners that we know of. None have been put in with us. Other than that, we know very little."

Gohan realized Bob, Willie, and Oscar were probably dead. It looked like he was next, but he refused to make it easy on the enemy. They would have to work if they wanted him dead.

"I have a plan. It's the only thing I can think of—escape. Wouldn't it be easier to escape from the hospital than from here?"

Dr. Thao was amused by the young American's confidence. "Yes, it would, but it still won't be easy. It's probably impossible. You must realize that you probably won't recover enough to consider escaping. I can't say if you'll recover at all. At best, we might be able to soothe your pain and allow your body to rebuild itself, but you've lost a lot, brave friend. I can't offer much hope."

One of the men in the dungeon spoke to Dr. Thao. He listened, then turned to Gohan. "I'm curious. How would you escape?"

"There's plenty of time to figure that out, doc. I need to know if you can get me into the hospital. Can you begin working on me and heal me as much as you can? That's all I ask."

Dr. Thao was amazed by Gohan's courage. He was almost dead, yet he seized a possible plan as if he were whole and refused to accept defeat. He was young, but he possessed more courage than the doctor had ever seen before. He was impressed.

Dr. Thao was only forty-eight, but the beatings and ill treatment from those who took over his village drained him of almost all energy and life. He didn't know what happened to his wife and daughter, and he didn't want to find out. He accepted the fact that their lives were probably worse than his. He had given up all other hope and had simply tried to help his comrades in the dungeon. Other than that, he waited for his time to die.

Now, with the young American who had such need, strength,

and resolve, Dr. Thao became reenergized. He decided to help the young man. The worst thing that could happen would be for the KGB man to kill him for interfering, but Dr. Thao was already prepared for death.

He motioned Gohan to be quiet, because someone was coming to feed the prisoners. The lid above was moved slightly aside, and blinding sunlight streamed down. The guard lowered a large, steaming cauldron, then another that didn't steam, then he left.

The men moved to the center of the cold, damp prison, and Dr. Thao turned to Gohan. "It's time to eat, my friend. Be patient. I'll help. They call it soup, but it's just water with some cabbage cooked in it. They remove the cabbage and serve us the broth. Then there's water to drink. It's better than nothing."

Gohan watched each man take a small portion in his cup. Each man also had a spoon. After receiving their portion, each man moved to his place against the wall and began eating. All were as emaciated as the doctor.

Dr. Thao spoke to them in their native language, then brought his portion to Gohan and fed him. Gohan looked up in surprise.

"You eat, too," Gohan said. "You can't starve yourself for me. If you don't eat, then I won't, either."

The doctor smiled. He took a spoonful for himself, savored it, then gave a spoonful to Gohan. They finished the meal that way.

When they were done, the other prisoners came to the doctor and poured what little they had left into Gohan's cup. Sometimes, it was only a drop. Then they moved back to their places against the wall.

Gohan watched in amazement and was overcome by the gesture. The men didn't know him, yet each one, although he was starving, shared a small part of his insufficient meal. As Dr. Thao fed Gohan the remaining broth, Gohan suddenly understood something about humanity that he couldn't put into words.

When he finished, he tried to sit up again and failed. He turned toward the other men in the room, enduring the pain the movement brought, and told them, "Thank you, men."

Soon, the guards retrieved the two cauldrons and closed the

lid overhead. Dr. Thao brought his face close to Gohan to talk.

"My young friend, we have accepted you as one of us. That might not mean much to you, but it's important to us. You may consider yourself an honorary Hmong."

"It means a lot to me, doctor. Please tell your friends that I consider it the highest honor to be accepted as one of you."

Dr. Thao nodded and smiled.

"Doctor, what's the best you can do for me? If you convince Nikko-Witch the Russian to put me into the hospital, will he let you tend me? I'd like that if it's possible. What's the best you can promise? I'm very stubborn. Whatever you think the maximum healing I can achieve, I'll do better."

Dr. Thao smiled inwardly. If all the patients he tended over the years had shown the same determination to become well, he would have become the most successful doctor on earth. Though the possibility for healing the young man was almost zero, Dr. Thao realized that his attitude gave him a chance.

"Let me say this. If you believe you'll walk again, there's a chance you might. We have some treatments to soothe pain and allow whatever healing would naturally take place to do so. The body has a phenomenal way of healing itself under the right circumstances. I can assist in that process."

"What kind of time frame, doc?"

"Realistically?"

"Yes."

"Barring any major setbacks, in order to heal enough that you can think of attempting to escape, you need two or three months. Please understand I can't promise. Your situation is worse than any I've seen. We must recognize the possibility that you won't recover. Are you prepared for that?"

"Not for a moment, doc. You said two or three months minimum, right?"

"Yes."

"OK. Now what I have to say is important. Do I have your attention?"

"Yes."

"We have one week. If you can get me into that hospital, I have to escape in a week. If not, those perverts will set me back again. Can you do it?"

"No, son. I can't perform miracles. Only God can do that."

Gohan wasn't surprised by the doctor's response. He thought of how the admiral always talked about God being there for him whenever he asked

"OK, doc. If God decides to perform a miracle, can you assist Him so I can be ready to get out in a week?"

Again, Dr. Thao smiled. "Yes, young man, if God performs a miracle for you, I'll assist Him in any way I can."

"OK. What's the plan?"

Dr. Thao motioned for quiet so he could think. He'd considered several plans during his imprisonment, but he discarded them recently when he saw how quickly the health of he and his compatriots had deteriorated. He nodded slowly, then looked at Gohan. "I'll attempt to make an appointment with the KGB officer and will tell him you'll die unless you're brought into the hospital. I'll also say I believe you will recover, but you must have correct treatment. He'll know that I can perform that duty better than anyone else. He doesn't know my background, so I'll let him think my specialty is burns. He might let me treat you then. Please understand that I can't read his mind. He might choose to let you die."

"Suppose you tell him I was talking with you?"

"Hmmm. I don't know. I'm considered a bit of a rebel. He wouldn't think of me as someone who'd turn against another prisoner."

"Unless you didn't like Americans."

"I'll think about it. Let's hope it doesn't become necessary. Hopefully they want to interrogate you further, and that'll be enough reason for them to allow you into the hospital.

"There's one other thing. There's a young nurse assistant working at the hospital, another Hmong named Ka Moua. Her father is the headman of our village. He's with us in prison."

When Dr. Thao looked left, so did Gohan. He saw an older man nod slowly.

"Ka speaks no English. She's aligned with a group of villagers led by her brother, Cheu, who have created a small underground army."

"How'd you find out about that down here?"

"Because of our condition, they allow the nurse assistants to come down to minister to us and salve any festering wounds. The Russian doesn't know that Ka is one of the headman's family. She worked her way into the hospital so she could nurse us, then she began sharing information with me.

"I don't say that so you'll rely on her for help. That may not be possible. It depends on whether I have an opportunity to speak with her. Once she sees you, she'll tell her brother. It's important that this information remain secret. You can't tell anyone, or you'll endanger her life."

Gohan laid back his head and sighed. Pain was etched on his face. The conversation had taken his mind off the pain, which was good. He doubted he had much chance of escaping, either, but the admiral said that was what a man had to do to stay focused in such a situation. It seemed to work, too. He felt better after talking with the doctor.

When he thought how badly he was injured, keeping a positive attitude wasn't easy. Seeing his injuries was a shock, but the doctor said that the rest of his body was even worse. He refused to allow that to stop him. He needed to escape no matter what.

"OK, doc. It sounds like a plan. Let's get it executed."

"Please, son, try to rest. Your body needs that as much as anything. Depending on what happens in my meeting with the KGB officer, if he sees me, it might be important that we speak no longer."

"OK, doc. I understand. What happens to you if you do this? Does this create a problem?"

"No, son. I'm a doctor. They'd expect me to do this."

He was lying. If Gohan attempted to escape, the doctor would be killed. He knew that and decided it was still the right thing to do. He looked at the young man as he tried to rest.

When they first put Gohan in the dungeon, Dr. Thao tore

off the young man's undershirt and covered his wounds with it. Now that he was resting again, he adjusted the undershirt to cover as much of his wounds as possible, hoping to keep flies and insects away.

He moved away and took a sitting position against the wall. He never asked why the American was there, but it was likely the American wouldn't have answered that, anyway.

When he was certain Gohan was asleep, or appeared that way, Dr. Thao called up to the Pathet Lao guard and said he had information for the KGB man concerning the American.

After a few minutes, the guard lowered a ladder. Dr. Thao had trouble climbing it, but he eventually succeeded. Then he was escorted into the compound and led to Nikolai Nikolayevich's office.

Walking from the prison to the compound was a wonderful feeling. It was evening, and the sun was down, but there was still light and warmth. Dr. Thao enjoyed that.

He was quickly ushered into Nikolai's office and told to sit in a chair before the KGB man's desk.

"Yes, what is it, doctor?"

Fortunately, Dr. Thao had studied in Moscow and spoke passable Russian. "It is the American who was tossed into our pit. He's dying, comrade."

"What is that to you? Why should you care if he dies?"

"I'm a doctor, comrade. I care if anyone dies."

"How bad is he?"

"He has massive head injuries that will impair his ability to think or speak unless they're treated. He has extraordinary internal injuries from the beatings around his stomach and midsection. They, too, can be treated, but they are critically serious. All this must be done immediately, or he has no chance of survival."

Nikolai walked to the cupboard and took out a vodka bottle, then poured some into a glass and drank. "Has he said anything to you?"

The doctor was silent, hoping that was the right message.

Nikolai slammed his fist into the desk. "Doctor, you'll answer me! If you don't, I'll throw you back into that hole, and you will die with him!"

Dr. Thao paused, cleared his throat, and spoke. "He told me about the beatings and spoke of his friends. He wondered what became of them."

Nikolai paused and walked to the window, looking at the grassy clearing and the jungle beyond. The doctor had gotten more information from the American, without trying, than he had through massive torture. If he could learn something vital from Sergeant Rice, he might earn a quick release from that hateful assignment.

"What else did he say? Anything?"

"Please understand, comrade, he's almost dead. It's all he can do to talk at all. We didn't have a lengthy conversation."

"Do you think he'd continue speaking with you if he were better?"

Dr. Thao sighed and shook his head slightly. "I can't answer that, comrade, because he isn't better. My medical specialty is burn cases. I have the ability to treat him, and, possibly, bring about enough healing that he can converse with me. I'd enjoy that."

Nikolai finished his vodka and looked at the doctor, trying to read his face, but the man lowered his head. He didn't look very healthy himself.

"Doctor, it appears you need some treatment, too. Would you be able to treat the American in your condition?"

Dr. Thao smiled. "Doctors, comrade, are like soldiers. We don't stay home from work because of a headache. If he needs treatment, and you allow me to do that, I will be able to."

Nikolai was pleased. Perhaps he had gotten lucky. The doctor was playing into his hands without knowing it. He quickly formulated his plan.

"I have a deal to offer you, doctor. If I allow the American to be placed in the hospital and I allow you to treat him, there are two other things that will happen. I will allow you to regain some strength by feeding you better, but there's a price. I want information. He's obviously willing to talk to you. You learn what I want to know, and I'll let you save his life. Once he recovers, he's mine. What do you say?"

"I'm a doctor, Comrade Nikolayevich!" Dr. Thao feigned indignation. "Not an interrogator! I told you what he said. I'll continue to do that, but I won't conduct interrogations."

Nikolai was impressed by the man's integrity. It also assured him the request wasn't part of a trick.

"I repeat, doctor, if I put the American in the hospital with you in charge of him, you'll be under constant scrutiny from my office. If I tell you I want certain information, you'll attempt to get it for me. I won't undermine your integrity as a doctor, but neither will I let you undermine my ability to run this camp.

"That is all. You'll be sent for soon."

He called for a guard to escort the doctor outside. "Allow him to sit in the sun for a few minutes, and prepare a bed in the hospital. As soon as it's ready, prepare to move the American there. The doctor will supervise the move. Do as he says. That's all."

Nikolai couldn't have been more pleased. When he learned what the drunken soldiers had done to the American, he was enraged. He wanted information from the man, not to kill him outright. Now it looked as if he would still get what he needed despite the idiotic way the soldiers handled the prisoner.

Ka Moua was lucky again. She slipped into the jungle and began her jog back to her brother's camp on the nearby mountaintop. She had good news and was overjoyed to have been ignored by the KGB monster.

The run back to Cheu's camp was enjoyable. She arrived and met him only to learn he, too, had good news.

They walked into Cheu's tent, and he ordered a meal for his sister. Captain Baker and Vu Xiong were sent for, too.

When Captain Baker walked into the tent, Ka's eyes widened. She looked to her brother, who smiled and explained.

"This is Captain Baker of the United States Navy," Cheu said. "He and four other Americans—the three who were killed and the one you say is at Ban Na Lom—are here on a special mission.

He will help us attempt to rescue the other American and take our village back from the enemy."

Ka greeted Captain Baker, then turned to her brother in great excitement, explaining all she knew of the other American. Captain Baker saw her expression and heard the excitement in her voice. He forced himself to wait patiently.

When she finished talking, Cheu turned to Baker. "Captain, Ka see American, hospital. He bad." He pointed to the back of his head and then to his stomach. "Very bad."

Baker expected as much. Gohan was hurt badly. It would be difficult to learn what he needed to know from Cheu, because his English was poor. At least he understood more than he spoke, which helped. But close wasn't good enough. Baker needed to know for certain.

"Is the American injured badly?" he asked.

"Yes. Sister say yes."

"Will he live?"

Cheu asked his sister, who paused before answering. Ka looked at the captain and shrugged.

Baker didn't like the answer. He needed to tell Gohan that someone was coming for him. That would help build his confidence.

"Cheu, can she give him a message?" he asked.

Cheu turned to Ka, spoke rapidly, and was rewarded with another shrug. "Sister no English."

"Can she tell him one word?"

Cheu interpreted, and she nodded slowly.

"OK. The word is *admiral*. OK? Admiral?"

Cheu looked at him inquisitively. "Admer?"

"Ad-mer-ull." Baker repeated it slowly.

"OK. Ad-mer-ull."

"Excellent, Cheu."

Cheu spoke to Ka, who replied, "Am-oh-low."

Baker spent ten minutes instructing Ka in the proper pronunciation. Finally, he was satisfied. They finished their meal together.

Ka looked forward to the coming day, when she would learn

more about the American. Captain Baker and Cheu would begin creating a plan to release Gohan and any other prisoners. Ka hadn't had such a good day since she began working at the hospital.

Finally, all their work would pay off. She was excited about having two Americans help them, even though one was dying. She was happy that Dr. Thao had been allowed to reenter the clinic and help treat the American. She shared that news with Cheu, and he was encouraged, too. Dr. Thao was well liked.

Feeling tired, Ka left Cheu's tent, said good night, and retired to her own tent. For the first time in many days, she slept well.

Chapter 18
New Life

THOUGH HE AWOKE OFTEN THROUGHOUT THE NIGHT, GOHAN managed to get some sleep. The pain was too intense to sleep straight through. He had learned that his new friend had talked the Russian into putting him into the small hospital.

I guess they think they can get more information from me, he thought, *so they're gonna let me go to the hospital. Way to go, Nikko-Witch. Bad news—I'm still not talking to you. But the good news is in the meantime, I'm gonna improve enough to escape from this lousy place.*

He wondered how Dr. Thao did it. He must have convinced them that Gohan was dying.

Well, Dummy, that's what the doctor told you, wasn't it? The question is, was it true? Am I dying, or am I about to recover?

He opened his eyes and looked around. He wasn't in the dungeon. He realized he was in the hospital already. He knew that. He must have forgotten. He hoped he wasn't losing his mind. The guards hadn't been gentle when they brought him in. After what Gohan had done to their friends, that was understandable.

When they finally dumped him onto the hospital bed and left, he passed out. That was some time ago, and it was dark now. He guessed it was evening. He tried to raise his head to look around, but the pain was too intense. He moved enough to see the length of the room and what was on the other side, but he couldn't turn his head because of the pain.

It looked like there were ten beds on the other side of the room, six on his left, one directly across from him, and three to his right, so he assumed there were the same number on his side. He couldn't see to the far right side of the room, so he didn't know what, if anything, was beyond those three beds.

On his side, it appeared that the last bed was only a few feet from the exit door. He saw the outline of a guard sitting in a chair with his back to Gohan. By the way his head slumped, he was probably asleep. Only three of the ten beds on the other side were occupied, but, because of the darkness and the angle at which he lay, he couldn't see them clearly.

There seemed to be no staff around. It looked like it was the middle of the night. He was thirsty, but he couldn't do much about it. At least he'd been moved to the hospital. He wondered if that meant he'd be fed better. No, probably not. The hospital was run by Ivan the Terrible, not the Little Sisters of Mercy.

Again he tried to lift his head, hoping to see the entire room. He'd be in there for a while and wanted to know as much about it as possible. He wondered who the other patients were.

Seeing his surroudings was important enough that he had to force himself despite the pain. When he tried to move, though, the pain was too great. His head felt frozen in place.

The one thing I have going for me right now is time, he thought. *It won't be as much as I need, but it's a lot more than I expected.*

He wondered how long it would take before his head felt better, enabling him to look around. He needed knowledge so he could plan his escape. The sooner he knew what was going on, the sooner he could formulate his escape plan.

He was anxious to see Dr. Thao again and felt glad the doctor was out of the horrible dungeon, too. At least, that's what he remembered. He hoped that was correct. Hopefully, while he was treating Gohan, he'd be allowed to live somewhere other than that underground hell.

That wouldn't be like these barbarians, Davey Boy, he told himself. *At least the doc will have a little freedom and maybe some decent food.*

He hoped Dr. Thao would be able to give him the information he needed about the room. It was good the man spoke English. He could tell Gohan about the part of the room he couldn't see— what was outside the doorway, and what was on the other side of it. There was a lot he needed to know.

How often did the guards change shifts? Did they sleep at night like the current guard? How far was it from the hospital doorway to the jungle's edge? Was there a fence to climb? What about the underground guerilla movement the doctor mentioned? How good were they, and how close were they?

He had a lot of questions that needed answers. He felt, with Dr. Thao's help, he could learn them. Gohan felt excited about his prospects for escape. That was a good feeling. Like the admiral said, anything positive was good.

He began to understand more of what the admiral said earlier. Even though Gohan knew he was in bad physical condition, he was still alive. He was also in good spirits, because he took all the positives he had and created a game plan from them.

As he began to summarize his situation, he realized that escape was possible, but its success would depend on help from other areas. He had to be physically fit enough to make the attempt, which meant the doctor had to rehabilitate him fast. That gave him hope—another positive thing to think about. Then, of course, there was God. As bad as things were, he hadn't done a good job of praying like the admiral had told him.

I'm sorry, God. But my head's spinning. There's so much I need to know and so little time. He took a deep breath and tried to slow down his mind. *Thank You, God, for saving my life. I know I should be dead now. I'm assuming I'm alive because of You. There's so much I need to know about You. But without the admiral, I guess I can't learn it.*

Suddenly, he knew that wasn't true. He didn't know why but he knew he could learn more about God even without the admiral. *Here? But, how?*

And just as clearly as before, he knew that the answer was in prayer. He needed to pray.

OK, God. I'm willing, but I'm not even sure how to pray. I learned the Our Father and the Hail Mary as a kid. Is that what I do? The admiral just kinda talked to You. That made more sense. Yeah, so I guess that's what I do, too. OK. Here goes.

God, here I am in Ban Na Lom, Laos, nearly dead. First, I should've been killed when those soldiers captured me, especially after all I did to them. I must've killed three or four of them. Why didn't they kill me? You? Yeah, I guess so. So, You saved my life. Then, after all that torture, I'm really surprised I'm alive at all, that is if I am. Doc said it was pretty bad. Yeah, and guess what, Davey boy? Your only hope was to get to the hospital and look where you are. God, You did that, too? Yeah, I guess so. What did the admiral say, 'no matter what the situation was, God had a way out of it,' or something like that.

So, now I have to get healed enough to escape. Does that mean You're gonna make that happen, too? Oh, man, I hope so. God, I don't understand a lot, but I guess I know now that, just like the admiral said, You care for me even though I've been kind of a jerk all my life. Wow!

I'm alive because of God.

He took a deep breath again. The pain was still there, if not worse. But, he sure felt better.

If he saw Dr. Thao in the morning, he'd talk to him. *Man, I hope so*, he thought. *Doc, I need you here. I have a lot of questions and very few answers. Maybe you don't know them, either, but you can get 'em. Then I can make an escape plan. We can do it, doc—you, me, and God. I can't wait to see you.*

He was planning already, but he couldn't write anything down. Fortunately, he had a sharp mind and good memory. He could do it, and he looked forward to it.

Doc, I hope you have something for the pain, he thought. *It's so bad, I can hardly think. Every inch of my body hurts worse than anything I ever felt. I need relief.*

He wondered what was happening back home, and whether he had been on the mission five or six days. He had already lost track of time. Realizing Sumi was probably over her illness made him feel better. He hated leaving when she was ill. Childhood illnesses didn't usually last long, at least not when he was a kid. Still, he had a little fear in the back of his mind, because he wasn't back home in America. He couldn't call good ol' Dr. Green and know everything would be fine.

Come on, Gohan, he encouraged himself. *That's silly, and you know it. Dr. Kentsu's a good doctor, and Okinawa's a civilized island. They have medicine as good as America's. Look at Dr. Thao. Here I am, lyin' in a makeshift hospital in an enemy prison camp in the jungle of a foreign country, and I meet a doctor who graduated from UCLA. He's the reason I'm still alive. Well, of course, God, too. Sumi's not in prison camp, and Okinawa's not a jungle. Get a grip.*

He was glad he thought that out. Sumi would be OK. Knowing Keiko and how lonely she'd be without him, she probably had Sumi in bed with her, snuggling up as they slept like babies. He smiled at the thought.

Keiko said they would move back to her father's estate, even though it wouldn't be for long. It might be longer now that Gohan was captured. He was glad she didn't know the truth about his situation. That would have made her life very difficult. No one, not even the admiral, knew his circumstances, so no one could tell her. That was comforting, too, in a morbid sort of way.

He tried to turn to a more comfortable position but couldn't. The pain in his head was terrible. It didn't seem to be focused there anymore. His neck, back, and face hurt. The pain in his legs and midsection throbbed with unbelievable intensity. He wondered how he managed to get any sleep at all. Maybe he hadn't. He might have just passed out from the pain.

God, there has to be a way to control this pain! Please!

He forced his mind to wander and tried to keep busy. What

was he thinking about earlier? Oh, yes! Sumi. And the time. It was five days. He thought so, anyway.

That meant the time for their pickup was past. He wondered if General Winthrop and General Mancini sent a team in to get them. His last messages told them the three marines had been killed or captured, and he still didn't know for certain. He added he and the admiral were going to look for them, promising to stay in touch.

Of course, he hadn't. What would they think? Did the admiral dig up the radio and send another message? He doubted the man knew Morse code. Suppose the rescue team came after five days and picked up the admiral, then left? Would they do that? He didn't know.

He didn't think the admiral would leave him there, so what did that mean? If they received his last message, they probably wouldn't come. They'd wait for another message. Would they assume that no further messages meant something happened to Gohan? Probably, they would. General Winthrop had said that if anything went wrong with the mission, the U.S. would destroy all records and disavow any knowledge of it.

So, no one was coming for him. He didn't know if the admiral was even alive. That meant escape was up to him.

OK, he told himself. *Now you know. You're on your own. That's fine. You can do it, Davey boy. You and God. Don't be afraid. Stop looking at negatives. There are too many of those. Look at the positives. Thanks, admiral. The stuff you told me sure helps. OK. What do I do next?*

He had to escape, so that's what he would concentrate on. First, he had to learn how to move and walk again. He had to move around, learn his surroundings, and figure out how to get out alive. Time was short, so he had to begin immediately.

Gohan took a deep breath, pushed down with both hands against the thin mattress, and forced himself up off the bed. Pain shot through every square inch of his body. As difficult as movement was, his emotions reached a joyful high as he felt himself lifting off the bed.

Wow! How about that, doc? It's a shame you aren't here to see this, he thought.

Hours earlier, he couldn't bear to see himself. He wanted to shout "Hallelujah!" but couldn't. Movement was painful, but it could be done.

Then his head seemed to burst with even greater pain, and he toppled to the floor, unconscious.

Dr. Thao awoke early, excited about the upcoming day. The young American's brashness and confidence had renewed the doctor's spirit. It was possible that all he would do would put off the inevitable. The poor young man was wounded so badly, it was almost impossible to imagine putting him back together. If he lived, he would, at best, be confined to a wheelchair for the rest of his life. Even that would never happen unless he escaped. Then he still needed correct medication and treatment.

The American's future was bleak, but there was no reason for the doctor to feel any guilt. Dr. Thao hadn't offered the young man false hope. He told him the truth about his condition, but the American refused to accept it.

Just being allowed to climb out of that pit and walk on the grass, feeling the day's warmth against his bruised, starved body, gave the doctor a ray of hope, too. He assumed he would be fed better, too. If they wanted the American to live, they had to keep the doctor healthy, too.

That idea brought the lovely scent of life back to him. He'd given up on survival and had decided to do what he could for his fellow prisoners until he died, probably from starvation. He assumed the worst for his attractive wife and teenage daughter. If they weren't already dead, their lives were far worse than his. He tried not to think about that.

Suddenly, he felt hope again and didn't know what to do about it. He didn't want to raise his hopes too high, because the American might die at any moment. If he did, Dr. Thao would return to the dungeon and would die there. If he succeeded in helping the man and he began to recover, the Russians would torture him again. If he were as stubborn as he appeared, he'd be tortured badly. How would Dr. Thao feel about that?

If he succeeded enough to enable the man to escape, would the guards blame him for it? He shook his head. He was a doctor and made a conscious choice to bring healing and comfort to others. Now, as he approached his own death, God gave him another chance to practice medicine.

That was how he would approach it. He would put every effort into rehabilitating the man, based on his stated desire to escape within one week. He wouldn't think about anything else.

Still, he didn't have a plan to follow. He'd never experienced anything as difficult in all his years practicing medicine. What could he do for the young man? His chances of healing enough to enable him to escape in seven days were zero.

He had to check what supplies were available at the hospital. He bought a large supply of cantharis tincture, which included properties that would help the injuries to the American's midsection. It would be difficult to apply due to the nature of his wounds, but that was the right place to start. And he would reset the broken bones, if there were any. He didn't know that yet.

He would need Ka for an assistant. She'd be helpful for many reasons, one of which was that the American would trust her once he knew about her. Dr. Thao would have to watch the applications closely. If healing seemed to be occurring, he'd begin the rehabilitation process immediately.

He nodded to himself. If there was even the slightest glimmer of hope, that was what he'd do. He didn't know why the American was in Laos or how he came, but he vowed to do everything in his power to help him escape. The rest was up to God. At least he could promise the man he'd be healthier when they finished with him than when he started out.

It wouldn't be easy, but he looked forward to the challenge. He owed something to the man for giving him back his hope. He was such a young man, in his early twenties at best. He wondered if he had a wife and children.

Dr. Thao couldn't promise him a long life, but he'd give him the best treatment he could find.

Someone grabbed Gohan. It felt like more than one person.

Oh, no, he thought. *They're taking me back to the interrogation room. Oh, God, I'm still dying from the last beating. What happened to the hospital? I thought I was in there. I thought doc would work on me.*

The soldiers all looked like copies of Nikko-Witch, and they constantly kicked Gohan.

How can they continue this? he wondered. *There's nothing left down there.* "Ohhh, God!" he screamed aloud. *What are they doing, trying to break me in two?*

Two or three at a time kicked him. The big Russian kept chugging vodka until it ran down his beard and onto his chest.

"Go ahead, you jerks!" Gohan shouted. "Not one piece of me will talk to you!"

Someone shook him and slapped his face.

Is that all the harder these wimps can hit? Gohan wondered.

Startled, he awoke. When he opened his eyes, he saw Dr. Thao's tender face smiling warmly at him. He spoke quietly so no one else could hear him.

"You were having a nightmare," Dr. Thao explained. "You're all right now. You're in the hospital, and we'll start treating you. With God's help, we'll bring about your healing. You fell from the bed, but you're fine now."

Gohan felt perspiration rolling down his face. *A nightmare? I thought for sure I was back in that room, being beaten to death.* He looked up as tears welled up in his eyes. "Thanks, doc."

What a startling change from seeing the faces of madmen who wanted to kill him to seeing the kind face of a starved Hmong doctor. Tears of relief rolled down Gohan's cheeks.

A nurse, a young girl from her appearance, stepped out from behind the doctor to gently wipe Gohan's face with a wet cloth. She was pretty. The moment he made eye contact, she looked

away. Gohan assumed she was fifteen or sixteen. When she finished wiping his face, she disappeared behind Dr. Thao again.

"Well, young man, since we'll be spending a lot of time together,
would you care to give me a name to call you?" Dr. Thao asked.

Gohan thought for a moment. The only thing he'd said to
Nikko-Witch was his name, rank, and serial number, so he'd stick
with that. "David."

The doctor smiled. It was good to have a name to go with a face.
Everything became more personal. That was important, because
Dr. Thao and Ka would become very personal with David in the
next few days.

"David, we're going to treat you with a cream to reduce inflam-
mation and pain and to increase your body's ability to heal itself.
At the moment, that's all we're doing. We'll treat you several times
a day, but it will be painful, because that part of your body is
extremely sensitive. You must endure the pain.

"Your head wounds are serious but not life-threatening. They
will require surgery, but, because of your condition, I can't give
you anesthetic. Do you understand?"

Gohan thought for a moment, then shrugged. "What's a little
pain, doc? I'm an expert at that now."

"I'm sorry, David. You don't need additional pain, but it's
important that we move ahead. I'll work on your head later today.
It'll be more painful than what you experience now, but there's no
alternative. It can't wait. We'll help you through it."

Gohan smiled, though he didn't want to think about more pain.
He wondered how much one person could endure. He'd know
soon. "OK, doc. Just remember, we've got only one week. I didn't
expect this to be easy for either of us. Do what you have to."

Dr. Thao motioned Ka to wipe Gohan's face again. As she did,
the doctor lifted the man's head to inspect his injuries. That gave
him the chance to speak into Gohan's ear.

"It's important, David," he whispered, "that other than when
I treat you, we don't spend time together, especially when the
guards are here and awake. There will be times when we can
speak, but we must be careful. They've told me I'll be sent back to

the dungeon each evening. I also have the responsibility of working with the Soviet doctor, helping him with other patients in the clinic.

"The girl is Ka Moua. She's the one I mentioned earlier. She speaks no English but will take good care of you. You can trust her, but don't try speaking to her. That would endanger her."

"Ka?"

"Yes. She's Hmong. Her brother, Cheu Moua, is the underground guerilla leader I mentioned.

"We must turn you onto your stomach, David. It will be very uncomfortable, but we have to do it. Then Ka will begin cleaning your head wounds. That, too, will hurt. We will apply salve to the wounds before sewing and wrapping them. Then we have to turn you over again. I know this will create terrible pain, but we must do it. Then we can apply the salve to your legs and midsection.

"After that, I want you to rest. The pain will make that difficult. Nevertheless, that's our program. Please try to get used to it. Rest is an important part of the healing process.

"OK, David. We'll turn you over now. Try to relax."

Yeah. Easy for you to say, he thought.

Suddenly, he realized that the emaciated old doctor, who didn't weight even one hundred pounds, and the pretty Hmong girl, who weighed even less, intended to turn him over. He weighed 190 pounds, although he probably weighed less because of his condition. Yet, they had to move him as delicately as possible. No one else came to help.

This is great, Gohan thought. *I've got Don Knotts, who's starving to death, trying to move me, with Olive Oyl helping.*

It was difficult, but they did it. It was painful for Gohan to lay on his stomach. He tried not to move, because any movement caused extreme pain to his midsection.

He felt them touching his head and realized he was fortunate to be in such circumstances and still receive special treatment. He looked forward to being healed and attempting his escape. He thought about what happened so far.

Let me get this straight, he thought. *We've got a nurse named*

Ka and her brother is Chew Moo-uh. He smiled. Well, they're probably saying the same thing about me. What kind of stupid name is David?

Gohan wanted to talk to the doctor and ask questions, which he would do as soon as they finished operating and turned him over again. Once he knew more, he could begin planning his escape.

The opportunity to work as a doctor seemed to have given Dr. Thao new life. The change was obvious. He was dramatically different from when they'd been in the dungeon.

Gohan wondered about Ka. She was very sad. Perhaps the Soviets killed her family, though doc said her father was in the dungeon. As pretty as she was, it was hard to tell what had been done to her.

He was glad to hear she belonged to a guerilla group. It was nice to know the Americans weren't fighting the war alone. He wondered what their plans were. He had a lot of information the general would want to know. That was why he had to escape. It was unlikely the U.S. knew what Gohan knew. What could he do with it? The answer was nothing. He needed to escape and take the information with him.

After an hour, Dr. Thao and Ka moved Gohan slightly, but they didn't roll him onto his back as he first assumed. Instead, the doctor placed a bag of utensils on the stand beside the bed and sat down to speak quietly with Gohan.

"David, I changed my mind. We'll do the surgery now. Relax. It will take about an hour."

Ka gave him a thick towel to bite on. As hungry as he was, he would have preferred an apple. He tried to keep his mind active, not wanting to think about them cutting into his head.

He wondered why no one had any information about the missing marines. The prisoners didn't know anything, and the good guerillas apparently didn't, either. Doc didn't, and probably Ka didn't. Maybe the marines were never brought back to the camp. If that was the case, they were dead.

Gohan felt doc working on his head and bit hard into the towel. Doc was right. The pain was intense. Tears rolled down

Gohan's face. He bit down harder, closed his eyes, and tried to will himself past the throbbing. It felt like someone was stabbing his head with a knife.

Well, what did you expect? he asked himself. *That's probably what he's doing.*

He thought about his family and pictured little Sumiko sitting in the rocking chair in his lap. She still had the sickly look he remembered from the last time he saw her. He couldn't imagine her well no matter how hard he tried. He enjoyed daydreaming about her, though, even with her tired, feverish face.

He rocked her and held her close. Keiko came and sat beside them, laying her head against his other shoulder. He remembered the song he sang to her before he left.

How appropriate, he thought.

He hadn't anticipated anything like what he currently felt and wondered if Sumi would remember the song if he died.

Sumi, I love you, honey. God, please don't take me from her.

Sumi was sweet in his dreams. As he sang, she smiled radiantly.

Even after we part
Should fate have it so,
We will be like flowers
Linked together, never to be torn apart.

He bit down harder, keeping his eyes closed. Somehow, that made it easier.

Keiko, Sumiko, I'll get out of here. I promise. I'll be back. These Russians and Viets aren't big enough to keep me from you. I promise I'm coming back.

Sumi started crying. He picked her up and laid her against his shoulder, and Keiko leaned over to kiss his lips. He felt his daughter's warmth against his neck. How he loved her and wanted her to be well. Her tears dried, and she smiled as he sang to her once again. He didn't know why he sang the famous old Okinawan poem, but that's what he heard in his reverie.

Nami nu kwim tumari.
Kajinu kwim tumari.
Shu-I tin ga nashi
Mium chi ugami.
Waves, be still,
And quiet, wind.
The king from Shuri comes
And we must pay him reverence.

The pain was terrible. What are they doing to me? Ohhh! There it is again! he thought.

What's that? Sixty-two? How long can this go on? When will these drunks get enough? Why aren't their legs tired? How much more can I take?

"David?" Dr. Thao called. "David? You're having another night-mare. It's OK, son. We're here and taking care of you."

Gohan opened his eyes and saw Dr. Thao and Ka. Then he began shaking. Tears rolled down his face. Ka wiped them with a damp cloth, and Dr. Thao smiled.

OK, David thought, *where are we now? What's going on? Oh, yeah. I'm having my head operated on.*

Gohan was tired. Despite the excruciating pain, he felt he could sleep. Doc finished sewing the stitches, then he and Ka turned Gohan over onto his back, which was much more comfortable.

Ka gently placed a pillow under his head and propped it up slightly. That hurt, but so did everything else. His head felt worse than before, but it was OK, because he was on the right track now. He could handle it.

Ka wiped his face again. Her eyes refused to look directly at him. There was a very sad story in them that he wasn't sure he wanted to hear. Thinking about that ended his drowsiness.

Doc pulled the thin, green sheet back and removed the damp, bloody cloth from the center of Gohan's body. Ka gasped, moaned, and turned away quickly. Gohan didn't see her for a while. Doc applied the cream. That, too, was unbelievably painful.

"OK, doc, now that you've had a chance to play around with me, how bad is it? As bad as you first thought?"

"No, not as bad at all," Dr. Thao answered. "You have some fractured ribs which will heal, but no other broken bones. That's wonderful news. The major problem is the beating you took to your midsection. As I said before, it will take a long time to heal. You'll have to be patient."

That was good news. No, that was great news. He could go forward with his plan.

"Doc," Gohan whispered, "there are things I need to know about the layout of the hospital. You're the only one who can tell me."

"David," he whispered back, "I'll stand so no one can see you talking. They can see me, but I won't reply. Talk slowly and quietly. I'll listen, but I can't speak. Understood?"

Gohan nodded, and doc shifted position. Gohan wondered who doc was shielding him from. He waited until doc began working on his stomach before asking, "Is my head better? It sure doesn't feel like it."

Dr. Thao smiled and nodded.

"Good. I'm trustin' you on that. I need to know the complete layout of this hospital—where every bed and door is, where the guards are, where the supply cabinets are. How often do the guards change their posts?

"Then I need to know the layout outside the building. How close are the other buildings? How far is the jungle? Is there a fence? If so, how high? Where are the guards outside? How often do they change their posts? You said earlier there was a spotlight. When does it come on and where do they shine it? How often?

"I need a weapon, too, probably a knife. It has to be sharp, but I don't want it until the last moment.

"How far is it to the guerilla group? How can I find them? Can we tell them I'm coming? Daggonit, doc! Do you have to be so rough? I'd like to have another kid someday."

Then he saw Ka returning and guessed she'd become ill when she saw his condition. *Everyone knows what I look like except me,* he thought. *Great. I'll probably get ready to escape, look down, throw up, and be recaptured.*

Doc spoke to Ka, explaining the procedure they'd follow for the patient. He patted Gohan's shoulder, nodded without speaking, and left.

Ka continued the work. She still didn't look at Gohan, but he noticed tears rolling down her face as she tended him. Was she that sensitive, or were his injuries that ugly?

Ka had never seen anything like it before. Dr. Thao warned her the American was hurt worse than anything she had seen in her experience, but she still hadn't been prepared for what she saw when he uncovered the young soldier. It embarrassed her that she became sick. But, with all she had seen in the war, she knew her embarrassment would fade soon.

She knew enough from her brother and the other American that it was important that David recover. She gently applied the cream to his affected areas, careful not to scrape or scratch, knowing how painful the treatment was.

There was so much damage to his body. She only hoped Dr. Thao could help him. She was self-conscious around him because of his condition, but mostly because she felt dirty over what happened with the KGB man.

That was one reason she didn't looked at David. It wasn't the way of her people to make eye contact, anyway. If she did, and he looked at her, she wouldn't know what to do except blush. She smiled weakly to herself and continued working on him.

Suddenly, she remembered the other American gave her a word to say. What was it? Umm-berr-ohh? That sounded like it. No, it was Add-merr-ohh.

She didn't want to say it at the moment, partly because she didn't want to look up and see him while nursing him. She'd tell him later. That would be soon enough.

Ka finished spreading the cream and carefully laid damp cloths over Gohan's bruised and wasted body, then pulled the green sheet up over him. Without looking directly at him, she bowed slightly, letting him know she was finished and was pleased to serve him. Then she left and joined the Russian doctor, who was tending an elderly village woman.

Gohan shook his head as she departed. *What's with her? Doesn't she know I'm on her side?*

He watched her walk away and looked as far as he could to each side of his bed. He still couldn't move his head much. Doc warned him against trying too soon, especially after they had just worked on it. It didn't appear there was much going on, anyway.

He summarized the morning's events in his mind and recognized that he had accomplished a lot. His head injury had been taken care of, they were working on his midsection, and he had given Dr. Thao a list of information he needed. He also met the liaison with the guerrilla group. And, of course, the wonderful news from Dr. Thao that he had no broken bones.

Thanks, God. You really are something. No wonder the admiral feels the way he does about You. How do I get to know about You the same way he does? I think I'd like that.

His plan was moving forward nicely. According to Dr. Thao, Gohan had to rest. Later, they would return to proceed with round two of his rehabilitation.

He decided to obey the doctor's orders. Without the enjoyable attention, the pain became more prevalent. He tried to think about good, peaceful, lovely, and wonderful things. Maybe that would help him sleep.

He remembered the last time he and Keiko went to Zamami Island, before Sumi was born. They enjoyed the day a lot and talked about it afterward, almost like a vacation to a faraway place, even though it wasn't that far.

They sat on the beach and watched the beautiful parrots for hours. He relived the entire day, knowing it would be enjoyable again.

At that moment, a passerby would have seen the slightest hint of a smile on Gohan's face as he closed his eyes and drifted off into reverie.

Chapter 19
To Rescue or Not to Rescue

THE PRETTY LIEUTENANT CHECKED IN THE IMPRESSIVE LIST of VIPs as they gathered for another top-secret meeting. The same two generals and the CIA man were back, but a new general joined the meeting. She looked at the list carefully, hoping to see that cute sergeant again, then felt disappointed when she saw his name missing.

She sighed. Her phone rang.

"207, Lieutenant Walsh. Yes, sir. Certainly, sir. Right away, sir. You're welcome, sir."

General Marshal Winthrop, Air Force Far East commander, sat in the center of the group. To his left sat Marine General Emilio Mancini, then CIA Assistant Director Kenneth Damsteegt. To General Winthrop's right was Retired General Adam Horring from the National Security Agency.

There was a knock at the door, and the lieutenant brought in a tray of coffee for the men, then left quickly.

"I think all of you know our deal fell through," General Winthrop began. "Now we have some decisions to make."

"What happened, general?" Damsteegt asked.

"We don't know. The first three days of the mission, everything went smoothly, and we received excellent information. It wasn't good news for us, but those men did their jobs.

"It looks like the Soviets have joined forces with Ho and will back him in this Vietnam thing. They're getting good information on what our boys are doin' there in Laos. They're creating a trail down the border there for Ho to get into South Vietnam. That's their main thrust. We know it now. The question is, can we stop it without getting involved in the war? Anyway, all that information has already been passed on. Then came a new transmission from Gohan, not Gomez. It was pretty standard info, except he added an emergency-only coded message indicating that the three marines—Gomez, Keller, and Bowie—were MIA. Evidently, they never returned after their transmission of the previous day.

"Gohan said he was shutting down the radio, then he and Captain Baker would look for the missing men. They said they'd report back in twenty-four hours, but they never did. Now we don't know what happened."

"They had clear instructions not to shut down and try to save their friends' butts," General Horring said. "That's bothersome."

"Yeah, to a degree. Remember, Gohan wouldn't have made that decision. That was Baker's. I'm pretty comfortable with anything Baker wants to do. If he decided to shut down, it was probably the right decision.

"Now maybe they knew there was no way we could come in to get 'em, because the situation was too hot. They might have decided to look for the marines, because there wasn't anything else they could do. Heck, we don't know. We weren't there. We chose the best boys we had, so we have to go with their decisions. Right?"

"I agree," General Mancini said. "You have to believe in your people when you put 'em in a position like that. You know when you go in it might blow up in your face. The question now is, what should we do?"

Damsteegt stood and began pacing. "General, you made it clear to the leaders of this mission that in the event something like this happened, we would disavow any knowledge of this. We have to do it. This mission is history. We got what we went in there for, so in that sense, the mission succeeded. As hard as it might be to quit now, we have to write those guys off and move on."

"I'll be darned if we do that, Kenneth!" General Mancini said. "You don't take your best men, put 'em in a dangerous situation to get what you need, then walk out when they need you! That may be how the CIA operates, mister, but we don't do it that way in the U.S. Marines."

Damsteegt, stunned by the general's outburst, looked around and saw he was alone with three multistar generals. "OK. You talk. I'll listen."

Mancini shook his head in disgust. "Bull. Why'd we have to meet here? I need a drink, and I know there isn't anything in those cabinets."

"Emilio, you're a marine," General Winthrop said. "This is an Air Force base, and I'm the commander. This is as important a military meeting as we've had in years. Wait just a minute."

Winthrop walked to the counter and picked up the phone. "Lieutenant Walsh, this is General Winthrop. I'd like you to bring us a bottle of J and B Scotch, a bottle of Jack Daniels whiskey, and a bottle of club soda with four glasses. On the double."

He listened for a moment. "What? Honey, I don't care where you get it. Call Brigadier General Haskins and tell him to get it for us if you have to. We want it right now. Thank you."

The other two generals laughed as he hung up.

"How'd you know I like J and B and soda, Marshal?" General Horring laughed.

"Because I've had important meetings with you before, Adam. We need to get together on this thing. We can't be on different sides of the fence. Emilio, I agree with you. Those boys went into a tough situation, and it obviously became a lot tougher after they arrived. They did what we asked, and now they're in trouble. We can't turn our backs on them. Adam?"

"Absolutely, Marshal. No offense, Kenneth. We aren't trying to gang up on you. We're lifers in the military, and loyalty means a lot. There's protocol, which you brought up, but that's only for a worst-case scenario. We aren't at that point yet. Marshal, do we have any other substantive information?"

"No. There's been nothing since Gohan's last transmission. I'd like to tell you something about Captain Baker, the team leader. If he thought goin' in for those marines would endanger the lives of the rescue crew, he'd never ask for 'em. That's the kind of man he is. Maybe that's what happened."

"If they haven't contacted us since," Mancini said, "we have to assume one of two things. Either their equipment was found, and they can't reach us anymore, or they were captured or killed. We still don't have information about the three marines. Daggonit!"

There was a knock at the door, and General Horring answered.

"Come in, Lieutenant," General Winthrop said. "How'd you find the stuff so fast?"

"Well, sir," Lieutenant Walsh said with a smile. "General Hastings keeps a supply in a locked cabinet in this building. He uses it for meetings, too. Since it's for you, sir, I'm sure he won't mind."

Winthrop laughed. "You didn't call to ask first?"

"No, sir."

"Good. Tell that crotchety so-and-so we enjoyed his booze, and we're sorry we couldn't drink any more of it."

The lieutenant left the men. She thoroughly enjoyed pilfering the boss' liquor supply. Not many people liked him.

Mancini swirled the Jack Daniels in his glass, sipped, sighed, and set the glass down on the glass-topped table. "I have a suggestion."

"Go ahead, Emilio," Winthrop said.

"We don't have to prepare for the worst. Kenneth already mentioned that. If all the men are dead, God rest their souls, then we have no alternative but to deny the mission and any knowledge of it. Marshal and I know what to do to create cover stories for the deaths. We don't need to worry about that, because that scenario's pretty well set.

"What we need to do is plan for at least some of them still being alive. If that's the case, we need to extract them. There are two ways to do it. We can go in now and take our chances, which isn't the best idea even if you have to try it in war sometimes, or we wait until they contact us again. Then the information they send will determine what move we take.

"If we decide to go in right away, we have some quick planning ahead. We need to determine when and how fast we go in. Do we go in today or tomorrow, or should we wait, buy time, and devise a better plan? If we go now, we have to plan for that.

"As I see it, there's not much sense worrying about anything else until those issues are decided. Do you understand?"

"Absolutely, Emilio," Horring said. "We aren't arguing that. It's more comfortable to set a time period and then go in. That gives us time to prepare better, and it also gives Baker and Gohan time to call us if they can."

Winthrop nodded. "I like it, boys. The last thing we want to do is go in there and botch somethin' up that those boys have cookin'. If they're in a bad situation, we don't want to wait long, either. How long, Emilio?"

General Mancini looked at Damsteegt, who nodded. The general had fought in two wars and was wounded three times. Although he'd never been captured or spent time in a prison camp, he knew plenty of soldiers who had. He also had a wealth of military experience. He knew Captain Baker was experienced in war and surviving as a prisoner. Mancini hoped that if the men were captured, it would be easier for them than during an officially declared war.

Looking up, Mancini saw Damsteegt pacing again, then he turned to General Winthrop. "As much as I agree that we don't want to upset anything Baker and Rice are doing, we still have to assume the worst. We don't know how they're being treated, but they sure won't get milk and cookies each night. We don't want to wait too long."

"Wait a minute, Emilio," Horring said. "If we think those boys are POWs and we send in a rescue team, we could stir up something that'll need a lot more authority than we have in this room."

Damsteegt walked to the counter, poured more scotch, added a little water, and swirled the mixture. After sipping, he looked at the three generals. "I've been staying quiet on purpose. I can't argue military strategy with you. That's your game. However, there's something we have to keep in mind, and that's the nature of the situation over there. Adam, you're right in what you said. That area's a volcano, waiting to blow, and we might be an inch away from war right now. As a nation, we're already preparing for that.

"We hope we won't be pulled into their civil war, but, if it goes that way, we're ready. We have a lot at stake. Let's suppose we can somehow calm the storm and get out of this mess without going to war with North Vietnam. Can you imagine what will happen if we send a rescue team into Laos without knowing if there's anyone alive to be rescued? What if we get in there and find ourselves in a skirmish with the North Vietnamese or the Soviets?

"I'm not saying we should leave those men to fry, but we need to be very careful before we act. Jumping too fast might be the wrong move. Adam was right, too. We need time to get approval on this."

"I hear you, Kenneth," Horring said. "He's right, men. What do you say?"

"Yeah, daggonit. I know he's right," Winthrop said. "I guess we'd better pull back a bit. We don't have to scrap our plans, but we need to postpone them a little while still preparing a way to get those boys out. Right?"

"Yes," Mancini said. "We need to have a team ready to go to Laos at a moment's notice. We might take the two considerations and combine them. We prepare a plan to rescue Baker and Rice and have a team in place and ready to take off within minutes of a phone call, but we don't implement the plan until we hear from either Baker or Rice.

"In the meantime, we need Ike's approval. That's hard, but Kenneth's right. If it turns out that we decide to go in anyway, we'll be prepared for that, too. For now, let's organize a rescue plan and get a team ready. While we do that, we can wait for Ike's word."

"Ike's been there, Emilio," Winthrop said. "We all know he'll approve."

They nodded. General Horring would brief the national security advisor and the president and get their approval. Assuming they said yes, Generals Winthrop and Mancini would formulate the rescue plan and gather a team to implement it.

The men finished their drinks and left the building. As Lieutenant Walsh cleaned up the room, putting everything away so General Hastings wouldn't know what happened, she wondered one more time what happened to the cute sergeant.

Chapter 20
Final Preparation

EVERYTHING WAS GOING ACCORDING TO PLAN. THE ONLY problem was it looked like it would take six months, not six days. Gohan wasn't disappointed, though, and still felt confident everything would work.

Dr. Thao gave him the necessary information. There were ten beds on the far side of the room, with eight on Gohan's side. At his far right was the doctor's station. The Russian doctor had his own office where he spent most of his time, usually asleep when he wasn't working. He liked to walk in the courtyard in the early evening, but he spent the rest of his time in that little room alone. Dr. Thao said he was writing a book.

On Gohan's side at the same end of the room were four wooden cabinets filled with supplies. The main exit door was at the far end of the room. There was a door at the other end, but it was always locked.

There was only one guard. When he wasn't patrolling, he sat in a chair on Gohan's side of the doorway so he could watch what happened outside the room. That made sense. The Russians wouldn't be worried about anyone in the hospital, just people trying to get in. Fortunately, the guard couldn't see Gohan's bed from his chair. Unfortunately, most of the guards spent their time walking around during the day and early evening. The middle of the night, however, was the best time for him to escape, because the guards were often asleep in the chair.

There were two steps down from the hospital floor to the ground outside. That might be difficult for Gohan, but at least he knew what to expect.

Once outside, the tower was in full view. During the day, the two guards didn't do much, but they were highly alert at night. One used the spotlight, sweeping it across the length of the fence, then over the open ground between the jungle edge and the compound, then on to the front of the hospital. That was probably why the guard kept his chair back from the doorway.

From there, the spotlight swept the rest of the compound. The full sweep took five to six minutes. Although two guards had been stationed in the tower during the day, recently that was changed to only one, but there were always two at night. Gohan assumed that Nikko-Witch was very paranoid.

Once out of the hospital door, Gohan would have to negotiate the steps and reach the side of the hospital before the spotlight returned. Because of the angle of the hospital, he couldn't be seen if he stayed against the side, or so Dr. Thao thought.

Gohan wouldn't be able to stay there for long. Guards were posted at the end of the compound all the time, because someone had been seen running into the jungle. There were also guards in the village, but they wouldn't be any trouble at night.

Ammunition was stored at that end of the compound. Gohan didn't know if that information was useful, so he filed it in his mind for later. From the side of the hospital, he would have to wait for the spotlight to pass him again, then he had sixty or more yards to dash to reach the fence. When he was in high school, he ran the hundred-yard dash in just over ten seconds, but he couldn't run much anymore. He couldn't even walk. He assumed those issues would be resolved before he left.

Once he reached the fence, he would use his knife to slice

through it and crawl under, then he would head for the mountain to meet Ka's brother. That assumed someone would hand him a knife. Dr. Thao hadn't said anything more about that, and Gohan made a mental note to ask again.

So far, Dr. Thao had been amazing. Gohan was sure he would find a weapon for him.

His first five days in the hospital were both great and terrible. The treatments Dr. Thao and Ka gave Gohan worked wonderfully. He felt the burning sensation slowly subsiding. Healing took its place, and his head was better, too. On a scale of one to ten, his pain went from a ten to about an eight. Unfortunately, that was only when he lay perfectly still, while he was being treated by Ka's tender touch, or was asleep. The rest of the time, Gohan was on an incredibly strenuous exercise regimen that more than made up for the lowered pain level. Dr. Thao said Gohan's chances of being able to walk within one week were a million to one, and then only if he rehabilitated at a rate only an insane person would consider.

Gohan did sit-ups that felt like someone was sliding a knife through his middle. The first day in the hospital, when Dr. Thao and Ka came back to treat Gohan's wounds again, he told the doctor he wanted to start rehabilitation as soon as possible.

"Whatever it takes, doc, is what we need to do," Gohan said. "I'm leaving in a week. You need to work on me with that in mind."

Doc took him at his word. After the evening treatment on Gohan's first day, Dr. Thao started him on an excruciatingly painful workout program.

"David, I'll hold your knees. I want you to do a sit-up."

Try as he might, Gohan couldn't do it. He soon became drenched in perspiration and was ready to give up and concede. Dr. Thao was right. Then Dr. Thao turned the tables and refused to quit.

"Come on, David. You said you're leaving in a week. You said you were ready, so let's go. It doesn't matter how much it hurts. We can't go forward until we start. Give me your hands. I'll help, but you'll do the work."

He took Gohan's hands and gently pulled as Gohan put all his energy into moving his torso. Finally, after almost ten minutes,

Gohan felt his chest moving toward his knees. He thought he'd die from the pain. He gritted his teeth, bit through his tongue again, and fought the pain as perspiration and tears rolled down his face. Finally, his fingers reached his knees.

Very slowly, Dr. Thao lowered him until he lay flat on the bed again. Gohan had closed his eyes during the ordeal, trying to overcome the pain. When he opened them, he found Ka staring at him. She, too, had tears on her face, but her eyes no longer were filled with sadness. Now they seemed to say that she understood.

They looked at each for a moment, and Gohan tried to smile. He wasn't sure if Ka noticed, but she quickly looked away.

"David, there's no time to rest," Dr. Thao said. "We must work. I'll exercise your legs."

He spoke to Ka in Laotian, although it sounded like Chinese to Gohan. She brought him a towel. It was time to eat cloth again. He bit down hard and waited for the worst.

Dr. Thao took both of Gohan's legs below the knees and pushed them toward Gohan's chest. The pain was unbearable. Gohan bit into the towel, balled his hands into fists, closed his eyes as tightly as he could, and moved his head back and forth as he moaned. Ka, sitting on the bed beside him, took both his hands in hers.

He opened his eyes, and saw compassion fill Ka's face. She saw the fear and hurt in his eyes, but holding his hands helped take his mind from the pain a little.

Ka was five-feet-two-inches tall, slender, and very attractive. She had high Hmong cheekbones, and her black hair was cut very short. Her eyes seemed a little less oblique than the other Hmong in the dungeon. Like them, she had a yellowish complexion. In America, she could have been a model. Gohan thought it was nice to look at her, not just because she was pretty, but because it kept his mind off the pain as the doctor worked.

He didn't know how often Dr. Thao bent his knees for him, but he was very glad when it was over. He assured Gohan that they would increase the number of repetitions each time. He would do all he could to prepare Gohan.

That was all Gohan needed. If Dr. Thao suddenly thought he

had a chance to walk out of there, Gohan knew it would happen. He could teach himself to embrace pain and recognize it as a friend. The admiral told him about that.

Thanks, admiral, Gohan thought. *You're never far from me.*

When Dr. Thao left that first night, Ka stayed. She rechecked Gohan's bandages, pulled the sheet up over him, and looked at him for a long time. She seemed ready to say something. Finally, her expression changed, and she said, "Am-er-oh."

Gohan shook his head in confusion.

"Am-er-oh."

He studied the sounds, but they didn't make sense. He smiled and took her hand again. "It's OK. Am-er-oh."

She grinned, glad that he understood his friend was with Cheu. Feeling happy, she bowed to Gohan and left.

Gohan didn't know what she meant, but that didn't matter. She knew he couldn't speak her language. It was probably Laotian for, You're doin' real well, cowboy. Keep it up.

In his fifth day, Gohan progressed to six sit-ups per session, and doc was moving his legs quite a bit. Gohan could sit up in bed now. Although that was difficult, it represented another step forward. Finally, he was able to see how bad his wounds were, and he wasn't surprised that Ka threw up the first day.

Earlier that day, Dr. Thao said Gohan could attempt walking the following day. "You'll have to be very patient, Gohan. You might not succeed at first. You've been bedridden awhile, and your injuries are still severe. We've made excellent progress, but we have to take this one step at a time. I honestly believe you'll walk."

Dr. Thao was amazed by Gohan's progress. More than once, he told Gohan what he had done so far was a miracle—and physically impossible.

Ka, too, became a friend. She was no longer shy around Gohan. Gohan felt great respect for her, and she obviously returned it. Despite his circumstances, he was as comfortable as possible. Having Dr. Thao and Ka there made all the difference.

Then Dr. Thao brought bad news. Gohan's worst fears were verified. Dr. Thao learned that Ka was being sent for by Nikko-Witch. Gohan knew what that meant. She couldn't refuse, so she put up with it in order to bring information to her brother.

Gohan's heart was broken at the news, then he became angry. He became even more determined not only to escape but to return and rescue Dr. Thao, Ka, her father, and the other villagers, then he would slit Nikko-Witch's throat and watch him die slowly.

Every time he saw Ka, Gohan wanted to cry. At her young age, she made such a commitment to her brother's cause that he felt she qualified for a special medal. If he had anything to do with it, she would receive it, too.

Then came more bad news. As Dr. Thao finished the exercises that afternoon, Gohan saw he wanted to talk. He spoke softly to Ka, and they moved to hide whatever Dr. Thao did next. He moved close to Gohan so they could talk.

"David, this is likely to be the last time I see you. Nikolai Niko-layevich, the KGB officer, is angry with me, because I haven't brought him the information he wants. He no longer believes me when I say you're making slow progress. It's possible that the Soviet doctor will start working with you tomorrow. We've come very far, my friend, and I owe you a lot. You gave me purpose and a reason to fight on. Good luck."

Gohan was stunned. He couldn't let Dr. Thao leave. He quickly gathered his thoughts. "Doc, listen. I owe you my life. Don't worry. I'll get out of here, and I'll come back for you. That's a promise. Tell your friends to hang on. We'll get all of you out."

Dr. Thao smiled. Gohan was serious, and he no longer doubted that whatever the remarkable young man set his mind to, he would do. He patted Gohan's shoulder. "Good-bye, David."

Gohan had to think fast. If doc was leaving, Gohan had to change his plans immediately. They had to move the timetable forward. "Doc, wait!"

Dr. Thao walked back slowly and leaned close to listen to Gohan's words.

"Tell Ka I'm leaving tonight. I need a weapon."

Dr. Thao was surprised, but only for a moment. He nodded, turned, and quietly spoke to Ka, then he looked at Gohan for a few seconds. Tears formed in the old doctor's eyes, and they suddenly sprang to Gohan's eyes, too. Then Dr. Thao walked away.

Ka stood perfectly still. For the first time, fear showed in her eyes. At least she now understood what would happen. She turned toward the nurse's area.

Gohan would have one more treatment and exercise session later that evening with Ka. Then, after everyone left, he'd go home, too. In a way, that would be better than the original plan. There had always been the fear that if he waited a little longer, his chances might evaporate. Now he had to leave immediately, and the idea brought a sense of peace. He was ready.

He had to rest, so he closed his eyes, but sleep wouldn't come. His heart pounded, and he wondered if the admiral had managed to escape. So far, Dr. Thao hadn't said a word about him. That probably meant he wasn't in the camp.

Was the admiral still in Laos? Gohan hoped his friend was hiding nearby, watching the village and camp.

Well, admiral, he thought, *you'll get a real eyeful tonight if you're close by. Keep that rifle handy, buddy. I might need some help.*

Gohan thought of Keiko and Sumi and couldn't wait to see them again. He wondered how much Sumi had grown. It was over two weeks since he last saw her, and it bothered him to miss any of her growing up.

He closed his eyes and saw her sitting in his lap on the little rocking chair at his rented house in Nakadomari. She was still flushed with fever and hot. He couldn't understand why he kept seeing her that way in his mind, but it didn't matter.

Determined to escape, he refused to allow any thought of failure to register in his mind. His plan would work, and he would reach the guerilla camp. Then he would get word back to Okinawa, and someone would come for him. Then he would go home. He imagined his homecoming.

"Gohan-san, you take more than two weeks. Why you so long in Germany?"

"I had a slight accident, honey. But everything's OK now. Is Sumi OK?"

"Yes. Dr. Kentsu make Sumiko better. Where you hurt, Gohan-san?"

"Oh, it's nothing. Let's get a boat and go to Zamami Island for a picnic."

"Yes. OK, Gohan-san, but you tell Keiko-san where you hurt. I am wife, and I want to know.

"Well, honey, I slipped on a banana peel and got eighty percent of my midsection ripped apart. Nothing serious."

Back to reality. He knew that wouldn't work. How could he explain it to Keiko? There was plenty of time to figure that out. Besides, just being home was good enough for him. It would be tough on Keiko, but she would be fine. She always was, wasn't she?

He tried to centralize the pain so he could rest. It was important for his body to be well rested. He wanted to be as sharp as possible when he escaped. It would be traumatic enough as it was, but he could do it.

He still had one more evening session with Ka. That would make him stronger. Sleep would be best, but he knew he wouldn't sleep.

Get some rest, Davey Boy, he told himself. *You'll need all the strength you can muster. You don't have to sleep, but at least you can rest. Come on, man, relax.*

Yes, sir. Is there a button to push to make that happen?

He tried to relax and keep his mind off the pain. Again, he visualized the escape attempt, trying to plan out every movement.

Only a few more hours, Davey.

He could hardly wait.

Time passed quickly. He realized he had been asleep and looked around. *Good. That's a bonus I hadn't counted on*, he thought.

Ka walked to his bedside and nodded hello in a businesslike manner. He wondered if someone were watching. She checked the bandages around his head, carefully uncovered him, and applied a treatment to his wounds. He watched her closely the entire time, but she never looked at him.

She was careful, gentle, and slower than usual, though. Gohan wondered what that meant. Had doc told her he was going early? It was clear he wouldn't learn anything from Ka. She hadn't looked at him once since she arrived twenty minutes earlier.

Ka finished her work, replaced the damp cloth covering Gohan, and covered him from his hips down. Then she climbed onto the bed and sat on his legs below the knees, holding his legs down as he went through his sit-ups. He did eight, two more than earlier that afternoon.

When he finished the eighth, he looked at her for a sign of approval, but she refused to look at him. He became concerned.

Is there a problem, Ka? he wondered. *Are you trying to tell me something? How will I know? You don't speak one word of English.*

Suddenly, he realized that during his time in the hospital, she said only one word, and he hadn't understood it. She must have known his name. Doc would have told her, but she never said it.

Oh, well. The idea is to heal so I can escape, not make friends, he thought.

She slid off his legs, grabbed him above the ankles, and pushed his legs backward into what he thought of as inside out deep knee bends. She went through twenty very painful knee bends with him, then, when she finished, she got off the bed and straightened the sheet.

With a damp cloth, she wiped him down. The exercise made him perspire heavily. As she wiped his face, she looked at him, but their eyes didn't meet. Her face showed no expression. She put away the cloth, looked around to make sure she wasn't being watched, then pulled a bag out from under the bed. Gohan watched intently, astonished as she went about her work and wondering what was in the bag.

Ka repacked the cloths around his legs, groin, and stomach, wrapping them tightly and securing them with tape from the bag. That was the first time she used tape, and he realized she was preparing him for his escape. He felt as if he were wearing a diaper, and it was very uncomfortable.

Ka put the supplies in the black bag again, pulled up the sheet, looked around the room, and then walked toward him. She gently wiped perspiration from his face and sat on the bed beside him.

For the first time that evening, she looked into his eyes. Hers no longer held the fear he saw before. She was all business now, and it showed.

She reached into her dress and pulled out a long, thick kitchen knife, sliding it under his pillow. Then she pointed at her blouse and skirt, then under the bed. He realized she meant that his clothes were hidden there, so he nodded.

Tears formed in her eyes, and her businesslike look was gone. A moment later, she leaned over and lightly kissed his cheek. When she pulled away, a tear fell onto his cheek.

She looked at him and tried to smile but couldn't. Then, amazingly, she spoke one word. "Gohan."

It shocked him but before he could think about what he had heard, she quickly turned away and walked toward the nurse's area without looking back.

Gohan sighed. It was a nice moment and a lousy time for it, too. He'd probably never see her or doc again. Unless he escaped, he would never see anyone again. Then it hit him. She called him Gohan. How did she know? The admiral. Doc had said that she ran to her brother's camp at night. The admiral must be there with the guerillas. Wow! That changed everything. She knew that he was going out that night and she would be able to tell the admiral and her brother.

Excitement began to shoot through his mind and body. Suddenly, he knew he was going to make it.

Thank You, God. Thank You, God.

Then, he calmed himself and began to think.

OK, Davey boy, let's make this work, he told himself. *First, we get out of here. Then we can come back and rescue all these good people. You'll see doc and Ka again, and the admiral, too. Then you'll see Keiko and Sumi, too. We'll do it, man. We'll make history.*

He nodded. It was time.

He knew Ka would leave immediately, then the hospital would become quiet. He would spend the next few hours rehearsing his plans until there was no room for error. He was wide awake and alert, and he would stay that way until it was time to make his move.

Chapter 21
Escape

IT WAS TIME. THE HOSPITAL WAS QUIET, AND KA AND DR. Thao were gone. The Russian doctor was asleep in his office. Two elderly Laotian women and one elderly Laotian man lay in the beds across from Gohan, but all seemed asleep. A girl of five or six years was in the bed to his right, moaning in pain as she'd done when they admitted her days earlier. Her mother was beside her, comforting her even at that hour.

A Pathet Lao soldier was in the bed by the doctor's office, the one Gohan shot when he was captured. According to Dr. Thao, the man would probably die. The other injured Viet Minh and Pathet Lao from the capture had been released earlier that week.

The situation was good. He hoped the mother wouldn't create a fuss, but why would she? The others had invaded and destroyed her village. She would think of Gohan as an ally.

The pain was about seventy-five percent of what it had been, so he could handle it. His clothing was under the bed, and his weapon was under his pillow. The guard appeared to be asleep. Gohan guessed it was two o'clock in the morning.

Slowly, he sat up. He hadn't had a chance to practice walking yet, so he'd have to be very careful. He felt he could make it. As he was ready to slide off the bed to retrieve his clothes, he realized that he hadn't even tried to stand since the beatings.

Well, bud, he thought, *we'll find out real quick how good you are. Let's go.*

He carefully slid to his feet onto the cold, wooden floor. Instead of trying to stand, he went to his knees so he could pull out the clothes under the bed. Pain stabbed him, but he pulled himself back onto the bed and laid out the clothes beside him. It was painful to turn his head, but at least it was possible. He looked around the room.

All was quiet. The mother glanced at him, then went back to her sick child.

He put on his socks and realized how important the sit-ups and deep knee bends had been. It was all he could do to reach his feet, never mind putting on his socks. On to his second sock, he couldn't reach the final two inches.

He brought his feet as close to his chest as he could, creating additional pain he didn't want, but no matter how many times he tried, he couldn't pull on the sock.

Frustrated, he sat on the bed and realized he was losing precious time. Should he go without socks or try again? He gritted his teeth, screamed inwardly at himself, and threw his upper body forward with all his strength, grabbing his left foot solidly. With the sock in his right hand, he slowly pulled it onto his foot. He exhaled, more loudly than he wanted.

Daggonit. Why didn't I think out this process before I started? Come on, Davey. There's no time to be stupid.

Now he was behind schedule. He'd given himself twenty minutes of extra time, but he'd used up most of it. He slid on his pants, then pulled on his undershirt and shirt.

Where'd she find these clothes? he wondered.

They must have come from a villager. They fit well enough to make do, but they were a bit small. Getting his shoes on was tough, but he did it. The shoes and socks were his, so they fit better than the other clothes. With his borrowed pants and shirt, he probably looked like a worker from the rice fields.

He glanced around, but nothing had changed in the room. He slid to the edge of the bed until his feet touched the floor, then he reached under the pillow for the knife. After examining it closely for a second, he slid it into the sheath Ka had slipped onto his belt.

What a great job she did, he thought. *She and doc belong in the Prison Camp Hall of Fame. OK, Davey Boy. Time to show your stuff.*

He pushed himself up from the bed and stood on two feet for the first time in a week. It hurt, but it felt good, too. He took a deep breath, leaned against the bed for support, then made up the bed so it looked like someone was still in it.

He looked around and saw the guard's head was slumped against his chest. He was sure he was asleep.

He waited for his breathing to slow to a normal rate. *OK. I have to start walking. Take it easy and try one step at a time. We're on schedule, so there's no hurry.*

He straightened up and took one cautious step forward. *Good job, Davey Boy. It's just like in the song. Put your right foot out, then your left, and do the hokey pokey.* He laughed to himself.

Just as quickly, he became serious. The first step was wobbly, but he made it. Pain seared through him, but he'd been expecting that. Doc told him it would happen.

He took a deep breath and tried two more steps. He moved his left foot forward, felt his body shift, then quickly moved the right foot.

It was too much, too soon. His vision blurred. He reached for something to steady himself, but there was nothing to grab. Instead, he collapsed to the floor with a thud.

He lay perfectly still, expecting the worst. It wouldn't have surprised him to hear sirens and people running toward him. But, he didn't.

God, please don't let Ivan the Terrible wake up. What the heck will I do if he comes over here?

He waited, but there was no sound. After waiting a little longer, he raised up to a kneeling position and found himself near the aisle at the far edge of his bed. The guard was still slumped over, sleeping in his chair.

Looking the other way, Gohan found the mother standing up, looking down at him. He put a finger to her lips, motioned her to be quiet. She nodded and sat down again.

Good, he thought. *I didn't think she'd be a problem. Well, boy, you don't have time for a practice session. You'd better get this walking business together fast.*

He paused and thought about the admiral.

God, I need Your help. I don't know how miracles work or how people get 'em, but I need to learn how to walk right now. Tomorrow's too late. Even five minutes from now isn't enough.

I hope that's not asking too much, but we either do it now, or I'm dead. Please, God, You've been magnificent so far. I know that I wouldn't be here if You hadn't intervened. Now, I need Your help again. Please get me out of here. Amen.

He gritted his teeth against the pain, which grew with every move he made. He slowly got up then took a few steps very carefully until he reached the edge of the aisle. He turned left carefully and moved toward the front of the hospital and the guard.

He pulled out the knife and had it ready. If the guard woke up and saw him, he'd have to throw the knife and pray he was lucky, because otherwise, he was dead.

He passed two beds without any trouble, but walking took longer than anticipated. He would rather be careful than fall again. His steps were short and slow.

He passed the last bed on the left and moved around it to get behind the guard's chair. He wanted to turn around to make sure no one was looking at him, but he was too close and couldn't risk being distracted.

He approached the back of the chair, took a quiet breath, and plunged the knife deep into the back of the Russian guard's neck. His free hand went to the guard's mouth to prevent him from calling out.

He pulled out the knife and snapped the man's neck to make sure he was dead. He put the knife away and placed the guard's head back into the sleeping position.

When Gohan turned, he found the mother and the old Hmong man staring at him. He looked at Gohan and smiled as Gohan removed the dead guard's weapons and belt, putting them on himself. He wasn't familiar with the rifle and pistol, but that didn't bother him.

He moved behind the guard toward the door and hid in the shadows, watching the tower guards use the spotlight. They scanned the fence at the edge of the jungle, and Gohan stepped back as the light swept across the hospital door and around the compound.

He moved to the steps quickly, then decided that caution was more important than speed and sat down to descend them so that he wouldn't fall. Once on the ground, he stood and moved to the side of the hospital, out of sight. Dr. Thao's information had been right. There were no windows on that side of the building, and the spotlight couldn't see him there, either.

He had a few minutes while he waited for the search pattern to come around again. So far, his plan was working, but the toughest part was next. Once the beam of light passed, he had only a few minutes to cross the open area, cut a hole in the fence, and get into the jungle. He didn't know if he could do it.

He was breathing hard. Although able to walk, he was not moving well and was very tired. He didn't know if he could run. If he fell again, he'd never make it through the fence before the light came back to him.

He removed the pistol from its holster and examined it, seeing how to use it. He did the same with the rifle. At least he had weapons if he needed them. He wouldn't be recaptured. He'd fire every bullet he had and take as many of the enemy with him as he could, but he wouldn't give up and allow them to torture him again.

He was ready. There was no turning back, and he didn't want to. He had to go through with his plan. For Dr. Thao's and Ka's sakes, he had to succeed.

The searchlight was coming back around, and the guards seemed to be changing positions. A new man would run the light for a while. Gohan watched the light move along the length of the fence. He had to be under the fence and away before it returned, or he'd be seen for certain.

The light swept across the grassy courtyard and past the hospital.

Now, Davey! he told himself.

He had difficulty starting out, having to pick up his leg and thrust it forward, but there was no momentum. He tried desperately to run but couldn't manage. The best he could do was walk.

After eight steps, he saw he'd never make it and returned to the hospital wall to think. *Daggonit, Davey Boy*, he screamed inwardly. *Are you a wimp?*

He was upset and surprised at how tired he was. He hadn't done much yet, yet he was in terrible pain. He leaned against the wall and tried to think out his situation, then sat down to rest his tired, sore legs.

As he thought over the problem, he realized it was all about pain. When he tried to run, pain shot through him so strongly that he could barely move.

You can overcome pain through willpower, Boy. Forget the pain. You don't have to experience every little pain that comes your way. What will you do, record it for posterity? Just grit your teeth and run. Come on, Davey. Forget the pain. Doc and Ka are counting on you, and so are Keiko and Sumiko.

Cheu Moua, Captain Baker, and the small guerilla band received word from Ka that Gohan would attempt his escape during the early morning hours. Cheu and Baker quickly devised a plan that would give Gohan help and support if he couldn't manage the escape alone, offer him armed protection if he were discovered during his attempt, and create an offensive onslaught if he were killed.

They moved into position at midnight. No one knew exactly where he would try to break through the fence, so they spread out. Ka warned them that Gohan wasn't strong enough to make it. The men were prepared to offer any help he might need.

Cheu and three of his men moved as close as they could to the camp. They were painted and camouflaged so well that the searchlight would have great difficulty finding them in the bush. They took positions just on the other side of the long, high fence. Captain Baker and the rest of the men were farther back, out of sight but ready to help.

They saw Gohan come out of the hospital, move down the steps, and then into the shadow alongside the building. They immediately moved to get into the right position to intercept him at the point in the fence he would run for.

Cheu and his men watched Gohan fail in his first attempt. He saw that Gohan would need help just crossing the open field. When Gohan retreated to the safety of the wall, and the search-light finished another pass along the fence, one of Cheu's men moved to the fence and cut the bottom three strands of wire over a three-foot area. Another man motioned to the group behind them to send up two more men.

Baker moved in alongside Cheu Moua.

"Let me go, Cheu. He'll recognize me. As soon as the light passes by him, I'll get to him, then I'll bring him out."

Cheu nodded his acceptance and they waited.

Gohan stood and slowly blocked out all sensation. He set his eyes on part of the fence straight across from his hiding place, glad to see there was jungle on the other side. The searchlight scanned the courtyard and went past him, and he took off.

As soon as Captain Baker saw him move forward, he retreated back to the safety of the bush.

He was running! It worked! He wasn't moving that fast, but at least he was running. The pain was beyond description, but that didn't matter. He felt a little wind against his face as he ran, and he suddenly realized how beautiful one word was—*run*.

His eyes were on the fence and the bushes behind it. He would make it! Adrenalin pumped through him as he reached the half-way point. His timing was good, and he knew he'd make it.

Then his vision started turning black. He couldn't see the fence. What was happening? He was running, but it felt like he was falling. Had he been shot? He hadn't heard a gun going off. What was going on? He couldn't see! Then everything went black, and dizziness took over.

Cheu and his men watched in concern as Gohan made his second attempt. He moved well and looked like he'd make it, then suddenly, halfway across the courtyard, he collapsed.

It was too late for them to run to him. They'd never get through the fence and back before the light returned. Four men in the rear group aimed their rifles at the tower guards. If the searchlight found Gohan, the guards would die immediately, then Cheu and his men would go in and try to bring Gohan out before the rest of the camp erupted.

They watched the searchlight beam return along the fence, completely missing the cut portion in front of the hidden guerillas. It moved across the courtyard and passed over the fallen American, missing him completely.

As soon as the light moved away, Cheu and three of his men moved through the fence, ran to Gohan, grabbed him, and carried him back out. The two snipers had their rifles trained on the tower guards in case they saw what was happening. In the meantime, two other men cut away more of the fence so the group could get through easily.

They brought Gohan out, then the men repaired the fence and retreated into the jungle. When they reached the second group, Cheu motioned them to move quickly toward their mountain camp. Baker came to help carry his wounded friend, but Cheu wouldn't allow it. The Hmong guerrillas were better suited for the job.

"Captain," Cheu whispered, "friend hurt and alive. Move fast."

Baker nodded, and the group moved away from the compound and made the long trek back to their camp.

Later, far enough from Ban Na Lom to be safe, the men moved at a slower pace. Captain Baker moved to the front to be with Cheu. He was impressed by the way Cheu and his men carried out the mission and knew he could rely on them. They were well trained, and he felt they could retake the village.

Cheu made a circular motion with his fingers pointed at his head, laughing softly. "Friend crazy, yes?"

Baker laughed, too. "Yes, sometimes I think Gohan's crazy, but a better word would be brave."

"Yes, brave. Friend Gohan brave and crazy, yes?"

"Yes." He smiled. Perhaps all heroes had a little of both in them.

Chapter 22
A Welcome Sight

GOHAN AWOKE AND SAW BRIGHT SUNLIGHT. HE WAS OUTSIDE. People were talking nearby, but he couldn't understand them. Where was he? Was it another nightmare?

He remembered running, knowing he would make it. Then something happened. He thought he remembered seeing the admiral, but that had to have been a dream. What had happened to him?

He feared he would find out he had been dead for a long time, and none of the things he remembered were real. If he was alive, though, he needed to know where he was.

Was he lying in the middle of the compound? Maybe they thought he was dead and hadn't bothered to move him. What should he do? They knew he tried to escape. They weren't going to celebrate the idea. They'd torture him even worse than before.

There was no sense putting off the inevitable.

"Hey!" he called weakly. "Anybody want a piece of me? I'm still kickin'!"

Someone laughed, and people moved toward him.

"That's only because we haven't buried you yet, you feisty rascal."

"Admiral! Is that really you? I wasn't dreaming?"

Baker and Cheu helped Gohan stand, then Baker hugged his friend. When Gohan realized he was safe, he started crying.

"Oh, God, admiral, what happened?"

"We knew you were coming. Ka, the nurse, told us. Cheu is her brother." He nodded to the Hmong beside him. "When you fell try-ing to escape, Cheu and his men came to get you before the guards noticed. We're safe in the mountains, miles from that village."

Gohan nearly fainted. He couldn't believe it. He escaped! He turned and hugged Cheu, much to the delight of his men. Then Cheu and Baker helped Gohan into a larger tent where a meal was waiting.

"Ka has kept us abreast of your situation, Gohan," Baker explained. "We need to feed you and build up your strength. She's still at camp, but Cheu has decided this is her last day. We want to find out how they're reacting to your escape. Ka will continue working with you until we bring you up to full strength. Right now, you need food and rest. You're badly beat up, buddy."

"What's the plan, admiral? Are we going in after them?"

"Whatever the plan is, there won't be any we. You need to be in a real hospital for months just to recover."

"No way, man. Let me explain something to you, admiral. There's a guy in there I call doc. I think his real name is Boua Thao. He's a doctor who studied at UCLA, and the only reason I'm alive is because he and Ka put their lives on the line in an attempt to get me strong enough to escape. He's one of the many Hmong who are imprisoned in an underground dungeon. It's cold, there's standing water in there, and there's no drainage. They sit in their own waste and are starving.

"I was with 'em, admiral, and I watched each of those starving men take a spoonful of his soup, which was really just hot water, and give it to me, depriving themselves. You know why? I was worse off than they were, but they didn't even know me!" Tears filled his eyes.

"I owe 'em big, admiral. We need to get that village back for those people and rescue those men, particularly doc, Ka, and her father. Then we need to take that Russian, Nikko-Witch or whatever his name is, and the rest of those perverted soldiers in there and feed 'em to the tigers.

"Don't try to tell me I won't participate. After what I've been through, you and Cheu and this whole camp aren't enough to stop me. OK?"

Baker saw the tears in Cheu's eyes and knew that he'd understood Gohan's speech.

"I'm glad we see eye to eye on this subject. I'm particularly glad to see you still recognize me as your commanding officer."

Gohan laughed. "I'm sorry, admiral. Do you have any idea what I went through back there? Never mind. You've been there."

"Yeah, I know. We'll talk to Ka when she returns, and we'll see how quickly she can get you into shape. In the meantime, eat and rest. When we plan our strategy, I want you in on it. We can do it, Gohan. These men are Hmong villagers, but they're good. Many fought with the Royal Lao Army, which was under U.S. control, so we've got a good group."

"Does Cheu understand you, admiral? His sister doesn't speak a word of English."

"He understands better than he speaks. He'll stop me if I'm going too fast."

Gohan glanced at Cheu, who nodded and smiled. They brought the food in, and Gohan recognized rice that was matted together with a rich sauce poured over it just like on Okinawa. There wasn't much taste, but at least it was nourishing. There was also a small portion of meat that had a strange texture to it. It tasted a little like wild deer.

He glanced at the admiral and raised his eyebrows.

"Boiled snake. Enjoy it. It's a delicacy."

The admiral motioned to Cheu, who spoke to his men. All left except Cheu, the admiral, a short, strong Laotian, and Gohan.

"Gohan," Cheu said, "this Vu Xiong."

Gohan held out his hand. "Glad to meet you, Vu."

Vu nodded without speaking. Gohan wondered if he understood English.

The admiral wiped his mouth on his sleeve. "Thank you, men. That was very good."

The Hmong warriors were pleased that Admiral Baker enjoyed the meal. Gohan saw he'd better do the same thing.

"Excellent dinner, men," Gohan said. "It beats anything Mom ever cooked. That snake tasted like chocolate chip cookies. Thanks a lot."

Baker laughed, then became serious. "Here's what we know, Gohan. You need to add to this if you know anything else. There were between forty and fifty soldiers at Ban Na Lom. We know about the guards in the tower. Our understanding is there are six sets of two guards at different places in the settlement and the compound. If we can create the right kind of surprise, we can cut down on those odds and make it an even battle. That means we strike at night when most of the guards are asleep.

"There's no reason to think they'll do anything special after your escape. They don't know about this group. You're just one American who escaped from the hospital, cut the fence, and crawled through. You're hiding somewhere in Vietnam or Cambodia by now. They might send out a search team for a day or two, but there's no reason for them to change their guard situation. They knew of four Americans—three dead and one escaped."

"Three dead? Are you sure?"

"Yes. Sorry, Gohan. I wasn't aware that you didn't know."

Gohan feared as much, so the news didn't come as a surprise. Still, he had hoped otherwise. "The whole place sleeps at night, admiral. We need to consider what they might add for extra protection. I struck at night only a day ago."

"True, but as long as the whole group isn't awake, that still leaves us in a good position," Baker answered.

"We also need a good picture of the rest of the camp. I didn't see that much, but doc gave me a lot of information so I could plan my escape. Do you remember where I came from when I tried to run for the fence?"

They nodded.

"OK. Directly behind that on the other side of the hospital is the underground prison. I was there, but I couldn't see much at the time. Doc said it's fifty yards from the hospital, near the fence at the back of the compound. You know where the large building is. The only room I know about is the one where they tried to turn me into two people."

"We've got pretty good information on the rest of the place, Gohan," Baker said. "Ka is there every day and is free to move around. Cheu and many of the men in our army lived in the settlement, too.

"Here's what we've got. We come in from the same direction as last night, then we'll spread out to cover the area we want. They have only two guards in the tower, though they might add a few more after your escape."

"Wait a minute, admiral. They put two guards at the south end of the compound now, twenty-four hours a day. Doc told me that."

"Yeah? That doesn't change much. There are guards in the village we have to take care of, too. All that comes first. If we handle it right, we can take these twelve guards without losing a man or alerting anyone. We don't want to become too spread out and lose our advantage."

"Captain," Cheu said, "two men, two guard." He slid his hand across his throat.

"Excellent, Cheu," Baker said. "He's sayin' that we'll use two-man teams to eliminate the guards. We'll send two men to take care of the two extra guards you just mentioned, too. We'll determine how we'll move at the last moment. That depends on where the guards are."

"We might need three or four additional groups of men for that," Gohan said. "If they place extra guards at other places after my escape, we need to take them out to maintain our secrecy. We need more men."

"We don't have any." Baker sighed. The mission wouldn't be easy no matter what. "Cheu, let's have six sets of men ready for ambush attacks. Can we do that?"

"Yes, captain. Have good men. Six, two."

"Good. Then we regroup after taking out the guards so we're back to full strength again. That means we'll have to move fast. Any delay could be disastrous."

"How about the hospital? They've got one guard in there. I took him out when I escaped. They might add more now."

"No, I don't think so. You were the only person capable of escaping. There's no one else in the hospital that's a threat." Baker turned to Cheu Moua. "Cheu, one of the teams will have to take out the guard in the hospital, too."

Cheu nodded and looked at Vu.

They spent hours planning and replanning until they felt they had something that would work. They would go in at the same time of night as Gohan's escape—two o'clock in the morning. Most of their men had already gone to sleep so they'd be sharp and alert when the attack came that evening.

Gohan showed the admiral his exercises. With the admiral's help, he did ten sit-ups and twenty-five deep-knee bends, although he did those from a standing position that time. He refused to stop, adding some push-ups to strengthen his arms. The strain on his abdomen kept him from doing better than he wished, but he managed four push-ups before he collapsed.

The effort exhausted him, so he was ready for a rest.

Ban Na Lom camp was in turmoil after the American escaped. They found the cut fence and the dead Russian guard at the hospital. After interviewing everyone in the hospital, it appeared they'd been asleep when it happened, including the Russian doctor. There was no indication the American had any outside help.

The situation was incredible. How could such a badly injured man, nearly dead a few days earlier, escape from a fenced compound guarded by fifty soldiers?

Nikolai sent for Major Ustinova and Cherkov, the sergeant in charge of the guards. Then he sent for Pavel, the KGB clerk, so that the meeting would be fully documented. According to KGB regulations, Nikolai had to send in a report immediately, but he would stall for a while. Pavel was obviously a pawn who would obey whatever Nikolai said. He wouldn't dare do anything that might make himself or his superior look bad.

If the other officers were at fault, however, the report would be sent to Moscow immediately. With luck, Nikolai would receive a replacement with at least half a brain, not like that idiot Ustinova.

Nikolai knew it might be too late to protect himself, but if heads were going to roll over the incident, he would make sure many other heads went with his. He would report the escape only after he understood what happened and could alter the tale enough to save himself.

"Nikolai Ivanovich Nikolayevich, how can I be of service?" Major Ustinova asked.

"Major, please sit down. We're waiting for Sergeant Cherkov."

A moment later, Cherkov knocked on the door and was ushered in. He nodded to Zortov and gave proper greetings to his superiors. "Major Ustinova. Nikolai Nikolayevich."

Nikolai looked at the three men sitting huddled on the short couch like whipped puppies and found the sight angered him even more. "Imbeciles! Idiots! How can a compound of fifty soldiers allow one badly injured American to escape? Ustinova, do you still have the ability to protect this compound? Are you aware of the importance of the work we're doing? Why did you send forty-eight men to bed and ask only two to protect us, especially when we know there are enemies in the village who have tried to rise against us in the past? Why do you think our dungeon is full of prisoners? Have you lost the ability to think? Has anyone told you that all our enemies are imprisoned?"

He slammed his fist against the table. "Zortov, pour me a drink."

"Nikolai Nikolayevich, I could use one, too," Major Ustinova said.

"No," he shouted. "You're the reason I need a drink and have had to call this meeting. I'm so angry with you, the only drink you might get will be a glass of poison so I can be rid of you."

Zortov handed the glass to Nikolai, who gulped down the contents and set the glass down. "What shall we do now, gentlemen? You know, of course, that this must be reported. How many men are out looking for the American?"

"We have three teams of six men out, Nikolai Nikolayevich," Sergeant Cherkov replied. "We expect them back within the hour. We'll let them rest while we send out another contingent."

"No, you idiots! Don't you see what you're doing? You've made us even more vulnerable here. Our purpose here isn't to catch the American, it's to keep that communications network functioning without interference. We must have a safe haven for the Viet Minh troops who'll soon be moving into South Vietnam. That is our responsibility. We have to guard this compound, not the Laotian jungle."

"Sergeant, when your men return, let them rest. Then I want the entire compound ready to turn back any attack the enemy might throw at us. Is that clear?"

"Yes, sir," Cherkov said.

"Major Ustinova," Nikolai said, lowering his voice as if speaking to a child, "do you think you can come up with a plan to preserve and protect this compound? Is that asking too much? Should I consider contacting General Samsonov and asking for a replacement? Alyosha and I are old friends," he lied. "I'm sure he would be happy to accommodate me."

"That isn't necessary, Nikolai. We're as concerned as you are about the breach in security. Please understand that we had no information that led us to believe the American could even walk. He was supposedly near death, and his recovery was supposed to have taken at least another month."

That made Nikolai even more angry, because the information came from his own office. He refused to let such a useless soldier put the blame on him. He swallowed the rest of his drink and pounded the table with his fist again. "Major Ustinova, if I need to make every decision in this camp, what do I need you for? Your only responsibility is to protect this camp, and I expect you to do it. Do I make myself clear?"

"Yes, Nikolai, very clear. I assure you this camp will be as secure as humanly possible."

"Put together a plan, and put it into effect immediately. I don't want to see you again. You two leave. Zortov, stay a moment."

Major Ustinova and Sergeant Cherkov walked out of the office as quickly as they could.

"Pavel," Nikolai asked quietly, "did you do as I requested? You haven't sent any information regarding the American to Moscow yet, have you?"

"No, sir. Nothing has been sent."

"Good. Let's keep it that way a little longer. I don't want to create an international crisis. If we recapture the American, there's no reason to let them know he escaped." He smiled, knowing Zortov wouldn't be a problem.

Zortov nodded. "What if the American isn't recaptured? What do we do then?"

"Then we have to tell them, but we won't put the cart before the horse as the Americans say. I want to rest and think awhile. In the meantime, bring me the doctor from the prisoners, the man who was treating the American. He's back in the dungeon."

"Haven't you questioned him already, sir?"

"Yes. I have no more questions for him. I don't even know if he was responsible for the American's escape. It's time to make an example of him so that nothing like this happens again. Send me three Russian soldiers and tell them to bring their rifles."

Zortov left the room. Nikolai went to the cabinet and poured another drink. After he downed that, he poured another and carried it to his desk, sitting in the comfortable chair behind it.

He wondered what his superiors would do to him when they found out about the missing American. He couldn't hide the fact forever. He had to find an answer that wouldn't incriminate him.

He could say the man tried to escape and died of his wounds, so they threw him in the river with the others, but could he find corroboration for that? Would anyone dare to attempt to disprove the story? Zortov would go along. He was too frightened to fight back. Ustinova was an idiot, so he was no threat.

Nikolai would come up with an answer. He had to.

Major Ustinova and Sergeant Cherkov walked to one of the tables in the courtyard and sat down without speaking.

Finally, Cherkov asked, "Major, why has he blamed us for the American's escape? Wasn't he the one who told us the man was so badly injured, he might not recover?"

"Yes, but you see, our KGB friend won't accept any blame. Therefore, he must blame us. As you grow older, you'll recognize that sometimes you must listen to people without hearing their words. Nikolai is an oaf who cares only for his own well being. No matter what happens, he will blame someone else."

"The KGB will learn the truth, though. They always do. If anyone is disciplined over this, it'll be Nikolai. He'll be the one who goes to a prison camp and live among the people he sent there. That would be justice, wouldn't it?"

Sergeant Cherkov smiled. "I don't understand politics, major. I just try to be a good soldier. What should we do now?"

"The first thing we do is ignore what Nikolai commanded. He's no military man and doesn't know how to run a military operation. Of course, we'll cease our outside operations, or he'll find out and have our heads. As for protection, we have two guards at the lower end of the compound during the day, correct?"

"Yes, sir. We went to twenty-four-hour duty, but that made no sense, so we stopped. They come in at ten o'clock."

"Very well. Let's keep them out twenty-four hours. Create the necessary shifts. That'll give us two guards at each end of the camp at all hours. Other than that, I don't think we need to change anything. The tower guards can detect any outside attack, which seems to be what Nikolai fears. We're secure on that score. A single man who escaped could elude many guards, but he certainly wouldn't try to escape where the guards are located, would he?"

Cherkov smiled. "No, sir. I'm sure he wouldn't."

"The truth is, the only war that's going on here is the civil war in Vietnam and the skirmishes in Laos. We're friendly with North Vietnam, because, like us, they're Communists. The Americans are friends with South Vietnam, because they aren't Communists. I'm sure the Americans don't want to become involved in a civil war here, and neither do we.

"What we're doing here is important, Dmitry, but we're trying to keep our distance from Vietnam's internal affairs, just like the Americans. We don't even know the full essence of our mission. The ministry doesn't always tell us those things. They like to keep that in the hands of the KGB, even though we're the ones who make the decisions. That's why we don't win many wars."

Seeing the sergeant looking at him strangely, he asked, "Are you concerned that I'm saying things that might have me sent to a prison camp? I see it in your face."

The sergeant, clearing his throat, looked around to make sure no one was within earshot. "Major, they do put men like us in prison for saying and thinking things similar to what you just said. You know that as well as I do."

"Yes, yes, but, after a while, you tire of the way things are done. We're a large, proud nation. We have the wherewithal to build an army second to none, but we never do it. Then we lie to ourselves about it, saying it's someone else's fault or circumstances beyond our control. Our history is kind to us only because we write it. Have you ever wondered what the rest of the world has written about us? I have."

Cherkov realized his commanding officer wasn't in the proper emotional condition to carry out his mission, but he'd never tell Nikolai that. Like the major, Cherkov wasn't sure the KGB man had the ability to command the post. Cherkov decided to stay as alert as possible and make sure everything worked smoothly, no matter what the major said. He would have to be careful, because he didn't want to appear insubordinate.

"OK, Dmitry," Major Ustinova said. "Get the men rested when they return, and we'll call off the search. If they find anything positive, let me know. I'll be out here. I need to think. Any new information could change our plans. Otherwise, create the new guard post at night and carry on as usual."

"Yes, sir. May I ask a question, sir?"

"Of course."

"What should we do if Nikolai checks the camp tonight or tomorrow and sees we didn't reinforce the positions as he said? Shouldn't we at least make an effort to follow his orders?"

Major Ustinova smiled. "Dmitry, you're a good soldier, a man who does what he's told, right or wrong. You need to be better than that, however. A soldier who wins wars only follows orders when they're correct. If you study military history, you'll find the best soldiers, no matter what country they came from, had a streak of rebellion in them and a streak of genius.

"When you know you've been given incorrect orders, you rebel to the extent that you make decisions that'll save your nation, the motherland. I've studied military history, including Alexander the Great, Napoleon, and the best German, Russian, and American generals from both world wars. I know how they think. They make decisions that win wars, and, when necessary, they rebel against those who attempt to force unwise decisions upon them.

"In every other country of the world, the man who does that is a hero. In the Soviet Union, you go to prison camp for it. However, you still must do what is right. Do you understand me?"

"Yes, major. Thank you." He turned. "What is this?"

A group of soldiers walked into the courtyard led by Nikolai. Dr. Thao and Pavel were with him, too.

Cherkov paled, praying it wasn't what it looked like.

Ka heard the commotion and walked to the center of the room, where she could see through the doorway into the courtyard. She saw the KGB monster, the soldiers, and then she saw Dr. Thao.

They moved Dr. Thao into an open area and left him standing as the rest walked away. The three soldiers walked toward the hospital a few paces, stopped, and turned, aiming their rifles at the doctor.

Ka saw many Hmong villagers standing outside the fence, watching, and she knew Nikolai must have sent for them, because they never would have come on their own. Then Nikolai began a long speech.

Ka gasped when she realized what was happening. When he finished with the doctor, he would send for her again. Then he would probably kill her, too, because she had also tended the American.

She hurried to the other end of the hospital, grabbed the black bag with Gohan's supplies, unlocked the door, and walked out, moving slowly toward the village. As soon as she saw the two guards ahead, she moved behind a wooden shed out of sight, then sprinted across the open yard into the jungle.

She ran as fast as she could, but she couldn't outrun the sound of shots behind her. In her mind, she saw kind Dr. Thao fall to the ground, blood pouring from his body. She stopped and leaned against a tree for a moment, crying.

She quickly gathered her strength and ran all the way to her brother's camp without slowing.

Gohan managed to get some rest and awoke feeling refreshed, though sore. He got up, found the admiral, and woke him.

"Come on, admiral. You have to get your little buddy into killing shape."

The admiral got up, cupped water from a nearby bucket onto his face, stretched, and walked outside. It was still light, but not by much. He helped Gohan through his exercises, but they were interrupted by a commotion from the edge of camp nearest the mountain trail.

They walked over to see what was going on, and Gohan saw Ka immediately. "Hey, Ka's here. Boy, she's a sight for sore eyes. Let's go say hi."

Ka was clearly tense and distressed. The admiral held Gohan's arm and led him back to the center of camp. "Come on. We don't know if this concerns us. It could be something personal. If not, Cheu will tell us. Let's stay out of the way."

Gohan nodded, and they walked over to what had turned into

the congregating center of camp, a small grassy area near a pile of neatly stacked Russian and American weapons.

After a few minutes, Ka went into the largest tent. Cheu walked to the two Americans and sat down.

"Gohan," he said softly, "Dr. Boua Thao dead. Killed, camp."

"He was killed at camp?" Baker asked.

"Yes."

"Who killed him?" Gohan asked.

"Soviet."

"The Russian KGB man?"

"Yes." Cheu nodded.

"Nikko-Witch!" Gohan spat, then sighed deeply and shook his head. He was so angry he was ready to start the mission right that second. He wanted Nikko-Witch for himself. He was ready to walk into camp and tear the Russian jerk apart.

Captain Baker saw Gohan's expression. "There are no personal vendettas in war, Gohan. You'd better remember that. We have a couple hours yet. Make sure you're settled down. Sit here for a minute. I want to talk to Cheu."

Captain Baker and Cheu stood and walked a few paces away, talking quietly. Cheu nodded and walked into the large tent. Baker walked back to where Gohan was lost in thought.

"Look, Gohan, I know this is tough, but it's also war. We don't have to like it, but we have to live with it. We have a job to do. Don't let your personal feelings get in the way of that job, or you'll become useless. Make sure you understand that. A lot of people are counting on us.

"Ka's getting something to eat. When she's finished, she'll come over and take care of rebandaging your wounds and helping you exercise. That'll be good for her. She needs to get her mind off this, too.

"We'll put the mission together in a few hours. After you've had your exercise, you'd better rest again. Ka will be with you, and she knows what to do. Listen to her.

"She's here for the duration now. She left the camp for good, but she wants to come along tonight. That means we have one more soldier. Cheu says she can handle it. He'll talk to her about revenge, too. She's still a greenhorn at this stuff."

"Greenhorn? Admiral, she's just a kid!"

"Cheu says she's seventeen. They don't keep records on that stuff here. You're OK, aren't you?"

"Yeah, I'm just not very happy."

"Yeah, well, neither are the rest of us. Now go to your tent. Ka will be with you shortly."

Gohan walked gingerly to his tent and looked at his new home. They brought in a special mattress so he could sleep. He assumed it was stolen from the hospital.

Lying on the mattress, he felt his head spinning. Too much had happened in a short time, and he needed to sort things out. What he really wanted was to scream. He was furious that doc had been killed. He knew he couldn't have saved the man even if he'd been there, and that increased his frustration.

The admiral was right. He needed to settle down. There was a job to do, and it wouldn't be easy. He felt the same way about the mission as he did about his escape. It looked impossible, but he honestly believed they could do it. The only problem was, when he escaped, he had friends who helped. With the mission, there wouldn't be any hidden friends. It was just their little group of Hmong against three times as many trained soldiers. Maybe that was why he loved Morse code so much. He never knew when the right combination of dits and dots would mean war.

When Ka came in with her bag of supplies, she stopped just inside the tent. She saw Gohan lying on the mattress, completely dressed. They looked at each other. Her face showed no emotion. It was completely lifeless.

Ka, the girl of many faces, he thought.

Gohan understood, though.

She walked toward him and knelt without looking at him. She removed his boots, pants, and shorts. Then she unbuttoned his shirt and pulled it around behind him. Starting with his head, she worked on his bandages. She was very gentle and very quiet, but she never looked at him.

She finished changing his bandages, then she moved into her customary position at his legs and began his exercises. After twelve sit-ups, Gohan surprised her by motioning her off his legs. He stood and began doing deep knee bends without her help, although she had to steady him a couple of times when he almost fell.

He did twenty-five deep knee bends, then he went to the ground and did five push-ups before collapsing. Ka helped him back onto the mattress.

She left and returned with a damp cloth to wipe the perspiration off his face. She wiped his arms and chest, then pulled the light cover over his waist before sitting beside him and looking into his eyes.

He didn't know what to make of her. She motioned for him to get some sleep, then walked to the tent opening and left without having said anything.

He sighed deeply. His body was sore from the exercising. Though he wasn't tired, he closed his eyes and, within minutes, fell asleep.

Chapter 23
Not So Sweet Revenge

KA SHOOK GOHAN AWAKE, AND HE JUMPED SLIGHTLY. HE WAS glad to see it was her. She checked his bandages, made some minor adjustments, and helped him dress. They walked to the tent door. She stopped, looked deeply into his eyes, and spoke the only word he'd ever heard her speak.

"Gohan."

"Ka," he answered.

They both laughed, then she suddenly became businesslike again. He knew it was time to go to war.

The rest of the team gathered at the center of camp. Someone was cooking food that smelled good as Gohan met the admiral near the stack of rifles.

"Hey, Robin Hood," Gohan said, "it looks like your band of merry men are ready for war."

"I think so. Sleep well?"

"Yeah. I'm ready."

"OK. While they prepare dinner, we have some business to take care of. I retrieved your transmitter and equipment. We need to send a message home. Do you remember that code system?"

"Sure. An elephant never forgets."

"OK. Come with me. It's set up over here." He led the way a short distance from Cheu's tent, then he handed Gohan a printed message. "Send this baby off. Tomorrow at this time, we'll be home."

Gohan glanced at the admiral's writing. "Where's this clearing you mentioned?"

Captain Baker pointed to the left. "Right over there, soldier. You can't see it from here, but that's where they'll pick us up, and that's where we'll be tomorrow. Dinner smells pretty good tonight. Send this off and join us at the buffet table."

"Right. What's today's specialty, sautéed monkey paws?"

Gohan quickly set up the equipment, then he altered the letters to meet the preset code they chose before leaving Okinawa. When he translated it, the message was ready.

SPECIAL/GEN MANCINI/GEN WINTHROP/TOP 1/ TSC/ASAP/ 3 DEAD/GOHAN CAPTURED/

TORTURED/SILENT/ESCAPED/

SERIOUSLY INJURED/BAKER OK/GOING IN WITH UNDERGROUND GUERILLA ALLIES TO GET REST OF LOCAL PRISONERS OUT/NEW RENDEZVOUS 4 MILES SE/TOP OF MOUNTAIN/CLEARING/MARKED W 2 FLARES/12 PM TOMORROW/HELI OK/IF NOT THERE ALL CAPTURED OR DEAD/LOVE BAKER/

He finished sending the message, then he joined the others for their evening meal. He was excited about the mission and would enjoy tearing that camp apart and putting the Russian, Pathet Lao, and Viet Minh Communists out of business.

He sat beside the admiral. Ka sat beside her brother. She had begun painting and camouflaging herself and already looked more like a soldier than a young nurse.

The sergeant major banged on the door and shouted, "General Mancini! General! Wake up, sir! It's an emergency!"

He finally heard noise inside but kept knocking until the door opened. General Emilio Mancini stood there, pulling on a robe. "Yes, Tom, what is it?"

"General, we just received an urgent coded message. I was told to get you ASAP. It's for your eyes only, sir. I have a Jeep outside with the engine running."

The general tried to get his brain into gear. It sounded like the message they'd been waiting for. "Good work, Tom. Let me throw on some clothes. I'll be with you in a minute."

The two men rode quietly in the Jeep a few minutes later. As they approached the gate at Onna Point, Mancini wondered if he would need any help, depending on how the message coded out. He had known Sergeant Major Tom Winchester for years, and the marines didn't make them any better. He was loyal, honest, and knew how to get things done.

General Mancini came to a quick decision. "Tom, you're not cleared for this, but I need someone to expedite things. Stay with me on this. I'll vouch for you."

"Yes, sir. I'm all yours, general."

"We'll be working together closely. How about dropping the military crap? Just call me Emilio, OK?"

"General, I've been a marine too long for that. You can offer me a drink, sir, and I'll take it, but I don't think I can use your first name. Sorry, sir." He smiled.

After clearing the main gate and entering the compound, the two marines were quickly ushered into Major Richard Parsons' private office and found Captain Peter Foust on duty.

"Come in, gentlemen," Captain Foust said. "Please tell me what you'd like, and I'll have it rustled up immediately."

Mancini appreciated the man already. "Thanks, captain. I'd like breakfast. SOS is fine, as long as it comes with hot, black coffee."

"Same for me, captain," Winchester said. "Thanks."

"Anything else? Extra phones? A runner? You name it, we've

got it. You can call for me anytime. Otherwise, I'll stay out of your hair."

Mancini really liked the captain. The military needed more competent men like him. "Thanks. I'll need two phones and two lines. The sergeant major and I will use them simultaneously to make calls. Other than that, please stand by. We'll call."

The message was in a sealed envelope on the captain's desk. General Mancini took it and pulled out the code from his wallet.

"OK, Tom," Mancini said, "we have to apply the code to this and find out what happened to our boys."

Sergeant Major Winchester looked at his commander.

"Sorry, Tom. You'll learn some things you might be better off not knowing, but I won't tell you more than I must."

"Understood, sir. Let's get on with it."

It took about fifteen minutes to transcribe the code. Their breakfast came, and they ate while they worked. A second telephone line was brought in and connected.

Once the coded message was written out, General Mancini read it aloud and whistled. "God, what are we getting ourselves into?"

"I don't guess there's any chance we decoded it wrong, sir?"

"No, Tom. What you see is what it is. Now it looks like they're planning to start a war, too."

"Do you know this Captain Baker, sir?"

"He's as good as they come, Tom. UDT. Former POW. That's the only comforting part of this whole mess. There must be a very good reason for him to start a war over there. He obviously thinks they can help the guerillas without anyone blaming us. Baker is smart and fearless. Gohan's fearless, too, but I don't know if he's as smart.

"We have work to do. I have calls to make. First, I want you to find out who the best medic we have available is. I don't care what branch he's in as long as he's loyal. This is classified stuff at the highest level.

"Find him and get his butt over to the beach. I'll warn our boys he's coming. You can tell him he's on a top-secret mission. He needs to know how to keep his patient alive, but he can't tell anyone about it. Get the name and number of his superior officer, too, and we'll take care of talking to him. Get on it."

Mancini pulled another piece of paper from his wallet and dialed the phone number written on it. A sleepy voice answered, "This is Colonel Wheeler. This had better not be a wrong number at this time of night."

"Brandon, this is Emilio. Operation Fiver is a go. Get it underway. Our ETA is two hours or less. That's not much time. You read me?"

"Loud and clear, Emilio. I'll need an hour."

"You've got it. I've got two add-ons. Tom Winchester is locating a good medic for us. I don't know who that'll be, but he'll get him from somewhere. He's needed. Also, in case we might need her, I contacted a woman who's an interpreter. Based on the situation, we'd better bring her along. I can make those arrangements. I'll meet you at the beach in an hour, and we can talk face to face, OK? One other thing—we're going in by heli."

"That's fine. I'll need to bump one. There's only so much room. Is that OK?"

"Sure. Do what you have to. You might have to bump two. I might go along on this one."

"OK. It's your call. See you there."

The general hung up and dialed again, hearing another sleepy voice answer.

"Yes?"

"Mrs. Holloway, this is Major General Mancini. I'm sorry for the bad timing, but we're leaving early tomorrow. I'll need you to do that interpreting work I mentioned. I'll send someone to pick you up. Can you be ready in an hour?"

"Certainly, general."

"Thank you, ma'am. We'll see you soon."

Mrs. Phoui Holloway was a Laotian woman married to an Air Force major stationed on Okinawa. General Mancini was very lucky to have found her and even more lucky that she agreed to come along, if necessary, to act as interpreter. There was a risk, but she already passed a security check, and her husband agreed to let her go.

280

She spoke French, Laotian, and Kammu. When General Mancini told her where they might be going, she mentioned the area was mostly populated by Hmong, who spoke a language similar to Burmese, and she could interpret that, too. General Mancini pulled out another piece of paper and made another call. "I have an urgent message for General Marshal Winthrop. Doesn't he have a personal secretary? I thought that was the number I dialed. Oh. I see. Yes, I'll wait. Thank you.

"Hello? Yes, I'm sorry to call at such an hour. This is Major General Emilio Mancini. I understand General Winthrop is in transit and can't be reached. Is that correct? I have a message that must be forwarded to him at the earliest possible moment. It can't wait under any circumstances. Can you do that for me?

"Thank you. Please tell him, 'Fiver is a go.' That's correct. Miss? I'm sorry, captain, this message can't be repeated to anyone else. Is that clear? Good. Thank you, captain. Please tell General Winthrop to contact me when he gets in. He'll know how to do that. Thank you. You've been very helpful. Again, I apologize for calling at such a terrible hour. Thanks again, captain. Good night."

He was unaccustomed to being so nice and was glad when he hung up. "How are we doing, Tom?"

"I can't get anyone at Kadena. That would probably have been our best guy, but I found a navy doctor at Camp Kuwae. He's on his way."

"Good work. The navy man'll probably be better, anyway."

Winchester smiled. "Sir? This is obviously a rescue, and the coded message indicated Gohan. Can I ask is that our hero from here at Onna?"

"Yeah, Tom, and whatever you've heard about him, he's the real McCoy. I'll take him with me anytime, anywhere."

"Well, sir, Gohan has a couple different reputations. I'll trust yours, sir. He sounds like the kind of guy we want to go get."

"Let's go thank the captain for making this easy for us, then we have to meet the team."

Cheu Moua's team was in position. There were six pairs of guerillas who had to silence the six sets of guards on duty at the compound. As it turned out, though, only five pairs were needed. One of the teams was led by Cheu, another by Captain Baker, and another by Vu Xiong. The fourth team was led by Jou Pang, another former RLA soldier.

Baker was satisfied. The ambush teams were strong. The rest of the guerillas were hiding only yards from the compound fence. Perched in bushes, they were safely out of sight but still nearby.

Gohan and Thek Moua, another Hmong, were the fifth team. They had their rifles trained on the two tower guards. In a worst-case scenario, if the guards learned what was happening, Gohan and his partner would take them out, using silencers on their long range rifles.

Vu and his partner sneaked to the lower end of the encampment and cut the fence just enough to crawl through. The two guards who were their targets were one hundred yards away, sitting on wooden ammunition boxes while they ate and talked.

The two Hmong waited until the searchlight moved past the hospital, then they crawled through the fence and slithered across the grounds until they were at the rear of the hospital, where they would be well hidden.

The two guards stood and walked along the camp's south edge that was shared with the village. Vu and his partner sneaked up to the two boxes the guards had just vacated and hid behind one, hoping the guards would stop at the first one as before. They did. After a short patrol, the two men returned and sat to talk quietly. One lit a cigarette.

Vu nodded to his friend, and slowly, the two Hmong guerillas sneaked up behind the Viet Minh guards. They thrust their left hands powerfully under the guards' chins, forcing their mouths closed as they slit their throats.

No sound came as the guards died. They slid the bodies behind the boxes. Then Vu moved quietly through the village into the jungle and back up the fence line for the rest of his team. His partner moved up the courtyard and behind the hospital. He crawled along the west outside wall until he reached the end of the building and huddled, waiting for the signal to complete his next assignment.

Cheu and his partner moved to the easternmost side of the village until they were within thirty yards of the two guards that were their responsibility. Simultaneously, Captain Baker's team moved to the edge of the jungle, fifteen yards from the guards they were assigned to. The guards sat together on the open ground. Somehow, they had to sneak up on them out in the open within their allotted time.

Jou Pang and his partner moved to the back of the encampment, where two soldiers guarded the rear of the village. The forest provided good cover, and they were soon only ten yards from their victims.

Cheu nodded to his partner, and they separated and crawled along the ground, moving toward the bench on which the two Pathet Lao soldiers sat, smoking, talking, and laughing.

When Cheu and his partner were within ten feet of the two men, they quietly rose from the ground, crouched, and moved forward. The soldier farthest from Cheu saw him as he came up behind the man's companion, but it was too late. Cheu and his partner pounced on the soldiers, their knives ready. Both men were dead before either could yell or shoot.

Captain Baker knew he had to move fast. They were too far from the Soviet guards sitting on the ground. There was no way to reach them unseen. They waited as long as they could, then his Hmong partner motioned that he'd go in front of the Soviets and motioned Baker to come up behind them.

Baker didn't know what the man planned, but he was ready. In a few minutes, the Hmong was lost in the darkness. To Baker's astonishment, someone groan loudly. The Soviets jumped to their feet, their rifles pointing toward the village and the direction of the sound.

Baker saw the Hmong walk toward the two Soviet men, clutching his side, talking to them, and motioning to his side as if he were injured. The Soviets exchanged a look, then they cautiously walked toward the supposed villager.

Baker crouched and moved as fast as he could toward the men, crossing the dark open space that separated them. The Hmong guerilla staggered to within fifteen feet of the guards, then collapsed. The Soviets slowly moved toward him.

Baker was fifteen feet behind the soldiers when one reached toward the apparently dead villager. As he did, the man leaped to his feet and thrust his knife into the Soviet soldier's chest. In the same motion, he cupped the man's mouth so he couldn't shout.

The second soldier moved to his friend's defense. Engrossed in the scene, he didn't see or hear Captain Baker coming up behind him. Before he reached the Hmong, Baker thrust his knife into the back of the man's neck, then snapped his neck to make sure he was dead.

The Hmong fighter moved quickly back into the forest to retrieve his weapon. He and Captain Baker moved toward the edge of the compound so they would be in position for the next phase of the operation.

The fourth Hmong team had the best position, sitting in the jungle only ten yards from two Viet Minh guards, who were smoking and talking. The men leaned against the compound fence, looking into the camp.

It should have been an easy job, but it wasn't. The Hmong guerillas moved quietly behind the soldiers. But when they were only five feet away, one Hmong lost his footing and made a sound that alerted the two guards.

Both Hmong leaped into action. Because he had his knife ready, Jou Pang subdued his man easily. He slit his throat and dropped him, turning in time to see the other Viet Minh soldier do the same to his Hmong partner.

The soldier turned toward Jou, who already had his right arm back and was bringing it forward. The knife hurtled through the night and pierced the man's head between the eyes. Jou was on him a second later, making sure he made no sound. After retrieving his knife, he moved toward the encampment to take his next position.

Vu brought in the remainder of the team except for the two sharpshooters and moved them to the village edge of the camp. They followed the two-man teams in as far as they could without being seen by the tower guards.

Xang Vue, Vu's partner, crouched and waited at the rear of the hospital. When Cheu signaled him from behind the dungeon, Xang waited for the spotlight to pass the hospital, then he crawled to the door and saw the sleeping guard inside.

He stepped in and slit the guard's throat quickly. He saw no one else inside and quietly walked through, noting that all the patients were villagers. At the far end of the building, he saw a Viet Minh soldier sleeping in a bed on the right and stopped. He slowly leaned over the bed and added one more dead Communist to the count.

He walked to the door of the Russian doctor's room, looked around, and saw two sick villagers watching him. He motioned them to be quiet.

Inside the room, the Soviet doctor had the odd feeling something wasn't right. He got out of bed and walked to the table against the wall, taking a small pistol from a drawer. Then he climbed into bed and sat there with the gun ready, waiting.

Xang opened the door and stepped into the room only to find the Russian doctor waiting with a drawn gun. He held his finger to his mouth, motioning the doctor to be quiet, then waved him out.

The doctor was confused. Assuming the man was a member of the Pathet Lao, he set down the gun and began dressing. As he buttoned his shirt, he realized the man had stepped into the room and was behind him. The doctor turned, but he was dead before he had a chance to respond.

Xang wiped off his knife on the man's shirt and moved back through the hospital. Once outside, he waved to his comrades and hid along the hospital wall again.

Phase one was complete. Phase two required two groups, led by Captain Baker and Cheu, while Gohan and Thek Moua remained ready to pick off the tower guards.

Gohan saw Xang go into the hospital and emerge a few minutes later. He waited until the searchlight moved past, then he saw Xang wave.

Gohan turned to his partner and nodded. Gohan lifted an M-14 with a twenty-round magazine. He wasn't totally familiar with the weapon, but he felt more comfortable with that than the Russian guns, which were more plentiful. Over time, Cheu's group had appropriated a lethal arsenal, including Russian AK-47s and SKS-45s, as well as some American weapons.

Gohan steadied his hand, waiting for the guard to turn toward him. He needed to kill him on the first shot, not just wound him. *That's right, buddy,* he thought. *Turn a little more. There you go. Perfect.* Without looking, he said, "Yes?" to his partner.

Thek had his man in his sights, too, and whispered back, "Yes."

The two muffled bullets rang out simultaneously. Gohan's guard threw his hand to his chest and slumped out of sight. The second guard reached toward his comrade. Then his face exploded, and he fell over the tower wall and hung there. No one noticed the faint sound the silencers made.

The teams moved quickly. Thirteen members of Baker's team moved forward. Within seconds, they were in position at the main compound building. Four went through the back door and stood outside the four inner doors. One door led to Nikolai's room, where he slept after drinking heavily. The other doors led to Nikolai's office, which was empty; Pavel's office, where he slept restlessly in his chair; and the empty interrogation room.

Nine men led by Baker moved to the other side of the compound and stood poised outside the north door of the barracks. Eight men and Ka, led by Cheu, were ready to burst through the south door, where the Viet Minh and Pathet Lao slept.

Xang, who had moved to the prison, was busy breaking the lid to the dungeon so he could release the sick, starved Hmong prisoners. Gohan and Thek crawled through the fence and were ready to handle anyone who came out the door facing them.

The groups were synchronized using a counting method the

Hmong understood. When Thek nudged Gohan and nodded, he was ready.

The four men in the rear of the compound burst in and killed the two Russians who slept there. Nikolai, who never had a chance, died before he could wake up. Pavel managed to leave his chair, but he died quickly, too. The four men moved to the barracks, two on either side, to assist their friends as they heard the gunfire there.

Baker and his men went through the doorway and stood outside the quarters where the Russians slept. There weren't very many of them, and he motioned to his men that they should kill them all. When they were ready, they burst into the room, firing. Surprise was complete, and it appeared all died. Few even woke up.

Sergeant Cherkov rolled off his bed the moment he heard something. He grabbed his rifle, rolled under the bed, and waited, choosing not to return the gunfire. After a few minutes, he heard someone shout in English, "Let's go!"

A few seconds later, it was over. He lay still for a moment, making sure they were gone, then he rolled out from under the bed and went to the door, his rifle ready. Terrible gunfire sounded from elsewhere in the building, but he wanted to check the damage in the barracks first.

Dressing quickly, he walked through, shaking his head in disbelief. Only one Russian had managed to grab his weapon, but he was still dead. Major Ustinova looked like he had been trying to pull on his clothes when they shot him. Why in the name of the motherland had he bothered? Cherkov was frightened, but he had to help the others. He went into the hall, moving cautiously toward the Viet Minh barracks.

Cheu and his men exploded into the barracks filled with Viet Minh and Pathet Lao soldiers, but some were awake and dressed, smoking, their weapons beside them. They quickly returned fire.

Cheu's team had to retreat into the hall earlier than planned. Fortunately, there was a turn in the hallway only twenty feet away, so his men found cover quickly.

Captain Baker's team joined them, and Cheu explained the situation.

Gohan and Thek Moua moved closer to the compound. Since nothing was happening outside, they decided to join their friends. They moved toward the main door. Gohan was moving awkwardly because of his injuries, but his adrenaline kept the pain from being an obstruction

They threw open the door and jumped back. Gohan peered down the hall. Seeing no action, they cautiously stepped in. Gunfire came from up ahead. They knew they would find the source soon, because the building wasn't that big.

They moved to the first turn and went around it to find at least a dozen Pathet Lao and Viet Minh, half in their underwear, moving toward the guerrila team, firing at the cross hallway corner to keep Cheu's men at bay.

Gohan and Thek immediately started firing, sending the Viet Minh and Pathet Lao scurrying back to their barracks room.

"We've got them on the run, Admiral!" Gohan shouted.

Hmong appeared from everywhere, returning fire to the soldiers, who retreated back into their barracks while taking serious casualties. The room had no windows or other exits, so Captain Baker knew he had them pinned.

Gohan and Thek rose off the floor and moved forward to join the others. As they did, Gohan heard a shot and saw Thek fall. Gohan saw a big Soviet running toward him with a knife in his hand. He immediately realized it was the same man who had captured him.

He must be out of ammo, Gohan thought. *Well, Ivan, this is no time to be a hero.*

He lifted his pistol and shot the Russian between the eyes, then checked Thek Moua, but he was dead. Gohan moved forward toward the others.

They had lost a few men and had some more injured. Captain Baker moved to the turn of the hall where Gohan and Cheu were talking.

"All right," Baker said. "We don't want to prolong this. It was supposed to be bang, bang, and we're out. We can either go in and get them, or we can get out without their knowing it. I don't mind telling you that I don't like that. We would have our backs to them and would be sitting ducks."

"Anyone have a grenade?" Gohan asked.

"Grenade?" Cheu asked. "Crazy."

"Gohan, a grenade could bring this whole building down on top of us," Baker said.

"You have a better idea, admiral?"

"No."

"OK. Listen up. Cheu, give me two grenades. You guys take off down the hall and get the heck out of the building. If you've got a brave man, leave him with me. If not, I'll do it myself."

Captain Baker didn't like the idea and was about to say so when the trapped Communist soldiers burst through the door, screaming defiance and firing down the hall at the Hmong guerrillas and their allies. Two of Cheu's men dived to the other side of the hall while returning fire.

Both sides were firing wildly, but the enemy kept coming until they turned the corner and were on top of the Hmong troops. Hand-to-hand combat broke out, punctuated by several shots.

Gohan jumped away from the group, too beat up to fight one on one with anyone. Keeping his handgun raised, he shot anyone who wasn't wearing camouflage paint.

A Viet Minh soldier came around the corner, screaming, and lunged at Gohan. Gohan, seeing the fear in the man's eyes, knew he had already decided he was a dead man, so he might as well take as many of the enemy with him as he could. Gohan had been in the same situation and understood. The Viet Minh had his knife raised, ready to run it through Gohan's face.

Gohan lifted his pistol and pulled the trigger, only to hear it click against an empty magazine. He dived to the right, and the

Viet Minh banged against the wall.

Gohan got to his right and held the man's arm just as he tried to stab him with the knife. Gohan banged the man's arm against the wall, but he couldn't dislodge the knife. He couldn't use his legs to kick with, because he couldn't raise them high enough to be any good.

The Viet Minh held Gohan's right arm. They were locked in combat, neither one gaining an edge. Gohan threw his weight against the man as hard as he could, shoving him against the wall. He pulled back, bringing the Viet Minh with him, then threw him against the wall with tremendous force, cracking the man's head hard.

The wall caved in. Gohan saw blood squirt from the back of the man's head. The knife fell out of his hand as he screamed and clutched his head. Gohan went to his knees and pummeled the man's groin with a sharp right-left combination. As the soldier fell to the floor, Gohan stabbed him with his own knife.

"Gohan!"

He turned as he recognized Ka's voice just as another enemy soldier ran toward him with his knife ready. The Pathet Lao was on Gohan in an instant. He couldn't avoid the man in time. There was a sharp sting in his right arm as the Pathet Lao struck the wall, stabbing Gohan in the process. Gohan moved, ready to fight, but the man didn't move. When he saw blood running down the back of the man's neck, he shoved him over with his foot and saw a gaping hole in his neck.

Gohan quickly recovered and got back to his feet. His arm was badly cut, dripping blood. When he looked for Ka, he didn't see her. He wondered if she shot the man who was after him.

There was no time to worry about that now. He saw more Pathet Lao and Viet Minh soldiers, so he snapped a magazine into his pistol and fired at them.

A few minutes later, there was less movement in the hall and a lot less gunfire. Gohan looked for more targets, but the only ones left standing were Cheu's guerillas. It was over.

Vu Xiong quickly issued orders, and two guerillas walked through and around the bodies, checking for signs of life. Occasionally, a shot rang out as the men made sure their enemies were dead.

Gohan was completely spent. Once the assault ended, realizing he was badly hurt, he leaned against the wall, trying to gather his thoughts. The noise had been deafening. With all that gunfire in the enclosed barracks, he wondered why everyone wasn't deaf.

He looked around. *Wow*, he thought. *What a massacre. How'd I ever survive that? Those guys were crazy.*

Bodies lay everywhere. He wondered how many his side had lost. Suddenly, he realized these were people he cared about.

He moved to the corner and saw Cheu on the floor with Ka. Gohan's heart almost stopped when he saw the blood on her clothing. He moved closer and saw she was alive. Gohan went to one knee and touched her arm. Ka looked at him, then closed her eyes.

Cheu grabbed Gohan's arm. "Captain! Go!"

Gohan stared at the guerilla leader, then realizing what he'd said, he looked for the admiral. He glanced again at Ka, but Cheu gently pushed him away.

"Ka OK, Gohan. Captain no OK. Go."

Getting to his feet, Gohan looked down the hall toward a group of Hmong guerillas gathered around someone. He moved toward them quickly, stumbling, then crawling, until he saw the admiral on the floor with his head in the lap of a Hmong soldier. The admiral's chest showed a lot of blood from a gaping wound. A guerilla tried to wrap cloth around it.

Gohan heard Cheu shout. The other guerillas motioned to Gohan that they were leaving. Two of them carefully lifted the admiral and carried him down the hall toward the door. Gohan wanted to help, but he had no energy left. He turned to look for Ka, but she and Cheu were already gone.

His head spun as he hurried behind the guerillas. He realized he was the last man out, the rear guard. He walked backward to make sure no one followed. They had been successful, but they had lost some good people. He guessed they had been fortunate. He shook his head, trying to keep his senses sharp. Barely able to walk, he doubted he could still fire his weapon if he had to.

They left the compound and walked across the courtyard, then passed through the fence and into the jungle. Gohan couldn't keep up. The pain grew worse, and his energy faded. He didn't care. They had done what they had to. Two people he cared for were hurt, and he didn't know how badly. The admiral looked the worst. Gohan hoped they could find help.

Cheu carried Ka in his arms while another Hmong guerilla walked alongside to tend her. She'd taken a bullet through the side and lost a lot of blood, but she was bandaged and they had stopped the bleeding. Fortunately, she passed out, making it easier to carry her back to camp.

Two other Hmong carried Captain Baker with a third man walking beside them to care for him. Two other guerillas were nearby, ready to help with the captain when the others tired.

Gohan tried to run to catch up to the others, but he couldn't do it. It didn't matter. He knew the way back to camp. It was more important for them to get Ka and the admiral back quickly to tend their wounds.

He decided he did want to be with them, so he forced himself to run. *Come on, Davey. It's like when you escaped. Force yourself. You're tired, but you can run a little. They're not that far ahead.*

He made up some of the distance, but felt himself becoming dizzy and had to stop, dropping to one knee. He was dizzy and all the pain he had forced himself to forget about, suddenly thrust itself on him. He vomited, but immediately felt better when he was finished.

He didn't think he would faint. He was just exhausted and very sore. Someone grabbed his arm. It was Vu Xiong, who had stayed behind at the village for a few minutes to give instructions to the villagers.

He motioned Gohan to his feet, then took his uninjured arm and began walking quickly, pulling Gohan along. Gohan felt as if they walked for days. Vu had to almost carry him the last mile. Finally, Vu brought Gohan to the center of camp, where others were already working on Captain Baker, Ka, and two other wounded men. He laid Gohan beside them.

Gohan didn't pass out, but he lay there for quite a while, recuperating from the hike. A Hmong brought a cold, damp cloth to wipe Gohan's face. That felt good and helped restore him a bit. Someone offered him a drink, which he gulped down. It burned his throat, but he didn't care, because it helped.

One of the men bandaged his injured arm. It was all he could do to keep his eyes open. Then, he remembered Ka and the admiral. He tried to rise but couldn't. Even though he was safely back at camp, he wasn't relieved. There was too much that wasn't right. It was no good to have killed the enemy if it cost him the admiral and Ka. He forced himself to sit up and look over at his friends.

Ka cried and screamed from the pain. The Hmong medic worked on her, but Gohan knew he was little more than a shaman who used herbs and opium. Gohan didn't know if that would really work, but someone had to help Ka. He motioned the man with the damp cloth to help him stand up and walk to her.

Cheu sat beside her, holding her hand, as the shaman cut into his sister's side to remove the bullet. Gohan wasn't surprised to hear her screaming. Maybe the man was more than a shaman after all. Maybe he cared enough to do the right thing.

Gohan felt his head spinning again. When he tried to look at Ka, his eyes wouldn't focus. He gulped down a drink, then knelt beside Ka and quietly said her name.

She opened her eyes and looked at him. When she saw who it was, her face relaxed, and she gave him a weak smile. He stroked her arm a few times. Her face was filled with pain but was also peaceful.

Gohan looked at Cheu. "Will Ka be OK?"

"Yes. Ka OK. Captain no OK."

Gohan looked at the admiral. He was fifteen feet away. Two Hmong men worked on him. He looked back at Ka, who motioned with her eyes to go to the admiral. Gohan patted her hand.

"I'll be back, Ka. Be brave."

A Hmong guerrilla helped him walk to the admiral. Gohan went to one knee again. The admiral had a hole in his chest big enough for Gohan's fist. The men had cleaned it as best they could, and it wasn't bleeding anymore. The admiral was resting.

A Hmong brought the admiral a cup of water. He lifted his head, allowing the man to give it to him, but most ran down his chin.

Gohan put his hand on the admiral's shoulder. "Hold on, man. We'll be out of here in a couple more hours. Just hold on."

He needed to be brave for his friend, but it wasn't working. Tears rolled from his eyes as he realized his friend and mentor was slipping away.

The admiral looked at him and smiled, making Gohan wonder how he could smile at a time like that. He was dying! Gohan felt overcome with emotion. He wanted to do something for his friend but didn't know what to do.

The admiral motioned him closer, and Gohan moved to within a few inches of his face.

"God doesn't make mistakes, Gohan," he whispered.

Gohan pulled back and stared at him. He didn't know what to say, so he nodded, saying nothing. The admiral motioned him closer again.

"God has something special for you, Gohan. Don't miss it."

Gohan looked at him. Although he was dying, his friend seemed peaceful. He was more concerned about Gohan than himself. Gohan realized he was in the company of a very great, very special man.

The admiral looked at Gohan, who wanted to say something but didn't know what it should be.

"Admiral?" he said.

The admiral waited, and Gohan's eyes filled with tears.

"Admiral, I love you, man. I love you."

The admiral's eyes smiled, filling with tears, too. He opened his mouth to speak, but nothing came out. When he opened his mouth again, a small stream of blood came out of the corner and rolled down to his chin.

Gohan reached to wipe it off. He saw the admiral's eyes close and knew his friend was gone.

He looked at the Hmong, who nodded. Gohan looked at the other Hmong, who helped him to his feet. With their help, he moved back to the center of the camp toward the other wounded. He managed a few steps, then collapsed in the villagers' arms.

Chapter 24
Going Home

Vu splashed water onto Gohan's face to wake him. Gohan tried to get up but couldn't. He hurt and was so tired all he wanted was to sleep. Slowly, his senses returned, and he knew there were things he had to do.

"Where are Cheu and Ka?" he asked.

Vu pointed to the tent where Gohan slept the previous night. Gohan motioned Vu to help him up, and the Hmong grabbed his good arm and helped him walk to the tent. After calling to Cheu, Vu motioned Gohan inside.

As he walked in, Gohan realized that someone had wrapped a bandage around his injured arm. He didn't remember it happening. With difficulty, he walked to the mattress where Ka lay. He sat beside her.

Cheu patted his shoulder as he stood. "Gohan, please come. I go plane. You come."

Gohan thought he understood, but he didn't care. He wanted to spend a few minutes with Ka. He knew Cheu wouldn't let the helicopter leave without him. Cheu left the two of them alone.

Gohan moved closer to Ka, caressing her face with his fingers.

"Are you OK, Ka?"

She smiled but didn't understand the question, but that didn't matter. They hadn't needed language before and didn't need it now, either.

He was careful not to touch her bandaged side as he moved his face closer to hers. "You're one of the most special ladies in the history of the world. Not only that, you're beautiful, too."

He spoke gently and lovingly. She didn't understand his words, but she caught the meaning and beamed a smile at him. "Gohan," she said softly.

"Ka, I have to go home. I have a wife and daughter. But, I'll never forget you. You're beautiful, wonderful, magnificent, and very, very special. I love you."

She smiled and reached out with her free arm, touching his cheek. He heard an approaching helicopter, and her face showed she heard it, too. They both knew it was time for him to leave. From his kneeling position, he took her hand and held it as he looked into her eyes. After affectionately kissing her hand, he stood and left without looking back.

The helicopter landed in the clearing, and six marines jumped out, their rifles ready. The doctor came next and threw a stretcher onto the ground. General Mancini and Mrs. Holloway followed.

Cheu ran to the copter, motioning them to bring the stretcher quickly. The navy doctor moved with four marines toward the Hmong who gathered around the two fallen Americans. General Mancini and Mrs. Holloway sat on a large rock with Cheu. Once he saw that she understood his language, he related the story from beginning to end. General Mancini listened intently without asking too many questions.

The marines put Captain Baker in a body bag and carried him to the helicopter. After examining Gohan, the doctor ordered the marines to place him on a stretcher.

"Doc," Gohan said, "there are several badly injured Hmong at their camp, right through the jungle there." He pointed. "We can't let them go without help. They saved my life, and the admiral and I considered them true friends. Can you do it, doc? It's important."

"Sure, Soldier. You guys get this man to the helicopter. I'll be back soon."

"No way, doc," Gohan said. "I go with you. How 'bout one of you guys lending me a hand? The camp's only a few yards from here."

General Mancini had told the men that Gohan and Baker were heroes at the highest level. The marines looked at the doctor, then at Gohan. Finally, a tall, black marine said, "Sometimes we listen to doctors, sometimes we listen to heroes."

They helped Gohan off the stretcher. One Marine helped him walk as he led them back to the small mountain clearing. Vu Xiong went with them and took them to the injured Hmong. The doctor spent over an hour in the camp, treating two seriously injured men. Cheu, General Mancini, and Mrs. Holloway joined them.

Vu and his men prepared a small meal of rice and vegetables for the Americans. As the others ate, the doctor, one marine, and Gohan went to Ka's tent.

"Doc," Gohan said, "the lady in there is Ka. She's the commander's sister and a nurse. When I was at my worst, she kept me alive. I owe her a lot. When it was time to go in and rescue her village, she became a soldier like the rest of us. She doesn't speak one word of English, doc, so you don't have to talk to her, just fix her up."

The navy doctor removed Ka's bandages and looked closely at her gunshot wound. He gave her an injection that she accepted grudgingly. When he finished treating her, he rebandaged her side.

"Young lady, you're pretty lucky," he said. "You'll be up and around in no time. Don't try to do too much for a few days, then after that you can start living a normal life again."

"Doc, she doesn't speak English," Gohan yelled from outside the tent. "You have to tell her brother, Cheu. He'll understand."

The doctor put away his utensils. When he looked at Ka, she nodded in gratitude. As they turned to leave, Gohan glanced in and looked at Ka, who smiled warmly.

What a trooper, he thought as he saw her lying on the mattress. *She's ready to start the next part of her life. Ka, you're really something.*

He started to leave, then turned back to look at Ka one last time only to find the friendly smile gone and her face drenched in tears. He left quickly while he still had control of himself.

They carried Gohan back to the helicopter on a stretcher. Cheu walked with the men. After getting Gohan inside, the navy doctor removed Gohan's clothing and began treating his wounds.

Cheu said good-bye to the Americans. General Mancini shook Cheu's hand and thanked him. The guerilla leader leaned inside to touch Gohan's arm.

"Gohan, thank," he said, his face filled with emotion. Then he leaned forward to kiss Gohan's cheek before nodding to the general and running back to where his men waited. The helicopter rose and headed toward safe territory.

Mancini turned to the navy doctor, who was cleaning Gohan's wounds. "How bad, doc?" the general asked.

The doctor's face was white. "General, I don't think I've ever seen anything this bad in my entire life. He needs immediate attention at a hospital."

"Relax, doc. The Hmong guerilla leader told me it was twice this bad when they finished torturing him. He's actually recovering well. Keep him comfortable and do whatever is necessary. We'll be home soon.

"We lost four good men on this mission. The one in that body bag was the best."

"He was the best ever, general," Gohan said. "They don't come any better."

General Mancini turned toward Gohan. "Gohan, you're everything they said you were. I'm proud of you. Cheu gave us a detailed picture of what happened. After you've had a chance to rest, we'll go over it with you.

"I have to ask one important question: was there anyone left alive in that compound?"

"No, sir. Vu Xiong, Cheu's top lieutenant, took care of that.

He told the villagers to get rid of the bodies. They'll do that, then they'll burn the camp and move to a neighboring village. If Ivan the Terrible or Ho what's-his-name decide to come back, they won't have any idea what happened. There won't be anyone to ask. It's pretty clean, sir."

Mancini nodded. "There'll be a lot of people who won't be happy about this. I want you to know I'm not one of them. You guys did a heck of a job."

"So did God," Gohan answered.

"What?"

Gohan smiled. "The admiral told me that God got him through the POW camp when he was in Korea. And he got me through this one, too. I didn't know much about God before this, but I know a lot about Him now. He did a heck of a job, general."

The general nodded, understanding.

"What happens next, general? To me, I mean?"

"Well, you'll be in the hospital for a while. You're beat up pretty bad. After that, life will return to normal."

"I have a wife and sweet baby girl I haven't seen in a while. Can they visit me at the hospital?"

General Mancini knew about Sumiko, but he didn't want to add to Gohan's tragedy right then. He needed time to heal physically and emotionally. Mancini was a tough man, but he couldn't do that to Gohan.

"I'm sorry, Gohan. But because of the nature of the mission, you'll have to be debriefed before you go home or speak to anyone besides our team. I'll be pitching for you, and we'll get through all that as fast as we can. That's the best I can do. I promise."

Gohan sighed. He was tired and wanted to sleep. He hoped he could, then he could wake up and find out it had all been just a dream. He needed time to put it all in perspective. It happened so fast that his head still spun. So many bad things had occurred in such a short time.

God, there are things I don't understand, he thought. *Why? First doc, then the admiral, then Ka. All three of them! Why? What did the admiral mean when he said God has something special for me?*

What's so special about losing three of the most beautiful people in the world?

At least Ka would recover. The navy doctor said her wound wasn't serious. She was special. Although Gohan never got to ask, he knew it was Ka who shot the Pathet Lao who was ready to slice off his head. She saved his life twice. He would never forget her.

In a span of only two weeks, he met three of the most magnificent people on earth, all of whom had an enormous impact on his life. Then, just like that, they were gone. Two were dead, and Ka was out of his life forever.

He wanted it all to go away, then he didn't. The time he spent with each of them and all the things those people had done for him were too precious to lose.

His body, mind, and heart had been hurt a lot. He found himself crying again. He didn't care if the others saw him. He knew the hurt was temporary. Although the memories hurt then, they would become good ones someday. The hospital would care for his outer pain. Spending the rest of his life with Keiko and Sumi would take care of the inner pain. He couldn't wait to be back home in Okinawa.